I0782372

JENNIFER CHIPMAN

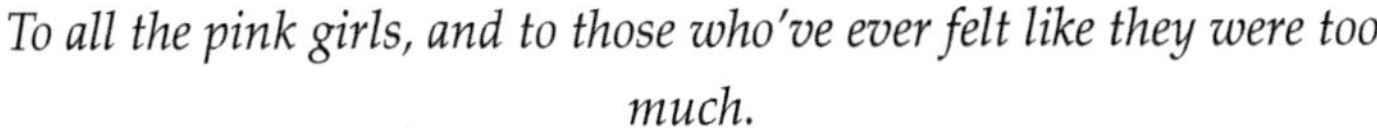

To all the pink girls, and to those who've ever felt like they were too much.
Don't ever change—you're perfect just the way you are.

Playlist

- Once Upon A Dream - Mary Costa, Bill Shirley, Chorus
- All I Want - Olivia Rodrigo
- Cupid (Twin Ver.) - FIFTY FIFTY
- Start of Something New - Drew Seeley, Vanessa Hudgens, and Zac Efron
- New Romantics - Taylor Swift
- Dancing On My Own - Calum Scott
- ceilings - Lizzy McAlpine
- Line Without a Hook - Ricky Montgomery
- Late Night Talking - Harry Styles
- Mess It Up - Gracie Abrams
- Temporary Fix - Jonas Brothers
- I Wanna Be Yours - Arctic Monkeys
- Daylight - Harry Styles
- You Belong With Me - Taylor Swift
- Fairytale - Alexander Rybak
- Today Was a Fairytale - Taylor Swift
- Golden Hour - Kacey Musgraves
- So Close - Jon McLaughlin
- we can't be friends (wait for your love) - Ariana Grande

- Cornelia Street - Taylor Swift
- Until I Found You - Stephen Sanchez, Em Behold
- bad idea - Ariana Grande
- As Long As You're Mine - Irina Menzel, Leo Norbert Butz
- Dress - Taylor Swift
- Golden - Harry Styles
- invisible string - Taylor Swift
- i'm yours - Isabel LaRosa
- All Of The Girls You Loved Before - Taylor Swift
- Cloud 9 - Beach Bunny
- Feels Like - Gracie Abrams
- I Think He Knows - Taylor Swift
- Sparks - Coldplay
- You Are In Love - Taylor Swift
- Oh, What A World - Kacey Musgraves
- Daylight - Taylor Swift
- Cinema - Harry Styles
- Lover - Taylor Swift

Contents

They say if you dream a thing more than once, it's sure to come true.

SLEEPING BEAUTY, 1959

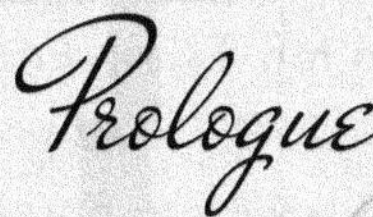

Prologue

AUDREY, TWELVE YEARS OLD

Parker!" I shouted across the street, the brunette boy turning his head at the sound of my voice.

Today, he was dressed in jeans and a black t-shirt, but I still thought he was the most beautiful boy I've ever met.

I'm going to marry him someday, I thought to myself.

He was my first crush and my first friend outside of my twin sister, Ella, and he was always down for adventures. A year older than me, and yet he never treated me like a little sister. I was already sad that he'd be leaving me for High School next year.

Parker's face rose when he caught sight of me, but then fell again.

"Hi," I said, coming to stand in front of him, fiddling with the strap of my pink overalls.

"Hey, Rosie."

Whenever he called me that, I blushed. Just like my nickname. Rosy cheeks—Audrey Rose—*Rosie.* He was the only person who used it, so it felt special.

"Why the long face?" I tightened my blonde high ponytail, so I had something to do with my hands.

"My parents just told me that we're moving."

"What?" I couldn't keep the look of surprise off my face. "But... you're my best friend."

He gave me a sad smile, his toe digging into the dirt beneath us. "You're my best friend too. I wish I didn't have to go, but..." Parker's shoulders slumped. "My dad got a job across the country. He's going out in two weeks to find us a place to live. They said I could finish out the school year, but then we'll join him."

"That *sucks*."

"You said it." He ran his hands through his hair, longer on top than on the sides. "But we'll always be friends, won't we?" Parker stuck out his pinky.

"Yes," I agreed, wrapping my pinky around his. *Pinky promise.* "Always." I smiled at him, even though I felt like my heart was breaking inside. *You can't go,* I wanted to cry. "When do you leave?" Even I heard my voice break, and I hoped I didn't start crying in front of him.

I'd always tried not to cry in front of Parker. I might have been a girly girl, always wearing pink and dresses, but I loved playing outside. We rode our bikes together, and I put on a brave face when I skinned my knees. We climbed trees together, and I didn't complain when I got sap on my hands or twigs in my beautiful, golden curls.

When we were younger, we played princess and the knight who stormed the castle to save her from an evil dragon. He slashed through thorns (vines) and scaled a tall tower (the tree house in his family's backyard) to save me from the beast (a large stuffed animal he pretended to stab). It was a good memory—one of the best.

"The week after school gets out. They want me to start high school in the new place."

I did the math in my head—*one month.* I only had one more month left with Parker.

When I looked up at him, it was with a determined gaze. "Guess we're going to have to fit as many adventures as possible in this last month then, won't we?" It was a bravado I didn't quite feel, but I was trying to put on a brave face for him. He was the one moving, and his sadness was warranted, but I didn't want to make it worse.

He gave me a brilliant grin, nudging my shoulder with his. "That's the spirit. It'll be okay, you'll see. And then you'll find a new best friend and forget all about me."

I sighed internally, wondering if that was possibly true. If I'd ever find another best friend who would replace him. At least I had Ella. She ensured I was never truly alone. Even if she was more introverted than me and preferred to stay inside and work on a craft project.

"I'll never forget you," I promised. "You'll always be my best friend, Parker. Besides, we can keep in touch, right? Mom said I could get a cell phone soon. And we can write? Or email."

He sighed. "Yeah. We'll stay in touch. And maybe I can come back and visit."

I nodded. "Yeah. Because I can't go on the carnival rides alone."

It was stupid, but I liked it when we rode the rides together. Sometimes, when I was scared, he'd slip his hand into mine and squeeze tight.

Parker laughed. "Alright. I'll come back for the carnival."

That summer, watching the Maxwells pack up their house, and their moving van drive away,... That was the year I learned about what it felt like for your heart to break. Despite his promise, he never came back. And our phone calls and emails slowly trickled away into nothing as we both got busy with life.

But I never forgot about the best friend who had held my heart in his hands.

And despite my vow to never feel that way again, I would get mine broken several times before I ever saw Parker again. When I fell, I fell fast and *hard*.

That was the curse of being a hopeless romantic.

CHAPTER 1

Audrey

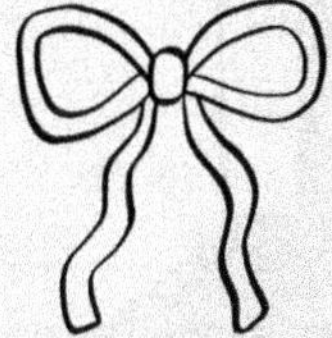

O*nce Upon a Time…*
I'd always dreamed about those words. Thought that one day, it would be the start of my story, and they'd be meant for me. That I'd be the girl in a glittering dress, with the man she loved standing in front of her with a bouquet of pink roses. So, I'd spent my whole life hoping and praying for my happily ever after. Imagining it like a dream.

But life wasn't a fairytale.

Because I was just Audrey Rose Ashford, your typical college student. Sorority girl, lover of all things pink, and a theater kid. I wouldn't get my perfect fairytale ending. Maybe that was okay. Life would still go on, just like it always had. True love or not, I was chasing after my dreams, the life I wanted so desperately.

"Good morning, Sleeping Beauty," my sister, Ella, called, opening the blinds to the window in our shared room.

I groaned, throwing my pillow at her instead of moving. "Five more minutes."

She clicked her tongue. "It's Saturday."

"Yeah, and?" I sat up, brushing my hair behind my ears as I narrowed my eyes at her. "Saturdays are for sleeping in."

"Did you forget what we promised we'd do this weekend?" She quirked an eyebrow at me, popping her hand on her hip.

"Yes…?" Honestly, I had. Between classes and sorority activities, I'd almost forgotten that Halloween was creeping up on us.

"You really *are* exhausted, aren't you?" Ella gave me that look —that older sister, *I'm disappointed in you look*—because even if she was only thirty minutes older than me, she was still the older, more responsible twin. I loved it, and I hated it simultaneously. "We're supposed to finish our costumes."

"Oh. Right!" Duh. We'd picked out the fabric last month on a whim of a shopping trip, and I'd fallen in love. Though that wasn't hard, considering it was pink and sparkly, my two favorite things.

I was convinced anything could be fixed with a bit of glitter.

Halloween was next week. Which meant an entire weekend full of parties and the best excuse to dress up. One I wouldn't be turning down. "Any chance we can get coffee before we start?"

"Already arranged." She pulled a cup from behind her back, brandishing it towards me.

"You're my favorite sister ever." Ignoring the cup, I flung my arms around her neck.

"I'm your *only* sister."

"Semantics." Grabbing my cup of coffee, I sipped on it, letting the caramel flavor pool on my tongue. After a quick shower and some caffeine, I'd definitely be ready for the day.

My twin was in a costume design program at Castleton University, which meant she made costumes for school, too. Though thankfully, she didn't mind an extra sewing project or two. It worked out for me because I couldn't sew to save my life. I'd tried a few times, but each project had only ended up in a shredded mess.

It was better that I stuck to the things I was good at.

Twisting my hair up into a clip, I blew my bangs off my forehead and went to the closet to change out of my pajamas. Our shared closet was full of pastel shades, though there was more pink and blue than anything else.

I was a sucker for all things pink, and I might have had a slight shopping addiction. Ella didn't complain, though, benefiting from our overflowing closet.

After a quick shower and pulling on a pink Pi Rho Sigma crewneck with leggings, I came back to our room to find Ella already hard at work on her sewing machine. All the pattern pieces were already cut out, and she'd started constructing the bodice pieces last week.

She bit her lip in concentration as she fed the fabric through the machine.

"Can I help with anything?" I asked, fiddling with my fingers.

She threw a mostly finished top in my direction. "Want to rhinestone this?"

"Hell yes."

What I said before about glitter? Double that for rhinestones.

As far as I was concerned, the more sparkle, the better.

WE LOOKED PERFECT. Looking at us in the mirror, I couldn't help but smile. For years, we'd always done matching costumes. This year, however, I was a pink witch, and Ella had designed a princess costume for herself. One she *still* hadn't put on, even though it was Halloween weekend and we had a party to get to.

"What do you think?" I asked, both of us inspecting Ella's makeup and hair in the mirror. If sewing and creating was her talent, makeovers were mine. I'd loved makeup ever since I was little playing with my Barbies, and now my friends always asked me to do theirs.

"I swear, you're my Fairy Godmother," Ella laughed, touching her cheeks. "Your transformations are like *magic*."

I looked down at my costume, twirling my hips so the dress

would flounce out. "Well, you made me *this,* so I guess you're mine as well."

"The perfect pair," Ella said, a smile on her face.

Laughing, I poked her in the shoulder. "Come on, go get dressed! It's getting late."

The party hadn't even started yet, but I was way too excited.

My twin rolled her eyes at me, unzipping her Castleton University sweatshirt and sliding her leggings off.

"No one gets there when parties start, anyway," Ella grumbled, picking up her dress and pulling it on over her hips before taking her bra off. "Zip me up?"

I nodded, and once Ella had her silver heels on, she turned to me. "Happy?"

"You used to dream about these parties, you know." I still loved them. Seeing friends, socializing, and getting compliments on my outfits. It might have been shallow, but they made me feel good, so no complaints here.

"Dreams change." Ella huffed out.

My voice was quiet when I responded, "Come on, not all guys are like that. You know it." She'd had a rough experience last year walking in on a guy cheating on her, and ever since, had been focusing more on classes instead of having fun. Tonight, I wanted her to let loose and forget about that. She was a catch, and anyone who didn't see that was an *idiot.*

"Finishing touch," I murmured, gently placing the tiara in Ella's bun. "An outfit fit for a princess."

She looked perfect. We both did. I loved the fluffy pink skirt on mine, the way it fanned out around me as I twirled, and even my pink witch hat.

"Shall we?" Ella asked, linking her arm through mine.

I grinned at my twin. "Heck yeah. Let's go!"

Heading out of our room, we walked arm in arm down the stairs of our sorority house.

While we didn't usually go to the Delta Sig fraternity's parties, I'd wanted a change of scenery.

Mostly because I didn't want to run into my ex, and I knew exactly what circles he ran in. I scrunched up my nose at the thought.

"What?" Ella asked, poking me in the arm.

I shook my head. "Nothing. Just glad our street's a little quieter." Honestly, the fraternity houses on the weekend were a constant barrage of pulsing music. The sorority house was a few blocks away, giving us the precious silence we needed so I could *sleep.*

Sometimes I joked that my favorite hobby was sleeping, but I was definitely grumpier when I didn't get my full eight hours of sleep every night. Ten hours? Bliss.

Ella bit her lip, rocking on her strappy silver heels. "Are you sure about this?"

"Of course—" I grinned. "It'll be fun! We'll just grab a drink and wander." I stopped walking, turning to face my sister. "If you're not having fun after that, we'll head back, okay?"

She nodded. "Okay."

Pivoting on my foot, I headed to the house, only to stop when a large frame blocked the path. I froze when he wrapped his arms around my waist.

My ex-boyfriend nuzzled his nose into my hair. "Aud. There you are, baby." He was slurring his words a little. Was he already drunk?

I tried to push him off of me. "I'm *not* your baby." Stepping back, Ella grabbed my hand, squeezing it tight.

"Course you are." He frowned. "You love me."

"No, Duke. We broke up, remember?" I shook my head. "You cheated on me." Among other things. Really, our relationship wasn't great to begin with. He'd never cared about me, only what I could do for him. I'd just been so infatuated with him that I hadn't seen that until it was too late. He *was* handsome, with swoopy dark blonde hair and blue eyes I'd let myself get lost in. But his good looks couldn't hide his horrible personality.

Tonight, he was dressed as a sexy cop. *Vomit.* Just thinking about sex with him made me want to throw up. He'd never even gone down on me. What had I been thinking?

"We have to go. Bye, Duke." Tightening my grip on Ella's hand, I started walking away, hoping he wouldn't follow us.

"You're going to regret this!" my ex shouted.

I rolled my eyes. "Seems unlikely!"

Without turning around or looking back, I navigated us onto the front porch of the Delta Sigma Iota fraternity house. Our friend Sutton was here with her boyfriend Forest, who was friends with the president, so I'd deemed it as safe.

"Are you okay?" Ella asked, squeezing my hand.

"Yeah." I let out a breath. "He's annoying, but he's harmless." This wasn't the first time, and I was sure it wouldn't be the last.

"Ro…" She frowned.

"Come on, let's just go inside. Everything's fine."

Now if I could just get my heart to believe it too.

GOING OUTSIDE FOR SOME AIR, I leaned on the porch railing, looking up at the night sky. The party was already in full swing when we arrived, making it easy to disappear into the crowds. After a few drinks, I'd felt less off-kilter.

The stars twinkled above me, and I closed my eyes. It was so easy to fake a smile, to be that bubbly, outgoing girl everyone loved. But I was tired. All I wanted was one night where I didn't have to pretend.

Where I could just be *me*. Though some days, I didn't even know who that was.

I hummed to myself, looking up at the sky. Sometimes I wasn't even aware I was singing to myself until someone else pointed it out.

The sliding door behind me opened and shut, and when the wood creaked, I turned to find a guy mirroring my position on the other side of the deck as he ran his hands through his hair.

"Oh." I rested my hand over my heart.

"I'm sorry," he said. "I didn't mean to frighten you."

"No." I shook my head. "You didn't. I just didn't expect anyone else to be out here."

He stepped out into the light.

I was frozen. There was no way. He simply couldn't be… *"Parker?"*

He looked surprised as his eyes traced over me before settling on mine, his gaze softening. "Rosie? Is that you?"

It had been almost a decade since I'd seen him, but I knew who he was instantly. There was no mistaking his smile. That messy brown hair. He used to run his hands through it when he was nervous. Did he still do that?

I didn't really know him anymore. But he'd been my friend. My best friend. The only person I'd ever been as close to as I was with Ella.

He looked the same, and yet completely different. Gone was the lanky boy I'd known, and in front of me was a *man*. Parker had filled out his frame, his biceps straining against his flannel shirt. Yep, it was official—my childhood best friend was *handsome*.

"Hi," I whispered the word, frozen in place. What was he doing here? There was no way we'd been going to the same school for the last two years and had never bumped into each other, right? "I can't believe you're here."

CHAPTER 2
Parker

New year, new me. At least, that's what I'd been trying to tell myself ever since I transferred to CU. My first three years of college weren't exactly the *greatest*, but I was determined to make senior year my best year yet.

Castleton had offered me a full ride between academic and athletic scholarships, and I hadn't been able to turn that down. I'd wanted a change and to leave Rhode Island.

So here I was.

I was going to focus on classes, lacrosse, and keeping my head on straight. My team, friends, and a social life came secondary to my primary purpose: getting my degree and starting my career. Nothing else mattered.

"Yo, man!" came the voice of my new teammate, Samuel. He also happened to occupy the room next to mine in the Lacrosse house and was constantly barging in to talk to me.

Maybe he knew I didn't really have any friends here. That I only went to the required team practices and bonding activities, and I left the latter early most of the time. After the way last school year ended, I wasn't exactly looking to make friends with my teammates.

"What's up, Sam?" I asked him, leaning back on my desk

chair. My textbook for my architectural design class lay open on the desk, and I'd planned to get a chunk of studying done tonight.

"We're going out tonight. You're coming with us."

I frowned, looking at the book in my lap. "Why?"

He shook his head. "What do you mean, *why*? You haven't come out with the team once since the semester started, Maxwell."

He was right. I hadn't gone out once. But that was because I had other shit to do. Studying, for starters.

"But…"

"Come on. Please?"

I sighed. This wasn't me. I used to always be the life of the party—the easy going guy on the team. Maybe I could be that guy again. "Okay," I finally agreed. "But I don't have a costume." It was Halloween weekend on campus, after all, and I'd been hearing people talk about what they were wearing to the parties the entire week in class.

"Don't worry, bro. I've got you covered." He slapped a hand on my shoulder, grinning.

Groaning, I ran my hands through my hair.

I already knew it was going to be a long night.

I'D LOST count of the amount of parties I'd been dragged to, house after house, as my teammates drank beer after beer. Finally, we'd gotten to one of the frat houses. I'd shed the stupid costume they'd given me at the last party, instead wearing my black t-shirt and flannel.

Grabbing a fresh beer from the kitchen, I wandered into the back of the house, finding a few of my teammates chatting with some girls dressed in short skirts.

It's not that I blamed them for chasing after girls, but I'd promised the coach when I accepted being on the team here that

I would be on my best behavior. My life this year was class and lacrosse—no distractions.

That didn't mean I couldn't look. No girl had caught my eye yet, though. There were a multitude of costumes here tonight, ranging from cute to skimpy versions of every animal you could possibly imagine.

And then I saw her. Long strands of blonde hair, like the color of sunshine. A sparkly, poofy pink dress that would have been absolutely ridiculous on anyone else. Pink heels that tied into bows at the ankles. And to top it all off, a pink witch hat.

"Who's that?" I asked, unable to tear my eyes away. Though I couldn't see her face, her presence lit up the entire room. Like the sun revolved around her, rising and setting based on her smile.

"Who?" Samuel followed my gaze, a smirk covering his face when he saw her. "The blonde?" I just nodded."Some theater girl, I think. Dunno." Sam's voice drew me out of my trance. He shook his head. "They're more trouble than they're worth. Stick to the ones who aren't so high maintenance."

I snorted. "I won't be doing any of that, Sam. No girls. Got enough going on this year."

He shook his head. "Whatever you say, man."

Rolling my eyes, I downed the rest of my beer. I wanted to go talk to her. Maybe it was the beer. I wanted to know if she tasted like sunshine.

I wasn't that drunk, right? Fuck, I needed to cut myself off. No girls. I'd been so good this year.

Smoothing a hand over my face, I crumpled the can of beer in my hands. "I'm gonna go find the bathroom."

"There's one upstairs. Normally the one down here has a line."

"Cool. Thanks, man."

He nodded, turning towards the kitchen. "I'm gonna go see if I can find some food in this place. I'm starving."

The path up the stairs was empty, and that was when I heard

it. Singing. A beautiful, melodic voice. I was entranced. A flash of pink. Bouncy blonde hair. And then she was gone.

Back down the stairs, into the throes of the party. Where did she go? I pinched my eyes shut— if only to hear it again—but the only sounds came from the party downstairs.

Damn. The girl had sounded like an angel. I wondered if I could get her to sing for me again.

Slipping into the bathroom—which, thankfully, was empty— I splashed some water on my face before taking care of business and then washing my hands.

The water was a wake-up call. I needed some air. Needed to not think about the beautiful blonde who I'd only caught a glimpse of. Was it her I'd heard?

It was like something I'd heard in my dreams, and I was dying to hear it again.

Needing a break from the party, I headed to the door that led into the backyard that I'd seen earlier, only to find someone else had the same thought as me. It was the girl in pink I'd seen inside. The beautiful girl who had been singing to herself upstairs before I'd lost her. She was leaning against the rail, illuminated by the moonlight.

Sliding the door open, I joined her outside, copying her position on the other side. I leaned against the railing, staring up at the stars. The air outside was crisp, given the temperatures this time of year, but I wouldn't complain. I had my flannel and a pair of jeans on, besides. It had been colder up in New England, so I was used to it.

That was when she noticed I was there. "Oh." She sounded surprised.

"I'm sorry," I said. "I didn't mean to frighten you."

Shaking her head, she said, "No. You didn't. I just didn't expect anyone else to be out here."

That voice… I stepped forward, wanting to be closer to her. To ask her to sing for me again.

The girl in pink froze, her eyes growing wide. *"Parker?"*

That stopped me. Her voice. I knew that voice. Knew *her*. She stepped closer, and my heart felt like it had stopped beating. She was here. The girl of my dreams. "Rosie? Is that you?"

How long had it been? When I'd moved away, I'd planned on keeping my promise to my childhood best friend. Keep in contact. Go back and visit. But it'd been hard. We'd moved states away, and I'd had lacrosse and school to keep up with.

"Hi." She whispered the word, her cheeks still the prettiest shade of pink I'd ever seen. "I can't believe you're here."

"You go here?" I blurted out. "To Castleton?"

Audrey nodded, leaning with her back to the railing. "I'm a junior. Majoring in drama."

Of course she was. A smile spread over my face. This felt a lot like fate. Maybe the universe had brought me here for a reason. "I just transferred here this year. Architecture. I'm on the lacrosse team, too."

"Wow." Her eyes widened. "So much has changed, hasn't it?"

I smoothed a hand over my face. Wasn't that the truth? "Yeah." But not everything. She was still the same Rosie Girl I'd known, down to her core. I could feel it. "What were you singing?"

She blushed. "Oh, you heard me?"

I nodded. *You sounded beautiful.* Words on the tip of my tongue. "Yeah. You always were an amazing singer, you know?"

"It was just a Taylor Swift song." Audrey brushed me off. "I don't even notice I'm doing it sometimes." She brushed a lock of golden blonde hair behind her ear, turning towards me.

"Do you want to sit?"

She looked around the porch, her eyes landing on the patio furniture. "Yes."

Tucking her legs underneath her on the wicker couch, she took her witch hat off and stuck it on the glass table.

"This is fun," I said, gesturing to her costume. "Little pink witch. I like it."

"You should see Ella," she said, smiling. "She made both of our costumes."

"She goes here too?" I asked, though I didn't know why I was surprised. They'd always been close, even for twins.

"Mhm." Audrey hummed in response. "She's majoring in costume design."

"That's cool." Reaching over, I brushed a thumb over her cheekbone.

"W-what was that for?"

"You had a fleck of glitter on your cheek."

"Oh." She looked down at her lap. "Occupational hazard, really. Sometimes I probably use too much glitter, but…"

But she loved it. It had always been that way. When we were younger, her bike had been pink with a little white basket. She'd worn her pink sundresses to play with me in the mud and go on adventures around the neighborhood. Audrey had always loved the color, sparkles, and being the center of attention.

Maybe that was why I couldn't take my attention off of her. Because she lit up my world in a flurry of pink, and I was entranced, like she had me under her spell.

Childhood best friend, I reminded myself. Even if we were more like strangers right now. It had been almost a decade, yet slipping back into a friendship with her felt as easy as riding a bike.

"Where's your costume?" she asked, raising an eyebrow.

"Ah." It was my turn to be embarrassed. "I sort of ditched it at the last party. It was stupid, anyway."

"I'm sure that's not true."

"No." I rubbed my forehead. "It was. My teammates made me wear these awful demon horns and fake vampire teeth."

Audrey burst out laughing. "A demon? God, that's the last thing I can imagine you dressing up as."

"It's been a few years since I did," I admitted. "I'm not really that interested in Halloween anymore."

"But you loved it when we were younger," she pouted.

Not really. I just loved making her happy, and *she* loved dressing up. I went trick-or-treating with her every year, content to be her protector. The last year before I moved away, we had a big Halloween party at my house, but the two of us had spent most of our time sitting on the swings in my backyard.

Back then, Ella and Audrey always wore matching costumes. I'd just dressed up as whatever she told me to be. It wasn't like I had a sibling to dress up with, so I didn't care as long as it made her smile.

Even though she was a year younger than me, she always got her way. Maybe it was her outgoing, bubbly, sunshiny personality. In comparison, I was quiet. Shy. Easygoing. Sure, I could be brave, too, but it had mostly been for her.

"Halloween was always fun growing up," I admitted. "You made it fun."

"Yeah." She was quiet. "Listen, I should—"

"Don't go," I practically begged, reaching out and grabbing her hand.

Audrey giggled. "I was going to say I should probably find Ella and tell her we're hanging out. That way she doesn't miss me."

"Okay." I nodded. "After that... do you want to get out of here?"

She grinned. "*Yes.*"

CHAPTER 3

Audrey

"Ella!" I shouted, spotting my twin standing off to the side. She'd always been more of a wallflower, desperate to blend in even though she was the best person I knew. I wished she saw herself the way I saw her.

"Did you see Sutton?" Ella yelled over the music.

Sutton was our friend who had initially rushed the sorority with us, but dropped out because it wasn't *her thing*. She was dating Forest Carter, a baseball player, and they seemed so happy together. That was all that mattered. He swept her off her feet like a true Prince would. Not that I'd know anything about that.

"I did!" I grinned. "Her fishnets are *awesome*. I dig it."

She had a bold style that would never flatter my complexion or golden hair—dark hair, pale skin, and red-as-sin lips that looked sultry and sexy simultaneously.

I wasn't sure sexy was even in my DNA. Cute? Sure. I knew how to be cute. I liked to think I was beautiful, too. But I'd never felt *sexy*.

But maybe that was just the way I felt after Duke had taken my confidence and stomped all over it. God, I hated that I'd ever thought he was the right guy for me.

He was nothing like Parker. We'd only been talking for a few minutes, reminiscing on our childhood memories, but all the reasons I'd loved being friends with him had come right back. Parker made me feel safe. Protected.

"You'll never guess who's here at CU," I said, still raising my voice over the music.

"Um…" Ella fidgeted with the strap of her blue dress as she struggled to come up with a guess. Not that I'd expected her to have one.

"Parker!" I exclaimed. "Parker Maxwell!"

She blinked. "The boy who lived next door to us when we were younger? Wasn't he like… your best friend until his family moved away?"

"Yes!" I gushed, looking across the room and catching Parker's eyes. He smiled at me, and I raised my fingers in a small wave.

He'd followed me back inside after I'd mentioned needing to tell Ella where I was. I didn't want her to be alone or worry about me. And I knew she would. But I hadn't expected Parker to ask me to keep talking, either.

"He must have been, what, thirteen when they moved?" Ella asked, and I nodded. "And now he's going *here*?"

It was a crazy coincidence that I'd run into him here after all this time. That he'd ended up transferring to the same university as us.

"You don't mind if I ditch you to catch up with him, right? Am I a terrible sister?" A wince slipped out of me. "I'm a terrible sister." After all, I'd practically forced her to come with me to the party, and here I was, ready to leave her behind.

Ella shook her head. "No." She just laughed. "*Go.*" I raised an eyebrow, ready to protest, but my twin just waved me off. "Seriously, I'll be fine. Maybe I'll go hang out with Sutton."

I nodded. Sutton was currently on the couch, chatting with a dark-skinned girl wearing a flapper costume, but I knew she'd welcome Ella. "I think I'm gonna go grab another drink," my sister added, heading towards the kitchen.

Blowing out a breath, I turned to find Parker standing in the corner, his hands shoved into his pocket. His eyes were focused on me.

Heading back over, I smiled at him, still holding my hat in my hands. "Alright. Where to?"

Parker's face lit up with a grin. "Tacos?"

I groaned at the thought. "Hell yes. I know just the place."

"Oh my god, I'm stuffed."

We'd both shoved into a booth at the local Mexican restaurant that mostly served college students, especially at this time of night. It wasn't much more than a hole in the wall, but the food was *good*, and given that the only thing I'd had since dinner earlier this evening was a few drinks, I had desperately needed this.

"This was fucking amazing," Parker agreed.

We slipped back into friendship so easily. Our entire dinner had been filled with laughter and grins. It was comfortable. Easy.

For a second earlier, when he'd asked if I wanted to get out of there, my body had heated. Like I'd thought he was asking if I wanted to hook up.

Of course he didn't. There was no way we'd ever be together, anyway. He was my friend. Even if I'd thought for a moment that he'd looked at me with heat in his eyes... that had dissolved when he'd realized who I was.

And, god, he looked like *that*. He could probably get any girl he wanted. That thought made me feel strangely possessive, and I didn't know why.

He was my friend. He'd probably slept around a lot during the last few years. It wasn't like I expected Parker to wait for *me*.

There was no way he knew of my childhood crush. That I'd wanted to marry him when I was younger.

I ran my hands over my pink poofy dress. My witch hat was sitting on the bench next to me. "So, lacrosse, huh?"

"Yeah. I started playing in High School. Got lucky enough to get a scholarship to play, so thankfully, I had a full ride to my school up in New England." He shook his head.

"*Had*?" I asked, not sure if he wanted me to pry.

Parker ran his hands through his hair, not answering my question. "I was lucky enough that Castleton offered me the same scholarship. And I was a red shirt my first year, so I still had two years of eligibility left."

Part of me wanted to ask why he transferred here, but I couldn't find the words. Instead, I finally asked, "So you'll be here for two more years?"

I didn't want to get my hopes up, but Parker had always been a grade above me. I'd already been preparing myself to say goodbye at the end of the year. It would have been just my luck, the universe putting my childhood best friend back in my life only to take him away from me again a year later.

He nodded. "Architecture is a five-year degree, so it just worked out that way."

Oh. I couldn't help the happiness that flowed from me. "That's great."

A laugh sprung free from his lips. "Rosie Girl, attached to me already?"

I blushed. "I already said goodbye to you once. I'm hoping I don't have to again." Looking out the window, I hoped I hadn't said too much. Hadn't revealed how desperate I was to have his friendship back.

"You won't," he promised, nudging me under the table with his sneaker. "You can't get rid of your best friend that easily, after all."

"Ella might be offended you're taking her position."

"Nah." Parker flashed me a smile. "She was just keeping it warm for me."

There were butterflies in my stomach, and he had no idea. God, I needed to control myself. My childhood crush was coming back to life too easily.

Friends, I reminded myself. We were just friends.

"Come on," Parker said, extending out a hand. We'd already paid for our meals, so we were free to go.

"Where are we going?" I asked.

He smiled. "You'll see."

OUR BEDROOM WAS STILL empty when I entered it. It was late—past three in the morning. Parker and I had stayed out late, catching up. Where was Ella? I frowned, going into the bathroom and doing my skincare routine. There was no way I'd be falling asleep with all this glitter on me, after all.

Grinning at myself in the mirror, I couldn't stop thinking about my night with Parker. How after tacos, we'd gone to the middle of campus, lying on the grass and staring up at the night sky. How he'd asked me to sing for him, and surprisingly, I'd agreed.

But what was more surprising was the way I'd kept going. How when I'd started singing a duet, he'd joined me.

In the quiet of the campus, our bodies pressed against the slightly damp grass, the moment felt almost sacred. His voice was deep, much deeper than I remembered it. But the last time I'd known him had been before puberty changed him into the man he was now.

God, he was talented. Did he even know it?

I hummed to myself as I washed my face.

The only thing that would have made last night better was if he had wrapped me in his arms and danced with me. I blushed at the thought. *Friends,* I scolded myself. I'd let myself have one last night of dreaming about him, and then I'd be good. Because Parker was my childhood friend, and there was no way I'd mess that up.

Still, when he'd hugged me tightly after walking me back to the sorority house, I'd buried my nose in his shirt, inhaling his scent. He smelled clean and crisp—all man. Like woodsy spice that I wanted to bottle up or burn as a candle.

God, friends didn't sniff each other like that.

Good night, Rosie girl, he'd said, his beautiful amber eyes keeping mine captive. *Sleep tight.*

Night, I'd whispered back, not wanting to break the moment —the night.

It was like something out of my dreams. He'd always been my *Dream Boy.* The one I'd written letters to in my diary growing up. I never wrote his name, but it was always him. His face I'd see. His heart I was wishing for.

"You're hopeless," I said, pointing a finger at my reflection in the mirror as I brushed my teeth. "Stop pining over your child-hood best friend."

He'd never acted like anything other than my older brother. And why would he? We'd been kids. Twelve and thirteen since he'd moved away. If his dad hadn't gotten a job, if he'd stayed for high school, what would have happened?

I sighed. No point lingering in the past. "No more dreaming about Parker," I told myself.

Even though I knew I couldn't keep that promise.

"Ro?" Ella whispered, waking me up. As much as I loved sleeping, I hadn't been able to fall into a deep sleep last night. Partially because Ella hadn't been there. Instead, I'd tossed and turned for the last few hours.

It wasn't even dawn yet.

Sitting up, I stared at her. Usually, she was the responsible sister. I never had to worry about her. Until last night. "Where were you? You didn't text me to let me know you were okay or anything." We had a pact—we always told each other we were okay. That way, the other person didn't worry all night.

Ella made a sheepish face, holding up her phone. "It died, and I forgot to plug it in." I took in her appearance. Same dress as last night. No shoes. Ruined makeup. Her hair was a mess. One look and I had a damn good idea what she'd been up to last night. Damn girl. At least one of us got some last night. "Did you have fun catching up with Parker?"

I tried to ignore the fact that she was changing the subject. I'd let her for now, but I'd get answers out of her, eventually. "Yes. Can you believe I found him again after all these years?"

She just hummed in response, and I raised my eyebrows at her as she changed out of her dress and into a large sorority t-shirt.

"So we're just not going to talk about you?" I asked, still waiting.

"Nope." She flopped onto her bed.

I rolled my eyes before climbing out of my bed and into hers, snuggling against my twin.

"Ella," I whispered, holding tighter when she sighed. "Are you okay?"

She opened her eyes, looking at me. I was worried about my sister. I didn't want her to keep secrets from me. "Yeah," she croaked out. "I'm fine."

"If you're sure..." I'd get it out of her later.

For now, I just stayed where I was, holding my sister.

CHAPTER 4
Parker

NOVEMBER

The last few weeks since running into Audrey at the party had been incredible. We'd fallen back into friendship, hanging out whenever we both had free time.

Audrey was incredible. The way she lit up talking about the theater department, her hopes, and her dreams, was contagious.

She made me want to be better. To strive to achieve my dreams, too. Working as an architect had been the end goal for the last few years, but it was only now that I was in my second-to-last year that I had realized how much I needed to focus. Academics had always come easily to me. I was book smart and barely had to study to get good grades. Now that I was in upper division courses though, things were different. Balancing that and being an athlete took up all my time.

Still, I couldn't resist being around her.

Putting down my weights, I pulled out my phone. Pulled up our texts and scrolled through them. They were mostly random shit. Us sending each other memes, random references to our childhood that made me laugh. It was good. Easy. The way it should be.

Nothing like my relationship had been last year. I should have known it wasn't right. That she'd been going behind my back with my teammate. More reasons I'd sworn off being involved with a girl. My grip tightened on my phone as I typed out a message.

PARKER

Do you have plans tonight?

AUDREY

We're supposed to have some sort of bonding event at the sorority house. Probably just watching a movie. Why?

Just wanted to see if you wanted to be my dinner buddy.

I hated eating dinner alone, and though I probably could have asked one of my teammates, I much preferred her company.

AUDREY

Yeah. Wanna meet at the Commons?

Hell yeah. I whooped, pumping my fist in the air, forgetting where I was.

Sam gave me a strange look, and Derek Stephens, our team captain, rolled his eyes. We were all working out in the gym facilities reserved for student athletes. We might not have games until the spring season, but we still had to keep up with our training and stay in shape.

"You texting your girl, Maxwell?"

I shook my head. "She's not my girl. Just my friend."

"Sure." Stephens shook his head. "That's what they all say."

I crossed my arms over my chest. It was true. She was just my friend. Audrey didn't think of me like that. She'd made that clear, pushing me into the friend zone. It was fine. Stopping to take a long drink from my water bottle, I wiped the sweat off my forehead. "Whatever. I'm gonna head to the showers." I had finished my workout, anyway.

"Bye, Lover Boy."

Rolling my eyes, I ignored them making kissy sounds. They were wrong. I didn't have time for a girlfriend. But I did have time for a friend.

One whose every word I hung on.

HER SMILING face greeted me as she waited by the door, wrapped in a white peacoat with a light pink scarf around her throat.

"Hi."

"Hey." I wrapped an arm around her shoulder, tugging her close to me in a side hug. She smelled like strawberries and roses, something I was trying hard not to notice. "You hungry?"

"Starving," she admitted. "I've been so busy today that I didn't even have time for lunch."

I frowned. "Rosie, you gotta eat."

She gnawed on her lower lip. "I know, I know. I'll be better, I promise."

Chuckling, I guided her inside, the smell of food immediately hitting my senses.

Audrey shrugged out of my grasp, and we both headed to grab food before meeting back up at the register.

"You can put them both on my plan," I said, handing the cashier my card.

"Parker," her eyes narrowed. "You don't have to pay for my food. It's fine."

I shrugged. "Do you know how big my meal plan is?"

"Still…" She had that cute little pink blush again.

"Rosie Girl," I sighed. "Let me. It's the least I can do for my friend."

"Fine." She rolled her eyes, picking her tray up as the cashier swiped my ID before handing it back to me. "Thanks, man."

He nodded, and Audrey and I headed to a booth for two, sliding in on either side. There were plenty of booths that would hold four people, but I didn't want any of my teammates joining us and teasing me in front of Audrey. They'd probably embarrass her, and I wanted to protect her from that.

Plus, I didn't want to know if she found any of them attractive. She was my friend, but I didn't think I could watch her date one of my teammates.

It would break me, and I wasn't sure if I could come back from that.

Shoveling food in, I ignored the thought as I ate my cheeseburger and fries. Once the season started, I'd have a strict diet and calorie plan, but for now, I'd enjoy something a little more greasy.

A shadow came over our table, and I looked up to find a tall blonde man standing over us.

"Duke." Audrey stiffened. "What are you doing here?"

"It's the cafeteria, Aud. Aren't I allowed to eat?"

But he didn't have a tray in his hands. And his intense focus on Audrey was unnerving me.

"Well, yeah, but…" She fidgeted, not meeting his eyes. When we'd sat down, she'd shrugged off her coat, leaving her just in a baby pink sweater. Instead of looking up, she played with the hem.

Fuck. She was clearly uncomfortable. Who was this guy?

"Do we have a problem?" I asked, standing up and drawing to my full height. He might have been tall, but I was taller—bigger. All of my lacrosse training had beefed me up, and I used my size to tower over him.

"Why are you eating with my girl?" He sneered.

"Your girl?" I raised an eyebrow. "Are you his girl, Audrey?" She hadn't even mentioned this guy to me.

"N-no." She shook her head. "We broke up."

Ah. So this was an ex. Fuck. I felt a flare of possession run through me. She wasn't mine, but damn if I wouldn't protect her. So, of course, I felt protective. That was all this was.

"You heard her," I said, staring him down. "She's not yours."

"Aud, baby. I just want a second chance." His floppy blonde locks and blue eyes might have been handsome, but he seemed sleazy. I hated guys like that. Ones that would take advantage of females.

I turned to her. "Do you want him to stay, Rosie?"

"Leave, Duke." She narrowed her eyes at him. "I'm not getting back together with you."

He rolled his eyes, leaning in close to the table. "You will," he said, and Audrey's face was ghostly pale. "Who else is going to want my sloppy seconds?"

My chest rumbled in warning, a low growl slipping out, and he looked at me. "No matter what she says, she's mine."

And then he spun on his heel, walking away.

When he finally left, I slid back into the booth, looking at her.

"Are you okay?"

She was shaking, practically seething with anger. But she took a deep breath before nodding.

"Is he always like that?" I asked, furrowing my brow. "Bothering you?"

"Well..." Audrey bit her lip. "Sometimes. Mostly, he leaves me alone." She shrugged, looking down at her glass. "It's just when he feels threatened that he lashes out. Or when he drinks and forgets we broke up."

"Rosie..." I sighed.

"Don't poke the bear, Parker. He'll get the hint, eventually." She shook her head. "I'm sure it was just that he saw me eating with you. He feels ownership over me still. But he should have thought about that before he cheated on me."

He cheated on her? Fuck. I really wished I'd punched him now. Who the fuck would cheat on a girl that radiated sunshine like she did? She was the most gorgeous girl in any room.

Looking down at her plate, she pushed around her pasta with a fork, avoiding my gaze.

"Audrey. Did he hurt you?" My words were soft, full of concern. "Did he hit you?"

She flinched, her eyes finally connecting with mine. "N-no."

Why didn't I believe her?

"Not physically," Audrey whispered. "He never laid a hand on me. He just..." She shrugged again. "Can we not talk about it tonight?" She croaked out. "I don't..."

"Okay." I placed my hand over hers, squeezing lightly before pulling away. "I'm here, you know? I'll be your protector any time you need it, Audrey."

She let out a breath, nodding, some of the tension easing from her body. "Thank you. You've always been such a good friend to me, Parker."

Friend. Fuck. Was that all I was ever going to be?

I'd have to learn to accept it. Friendship with her was better than nothing. At least this way, I got her smiles. Got to be around her sunshine.

DECEMBER

"I can't believe the semester's already over," Audrey said, rubbing her nose on her sweater. "I don't want to say goodbye again."

It felt like nine years ago when I'd told her I was moving. "Hey," I said, placing my hand on her shoulder and speaking softly. "It's okay. I'm coming back this time. You'll see me next semester." I squeezed lightly before taking my hand off of her.

She nodded. "I know." Fiddling with the bottom of her sweater, she looked at the ground. It was the first time since meeting her again that I'd seen her wearing jeans. I wasn't even sure she owned a pair. The girl was always in dresses with tights or leggings.

"I wish you could come with us on break," Audrey whispered. She and Ella were heading to Vermont for a ski trip with their friends. Their car was loaded, and we were standing at the back of it, saying goodbye.

"It's okay. I get it." I shoved my hands in my pockets to resist touching her. "Besides, my parents would be upset with me if I didn't come home." I hadn't gone back for Thanksgiving, either. And spring would be busy enough that I probably wouldn't see them unless they came down for one of my games.

Given how upset my Dad still was with me about the situation at my last school, I didn't see that happening. I hadn't run away, exactly, but sometimes it felt like I had.

My mom was excited to have me home.

"I'll text you," I promised. One I wouldn't break.

She raised an eyebrow. "You said that before."

I clutched my heart. "I was thirteen and an idiot. Believe me, I regret losing those years of our friendship. But you're stuck with me now. Besides, who else would I get dinner with?" I cracked a smile.

"True." She sighed, and then wrapped her arms around my waist, hugging me tight.

We didn't touch. Not like this. But I let us have this. I curled my arms around her back, buried my nose in her hair, and inhaled deeply. *Strawberries.* The smell of her shampoo was addicting.

I stepped back, running my hands through my hair. "I'll see you in a few weeks."

"Yeah."

She turned, walking towards the house where I knew Ella was still inside. "Hey, Parker?"

"Hm?"

"Thanks for finding me again." Her smile was bright. Radiant. She pushed a strand of hair behind her ear, her violet-hued blue eyes bright.

I chuckled, dipping my head. "Anything for you, Rosie Girl."

It might have been a coincidence that I'd transferred to her school, but I meant those words. I'd do anything for her. She just didn't know it yet.

But she would.

Best friend or not, I was going to keep Audrey Rose Ashford's heart safe. No matter what it took.

CHAPTER 5

Audrey

Made it.

Good. Glad to hear it.

What are you up to?

Not much. Just finished a workout. You?

Ella's freaking out because Cam's here.

The frat guy? I thought you said she liked him.

She does, she just won't admit it.

He's totally down bad for her.

Crying at the gym.

Is that the Taylor Swift song?

… Yes. Have you been listening?

You do realize how often you sing her music, yeah?

Oh.

It's pretty good. My mom likes it, too. We've
been listening to her newest album all week.

Pretty good? Gasp. That's my queen you're
talking about. She's amazing.

What's your favorite album?

Lover. Hands down. That's not even a question.

PARKER

What's your favorite holiday drink?

AUDREY

What sort of question is that?

I dunno. Mom's insisting eggnog is the best. I
think that stuff is nasty.

Hmmmmm.

Do NOT tell me you like eggnog, Audrey Rose. I
will defriend you.

GASP. You could never.

You're right.

Because you're stuck with me, Rosie Girl.

For the record, my favorite is a hot toddy.
Sutton says hot apple cider is the clear choice.

Also, she says hi.

AUDREY

I wish you had come. This place is boring without you.

PARKER

Break will be over before you know it, and then you're stuck with me, Rosie.

I don't think I'd quite call it *stuck*...

I happen to like hanging out with you, you know.

Spoken like a true friend.

Ha ha. You like hanging out with me too. Admit it.

Of course. Why else would I ask you to have dinner with me every night?

AUDREY

Favorite holiday movie. Go.

PARKER

Do I have any parameters?

No. We're just debating what to watch tonight. James and Adam keep arguing.

James and Adam?

Cam's best friends. The three of us are the single ones up here. The couples ditched us.

Couples, huh?

Well, I basically caught Ella and Cam making out. So even if they haven't said they were official yet, they're as good as together.

Hmmm. And what are these James and Adams's last names?

You're sounding like an overprotective brother right now.

Not your brother.

Just your friend. Looking out for you is what I do.

Right.

Last names, Rosie.

eyeroll James Erikson is the quarterback of the football team. Adam Prince is apparently the heir of some giant corporation.

Alright. They're good guys?

Yes. Now tell me your favorite holiday movie.

Home Alone.

What's yours?

The Santa Clause 2.

Not the original one?

Nah. I love a good love story.

I remember that. You always did.

Alright. Movie's starting. Talk to you later.

PARKER

You know, I'm only a few hours drive from you.

AUDREY

How many?

Less than five.

Parker, you can't drive five hours just to see your friend.

But what about my *best* friend?

Oh, I have the title again?

You know it was always yours.

Hmmmm… Do I?

Gotta go. Everyone's going skiing.

What about you? You going to go on a few runs?

Maybe. I'm pretty good on my feet, you know?

I'd pay to see that.

Haha. Shut up. Talk to you later.

Have fun, Rosie Girl.

PARKER

I was serious, you know. If you want, I'll drive up there.

You don't have to do that. Besides, the trip is almost over.

I'll see you in two weeks, remember?

We'll be back on campus before you know it.

Fine.

AUDREY

Driving home now.

PARKER

Be safe. Who's taking the first shift?

Me.

Watch the road. The weather's been bad. Not sure if they've plowed yet.

I'll be careful. Promise.

PARKER

Merry Christmas, Audrey Rose.

AUDREY

Merry Christmas, Parker Phillip.

What are the Ashfords up to today?

Opened presents this morning. Now Mom, Ella, and I are watching old Christmas cartoons.

Fun. I'm about to go work out.

On Christmas? What is wrong with you? You're supposed to be drinking hot chocolate and opening presents.

Or eggnog. You know. Since you love it so much.

...

I'm going to pretend you didn't just say that to me.

I gotta stay in shape. Season starts soon, after all. We'll go straight into regular practices when we get back to school.

Right. I almost forgot.

You gonna come to my games, Rosie Girl?

Are you gonna come to my performances?

Definitely. Wouldn't miss a single one.

AUDREY

Ella ditched me to drive back to campus early with Cam.

sniffles Can't believe my twin ditched me for a guy.

So you're driving back alone?

Probably, yeah. It'll be fine. It's not too far, anyway.

I don't like it.

Well, it's not like you can drive here and come with me.

Why not?

...

Parker. I don't need you to come here just so you can drive with me.

Besides, you have to be back at school early for practice.

Parker.

???

Fine. But I'm calling you, and you're going to
talk to me on the phone the whole time.

What about my Taylor Swift jam session?
You're robbing me of that.

Fine.

But I expect you to call me and check in.

J*anuary*
Fidgeting with the phone in my lap, I typed out a text
to Parker.

AUDREY

Leaving my house now. ETA 3:00 PM.

PARKER

Drive safe.

See you soon, Rosie.

My cheeks flushed, even if he wasn't around to see it. We'd
gone from being strangers to friends who got dinner a few times
a week to texting each other every minute of break. It wasn't like
we were even talking about important things, either. It was just
mundane questions as we got to know each other again. Like it
was important to both of us to catch up on every detail we'd
missed over the past decade.

But we hadn't talked on the phone. And despite his offering, I'd refused to let him visit. Refused to let him drive me
back to school. Because I needed some barrier between us.

Something to keep my little crush from blossoming into a full flame.

He was stoking the fire, being thoughtful, caring, and protective. When I thought about how he'd growled at Duke, protecting me from my ex-boyfriend, it made all those old feelings come back.

My best friend, he'd called me. *You know it was always yours.* My heart melted at those words. But did I really believe him? That he'd never had another best friend in all the years we'd lost contact? I'd had Ella, after all. And life had moved on.

Now that he was back in my life, though, it felt like everything was different.

I jammed to Taylor Swift on my drive—mostly my favorite album, *Lover*, though I loved all of her work equally—and tried not to let my thoughts be clouded by Parker Maxwell.

That was easier said than done, however.

I just needed to remind myself that we were best friends, and there was no way we'd ever be anything more than that.

AUDREY

Made it.

STARING up at the pink sorority house with my bag in my hands, I gnawed on my lower lip. It was crazy to think that I was starting the spring semester of my junior year. After this, I'd only have one year left at Castleton. I loved this place, loved my school, and as much as I couldn't wait for the next chapter in my life, I knew I'd miss this, too.

"Ro!" My sister grinned, leaning against a railing. "You made it."

I stuck my tongue out after her. "Only after being ditched. Hope it was worth it."

"It was great." Ella sighed, a dreamy look on her face.

God, it was so unfair that she was getting laid regularly, and I couldn't even remember the last time I'd been kissed. I scrunched up my face, realizing it was probably Duke. Ugh. What I wouldn't do to forget that his lips had ever touched mine.

Maybe what I needed was a hookup. That would solve my problem, wouldn't it? Give me my confidence back. I didn't need to love someone to sleep with them, right?

It seemed like it had worked out for Ella. Even if she *was* toeing a line she shouldn't cross, dating the fraternity president that she'd been paired up with.

Joining her on the porch, I hugged my twin before following her inside, heading upstairs to dump my stuff in the bedroom we used to share. Ever since she'd moved into the presidential suite, I'd had mine to myself.

I had to admit it was a little lonely. But I was making do. At least, I was hoping I'd get used to it. Luckily, Ella was only a floor away from me. It was hard to imagine that one day, I'd go from spending every moment with my twin to hardly seeing her.

Thankfully, we had another year and a half of college left.

"So, what's the plan for the night?" I asked, dropping my bag onto the floor. Ella sat on the bed that used to be hers, though I'd covered it in plain sheets. Not that anyone slept there. I normally just used it to lay out my outfits. "Do you and Cam have plans?"

She blushed. "I was thinking we could do something, actually. Spend some time together before the semester starts, and we're both so busy we forget to even eat or sleep."

"Only you, Ells." I rolled my eyes, sitting across from her. "There's no way I could ever forget to sleep."

Ella laughed. "Are you excited for the semester? The spring musical is creeping up on us."

I nodded. "It's a lot of responsibility, but I can't wait. What about you? How are the costume designs coming?" She'd been working on them over break, taking her sketchbook to the ski lodge and working on them as her boyfriend stared at her like a puppy dog.

It was adorable, really, even if she'd ditched me and spent every night in his bed.

"Good. I still can't believe of all the proposals submitted they picked mine."

"I can. Because you're seriously talented, Ella. And I'm not just saying that because you're my twin, and we share one hundred percent of our DNA."

It was my twin's turn to roll her eyes.

We were identical, down to our blonde hair and height. The only easy way to tell the difference was our hair—I had straight across bangs—and the slight hue variations in our eyes. They were both blue, but mine were a deeper hue that appeared almost violet in some lights.

I collapsed backward on my bed. "Do you ever feel like you're going to blink, and it'll all be over?" Staring up at the ceiling, I heard the mattress creak next to me and felt the dip as Ella lay at my side.

We didn't fit on a twin-sized bed—not well, anyway—but sometimes it felt good to cuddle up next to my sister. Hug her. I didn't need to tell her how much she meant to me—we both knew it was more than words—but I liked to, anyway.

"It's going to be weird when we graduate, isn't it? Then I won't get to do this with you every day."

Ella wrinkled her nose. "What do you mean?"

I turned to face her. "Well, it's not like I'm going to move in with you and Cameron post-graduation."

She bit her lip. "I guess not." I noticed that she didn't deny that she wanted to live with him. Guess that meant it was serious. "Still. We've got time."

Sighing, I turned over, reaching for my phone but realizing I'd left it in my purse when I'd walked in. Getting up, I went to retrieve it, noticing a bunch of unread texts. My parents—just checking in to make sure I'd arrived safely, and then a few from Parker.

PARKER

Welcome back, Rosie Girl.

Hope the drive went well.

What are you doing tonight?

AUDREY

Smooth.

I'm hanging out with Ella. It's girl's night in and we're watching a movie.

Alright. Have fun.

Night.

Ella and I ended up snuggling up in her bed—it was bigger than mine, after all—and watching a movie until we fell asleep.

My dreams that night definitely did *not* feature Parker riding in on a white horse with a sword in his arm to save me from an evil dragon. Maybe I'd been watching too many fairytales.

That was probably it. There was no other reason why I'd be dreaming about my best friend like that.

Not a single one.

CHAPTER 6

Parker

Spring semester meant lacrosse season was starting soon, so our practices were in full swing. I'd spent the last week on campus, getting back into the swing of things before the semester started, but classes were officially back in session as of today.

Samuel slapped my back as we headed back into the locker room after practice. "How's your girl?"

I shook my head. "She's not my girl."

Even though that wasn't true. She *was* mine. She just didn't know it yet. I'd been in love with that girl for my entire life. My best friend. When I was nine, I'd declared to my mom that I was going to marry her someday. Now, though, I knew that was all just a dream.

We were just friends. That was all we'd ever been. And I knew that was all I'd ever be to Audrey, so I was making do. She'd made it clear that we were friends, and I was okay with that. With lacrosse and my degree, I didn't have time for a relationship.

That was what I kept telling myself. That I'd take whatever I can get when it comes to her.

Sam made a noise in the back of his throat. "Sure. You definitely don't like her. I saw the way you looked at her at the Halloween party, remember? And you spend all of your time with her."

Groaning, I dropped my helmet onto the bench, my gloves quickly following behind so I could run my fingers through my hair. "She's my best friend. I've known her since I was a kid. That's all it is."

Since she chased after me with her pink ribbons in her hair. Since she'd followed behind me on her pink bike.

He shrugged, stripping the rest of his gear off and heading towards the showers. "Keep telling yourself that, man."

I was trying. Maybe, one day it would be true.

Last night, when she texted me she was back to campus, I'd stared up at the ceiling in my room, deliberating what to say—resisting from begging to ask to see her.

How had I gone nine years without seeing her when even one month apart felt like this? I liked my life full of her glitter and pink, how she'd always blush just for me, and how everything just felt so easy around her. Like I could be myself. I didn't feel like I needed to be anyone else.

But she'd spent the night hanging out with her sister, and who was I to object to that? Audrey and Ella were close. Growing up, they were practically joined at the hip. Always matching in their little color coded outfits. But I didn't need the pink to tell Audrey apart. There was a sparkle in her violet-hued eyes that couldn't be mistaken for anyone else.

Dumping the rest of my gear into the locker, I grabbed my stuff to also head to the shower when our Coach, Stefan Holmes, popped his head into the locker room.

"Maxwell," he called. "Can I see you in my office when you're done?"

"Sure," I said, dipping my head. Worry churned in my gut. I wasn't in trouble already, right?

I thought I'd been playing well. Meshing with the guys. Sure, I hadn't really attended many of the parties or group hangouts, but now that we were getting regular practices in, I felt good.

Better than I'd felt at the end of last season in Rhode Island.

After showering and collecting my bag, I headed to his office, hair still damp.

"How are you feeling after practice? Getting used to the new dynamics?"

I nodded, because what else could I say? "It's been an adjustment, but I like it here."

Surprisingly, that was true. I liked being a part of the Castleton Chipmunks Lacrosse team, too. The guys were cool. I'd been keeping my distance because of what happened last year, but that wasn't fair to them. I'd make more of an effort this semester.

And maybe I'd bring Audrey along as a buffer. As a *friend*, I reminded myself. Nothing more.

"Still no *distractions*, right? Like we talked about?"

I swallowed roughly. "No, Coach. No distractions." No girlfriends. I had enough on my plate with classes and lacrosse. My schedule for this semester was already full.

Never mind that a beautiful blonde in pink came immediately to mind.

"Good." He hummed, tapping on his desk with his fingertips. "I want to see you out with the team more. Not just at practice or in the weight room."

"Okay."

Coach Holmes looked surprised at how easily I agreed. "Alright. You're free to go then. See you next practice."

"See ya, Coach." I grabbed my bag, heading outside. I had another class before my day was over, and then I planned to hit the gym. But all I really wanted to do was see Audrey.

PARKER

Dinner later?

AUDREY

Don't you have practice?

Not tonight.

Okay. Ella's busy with Cam anyway. What time?

Seven? I'll meet you at the house and we can walk over together.

Okay.

What would have happened if we'd stayed in contact all those years? I could have come to Castleton from the start. We could have gone to college together. And even just thinking that was like a punch to the gut, because it wasn't like I'd intended to go nine years without talking to my best friend.

Maybe we would be together instead of being deep in the friend zone. I sighed, looking up at the sky.

It was worth it, though—being her best friend and a safe place for her. No matter what happened, that was what I wanted to be for her.

This place was becoming my home. Maybe it was Audrey; maybe it was just that I liked the way when the breeze rolled in just right, you could smell the ocean—a reminder that it wasn't too far away—or maybe it was that it finally felt like that fresh start I'd so desperately needed.

So instead of pulling my phone out, I left it in my pocket as I walked back towards the lacrosse house, taking in this place like it was *mine* for the first time.

Like the sun had parted for the first time, and I could finally see.

STARING up at the pink sorority house, I waited for her to come outside. We'd agreed to walk to the dining hall together to grab dinner, and I'd come over after a quick shower post-lifting weights. I'd pulled on a pair of dark wash jeans, a black long-sleeved t-shirt, and my favorite red hoodie.

When Audrey came out, she was wearing a pink sweater dress with tights and riding boots, all bundled up in a fluffy coat.

"Rosie." My heart thumped in my chest, and I rubbed at it. "Hey."

"Hi." She smiled, and it was like my entire world lit up. That was what her smile did to me. "How was your break?"

"You know, the usual." Boring. "How was yours?" I asked. Like we hadn't talked every single day. Like I didn't wait by the phone for her to text me back.

"It was… pretty great, actually." Looking down at her feet, she fiddled with the hem of her sweater. "I'm happy to be back, though. There's just something about being back on campus that I love." She inhaled deeply, like she was taking all of it in.

I did the same, enjoying this place. It was my second semester here, and I'd quickly grown to love it. There was a charm to Castleton and the way everyone seemed to know everyone. We hadn't had that at my old school. Plus, the campus wasn't in the middle of a giant city, making it feel quaint. We were bordered on one side by a neighborhood that mainly featured students, faculty and staff, and a densely wooded area sat on another. Plus, not too far away was the ocean. It was like the best of all worlds.

"I'm happy to be back, too."

She hummed but didn't say anything for a few minutes as we walked. I enjoyed the silence. It wasn't uncomfortable or strained. It was just… peaceful, like we could enjoy each other's presence without needing anything else.

I shoved my hands in my pockets to keep myself from reaching out for her hand. Friends didn't do that. Even though I desperately wanted to feel her palm against mine.

"How's practice been?" Audrey finally asked, breaking the silence.

I nodded. "It's good. You know, I was worried about fitting in with my new team, but they've all been great."

Audrey's face curved into a warm smile. "Of course they are. Because you're great."

Laughing, I shook my head. "You haven't even seen me play yet."

She shrugged as I pulled the door open to the dining hall. "Sometimes you don't have to see something to believe it."

Running my fingers through the hair as we headed to the counter to grab food, I contemplated that thought. If it was possible to know something was true without the prior evidence.

But even without having played a game yet, I knew the guys on my team were good. That it was more than just a sport for them. I could feel it in the air at practice, in the way my teammates treated each other.

There was a sense of camaraderie here that felt like belonging.

"Maybe you're right." I grabbed a plate with a pork chop, rice, and veggies and loaded it onto our tray as Audrey scooped up a bowl of chicken Alfredo.

"Always am," she said with a beaming grin. It was like sunshine, bringing warmth and a glow to my face.

We settled into a table in the back corner, not saying much as we took our first few bites.

"You know, you never told me why you left your last school. How you ended up here." Audrey twirled her pasta around her fork as she watched me, like she was studying my reaction.

I cleared my throat. "Just needed a fresh start."

She frowned. "But… what happened?"

I wasn't ready to talk about it yet. She'd probably look at me differently. With pity in her eyes. Or worse, and she'd blame me too. Just like my teammates had.

"It doesn't matter." I waved her off. "Tell me about your musical. You have rehearsals starting soon, right?"

Audrey blushed. "It's not *my* musical. I might have been cast in the lead role, but there's so many other people who it couldn't run without. The other cast members, the crew, the orchestra, the lighting and sound—"

"Right. Of course." I smoothed my hair with my hand, feeling like an idiot who'd just put his foot in his mouth. Of course, it wasn't hers. Except it would be, wouldn't it? I'd told her I'd go watch her perform, and I knew that there was no way I'd be able to tear my eyes away from her on the stage. Not when she shined so brilliantly. God, just hearing her sing was incredible. "Are you excited?" It was the only question I could think of asking.

Her violet-hued eyes lit up. They were such a beautiful color, that deep blue that read purple, that it was hard to look away from them. "So excited. Did I tell you Ella is designing all the costumes for the play? She's shown me the sketches, and holy wow, they're beautiful." Audrey babbled on about the things she was excited about. The score. The sets. How magical the story-line was.

It was based on her favorite fairytale, and she'd told me that it felt like kismet when she was cast as the lead.

Long after we'd finished our food, I sat there, trying to remind myself that she was my best friend. That I had no busi-ness noticing how her laugh made my insides warm or her smile felt like the sun coming out from behind the clouds. But her happiness was contagious, and I was just grateful to be in her presence.

It was enough.

It had to be.

Because I couldn't live in a world without Audrey Rose and her sunshine. Not ever again.

CHAPTER 7

Audrey

Did you eat lunch today?

Yes.

Well, depending on what you classify as lunch.

Rosie, what am I going to do with you?

Meet me for dinner?

Yeah. Definitely that.

Stowing my phone back in my bag and doing my best not to smile at Parker's overbearing tendencies, I focused my energy on my advanced musical theater class. We met in the theater building, seated in the front rows of the auditorium unless we were on stage. This building—this stage—felt like home to me after almost three years on this campus, and it never really felt like the semester had begun until I'd walked across the wooden floors.

This was what I wanted to do after I graduated. Perform. Hopefully on Broadway, but I wouldn't be too picky. Still, the idea of getting to do musical theater for a living sent a rush of rightness down my spine. It might not be an easy road to get there, but I was ready for the challenge.

We were already two weeks into the semester, and it felt like everything was flying by in the blink of an eye. Like if I blinked, it would be February tomorrow. I had my notebook in my lap, taking notes and doodling hearts in the margins.

The hour flew by quickly, everyone shoving their papers in their bag and getting ready to head to their next class as we finished up. I didn't have another one for another hour after this, so I didn't have to rush as much.

"Audrey?" Professor Woods called out my name as I was grabbing my stuff. "Can you hang back?"

My cheeks warmed. Shit. I hated being called out like this in front of everyone. Nodding, I dropped back into my seat until the room had emptied.

She leaned against the table at the front and sighed. "I'm afraid I have bad news."

"Oh." I bit my lip. "Did I do something wrong? Because I—"

"No." She held up a hand. "You're doing great, Audrey. I'm very impressed with how hard you've been working these last few months. Ever since you were cast, really."

"So… what's the problem?"

"Your co-star… Will. He was just put on disciplinary probation."

"Shit." That meant he was basically suspended from school until he got his grades up, and he couldn't be a part of any extracurriculars, including the spring musical. I was getting class credit for the production, but not everyone involved was. "What does that mean for the show?" We'd gotten the scripts last semester, but rehearsals hadn't started yet. Still, this was a big production.

"Well…" She winced. "You know how this normally goes.

The understudy gets the part, and we'd find a new understudy from the ensemble."

My heart stopped. "No." It felt like all the color had drained out of my face. "*Please*, no."

Because the man who'd been cast as the stand-in was none other than my asshole ex. Duke. He'd been hoping for the lead part from the beginning, but I'd been able to breathe easier when his name hadn't been on the list.

Now, though... I could feel all my muscles tense up.

She patted me on the leg, her voice soothing. "That's why I wanted to approach you first, dear. Since it's still the beginning of the semester, and not everyone has learned their lines yet, I thought maybe we could do something else."

"Yes. Whatever it is, yes." I dropped my voice into a whisper. "Please don't make me act opposite him."

"It goes against protocol, but I have an idea. And since I'm the department head, I can get away with it." She winked at me. Her eyes were soft—caring—when she shook her head. "If you can find a replacement who can take on a role of this scope, I'll be happy to make the change. We already have such a hard time getting men to try out as it is."

"Me?" By myself? How the hell was I going to accomplish that? I didn't know any guys on campus with copious amounts of free time *and* could sing and dance.

Well... Parker's face flashed to my mind, thinking of when we'd laid on the grass and sung that duet. But I hadn't heard him sing since. Plus, he was busy with lacrosse. I couldn't ask him to do something like this for me. Not that he'd ever even consider it. He might have been my best friend, but some things were just too much.

She patted my shoulder. "I'll keep my ears open too, Audrey. Just let me know if I can do anything for you."

I nodded, watching as she walked away, staying in my seat in the silence of the classroom. There wasn't another acting class after ours, which I was grateful for. It gave me the time to compose myself.

To figure out what I was going to do.

"WHAT'S WRONG?" Parker asked, looking up from his chicken, rice, and veggie bowl. He'd met me at the sorority house and we'd walked over to the dining hall together, like we were settling back into our routine from last semester. Even if it had only been for the last month and a half of the semester, I'd gotten used to eating dinner with him. It was nice not having to eat alone.

Especially when Ella had been busy with Cam and sorority responsibilities.

I frowned. "What do you mean?"

"You've been quiet all night." He raised an eyebrow. "And you're *never* quiet."

"Oh." I poked at my salad. He was right. Ella was the quiet, subdued twin. She was the one who preferred to be a wallflower. I was the opposite. I loved to stand out. To be the center of attention. I loved to talk. My mom always joked that I loved to hear myself speak.

Tonight, though, I couldn't stop thinking about the spring musical. That I was most likely going to have to spend a lot of time in close quarters with my ex-boyfriend. One who couldn't seem to get over me, even if he'd been the reason we'd broken up in the first place.

"I just got some bad news today," I finally admitted. "The other lead for the musical this semester dropped. And if there's no one who auditions, then the understudy steps into the role."

"And?" He looked confused. "I don't understand. What's the problem?"

"The problem is the understudy is my ex, Duke."

Parker furrowed his eyebrows. "Why? Is he even in the theater department?"

I laughed. "No. He's a business student. You don't have to be a theater student to audition. He doesn't know the first thing about theater; he's just determined to do whatever I do, I guess. Maybe he gets some sort of secret rush from stalking me." If I didn't laugh, I'd cry, so I just shook my head—like that would make the thoughts go away.

"That's fucked up." He grit his teeth. "He auditioned just to make you uncomfortable? Audrey, you need to get a restraining order."

I sucked in a breath. "I can't." I'd tried last semester. After Halloween, when he'd grabbed me on the sidewalk, I'd gone to the campus safety building and asked for help. But it wasn't enough. And all I felt was ashamed.

"What?" Parker's expression was pure rage. *For me.* "What do you mean?"

I winced. "He hasn't hurt me." The admission was whispered. I looked away, not wanting to look at him as I said the words. "Campus safety won't do anything unless there's proof of physical violence."

And besides him grabbing my wrist, he'd never hurt me. I'd never been beaten black and blue. I should be grateful for that, they'd said. He wasn't violent.

No, he was just a chauvinistic pig. But that didn't warrant a restraining order.

"Audrey..."

Shaking my head, I diverted all my energy into eating my salad. I tried to ignore the way his eyes were on me. How I could feel him staring at me—like he was trying to make sure I was okay. That I wouldn't break.

I didn't want to cry. Not in front of him. I couldn't. Because the second I let go, I'd shatter. And I wasn't sure I was ready to put all the pieces back together.

"What if I do it?"

My jaw dropped open, and I gaped at him. "What?"

"The musical. I'll do it."

"Parker. You can't. You don't even know the first thing about acting."

He raised an eyebrow. "I can learn."

I shot him a look. "What about lacrosse? You don't exactly have time to be a part of a musical. What will you do about the season?"

He shrugged. "I'll talk to coach. Make it work. Besides, don't you think my best friend is more important?"

"Well…" I bit my lip. It was nice that someone else cared enough to put me first like this. Sure, Ella always had, and I knew she always would.

But I didn't want to involve her in this. Not when she was so happy now.

"Besides, there's no fucking way I'm letting Duke hurt you. Not anymore. I've got your back, Audrey. That's what best friends are for, right?"

I blushed. "Yeah. Thanks."

Best friend, I reminded myself. He was my best friend. I couldn't like him. Not like that. But when he stood up for me and proclaimed things like that, butterflies erupted in my chest.

Still, I couldn't take him up on his offer. I'd have to find another way.

AFTER WE FINISHED up at dinner and Parker walked me home, I went inside the sorority house, dropped onto my bed and stared up at the ceiling. The semester had just started, and it was already off the rails.

I knew what I needed right now, more than anything: my sister. Part of me missed when she'd only been a bed away instead of a floor. Taking two stars at a time, I headed to her room, barging inside without knocking. "Ella—"

She let out a small moan, and oh, God. I shrieked, covering my eyes. Cam was here.

What was I thinking coming into my sister's room when she had a boyfriend?

"Oh." Peeking out from behind my hands, I felt a little better when I noticed he still had his pants on. Ella was in his lap, and he had his hands on her shoulders, massaging them. "Hey, Cam," I said, and he nodded.

"Audrey. What's wrong?" Ella frowned at me as I started frantically pacing back and forth across my floor. I ran my fingers through my hair, tugging at the strands. "What happened?"

"The other lead dropped out of the musical. He's on academic probation, so they won't let him perform. And if they don't find someone to replace him, I'm stuck with Duke," I finally said, blowing out a puff of air, my bangs rising from the motion.

"Really? Is there no understudy?"

"There is." *Duke.* "But since we've barely started running lines, he already volunteered to fill the role *officially.*" I rolled my eyes. "Like I want to kiss him on stage." Wrinkling my nose at the thought of ever kissing him again, I finally had to shake my head like I could get rid of the mental picture. "Anyway. I don't know what to do."

"Is there nothing that Dr. Woods can do?"

If only I hadn't already tried that. She was the department chair, the one who taught my class, and in charge of the spring musical.

"No. And Duke won't leave me alone. He keeps trying to get me to agree to get back together. I don't know what to do, and Parker—"

Said he'd star in the musical with me. Which was insane. Even if it was the answer to all my problems.

"Parker?" Ella asked, raising an eyebrow. "Are you guys…?"

"No." I felt my cheeks warm. "Never mind. That doesn't matter."

"Well..." My twin frowned. "I wish I could help more, but I don't have any suggestions."

I sighed, and Ella opened her arms, enveloping me in a hug.

"Thank you. That's all I needed," I murmured into her hold. I didn't need someone to fix it. I just needed someone to listen to me.

And I needed my sister.

"I'm always here for you, Ro. You know that."

I squeezed her tighter. "Love you."

"Love you too," she whispered back.

Saying goodbye, I went back to my room, knowing exactly what I needed to do.

Tell Parker *yes*.

THE NEXT DAY, as if he'd somehow found out my schedule and knew exactly where I'd be, Duke was standing outside the theater building, leaning against the wall as I came outside. Campus was quiet since the next class had already started, so there weren't too many people lingering around the building.

I'd just come from talking with Professor Woods, telling her about Parker. She was skeptical, even though I told her he could really sing. But maybe that had to do more with the fact that he was a jock.

Even I was surprised he'd volunteered to step into the role. Either way, she was on board as long as he came in for a formal audition.

Avoiding Duke's gaze, I raised my chin and continued walking forward.

He jogged up beside me, his backpack slung over one shoulder. "Aud. Come on. Talk to me."

"Why are you here, Duke?" I asked, still not looking at him.

"To get you to take me back." His tone made it seem like it was obvious.

I scoffed. "No." Crossing my arms over my chest, I spun to glare at him. "You cheated on *me*, Duke." And he gaslit me into thinking it was *my* fault. Strung me along because he knew I was infatuated with him. But I didn't love him, not anymore. Those feelings had turned to acid, and now they just burned. But maybe I'd never really loved him. Not the way you were supposed to.

"Baby, it didn't mean anything, and you know it. She didn't mean anything, Aud. The girl I want to be with is you. I told you I was sorry—"

Should have thought about that before you put your dick in another girl, I wanted to scream. But that wasn't the only problem. No, it was the way he treated me. Like I was just some pretty trophy for his shelf.

I was tired of that. Even if I was pretty, popular, and loved the color pink, it didn't mean I was an airhead. And it definitely didn't mean I just wanted to be someone's arm candy.

No, I had my own dreams. And there was no room for a man like Duke at my side—no way in hell.

"Did you?" I asked, point blank. Because he'd never apologized once for breaking my heart. For shattering my trust.

"I'll be your knight in shining armor. C'mon. Just like old times. And you'll get to kiss me every night." He wagged his eyebrows.

I almost threw up in my mouth. I never wanted to kiss him again, which was exactly why I didn't want him to be my co-lead in the musical. "Gross. *As if.* Duke, we're over. Just like I told you the last time." When would he take a hint. "It's been *months*. Why won't you just move on?" All I wanted was for him to leave me alone. Seriously, I didn't think it was that hard.

"Because you're mine."

"No. I'm not." And then I said what might have been the dumbest thing to slip out of my mouth. "Besides, I'm with someone else now." A lie. But maybe if he thought I was off the market, he'd leave me alone.

"What?" He growled. "You mean that jock asshole? I don't like how he puts his hands all over you."

Stopping, I planted my hands on my hips and glared at him. I wouldn't give him the satisfaction of telling him yes or no. "You mean my *best friend*, Parker? Newsflash, Duke. We were friends long before you ever existed in my life, and we'll be friends for long afterward. Parker's important to me. So you can just fuck off for all I care. Go find someone else to fuck."

"Audrey." His eyes were burning with rage, and he stepped closer towards me.

I took a step back towards the building, and he continued forward. One step. Another. Until my back was pressed up against the tile, and Duke grabbed my wrists, pinning them up against the wall. "Are you fucking him?"

I spit in his face. "None of your damn business, asshole."

Duke snorted. "Then you haven't." He looked smug, and I ripped my arms away.

"Leave me alone, Duke. I think I've made myself pretty clear when I said that I'm. Not. Interested."

Heaving my bag over my arm, I set off on campus, hoping he wouldn't follow me. Hoping that everything would be fine.

Why had I told him I was dating someone? Ugh, I wished that was true. Maybe that was what I really needed to get him off my back.

AUDREY

Are you sure you're up for being in the musical?

It's a big responsibility, and I know you have lacrosse. I don't want it to interfere with your schedule or make any problems for you.

PARKER

Will it help?

Yes.

Then it'll be fine. I'll talk to Coach.

Thank you.

Of course. What are best friends for?

One more small, teeny thing.

Uh huh?

Can you come in tomorrow for an audition? It'll just be with my professor in charge of the musical, but she wants to hear you sing.

Oh. Okay. Yeah. I can do that. Just let me know what time, and I'll see if I can fit it in.

Any suggestions on music?

Want to talk it over at dinner?

You bet. Meet in an hour?

Sounds great. You're the best.

CHAPTER 8

Parker

Audrey's face was pale when I slid into the booth opposite hers in the dining hall. She was wearing a thick pink headband in her hair and a white sweater covered in textured dots. I liked how she was always wearing her favorite color—like her world existed solely in shades of pink.

I expected her to be happy, all rosy cheeks and sunshine like normal.

"What's wrong?" I set my food down in front of us. "I thought you'd be happy."

"What?" She looked up at me, biting at her manicured thumbnail. "Oh. I am happy. It's just…" Audrey ran her fingers through her long blonde strands before exhaling. "I ran into Duke outside the theater building." There was a wince to her words.

I felt a growl forming low in my throat, but I did my best to clear it away. I didn't like that guy. Something about him, about how he wouldn't leave Audrey alone even though she'd told him *no*, rubbed me the wrong way. Especially when she'd admitted she'd tried to get campus safety to make him leave her alone, and they'd told her they couldn't do anything. What the fuck was up with that? He was basically stalking her, but there wasn't anything that could be done unless he hurt her.

Not saying anything, I waited for Audrey to continue. I needed to hear her out before I blew up about something that was none of my business.

She could take care of herself. I knew she could.

It was just that I wanted to take care of her, to be by her side. Holding her hand. That was what best friends did, right?

She blew out a breath, one that disturbed the bangs across her forehead. "I might have, sort of, accidentally… told Duke I was seeing someone."

"Okay?" I furrowed my brows. For a split second, my stomach dropped. Was she? Was there some guy I didn't know about? If some other guy took advantage of her—

I didn't let myself finish that thought.

"I'm *not*," she insisted, staring at me with a serious expression on her face. "I'm not seeing anyone. He was going on about us getting back together, and I just made it up."

"Alright." I shrugged, a plan forming in my mind. A way that I could keep her safe. Keep assholes like Duke away from her. Be by her side.

"Why are you being so casual about this?" Audrey raised an eyebrow.

I dipped a fry in some ketchup. "Date me."

Audrey looked confused. "Huh?"

"You should date me. I'll be your boyfriend."

"What?" She grimaced. "Parker, you're my *best friend*."

"How could I forget, sunshine?" I leaned over and flicked her nose. "I'll be your *fake* boyfriend," I clarified. "So Duke leaves you alone."

"You want to… fake date?"

"Yeah." I went back to eating my food, knowing she needed time to process this.

She bit her lip, worrying it in between her teeth. "I couldn't ask you to do that." Her food was completely forgotten in front of her, like she was so distracted she couldn't even remember to eat.

I'd noticed that she got so busy that she forgot to eat during the school day last semester. It was one reason I texted her and asked if she wanted to get dinner almost every night. Our schedules might not always line up for lunch, but I was making sure she got fed.

I crossed my arms over my chest. "You're not asking, Rosie. I'm offering. And besides, it makes sense. We're spending all of this time together, anyway. And now I'm doing the musical with you."

Assuming the audition went well. I still had to prove I could do it.

"How long would we even do this for?"

"Till the end of the musical, I guess." Even if it was fake, at least I'd get to be by her side. That was what I was telling myself.

"Right. That makes sense."

"Hey." I rested my hand over hers, and when she looked at me, her eyes were filled with so much uncertainty. I hated that. "Are you okay?"

She shrugged, stabbing at a piece of pasta instead of responding to me.

"It's okay if you're not, you know," I whispered. God knows I wasn't okay, not after last semester. Maybe she'd understand why I wanted to help her if I told her. But I couldn't make my mouth form the words. Not yet. It was still too raw. Too real.

"It doesn't feel like that," she admitted. "I feel like everyone expects me to be happy all the time."

"You don't have to be," I insisted. "You don't have to be anything with me other than yourself. You know that, right? I'm friends with *you*, Audrey. Not whoever people expect you to be. I like the girl who loves wearing pink but also was never afraid to play in the dirt with me when we were younger. When we were biking, you'd cry when you scraped your knees, but it never stopped you from getting back. What's stopping you now?"

"I don't know," she murmured. Something was holding her back. I knew it was. What had happened to make her draw into herself? To lose the sparkle in her gorgeous violet-hued eyes? I wanted to help her get it back.

Squeezing her hand, I let go. "I'm here. Whenever you need me, I'm always here."

"Thank you." Audrey relaxed, dipping her head. "Can I… think about it? Your offer?" Her voice was quiet. "The fake dating thing?"

"Of course you can."

She nodded, and then finally dug into her plate of food. I was content just to watch her. Audrey was clearly going through something, and I'd show her I was here the best way I knew how: by being by her side.

"So. About that audition," I finally said once she'd finished eating, clearing her plate.

Her lips tilted up in her first genuine smile of the evening.

And I did my best to distract her from thoughts of Duke, from anything that would take away from that smile on her face.

WHEN WAS the last time I'd sung in front of an audience? *Never.*

But here I was. Standing in front of the director for the musical, Audrey's professor—also the head of the theater department—auditioning to be in the show.

I had no fucking idea what I was doing. None. But how hard could it be, really? Maybe I'd never had professional voice lessons like Audrey, but I'd been in plays as a kid. And I'd been around for her lessons. Surely, I'd picked up a few things over the years.

Otherwise, all of that singing in the shower was for nothing.

Last night, I'd stayed up late, practicing the song I'd selected with Audrey's help. If any of the guys in the lacrosse house had noticed that I'd been listening to the same song on repeat, they hadn't commented on it. Even if they had, I'd deny it.

Fuck, I was an idiot. For offering to be Audrey's fake boyfriend. For volunteering to prance around this stage and perform in a musical. How was I going to balance all of this?

No distractions. Coach's voice ran through my mind. This was a giant fucking distraction, and I knew it.

But the way Audrey was smiling up at me as I stood in front of them… it was all worth it.

Maybe it was because of all my time playing lacrosse, but I didn't have an ounce of nerves as I stood on stage, looking out across the room. Of course, it was empty, save for my best girl sitting in the front row with her director, but I knew better than anyone what performance anxiety could do to an athlete.

Still, I was out of my element. This wasn't the same as running across the field or trying to get the ball in the net. And yet, I knew it was more important.

Not to me, but to the girl sitting in the front row, who was looking at me like I hung the moon in the sky. For her, I'd do it. I'd do anything. What she didn't know was that she was my sunshine. The reason I looked forward to each day. Ever since she'd come back into my life, that had been the case.

So I sang.

I sang like I did when I was a child, sitting next to Audrey at the piano, back when we were carefree and without a care in the world.

"Thank you, Parker," the woman sitting in the front row next to my best friend said with a smile as the song ended. "That was great. Now, why don't you two sing something together?" Professor Woods looked between Audrey and me. "That way, I can get a feel for the chemistry you'll have on stage together."

I looked at Audrey, the question in my eyes. *Do you want to do this?*

Yes, hers seemed to say back as she joined me on stage,

rushing over to the girl who sat at the piano accompanying us. I couldn't hear what she was saying, but I knew she was telling her what song to play.

"What are we singing?" I whispered to her as she stood across from me.

Audrey smiled, extending her hand. Wordlessly, I took it, the warmth of her palm relaxing me. "Ready?" she murmured, and I nodded.

The first few bars played, and I instantly recognized the tune. Of course.

Of course, she'd picked this song.

I couldn't look away from her. Not as she sang the first few words. God, she sounded like an angel. Looked like one, too, with the stage lights casting a perfect halo above her head, illuminating her blonde hair.

When we finished, we stepped off the stage behind the curtains.

"How'd I do?" I asked, running my fingers through my hair.

Audrey grinned. "You were great."

"So were you." I nudged her with my shoulder.

She gnawed on her lower lip. "Are you really sure you're okay doing this? It's not too much?"

"Audrey." I laughed. "Don't go trying to get rid of me already. I'm *in*, okay? I won't let you down."

Her voice was hardly more than a whisper when she responded, "I know."

"Shit." I looked at my watch. "I gotta get to practice. Coach is going to kill me."

Audrey winced. "Have you told him yet?" There was a frown on her face. Like she knew what I was doing. Delaying the inevitable. But she couldn't know the real reason I was avoiding the conversation. After all, I hadn't told her my stipulations for transferring onto the team. The shit I'd gotten into last year.

I cleared my throat. "No. I was planning on doing it today."

"You got this." She gave me a thumbs up. "You got this, Parker. Have a good practice."

With a wave, I headed off in a jog towards the field, hoping like hell I wouldn't be late.

"Hey, Coach."

"Maxwell." He had his arms crossed over his chest as I rushed into the locker room to change. "You're late."

"I know, I'm sorry—it won't happen again."

Coach dipped his head. "Remember what we said? No distractions?"

I cleared my throat. I needed to tell him about the musical. That I'd done all of this for Audrey as a favor. But nothing came out. "Right," I finally said. "I know."

He raised an eyebrow.

"It's not a distraction, I promise. Just doing a favor for a friend."

After studying me for a moment, he dipped his head, heading out to the practice field.

I pulled off my sweater and dropped it onto the bench. My jeans quickly followed as I dressed in all of my gear.

There was one thing I knew for sure—this was going to be a long season.

CHAPTER 9

There was a new skip in my step. Maybe I was still on cloud nine after signing with Parker the other day, but everything had felt easier. Lighter.

I still couldn't stop thinking about his offer. *Date me. I'll be your boyfriend.*

Your fake boyfriend.

All I wanted to do was talk about it with Ella and ask her opinion, but every time I opened my mouth, nothing came out. It wasn't like I was intentionally keeping it from her—especially when I knew she'd understand the reasoning behind it. She'd seen Duke's behavior on Halloween weekend firsthand, after all. But this was different. Especially when she was so happy with Cam. The two of them spent all their free time together these days, and I was so happy for her. She had found her Prince Charming; even if she was still dancing around her feelings, it was clear how much they cared about each other.

How could I tell my sister that I was so pathetic I needed my best friend to pretend to date me to get my ex to leave me alone? Part of me still couldn't believe I'd let that slip out to him or how easily Parker had agreed to it.

Surely, there was someone on campus he wanted to date

instead of *faking it* with his best friend. The thought made me scrunch up my face, even though I didn't have any feelings for him. Sure, I found him attractive, but that was as far as it went.

It wasn't real. That was what I had to keep reminding myself. Even if he'd offered to get Duke to leave me alone, he didn't have feelings for me. He probably still saw me as a little sister, like the little girl who'd followed him around the neighborhood like she had nothing better to do. Who cried when she scraped her knees after falling off her pretty pink princess bike. I grimaced, thinking about how annoying I'd probably been.

He seemed to regret the nine years where we didn't talk now, but maybe back then, he'd been relieved to have some distance from me.

"You're just being dramatic," I muttered to myself as I walked across campus, bundled up from the cold January weather. I couldn't wait for it to get warmer. I thrived in dresses and though I had several pairs of fleece-lined tights, winter had never been my favorite season. Spring would be here before I knew it, though, and so would the musical.

I hid my face in my hands as I thought about how quickly Parker had agreed to be in the musical. That he'd auditioned for *me*. Even if he was busy with lacrosse and his studies, and definitely would not have time for this.

Finally at the theater building as I headed in for my next class, the billboard in the lobby caught my eye. Leah and Mary, two other girls who were in the musical with me, were also looking at it.

A new piece of light pink paper had been added: the updated cast list. I sucked in a breath. Technically, they'd been required to open up auditions for everyone to fill the role, so there was always a chance that I'd be acting with someone else.

"Hey, Audrey," Laura said with a smile, blocking my view of the list. "Did you see they posted the new cast list? It's such a bummer that Will's on probation, huh? Disrupting everything, and we haven't even started running lines yet." She frowned.

"Better now than in two months, though, right?" I asked. Certainly, it was better that we'd gotten this news with enough advanced notice to replace him.

"Sure, sure." Laura agreed.

Meri nudged her with an elbow and then turned to me. "Do you know the new guy? Haven't seen his name on any casting sheets before."

My heart sped up. New guy. And right there on the list, the second name under mine it was printed, *Parker Maxwell.*

"Yeah." I nodded, a smile lighting up my face. "He's my best friend."

"Oh?" Mari quirked an eyebrow. "How come we've never heard of him before?" She and Laura were both seniors in the theater department, and they'd taken me under their wing my freshman year. Florence was the other member of their trio, though she was currently absent.

"Well, we sort of lost touch for a while." I tucked a strand of hair behind my ear absentmindedly. "But we grew up together. He just transferred to CU in the fall." Snapping a picture of the list on my phone so I could show Parker later, I nodded to them. "Gotta get to class. See you later."

"See you at rehearsals!" Laura called out as I started walking towards the hallway. "You're going to be amazing, Little Rose!"

I blushed as I headed into class, trying not to think about how the nickname they'd given me freshman year was oddly reminiscent of Parker's childhood nickname for me.

Not that I'd thought about it until this point.

Pulling out my phone, I typed a message to my sister.

AUDREY

Parker's going to do it.

ELLA

Sorry, do what?

Be the lead in the musical with me.

Do you think he'll fit in the costume?

Oh.

I think so? I'd have to measure him to be sure, though.

Okay. The costumes are all in the studio, right?

Yup. I have a few finishing touches to put on before dress rehearsals start, but other than that, they're almost completely done.

You're the best. What would I do without you?

Definitely not be so fashionably dressed.

Speaking of, have you seen my white sweater with the little bows on it? I wanted to wear it.

Why? Have a hot date?

Maybe...

I borrowed it. I'll bring it up when I'm back at the house.

Thanks.

GRINNING, I held up the piece of paper in my hand as Parker walked towards the sorority house. He'd just come from the gym, and his hair was damp. It was hard not to appreciate him like this. Especially when his black long-sleeved t-shirt was clinging to his arms, showing off every well-earned torso of his upper body.

Damn, if lacrosse made guys that buff, maybe I'd enjoy his games more than I thought.

"What's that?" Parker asked, raising an eyebrow at the paper I was waving in the air.

I'd printed it out from the email I'd gotten when I got back from class because there was just something about seeing it in physical form. Plus, I wanted it for my scrapbook. I had an entire box of momentos I'd kept from the school year to use in it over the summer.

A grin spread over my face. "The cast list for the musical."

"They put it up?" He looked unsure, and after the way he sang a few days ago, I didn't know why. God, he had no idea how good he was. His voice was deep, a beautiful baritone—nothing like how he'd sounded when we were kids.

I nodded, a grin splitting my face. "You got it!" Squealing, I ran to close the distance between us and threw my arms around him.

He wrapped an arm around my back, crushing me to him.

"Thank you," I whispered, not having enough words.

"Of course," he murmured back, his lips pressed against my hair.

I could almost imagine him pressing the faintest of kisses into the crown of my head. But I knew that wasn't what this was between us. And that was okay. I was under no delusions about our friendship or what I expected from him. I was just glad he was back in my life.

As we pulled away, I shook my head. "You have no idea how much this means to me. Really, I can't thank you enough."

"You don't have to, Audrey." He squeezed my shoulder. "That's what best friends are for." He lifted a to-go bag. "Plus, I brought sustenance."

"Oh, good." I reached for it greedily. "I'm starving." Biting my lip, I looked between us and the sorority house. "Do you want to... come inside?"

The house was quiet since most of the girls were still out for the afternoon.

Which was good, because I wanted somewhere private to

have this conversation. At least, not on campus, where I had to worry about someone listening in.

Parker blinked. "Really? That's not like, against the rules?"

Laughing, I shook my head. "Only if you tried to stay overnight after curfew." Not that I'd ever had a guy over before. When Duke and I had been dating, I hadn't had a room to myself, and he'd wanted us to spend all our time at his place. "Then Ilene would have some words for you." While I loved our sorority advisor, Ilene was not one to mess with the rules.

Even though I knew for a fact that last semester, when Ella had been in bed sick with a fever, Cam had definitely spent the night taking care of her.

So I left my door open as I let Parker enter my space. He let out an amused chuckle, and I wondered what it looked like from his eyes. After Ella had moved into her own room, I'd lucked out without another girl moving in and had taken over the rest of it.

My bulletin board was decorated with pink roses and bows that I'd tied myself. I had a stack of friendship bracelets from the Taylor Swift concert last year on the corner of my desk. There was pink everywhere: my bedspread, the tiny pink bow pillow—even in the little paintings I'd added to the walls. The details that made this place feel like mine.

"I like it," Parker finally said.

"Yeah?" I mumbled. "It's not too much pink?"

He blinked. "Is that possible?"

I shrugged. I'd been told I was *too much* more times than I could count. Maybe at some point, I'd started believing them.

Parker's gaze zeroed in on my desk. "What's all this?" he asked, running a finger over the basket and craft supplies.

"Oh." He wouldn't know since this was his first year at CU. "Every year, we do a Valentine's Day date auction to raise money for our philanthropy. Each sorority sister takes part. I'm just trying to get a head start. That way, I don't have to do it at the last minute in a few weeks." The semester was already flying by fast enough as it was.

He raised an eyebrow. "So someone… buys a date with you?"

I picked up the spool of pink gingham ribbon I was using to weave through the basket. "Yeah. We make a basket, and then whoever buys it gets to go on the date we planned."

"Huh." Parker looked intrigued. "And what is yours?"

Blushing, I fiddled with the ends of the bow instead of looking at him.

"Come on," I said, wanting to avoid the rest of the conversation. Telling him about my date felt too personal. Because then I'd also have to admit who I'd been picturing when I planned it. "We should eat."

He seemed to accept it, dropping onto the bed across from mine. It was hard to ignore how big Parker was when he lounged on it. I grabbed the paper bag I'd carried inside, pulling out sandwiches and bags of chips. I read the labels on them, tossing Parker his usual order. My heart felt warm as I realized he'd ordered mine for me, too.

It was strange to think that in a year of dating Duke, he'd never once ordered me food without asking me what I wanted.

And yet, after less than three months since we'd started hanging out again, Parker had memorized what I liked to eat.

Even though it was such a small thing, a gesture that shouldn't mean anything, it did.

Because it was becoming more and more apparent to me how Duke had never been a good match for me. How he'd never cared about me the way I'd cared about him. Maybe it was just a status thing for him like I was Elle in *Legally Blonde*. Some pretty blonde he could have on his arm when he was a hotshot businessman.

And I knew in my heart that Parker was nothing like that.

"Parker," I said softly, and he looked up at me from munching on his sandwich.

"Hm?"

"How would we do this?"

"Do what?"

I shrugged. "Fake date. You know. Pretend to be together. We didn't exactly iron out all the specifics." Wrinkling my nose, I avoided his gaze. "If you're going to be in the musical with me, we really have to sell it. Otherwise, Duke is going to know, and he'll be suspicious."

The last thing I needed was him giving me hell because he found out it was fake.

Standing up, he came and sat down next to me, sandwich forgotten. His face was serious.

"If we do this," I whispered, "We can't tell anyone it's fake."

"What about your sister?"

Ella would understand. Eventually. I hated keeping this from her, but I knew in my gut we had to do this. So I shook my head. "Her either. She's so wrapped up in Cam, and I just…" I didn't want her to pity me.

"Okay. I won't tell anyone." He reached over, squeezing my knee. "So we're doing this?"

"Yeah." I let out a breath. It felt like I hadn't taken a full one in weeks and could finally breathe again. "Yeah. If you're still up for it."

"Of course I am, Rosie. It would be an honor to be your fake boyfriend."

I giggled. "Don't go falling in love with me now," I joked.

His face fell. "Audrey."

I nudged him with my shoulder. "I was trying to be funny."

Parker massaged his temples like he was trying to find his patience. "Sure, sunshine. But you can't fall in love with me either."

"Not a problem," I answered. "You're my best friend. I won't let this get messy."

He nodded, and then we both resumed eating, neither of us making eye contact.

Parker Maxwell was my best friend.

And, after today… my fake boyfriend.

CHAPTER 10
Parker

FEBRUARY

Everything was normal. My first lacrosse game was later this week, and classes were going well. The only thing that was different was the girl lying across my bed, studying the script in her hands.

My best friend. And as of last week, my *fake* girlfriend.

I sat at my desk, trying to figure out exactly how we'd gotten here. Somehow, it all felt so surreal. Even before, when we were friends, we didn't hang out like this. We met up for meals in the dining hall and walked around campus together, but I'd never had her in my space before.

Not like this.

On my bed.

With the door closed.

Looking so sweet in her pink corduroy overall dress that she'd paired with a white turtleneck and tall, tan boots. Her legs were a million fucking miles long, and I wasn't even sure she knew how hot those boots were.

I pulled at the hoodie around my neck, fanning myself with the fabric.

"Parker."

"Hm?" Her sweet strawberry smell filled my lungs, over-riding any sense or thought.

Oh. She'd asked me something. "Sorry, what?"

"What do you think of the script?" Audrey inclined her head to the side. I'd had it for almost a week now after officially being announced to be taking over the role.

I leaned back in my chair, the script in question sitting on my desk. I'd read it three times already and was still stuck on one specific detail.

"We have to kiss," I said instead of commenting on the story-line. "In the second act, we…" Our characters were romantically intertwined, so why had I not considered this before accepting the role?

Audrey nodded, understanding dawning in her eyes. "Uh-huh."

I hummed. "We're pretending to date. Which means we should be comfortable kissing each other." I couldn't take my eyes off her soft, full pink lips. She was wearing her usual sparkly lip gloss. I wondered if it would taste like strawberries and cotton candy, sweet like the way she smelled.

Her voice was barely above a whisper when she responded, "Yeah."

"So we should, um, you know… practice."

"What?" Audrey's brows raised.

I could feel my cheeks growing warm. God, why was this so embarrassing? "If everyone thinks we're dating, won't it be weird if the first time we kiss is on stage at rehearsals? We need to look like we know what we're doing."

She fidgeted with the pink scrunchie on her wrist. One she always wore. "Yeah, but—"

"Rosie." I tugged on one of her blonde curls. "It's just fake, right?"

She sat up on the bed, nibbling on her lower lip. "Yeah, I guess," Audrey sighed, her body relaxing slightly. "Okay. Let's…

practice." She ran her tongue over her lips like she was moistening them, and I held back a groan. "Just like rehearsals."

Standing up from my desk, I joined her on the bed, and she backed up till she was against the wall. I placed a palm on either side of her on the mattress. Caging her in. My heart was thundering in my chest, and I hoped she couldn't hear it.

My finger hooked under her chin, bringing her eyes up to meet mine. "You good?"

"Y-yeah." Her voice was breathless. "Let's just do this. Get it over with."

Dipping my head low, I brushed my lips against her ear. "First of all, we're not just *getting it over with*, Rosie Girl. Okay?"

Her eyelashes fluttered, and she nodded.

"I'm going to kiss you now."

"Okay." The word was a tiny whisper, but it was all the permission I needed.

I pressed my lips against hers, just a slight brush, and Audrey closed her eyes, tilting her chin just an inch as if in invitation.

"Parker…" My name slipped from her lips, breathless.

Yes, I thought, brushing my lips over hers again. The lightest of touches. The ghost of a kiss. Just enough to leave us both wanting more.

Her hands wound around my neck, her fingers combing through the back of my hair. And then I didn't hold back, coaxing her mouth open with mine, devouring her with open-mouthed kisses and taking what was *mine*. Like all along, she'd just been waiting for me to find her.

Audrey might not have been my first kiss, but *damn*. I wanted her to be my last.

I was right. She tasted sweet, and I didn't even care that her lip gloss was probably on my lips, too.

When we pulled apart, she blinked away the haze that had clouded her eyes.

"Wow." She ran her fingers over her lips. "That was…"

I felt smug. "Good?"

She laughed, pushing at my arm. "You're a good kisser, Parker Maxwell. Who'd have thought?"

It was the reminder I needed that we were *best friends*. That this wouldn't be weird. I wouldn't let it be.

We'd promised that we wouldn't fall in love with each other, and damn if that wasn't the hardest promise I'd ever made. But there was a difference between loving someone and being *in love* with them.

No matter what I felt, I pushed the thoughts away.

WE'D RUN drills tonight since our first game of the season was only days away. All I could think about was that kiss earlier. That damn kiss. *Fuck.* I wasn't sure what the hell was wrong with me. Why couldn't I get the feel of her lips on mine out of my mind?

Rubbing at my shoulder, I looked across the locker room.

"You good?" Samuel asked, bumping me with his knee as I sat on the bench. I'd stripped out of most of my gear, leaving me in just a t-shirt and my shorts.

I exhaled roughly, nodding. "Yeah. Just pulled something tonight."

He made a noise under his breath. "You seemed a little distracted."

I winced. Damn, if he noticed, had everyone else?

"Parker!" Taylor—one of our defensemen—shouted from across the locker room, interrupting my conversation with the teammate at my side. "Are you coming out with us tonight?"

The guys on the team were all heading to the bar to celebrate one of our last free nights before the season started.

"I don't know." I frowned, looking down at the floor. Running my hands through my hair, I looked between the guys. "I, uh, have plans. With my... girlfriend." Coach would want me to go out with them, to bond with the team, but I had standing dinner plans with Audrey. And I hated to cancel them.

But maybe it was time to come out with it. We'd agreed to this charade a week ago, but hadn't publicly done anything since. Dinner on campus didn't count.

"The blonde?" Samuel raised an eyebrow. "No surprise there."

I frowned. "What?" I hadn't even told any of them we were dating yet.

"Come on, dude. It's been obvious you liked her since the Halloween Party."

Well, he wasn't wrong about that. I couldn't deny it. *Still.* "It's still new. We were best friends when we were kids."

"Bring her to the party on Saturday," Derek said, slapping me on the back. "After our first game."

"I don't know if she'll—"

"Of course she'll want to come." Taylor grinned. "We're the *best*. Who wouldn't want to hang out with us?"

I laughed.

"You sure about tonight?" Derek asked. "Whole team's going."

"I'll be there," I promised. After dinner with Audrey.

Grabbing my towel to head to the showers, I looked up to find my coach leaning against the lockers. "Maxwell." *Shit.* Coach had that *I'm-disappointed-in-you* look. The same one he gave the guys when they showed up to practice hungover after a long weekend. "What's this I hear about you being in the musical?"

I winced. "I was going to tell you. It's not a big deal. Just one weekend in early April and some rehearsals. It shouldn't conflict with any games, I checked."

"Thought we said no distractions."

"We did, Coach. But my best friend—"

"A girl?"

I nodded.

"His *girlfriend,*" Taylor said, waggling his eyebrows.

Fuck.

Coach raised an eyebrow.

"I promise I won't let it be a distraction. If it gets to be too much, I'll back off."

"Alright, Maxwell. I'm counting on you."

My chest felt tight. Because someone else was counting on me, too... *Audrey.*

"Rosie!" I shouted, jogging to catch up with her after glimpsing her pink cardigan with little bows on it and blonde hair. She was unmistakable.

Her phone was out, and I noticed it had a new pink sparkly case on it, and she'd added a pop socket that looked like a pink bow. Damn if that wasn't as endearing as shit.

"Parker." A small smile ghosted her lips as she stopped to face me. "Hi."

"Hey, sunshine." I slid my finger through the belt loop of her jeans, tugging her close to me.

"What are you doing?" Audrey whispered under her breath. We were only inches apart, standing in the middle of the sidewalk on the quad. I was still holding onto the loop of her belt and hooked my finger through the other side, too.

"We're dating, remember?" I murmured back. "Just smile. I told my teammates today."

"Oh." She blinked up at me. "Okay. Right."

I leaned in, pressing a kiss to her forehead. "Relax," I breathed into her ear. "I'm going to hold your hand, and we're going to walk into the dining hall together, okay?"

She nodded, and I interlaced our fingers before we started moving again.

"How was your day?" I asked, breaking the silence.

"Good. I only had one class, and then I got lunch with Ella."

"That sounds fun."

She squeezed my hand. "Yeah. It was nice." She tucked a strand of hair behind her ear with her free hand. "How was yours?"

"Better now." I squeezed her hand back. We were still new to this fake dating thing, but I liked it. "You know, we should really make each other our phone backgrounds," I said, hoping like hell she'd agree.

She stopped in the middle of the sidewalk, her mouth gaping open as she looked at me. "Who are you, and what have you done with my best friend?"

Was it that crazy that I wanted to be able to look at her any time I unlocked my phone? But maybe she liked her cutesy pink background and wouldn't want me on it.

"Well," I cleared my throat. "As your boyfriend, I think that—"

Audrey giggled. "*Parker*."

I shoved my hands in my pockets. "Yeah, maybe it was a dumb idea."

"No. It's just..." She bit her lower lip like she was debating on her next words. "It's sweet. And I'm still not used to you being like this."

I slid my hand over her cheek, cupping it tightly. "Well, you better get used to it, huh? Because I'm going to treat you right, Audrey Rose. Okay?"

"Okay," she whispered, rising onto her tiptoes to press her lips against my cheek. "Thank you."

A few other students passed by us on the sidewalk, and Audrey dropped back to her feet, waving hi to a few of the girls she must have known as they passed us.

She looked up at me, a curious expression on her face. "So, the season starts soon," Audrey finally said. "How are you feeling?"

"Yep. Saturday. Coach has been drilling us hard the last week." My muscles were a little sore, but mostly, I felt good. I was ready for this year. Ready to help lead the team to victory. I might not have been the captain, but damn if I wasn't focused on getting everything right.

A light pink dotted her cheekbones, though it was probably just from the chill in the air. It wasn't like she was affected by me. Well, not like that.

"Audrey," I murmured the word, and her eyes darted to mine.

I knew her. I'd been studying her blush since I was too young to know what it meant. But she'd always been easily flustered. Easily embarrassed. I enjoyed teasing her because I loved those rosy cheeks.

Today, though? I hadn't been teasing, which made that blush even more amusing.

"Huh?"

"What are you thinking about?"

Her face deepened in color even more. "Nothing."

Maybe she was more affected by me than I'd thought. Maybe my attraction wasn't completely one-sided.

But what was I going to do about that? No matter what, our friendship came first. I'd never do anything to jeopardize that.

Even if that meant accepting that Audrey Rose Ashford would never be mine.

CHAPTER 11

D rilling us hard the last week. Innocent words. And yet, why did I blush at them? Why did my brain go down a dirty path that he clearly hadn't meant?

"Audrey," Parker said, his voice deep, distracting me from my thoughts.

I looked up at him, wishing the earth would swallow me whole. "Huh?"

"What are you thinking about?"

"Nothing." I hid my face underneath my white fuzzy jacket, not wanting him to see how flustered I was. After we'd kissed the other day on his bed, I hadn't been able to stop thinking about his lips on mine. Wondering what I could do to get him to kiss me again.

To feel him—all of him—with his weight on top of me.

Even though it was *wrong*. We were best friends. He'd just kissed me as practice. It didn't mean anything.

We got to the dining hall door, and Parker stopped in front of me to open it. He let me walk in first, then he slid behind me, hand on my back.

I didn't know why my cheeks were on fire. Nothing about what we were doing was different than normal. It was just that

I'd never gone to dinner with him thinking about him being my boyfriend, either. And suddenly, everything felt way more real. The way his hand burned through my sweater.

The way he'd slipped his fingers into my belt loops and tugged me closer to him.

He followed behind me in line as I grabbed food, carrying the tray with both of our meals after we'd ordered. Really, Parker would make someone the perfect boyfriend someday. But this was all fake. It was just an act.

After he'd paid and we found an empty booth, I slid into one side, expecting Parker to sit opposite me. Except... he sat right next to me, both of us sharing the same side.

He'd taken two bites before he said, "So... about my team."

"Hmm?" I asked, looking up from my food.

He shook his head, a ghost of a smile forming on his lips. "My first lacrosse game is Saturday."

I nodded. "Yeah, I know." I'd written his games down on my planner at the beginning of the semester after he'd asked me to go. That was what best friends did, after all—they supported each other. "I'll be there."

But Parker just gave me a sheepish look. "We're having a party afterward at the house. To celebrate the start of the season."

"But what if you lose?" I wrinkled my nose in confusion.

"Rosie." He pinned me with a stare that made me feel things I should *not* be feeling. "They're horny college athletes. Do you think they care if they win?"

"Oh." They probably just wanted to get drunk and hook up with girls. "I guess not."

I tried not to think about Parker like *that,* too. If he fell into the same category. Was I keeping him from being with someone? Sure, we'd gotten dinner a bunch of times last semester, but it wasn't like I was with him every waking moment.

And yet, the idea of sharing him, of him sleeping with anyone else, made me lose my appetite.

"Will you come with me?" Parker finally asked, and I looked back at him to see him anxiously watching me. Those amber eyes bore into mine, and I knew my answer before it left my lips.

I bit my lip. "It would only make sense that your girlfriend was there, right?"

"Right." He gave a nod, like the matter was settled.

I cleared my throat. "You know… if there was someone else you wanted to, um…"

"Hook up with?" Parker finished my sentence for me, looking surprisingly indifferent. "There's not." He shrugged.

"But if there is?"

"There won't be, Rosie Girl. Not for me. And while we're doing this, I won't even look at another woman, okay?"

That settled my nerves. I dipped my head, liking the sound of that.

He wasn't mine, not really, but while we were faking it, at least I could pretend he was.

"I'll be there," I offered.

Parker seemed to relax. "Thank you." He pressed a kiss to my cheek.

Like he was grateful for me, even though I was the one who needed to thank him.

THERE WAS one thing I knew for certain: I had *no* freaking clue how lacrosse worked. Still, the energy on the field was fun. And more than anything, I liked cheering on my boyfriend, even if it was all fake.

I stood in the student section, surrounded by hundreds of other Castleton University students, all cheering on our men's team. It was the home opener and their first game of the season.

And maybe this fake dating thing was still new, but I wanted to be here to support Parker. Either way, I'd promised him I would be here as his best friend. So I was determined to be the best damn girlfriend I could be.

I'd pulled on my favorite Castleton University sweatshirt and a pair of jeans that had bows embroidered on the pockets. They also made my ass look *great,* though that wasn't the reason I'd put them on. Well, not *entirely.* My hair was up in a ponytail, tied back with my favorite pink scrunchie.

Thankfully, he was easy to spot. Although I probably would have recognized him anywhere, regardless of his last name sprawled over the back of his white jersey, along with the number 59 in light blue. There was just something about his presence. He was tall at six foot three inches, towering over me even when I had heels on. Thanks to the short-sleeved jersey, his arm muscles were visible, and those biceps were on full display.

Damn, he looked good.

For once, I was out of my element. Though I knew plenty of the students surrounding me—it wasn't that big of a school, and I was a naturally extroverted person, making friends easily—it was my first time at a sporting event. Would it be that obvious?

Parker had played sports even when we were younger, in middle school, but I'd had so many of my own activities back then that I'd never gone. Dance classes, vocal lessons, and even learning how to play piano. Sometimes I wondered if I'd done too much. If I hadn't sat back and really enjoyed life.

Even now, my whole life was theater. I lived and breathed it.

Until Parker, I hadn't taken much time for myself. He didn't know how much our dinners meant to me. That it was the only time I felt like I could just be me instead of worrying about smiling and being the person everyone expected of me.

When the first period started, the opposing team gained possession of the ball, and then they were off. I tried to follow what was going on, but mostly, I just cheered whenever Parker had the ball or tried to make a shot on goal.

At the end of the first, we were up by two, and I watched as

Parker wiped a towel over his sweaty forehead. There were only a few minutes of break before they started playing again, and I watched in fascination. I definitely regretted not researching lacrosse before the game to learn some of the rules. Parker talked about his practices and the team often enough when we'd hang out, but mostly I felt like it all went over my head.

Still, at least I could appreciate the well-toned thighs and arms the players had. Not that I was staring at any specific player. If my eyes lingered a little longer on Parker's forearms and how incredible his ass looked in those shorts, well… No one else needed to know that. He was my best friend, but that didn't mean I didn't have eyes.

And Parker was *hot*. He was absolutely incredible to watch on the field, too. The way he ran around, keeping possession of the ball, was so confident. He had an air of surety—like nothing could phase him. God, that intense focus had me swallowing roughly, wondering what it would be like to have that focus on *me*.

After all four periods had finished—sixty minutes of game time total—our team had won, 15-8, and the energy in the student section was *electric*. Everyone was screaming, cheering for our guys, celebrating with the person next to them, even as the stands emptied.

I made my way down to the field, waving hello to some girls I knew from class or a few fellow sorority sisters I recognized. They probably were all wondering what I was doing here since I didn't usually attend sporting events.

Soon enough, they'd all find out that I was here for my boyfriend.

A little rush of excitement ran through me as I reached the edge of the field, my stark white tennis shoes toeing in the grass.

Parker was with his teammates as they all high-fived each other, celebrating, and I held back. Would he want me to interrupt this moment?

But then he looked over, his eyes catching mine, and his face lit up. Like he was happy to see me. A few of his teammates slapped him on the back as he jogged over, holding his helmet and stick in one hand.

"You came to my game." Parker's voice was almost breathless when he reached me.

"I told you I would," I said, fidgeting with my ponytail.

"Still." He grinned, running a hand through his damp hair. "It was nice to see my girlfriend here."

I felt warmth creeping into my cheeks. "You're welcome. You were awesome out there, you know." He'd scored the winning goal. That was my favorite part to watch. Even I'd jumped from my seat to scream my lungs out for him. "I didn't really know what was going on, but I had fun."

He did his best to look bashful. "Thank you for coming. You still coming to the party later?"

I nodded. "If you want me there, I'll be there."

Parker leaned forward, pressing his lips to my cheek before pulling back. "See you there." He looked towards his teammates and then back to me. "Text me if you need me, okay?"

"Okay," I whispered the word, watching him head back across the field to the guys before they headed back inside to the locker rooms.

AUDREY

I'm here.

I WAS STANDING in front of the lacrosse house, my eyes focused on the doorknob, but I couldn't make myself move. Because I knew after this, everything would change. After this, we'd really be fake dating. Everyone would know. I'd be in another public relationship—this time with an athlete. He might have been new to campus, but after the game today, there was no mistaking who he was.

Was I ready? No.

But I needed to be.

The door opened, and there was Parker. He'd changed, wearing a pair of jeans that molded to his thighs and a red flannel that hid the delicious upper arms I'd seen at his match earlier.

He raised an eyebrow at me as I gawked at him. "What are you doing out here? It's cold. Come inside."

God, what was I even doing? "Okay." I followed him into the house, the warmth immediately surrounding me. He stood behind me, slipping off my jacket before draping it over one arm.

"Hi," I said when he turned around, fidgeting with my necklace pendant.

He pressed a kiss to my cheek. "Hey." Parker looked me up and down, and I frowned, looking down at my shoes. "Is something wrong? Do I not look okay?" After the game, I'd taken off my sweatshirt, leaving me in a cute white long-sleeved shirt.

"You look great." He tugged at a piece of hair I'd curled before coming over here. "But where's your pink?"

I blinked. "I... What?"

He furrowed his brow. "You're always wearing pink. Even if it's just the scrunchie that's always on your wrist."

Oh. He'd noticed that?

"I'm still wearing pink," I mumbled.

"Where?" He raised an eyebrow.

I blushed. "Somewhere you can't see?"

"Is that a question, Audrey?" There was a hint of amusement in his eyes, like he knew exactly what I was saying. Like he had x-ray vision and could, in fact, see where the pink was.

"No," I murmured, shaking my head.

Parker chuckled, grabbing my hand and interlacing our fingers. "Come on. I want you to meet the guys."

"Okay."

And then I followed him into the lacrosse house, holding tight to his hand, feeling like he was my lifeline in this brand new world.

CHAPTER 12

She had no idea how adorable she was. No fucking clue.

Nor did she know how much it affected me to know she was wearing pink fucking panties. I held back a groan, holding her hand tighter as I brought her into the living room, where the rest of my teammates were gathered.

Though we didn't all live in the house, it made sense that we'd all hang out here after games. The underclassmen mostly lived in the dorms, while some juniors and seniors were in apartments off campus, making this the easiest place for all of us to gather.

"Hey, everyone," I called to the room, all eyes turning to Audrey and me. "Want you to meet someone." I squeezed her hand as she stood at my side, giving a small wave to my teammates. "This is Audrey Rose. My girlfriend." Looking down at her, I winked, and she gave me a small smile back.

"Hey," Audrey said, any hint of shyness gone. Of course, she was the extroverted one in our relationship. I'd always been the quiet guy. Only now was I feeling more comfortable with the team. "You guys played great today."

Samuel grinned. "You watched the game?" He was sitting on the couch, a pretty brunette draped over his lap.

She nodded. "Yeah. It was fun." Looking at me, she cocked her head. "Though I'll admit, I didn't really know what was happening."

Taylor piped up with, "I'm sure we could teach you."

I hated that idea. Because if anyone was going to teach my girl the rules, it would be me. I wasn't letting any of these fuckers do it. I grumbled, close to her ear, "I'll teach you. Because you're *my* girl."

Audrey just nodded, and I tried to ignore the flare of possession I felt running through me. She wasn't really mine, so I had no right to be territorial over her time. But after last year, the last thing I wanted was for my girlfriend to spend an extended amount of time with my teammates. Call me paranoid, but I wanted her all to myself.

"I liked watching you," she whispered, standing up on tiptoes so her mouth was level with my ear.

Fuck yeah. My chest puffed out, feeling pleased to know that she'd watched me. I didn't think I'd mistaken the way her eyes had roamed over my body as I walked away from her earlier on the field, but this was practically a confirmation.

Derek, the team captain, stood up, extending his hand towards my girl. "It's nice to meet you, Audrey." He was a senior, graduating this year, which meant the position would go to someone else next year. Maybe that someone would be me if I didn't fuck everything up. I was pretty sure that was why our coach had been so hard on me.

She accepted his handshake. "Hi. Thank you for letting me come."

"Of course. We told Maxwell he couldn't hide you away forever. Besides, everyone's welcome." There were plenty of people here who weren't on the team. Friends, girlfriends, and other university students. We were celebrating, so plenty of people were drinking, but it wasn't so loud yet that we couldn't hear each other talk. Though it was still early. I was sure the music would be louder in a few hours.

"Do you want a drink?" I snaked an arm around Audrey's midriff, tugging her closer to me.

She nodded. "Sure."

I tugged her into the kitchen, grateful there was no one else around, as I grabbed myself a beer. There was a six-pack of hard strawberry lemonade in the fridge, and I held up a bottle for her. "How's this?"

"That would be great, actually." She looked relieved as I popped the top off with a bottle opener, and I laughed.

"Did you think I was going to give you a beer?"

Audrey shrugged. "I don't know. Maybe."

"Do you even like beer?" I took a sip of mine, used to the taste. It wasn't the shittiest beer I'd ever had. Thankfully, we'd sprung for something that wasn't the cheapest, but it wasn't *great*, either.

I knew she didn't. We might not have gone to parties every weekend, but I'd spent enough time around her to notice what she drank. It was mostly fruity beverages.

She wrinkled her nose. "No. But no one ever cared about making sure I *liked* my drink before."

"Duke?" I asked, popping my index finger under her jaw and tilting her chin up to look at me.

She nodded before taking a sip. "I'm used to it."

"You shouldn't have to be." I clenched my jaw.

Her eyes brightened as she stood up on her tiptoes, kissing my cheek. "Thank you, Parker. You're a good guy."

"A good *boyfriend*, you mean?"

She looked around as if worried someone else was eaves-dropping before nodding. "Yeah. That too."

"Come on, girlfriend. Let's go back in there."

"What am I supposed to say if someone asks about us?" Audrey asked, rubbing the rim of the bottle with her thumb.

"The truth." We hadn't really talked about this part in our agreement. I leaned my head down so my lips would brush against the shell of her ear. "Except for the fact that it's fake."

"Okay." The word was hardly more than a breath, and I tucked a strand of her blonde hair behind her ear before threading our hands together again and heading back out to the living room.

Sitting on the couch next to Samuel, I placed my beer on a coaster—we might have been athletes, but we weren't animals.

Audrey looked around, eyes wide. No doubt noticing what I'd already figured out. There were no open seats. I could see the indecision on her face as she looked around the room.

"Come here," I murmured, gesturing to my open lap.

Audrey's cheeks flushed pink like she couldn't possibly sit on me, her *boyfriend.* As if it was somehow scandalous to sit on my lap.

"Are you sure?" she whispered, and I wrapped my arm around her waist, tugging her backward so she stood in between my legs.

"Positive." My voice was low, more of a grumble than anything else. "Sit on my lap, baby."

I didn't think she was going to, but then she lowered herself onto my thigh, hovering like she didn't want to give me all of her weight. But I used my hold around her waist to tug her back against me fully before curling a hand over her thigh. Possessively.

Like I was daring the rest of these fuckers to make a move on my girl.

My teammates had no idea what happened last year, but I wouldn't make the same mistake again. She hadn't been right for me, anyway. I knew that, yet still, I'd stayed with her.

"Parker," Audrey whispered in my ear.

"Mhm?" With my free hand, I played with the ends of her hair. It was an unconscious movement, but I couldn't stop touching her. Now that we were dating and free to, I was finding excuses to have my hands on her all the time.

What would she think if I always asked her to sit on my lap? I could smell her perfume, the sweet scent like champagne and berries mixing with her strawberry shampoo. Sweet. She smelled so damn sweet.

I didn't hear a single conversation around me. Not when I was so painfully aware of Audrey's weight on mine. How good it felt like this.

She took a long gulp of her lemonade, and I did the same with my beer before setting it back beside me. Tonight, I wouldn't get drunk. During the season, I had a strict two drinks per night limit: beer or cider only—no hard alcohol. So I was content just to watch her.

"Parker," Audrey said my name again, and it finally broke me out of my trance.

"What?"

She giggled. "You're staring."

I hummed, pushing a hair back behind her ear. "So I can't stare at my *girlfriend*?"

A pretty blush dotted her cheeks. "No. I mean… You can. It's just…" She ran her tongue over her lower lip, and it drew my attention to those plush, pink lips. So kissable. They were just begging for my attention.

I rubbed my thumb over her bottom lip before pulling away. "It's just what?"

"Nothing." She shook her head before resting it on my shoulder. I adjusted her legs so they draped over my free knee so she didn't have to straddle me, and she cuddled in closer. Damn, but I liked this.

I glanced over at the couch next to us, seeing my teammate also cuddled up with his girl. Everyone might have been celebrating around us, but we were just in our own bubbles.

Sam's girlfriend, Danielle, was a cheerleader, her high ponytail still in her hair as she laid her head in his lap. Though the cheer team didn't officially participate in our games, she'd still been there anyway.

I liked that. She seemed nice enough from seeing her around

the house. I wondered if Audrey and I would ever be like that. Look that comfortable with each other.

Danielle was wearing Samuel's lacrosse t-shirt with his last name on the back and his number. No girl had ever worn my jersey before. But maybe it was time to change that.

A FEW DAYS LATER, I stepped foot in the theater building for the second time, joining the entire cast and crew of the spring musical. It was my first time here in my new role.

"You ready for this?" Audrey whispered to me as we took seats in the front row.

I squeezed her hand, not letting go as we sat down.

Looking around, I noticed her ex was in the row behind us at the end, glaring daggers at me. So I leaned over, kissing Audrey's forehead.

"What was that for?" she whispered.

"Because I wanted to." I smirked at her. "Plus, your ex is staring at us. Don't look."

"What?" She turned her head, and I clicked my tongue against the roof of my mouth.

"Don't pay attention to him. Let him know exactly how little you think about him." Audrey let out a breath, and I squeezed her knee. "I've got you, sunshine. Okay?"

He needed to back the fuck off because I wasn't going to play. If he came after her again, he was going to have me to deal with.

Everyone settled down as Professor Woods took the stage. It was clear she had stage presence and poise, and I was sure she'd graced the stage herself numerous times. "Welcome, welcome, everyone, to our first rehearsal of the season!"

Everyone around me cheered, and I looked over at Audrey. This was her wheelhouse.

I was incredibly out of my depth here. And I realized how

overwhelmed she'd probably been at my game this weekend. It was how I felt now. Damn, I should have prepared her better.

Though I'd had the script for a few weeks now, this was our first official meeting. I was surprised these hadn't started the second the semester had, but maybe losing their lead had delayed some things. Fuck if I knew.

"We're going to start things off with a little bonding exercise for everyone to get to know each other." Mary, the student director of the musical, announced to all of us.

To a chorus of groans.

I was pretty sure there was nothing college students hated more than icebreakers and bonding activities.

"I know, I know," Mary said, rolling her eyes at us. "But it's going to be fun. I promise." She grinned. "And then we're going to do our first read through of the script."

For the icebreaker, she brought all of us up onto the stage, sat us in a circle, and we played a silly name game. We all introduced ourselves with our first name and an animal that started with the same letter and then had to repeat everyone's names who had already gone. I chose Parker the panther, wanting a strong, masculine animal.

Audrey, the axolotl. I chuckled—even that was pink, which felt fitting.

Surprisingly, by the end, I actually remembered almost everyone's name. Given how many people were involved in this production, it was incredible.

I never would have imagined myself here, but as we went through the script for the first time and I watched the way Audrey's face lit up as she said her lines, I couldn't imagine anywhere else I'd rather be.

CHAPTER 13

Audrey

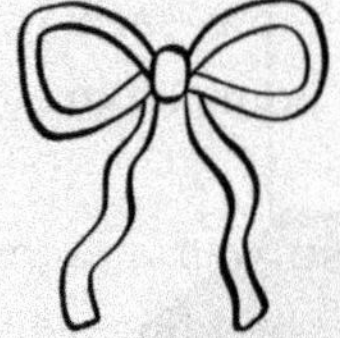

Our last few rehearsals, we'd been working on blocking and learning the music and choreography for the musical. We'd keep doing it for the first few weeks, going through all the scenes to get comfortable with everything.

I was surprised how easily Parker kept up. Sure, he could sing, but that didn't mean this was easy. But I hadn't needed to worry at all. He was a natural. His body moved gracefully, memorizing the choreo like it was *nothing*. When I asked him about it, he'd just shrugged and said, "*I guess learning all the lacrosse plays made it easy.*"

Still, I had to give him credit. I had no idea how he was juggling everything. He had his first away game last weekend, and I'd tried not to notice his absence while he was gone. We'd texted through it, but I missed him throughout the day. To distract myself, I'd gotten dinner with my twin, and the sorority had a movie night, all of us piling onto the couches to watch *Mamma Mia!*

It was one of my favorites, though I wasn't too hard to please as long as the movie came with a happily ever after for the main couple. I read romance novels for the same reason. I was a big fan of the HEA.

Real life was sad enough. At least in fiction, the girl could get swept off her feet by the perfect guy who would promise to love her and never leave her. And I didn't think it was too much to ask for, not really.

Today, we were rehearsing one of my favorite scenes of the musical—and one that made me the most nervous because at one point, the entire ensemble stepped off the stage, and it would just be Parker and I. Which meant that everyone else would watch us.

"You ready?" Parker squeezed my hand from the wings as we both waited for our cue. I would go out first since my character had a solo before his character would arrive and our duet would begin.

"Born ready," I said, rolling my eyes even as I felt the anxiety run through me.

I never had stage fright. It didn't even exist in my vocabulary. There was a reason everyone had always said I was born to be on stage. I thrived in the spotlight, and I loved all the attention.

But suddenly, everything felt *real*. Because the man at my side was more than just my co-star or a friend. And that made everything different.

He brushed a strand of hair away from my face before kissing the side of my head.

I was wearing one of my favorite flowy pink dresses with a chunky cardigan along with my character heels.

My heart was beating fast in my chest as I got my signal, stepping out on stage and letting the rest of the world go quiet. I just performed, letting my feet move without thinking. That was what I'd always been good at. Everything else faded away, and it was just me and the stage. Sometimes, it was the only time I really felt like me. Sure, everyone was watching me, and that was its own kind of pressure, but I also didn't have to think about how I was portraying myself. What I was saying or doing.

I got to slip into being someone else, and it was incredibly freeing.

Parker stepped out on stage, and for a moment, I let myself pretend that he was truly mine. That he was my prince here to save the day. Even if it was only a dream, it was a wonderful one.

Best friend, I reminded myself. *He's your best friend.*

We were in a good spot. Even if it was still strange holding his hand on campus and pretending like we were dating anytime someone else was around. Still, in private, we were just us. We'd watch fantasy shows or movies together and he'd tell me about how different they were from the book. Parker was a jock, but he was also a secret, quiet nerd. The moment I'd realized he was shy around people was an eye opener. He wasn't reserved with me, but I'd seen how he was with his team. Quiet. Like he was worried about something.

Right now, though, his entire attention was focused on me as he moved around me, holding my hand as we danced. I couldn't look away, even as the steps slowed, and I placed my hand on his chest.

His firm, warm, *hard* chest. He was wearing another plaid shirt and jeans combo, with the shirt left open to reveal the undershirt that clung to his muscles.

He wrapped his hands around my waist. My eyes darted down to his lips, and I ran my tongue over my lower lip, moistening it. Because I knew what was next.

He'd kiss me.

The two leads would share their first kiss of the musical.

"Everyone's watching us," I murmured, unable to look away from his handsome face. I'd always found him handsome, but this was different. Maybe because he'd never looked at me like *this.* Like he wanted to kiss me so desperately. Like there was nothing else in the world he'd rather be doing.

"Rosie," Parker whispered against my ear, tucking a loose

strand of hair behind my ear. "Breathe. It's just you and me, right?"

I'd never been nervous on stage before. But I'd also never been pretending to date my best friend slash co-star either. Giving him a tiny nod of my head, he pulled me in tight.

Everything else faded away as he held me in his arms. The rest of the room quieted, and all I could see and hear was him. It didn't matter that in the audience were all of my friends from the last three years in this program. It didn't matter that my ex was sitting there watching us or my professor.

All that mattered was the way Parker pressed his lips against mine. I wrapped my arms around his neck, pulling him tighter—just like was written in the script. It was a closed-mouth kiss, and there was no tongue, but somehow, this felt even more intimate than when we'd practiced on his bed.

God, I wanted him to slip his tongue inside. To taste him. Would he taste like coffee and sin? Last time we'd kissed like this, I hadn't really gotten to explore. To memorize him.

But damn, I wanted to.

This was dangerous.

Because no matter what, he was still just my fake boyfriend.

Everyone whooped and cheered for us, and we pulled apart.

Parker had the faintest blush on his cheekbones, and he ran his hands through his hair.

"Yeah, yeah," I deflected, trying not to draw attention to how much I liked kissing him. How much I wanted to do it again. Because we were supposed to be dating, so this should be normal.

Even though my racing heart and the butterflies in my stomach told me it was anything but normal.

No one had ever affected me like this.

No one had ever been Parker Maxwell, though.

EVERY YEAR, our sorority put on a Valentine's Day Date Auction, with all the money we raised going to our philanthropy. It was one of our big fundraisers of the year, and I'd been working on my basket for weeks. I hadn't wanted to leave it for the last minute.

There were so many themes in my sorority sister's baskets: Suzie had a movie date theme with popcorn and candy, while Peggy's was a pizza night date with all the ingredients to make their own pizzas. There was such a wide variety that my more traditional picnic date felt lame in comparison. But it was fine. Even if no one bid on me, I didn't care.

Ella stood next to me, wearing a blue gingham dress, peeking out of the curtains like she was trying to see who was out there. Her basket in her arms was for a night under the stars, with a cozy blanket and s'mores supplies.

"Don't worry," I said, squeezing her shoulder. "Cam's here for you."

"I'm not worried," she mumbled, letting the curtain drop. I raised an eyebrow, but she said nothing else. But there was no doubt in my mind that her boyfriend would be here for her. She'd spent more time with him this semester than she had with me.

Which, I supposed, was fair, considering I'd been doing the same with Parker.

Was Parker here for me? I'd mentioned it before, and he'd sounded interested, but it wasn't like I'd sent him a calendar invite or a reminder about tonight.

"I'm really glad you have him."

She gave me a small smile. "What about you and Parker, huh? I've been hearing rumors."

I blushed, waving her off. "It's nothing."

Ignoring the fact that I'd sat on his lap last week at the lacrosse party and he'd taken me out on our first date a few nights ago. Fake date, but that didn't matter. Not with the way he'd taken everything so seriously. He was the perfect gentleman, and I was pretty sure I was slowly growing obsessed with the way he kept holding my hand whenever we were together.

Like he knew just how comforting his touch was.

Ella looked at me, cocking her head to the side, but I stayed quiet.

"Alright, girls," Ilene said, ushering us all into our places behind the curtain. "We're going to start soon. Just like we practiced, okay?"

"Don't worry, Ilene," Ella reassured her. "Everything's going to be perfect. And the room is almost full."

Our advisor just nodded, letting out a deep breath like she was centering herself. "Everyone ready?"

We all nodded in agreement, and then the event started. One of the fraternity's advisors had agreed to be the MC for the night, but Ella was up first to introduce the event and our philanthropy since she was the President of our chapter.

"You got this, Ells," I squeezed her hand. "Go get 'em, sis."

She winked at me before stepping out on the stage, tossing the blonde curls that were identical to mine over her shoulder. I'd done her hair and makeup before we'd left the sorority house, and she looked absolutely gorgeous. Well, maybe I was biased, considering we shared the same face. But still, my twin was incredible. Ella liked blending into the background, but she was a born leader. She was fiercely defensive of her friends and she cared more than anyone I knew. But she was also extremely talented and creative.

I hoped that one day, she'd see herself the way I saw her. The way I suspected Cam saw her.

"Welcome to the annual Pi Rho Sigma Date Auction!" Ella announced to the crowd, who cheered. "If you've joined us before, you know what to expect, but for our first time attendees, tonight's event is to help our philanthropy, raising money for survivors of domestic abuse. Each of our members has prepared a date basket containing the perfect ingredients for the date you'll go on."

I watched her from behind the curtain, smiling as she explained the rules and how the evening would go.

Of course, once she finished, Ella was the first to go, presenting her basket and telling the crowd about their date. Not that she needed to bother. I knew exactly who would be going home with her.

"For a lovely date with the Pi Rho President, Ella, the bidding will start at one hundred dollars!" our MC started. "Do I hear one hundred?"

I couldn't see the crowd, but I could hear them.

"One hundred!"

"One fifty!"

"Two hundred!"

None of them were Cam. I frowned.

"We've got two hundred! Don't forget, all proceeds are going to the Pi Rho Sigma philanthropy to support Survivors of Domestic Abuse. It's a fantastic cause! Do I hear two fifty?"

"One thousand," shouted a new voice. *That* was Cam. I chuckled. Of course he would. Damn, he loved my sister.

"One thousand going once," the MC called out. "Going twice." There wasn't another peep from the crowd. "Sold to the gentleman in the third row."

Ella came back a few moments later, cheeks flushed.

"Well, we're definitely off to a good start!" I heard from outside as Suzie opened the curtain and stepped out.

"Damn, girl," I said, waggling my eyebrows. "Your boyfriend's down bad."

"Shut up," my twin mumbled, shoving at my shoulder playfully.

In response, I threw my arm around her, pulling her into a hug. "Love you."

"Love you too, Ro." Her voice was soft, full of emotion.

I hung back with her until it was my turn, grabbing my basket and heading out on stage.

"You got this, babe!" Peggy cheered for me, and Ella gave me a thumbs up.

Taking a deep breath, I opened the curtain, the bright lights keeping me from seeing most of the crowd. Except there... in the front row.

There was Parker. Grinning up at me in a Castleton University sweatshirt with dark denim jeans, hair damp like he'd come here straight from practice. But he was here.

For me.

My heart fluttered in my chest as I stepped in front of the podium to talk into the microphone. "Hi, I'm Audrey Rose. My basket is a Valentine's Day picnic, complete with heart-shaped sandwiches." God, this was stupid. What had I been thinking? No guy would want to bid on this. I forced a smile on my face as I finished describing the rest.

I looked at Parker, who was nodding encouragingly.

The bidding started, and I wasn't surprised when Parker's hand was the first to shoot up. Unlike Cam, who'd gotten the last word in, Parker immediately countered back to anyone who tried to bid on mine.

And then there was the one voice I didn't want to hear. "Three hundred."

Holding back a groan, I tried not to look. *Don't pay attention to him. Let him know exactly how little you think about him.* Parker's words from earlier this week rang through my mind. But I knew it was Duke. I just didn't understand *why*. Why was he so obsessed with me? Why couldn't he let me go?

"Five hundred," Parker said smugly from the front row, glaring daggers at my ex.

The MC just laughed, and when no one else attempted to outbid him, my date was sold. To my best friend.

Who was waiting for me with a big, goofy expression, his arms open wide, like he knew just where I wanted to be.

In his arms, always.

CHAPTER 14
Parker

When Audrey had told me that their date auction was an annual event, a fundraiser for her sorority's charity, I hadn't imagined anything like this. It felt like half the school was here, crowded into the auditorium to watch the show.

And damn, if I hadn't felt a flare of possession when she'd gone up on stage. I couldn't help it. She looked perfect, like a pretty pink princess, especially with the lights behind her illuminating her golden hair.

I couldn't help but think about how right it had felt to hold her in my arms the other day during rehearsals. How right it was to kiss her in front of the entire cast and crew of the musical.

To claim her as mine, even if it was just in our roles.

We were dating, even if it wasn't real, but I hadn't even taken her out yet on a date. A real date. I frowned at the thought. Sure, we were visible on campus. We walked together, shared dinner most evenings together, and spent most of our free time together. She let me hold her hand, interlacing our fingers as we walked with no space between our bodies.

It wasn't enough, though. I was still failing as her fake boyfriend. I needed to step up my game.

Maybe that was why I'd bid on her basket. Not because I couldn't bear the thought of anyone else going on a date with her, but because I'd wanted to prove that she was mine.

The look she was giving me as she came out from the back told me I'd made the right call. I didn't regret spending all that money if she looked this happy afterward. Truly, there was nothing better than the feeling of your girl walking straight into your waiting arms.

I swept her up into a hug, holding her tight against my body.

"You did so good up there, sunshine," I whispered against the top of her head. "I'm proud of you." I wanted to give her the words because I was beginning to suspect that no one told her how amazing she was. Sometimes it felt like she thought she needed to tone herself down. To be less than the amazing person she was. I wanted to prove to her that the only people who would ask her to change weren't friends at all.

To support her in every decision and every choice she made. If she wanted to wear pink every day, to wear her shimmery eyeshadow and sparkly lip gloss because it made her happy, that was no one's business but hers. All I wanted was to see her happy.

"I can't believe you just dropped five hundred dollars on me," Audrey mumbled as she pulled away slightly so she could look up at me.

I shrugged. "It was for a good cause. Plus, I wanted my date." I smirked at her. "No one else was getting my heart-shaped sandwiches."

Because damn, one look at her up there, and I'd known that there was no way in hell I was going to let anyone else win a date with Audrey. Fake or not, she was my girlfriend, and I wanted all of her dates. All of her smiles.

All of those pretty little blushes she gave me.

She wrapped her arms around my back, hugging me tight. "Thank you."

Brushing her bangs out of her eyes, I pressed a kiss to her forehead. "Of course, Rosie Girl. I've got you."

"I know," she murmured.

"So, how about that date?" I wiggled my eyebrows.

"Now?" Audrey laughed. "It's late. And don't you have a game tomorrow?"

We did. And next weekend, we had our first away game of the season. I sighed. "Raincheck, then?"

"Whenever you want, *boyfriend*," Audrey winked at me.

Wrapping my arm around her, I tugged her close as we headed out of the auditorium, leaving all of it behind us.

"Did you eat?" I asked, looking over at her. If there was one thing I knew, it was that she was constantly forgetting to feed herself. When she got busy, it was the last thing on her mind. But she had me now, and I'd always make sure to take care of her, even when she forgot herself.

She shook her head. "No. I got caught up setting up and—"

I nodded, guiding her to my car.

"Parker, where are we going? You have a game tomorrow. You should get some sleep." Audrey crossed her arms as she stopped in the middle of the parking lot.

"I'm going to feed you, Rosie, and then I'll take you back to the sorority house and watch you go inside to make sure you're safe, okay? And once I see your light turn on in the window, then I'll go." I tugged at the end of the pink bow she had in her hair. "Okay?"

Her eyes met mine, and I expected more of a fight, but then her arms dropped to her side, and she just nodded.

"The dining hall is mostly closed, though." She scrunched up her nose. Audrey was right—after a certain point, the only thing that was left open was the grill. And while I never minded a good burger, I knew the only thing she really liked from there was grilled cheese or chicken nuggets when she was in the mood. "So where will we go?"

Guess I was getting my date after all. I grinned. "Tacos."

If there was one thing I knew, it was that Mexican food would always make things better. Plus, I liked that it was where we'd shared our first dinner together after the Halloween party where we'd run into each other. It felt like *our* place.

I liked the idea of us having places. Anything that would tie us together. When this was all over, would she still go to those places and think of us? Or would it be places we never stepped foot in again?

Slipping my hand onto her lower back as we got to my car, I opened the door for her and let her get inside. She'd already buckled up before I came around and slid into the driver's side.

Audrey blew out a breath, messing up her bangs. "I have to admit, I was really worried about tonight."

"Why?" I frowned.

She shrugged, looking anywhere but at me as I pulled out of the parking lot. "Last year wasn't great. I know you weren't here, but..." Nibbling on her bottom lip, she hesitated.

"Your ex?" I guessed. I'd told her once that I'd be her knight in shining armor, but I'd never realized how true it was until now. How easily I'd made the decision tonight to prevent her ex from winning time with her. "What would you have done if he'd won?"

"It's not like we're forced to go on the dates, but I would have had to talk to Ilene, my sorority advisor."

"Does she know?"

A nod. "Yeah. I told her everything that happened last semester. She told me, well... Do you know what love bombing is?"

I shook my head, though I had an idea from the name. Still, I wanted her to keep talking. "No. Tell me."

"It's when you overwhelm someone with declarations of love, gifts, and excessive attention to make them fall for you."

"He did that to you?"

Her voice was quiet. "Ilene pointed it out. I thought he was sincere at first. Fall semester was great. And then... things changed."

I clenched my teeth together. "How?"

"He got more controlling, I guess. He'd be mad when I was hanging out with people other than him. If I wore certain things, he'd berate me for my outfit choice. If I was talking to other guys after class, he'd accuse me of cheating. Call me a slut."

I pulled into the parking lot of the taco place, putting the car in park but not getting out of the car.

"He's a narcissist," I stated. Not a question. Just an observation.

Audrey fiddled with her hands on her lap. "Yeah. And for whatever reason, he won't let me go. Like he sees me as his property." She shut her eyes. "I never should have gone out with him. Or slept with him. I was such an idiot."

"Hey." I rested my hand on her thigh, squeezing lightly. "That's my best friend you're talking about."

She gave me a small smile.

"You're not an idiot," I reassured her. "And we'll get him to leave you alone."

"How?" Audrey seemed so small. I fucking hated that.

I gave her a peck on the cheek. "By showing him that we're together."

"WHAT ARE WE DOING HERE?" Audrey whispered into my ear the next Monday as we stood in the busiest coffee shop on campus, her hand laced tightly around mine. She was holding onto it like I was a lifeline—her lifeline—and for some strange reason, I liked that.

I leaned down, dragging my lips against her ear. "Showing people we're together, sunshine."

She inhaled sharply as I placed a kiss on her neck before standing back to my full height. I'd always been tall, even as a kid, but now I practically towered over her. If I stood behind her, I could almost tuck her completely under my chin. It was strange how much I wanted to wrap my arms around her and keep her safe from the world.

"People already know we're together, Parker."

I hummed in response, taking another step forward as we waited to order.

"Do they?" I was pretty sure the circles of people who knew we were dating were the lacrosse team and the cast and crew of the musical. But even that wasn't enough. I wanted the entire campus to know she was mine.

Especially Duke Prescott, who hadn't gotten the memo yet that Audrey wanted nothing to do with him.

"Yes?" She sounded unsure, her cheeks the most adorable shade of pink.

Finally, it was our turn to order, and I took a step up, Audrey joining me at my side.

"What would you like?" The barista asked, looking at me. She completely ignored Audrey, smiling at me like I'd give her the time of day.

What she didn't know was the only girl I had eyes for was the one standing right next to me, wearing a pink sweater dress adorned with white pearls and tan heeled booties.

"My girlfriend will have a hot white chocolate mocha," I said, emphasizing the first two words a touch louder than I needed to. "I'll have a flat white."

"Perfect. Anything else?" She fluttered her eyelashes at me.

Audrey cleared her throat. "Can I get one of those strawberry tarts?"

Finally, the barista looked at her. "Sure." Her tone with Audrey wasn't as sweet as it had been to me.

Squeezing Audrey's hand, I kissed the side of her head before letting go. "Why don't you go find a seat, sunshine, and I'll pay?"

"Sure, baby," my girl agreed, giving me a little smile and the sweetest blush. "See ya in a sec."

I handed the barista my credit card, paid and got Audrey's pastry before I headed back to find her at a table by the fireplace. It was a cozy spot and one where everyone could see us.

I set the pastry down before sliding in next to her, wrapping my arm around her. "Smart spot, *baby*," I teased her.

"It just slipped out," she said, blushing even harder than before.

"It's okay, I liked it," I reassured her, tugging on a blonde curl. "You can call me anything you want, Rosie Girl."

She hummed in response, taking a bite of the puff pastry tart covered with cream cheese and strawberry. A little moan left her throat, and her tongue darted out to lick the little dollop left on her lower lip.

"Good?" I asked, watching with rapt attention.

Her head dipped in a nod. "Want to try it? These are my favorite."

"Yeah," I answered, hoping my voice didn't sound as gravely as it felt.

Instead of handing it to me, Audrey angled the pastry towards me, holding it up to my mouth. I took a bite right next to where she'd eaten it, and she was right. It was good.

"Mmm," I said after I swallowed, wiping my lip with my thumb before licking off the extra strawberry juices. "Delicious." I eyed her lips. "Just like you."

"Parker!" Audrey scolded, playfully smacking me on the arm before setting the pastry down on the plate.

I tipped her chin up with my finger, making her meet my gaze before pressing my lips to hers. I didn't deepen the kiss, just let it linger there. Her eyes widened as I pulled away, tucking a strand of hair behind her ear.

"There," I whispered against her mouth. "That'll do it."

Winking, I stood up to go fetch our coffees, wishing I could do more.

That it wasn't all just for show.

CHAPTER 15

Audrey

I blushed. He didn't tell me to *wear something nice*. No, he'd told me to wear something I felt good in, and that made a world of difference. Because I knew that when it came down to it, it didn't matter to him what I wore. Not when he made comments like *where's your pink* and made me feel so seen.

Though I had no idea what he had planned, I pulled a dress out of my closet, wondering if he had any idea how he made me feel when he said things like that. How much the butterflies exploded in my chest.

It was only four, and I'd finished all of my classes for the day, giving me plenty of time to pull my hair up into a half-up, half-down up-do, swiping on my favorite shimmery eyeshadow and pink sparkly lip gloss. Since it was still cold outside, I pulled on a pair of warm-fleece lined tights under my dress before staring at the shoes in my closet.

Ella and I used to have all our clothes crammed inside, but when she moved out, she'd taken a lot with her. It was even more noticeable now how little variety I had in my clothes and colors. There was pink, a few pieces in purple, white, black, and tan. Sure, I had a few things in other pastel shades, but I liked what I liked.

Words Duke had said in the past came rushing to my brain. *It's too much. You shouldn't wear pink all the time, babe.* I rolled my eyes, thinking about how different the two men were.

How Parker had asked me where my pink *was*. Like he accepted it as a part of me. Like he knew it made me happy.

And it did. I smiled as I slipped my dress on over my head, smoothing out the skirt. It was a long-sleeved pink dress, with pearl accents on the sleeves and a tight-fitting skirt that clung to my curves, showing off my waist and hips. I'd bought it last year, but never had the occasion to wear it yet.

Maybe I'd just been waiting for an excuse like this. *Our first date.* Fake or not, we were going out.

After I'd finished getting dressed, I headed downstairs, pulling on my favorite white coat. I was really over the chilly weather. Spring couldn't come soon enough.

A knock sounded at the door, and before I could head to open it, someone else did. It dawned on me that he could have texted me to tell me he was outside. But no. He'd come to the door, even knowing most of my sorority sisters would probably be home in the evening.

"Hey."

And there he was. Parker, my best friend. Parker, my fake boyfriend. Dressed in a dark gray button up with black slacks, holding a pink bouquet of roses in his arms.

"Parker," I whispered, my eyes darting back to the house where I was sure half the sorority was watching. "What are you doing?"

"Taking my girlfriend out on a date." He grinned, a cocky smile that made my heart flutter.

Because damn, he was perfect. And one day, he'd do these things for someone else. I needed to remember that.

"These are beautiful." I buried my nose in the flowers.

"Thought you'd like them. They reminded me of you, Rosie Girl."

I blushed. "I should put them in water before we go."

He nodded, and I scampered into the kitchen to find a vase and fill it with water. Dropping my purse on the counter, I opened the cabinet where we kept them.

Parker didn't stay by the door—no, he followed me into the house, leaning against a barstool as I busied myself with the flowers.

Suzie caught my eye and mouthed, *hot damn.*

I know. Damn, but I knew. He was *hot.* It should be illegal how good he looked like this, really.

"Ready?" Parker asked when I set the vase down on the counter, fluffing the flowers.

Suzie winked at me. "You two go have fun. I'll put these in your room, Audrey."

"Thank you," I said, nodding to her.

I came around the island and grabbed my purse. Parker placed his hand on my lower back, guiding me out to the door. He opened it for me, and his hand didn't drop.

Not until we got to the car, so he could open the door to his car for me. It was a practical car—nothing flashy, but it was nice all the same. He offered me his hand, and I slid into the seat.

Once I was settled, he closed it softly before rounding the car and getting into the driver's seat.

But he didn't buckle up and start the car. No. He reached over me, grabbing my seatbelt and dragging it over my body, clicking it in.

How was I going to survive the night when he was acting like this?

He grinned at me before buckling his own.

"Where are we going?" I asked as he started the car.

"It's a surprise," Parker said, keeping his eyes focused on the road.

His right hand rested on the center console, and I crossed my legs.

"You know you don't have to take me on an actual date, right? We can just do stuff on campus."

He glared at me. "Audrey Rose. You deserve to be taken on a date. So let me."

There was no point in arguing with him. Not about this. So I just let him take me on a date, one that didn't feel fake in the least.

He took me to a fancy teppanyaki place, where I ordered the shrimp and the chicken, as well as a bowl of fried rice. Not one person from CU was here, and we spent the whole night laughing, sharing our inside jokes. We had so many of them from childhood, but we were making new ones now, too.

I thought about the tree in his backyard—the one we'd carved our names into, because we were going to be friends forever. A big part of me wished we'd never lost those years after he moved, but maybe it was supposed to be like this. Maybe we needed to lose each other in order to find each other again.

We were different people now. I'd grown up. The rose-colored lenses I used to wear no longer applied to the world. Maybe I was less naïve now.

I still dreamed of a happy ending, of that great big love story

I could only hope was out there waiting for me, but I also knew this was real life—not a fairytale.

Even if today felt a lot like one.

AFTER WE'D FINISHED EATING our meal—which was delicious—and headed back out to the car, Parker pulled out a gift bag I hadn't even before, placing it in my lap.

I raised my eyebrows. "What's this for?"

"I didn't get to take you out for Valentine's Day, but I wanted to get you something."

"Oh, I..." I hadn't even thought about us getting each other gifts. Mostly because we weren't in an actual relationship. Still, how could I turn him down?

He had a faint blush over his cheekbones, and I found it adorable.

Opening the bag, I pulled out a piece of white material. Parker looked away, scratching the back of his head. "It's a jersey. My jersey. For you to wear." Sure enough, the back read Maxwell with his number—59—stitched onto it in light blue. "My girlfriend should wear my jersey when she comes to my games, after all."

"*Fake* girlfriend," I reminded him.

He gave me a stare that I felt straight down to my toes. "No one else knows that though, do they? Wear it to the next game. Please."

This felt like more than that, though. Like it meant some-thing. Him giving me his jersey felt... *special*.

I dipped my head in agreement. No one else knew this was fake.

And part of me wanted to wear his jersey to the next game. Wanted to claim him as mine. Wanted the girls who sat next to me, talking about how much of a catch he was, to know he was off the market.

Because Parker Maxwell was mine. Even if it was just for a little while.

I nibbled on my lip. "Are you sure?"

He tugged a strand of hair, smiling down at me. "Of course I'm sure, Rosie Girl. I want you to wear it."

"Okay then," I agreed, hugging the garment to my chest. "I will." Though I didn't know why it was so important to him I wore it, I would. He was doing so much for me, and it was such a small thing to do for him.

Leaning across the center console, I pressed a kiss to his cheek. "Thank you."

He hummed in response. "Anything for you, Audrey."

I had a feeling that he meant it. That he really would do anything for me.

Hopefully, Parker couldn't hear how my heart was beating wildly in my chest.

"Want to head back to campus?" he asked, and I just nodded.

It wasn't like I could tell him *no; I want to spend more time with you, just like this.*

Because tonight had been perfect. A fairytale of a date that I wanted to remember forever.

I hugged his shirt to my chest, knowing I was going to bury my nose in it tonight because it still smelled like him. Like the clean, crisp scent of his laundry detergent plus the woodsy, smoky smell that always clung to him. He smelled like a *man,* spicy in all the best ways.

But I couldn't exactly sniff his shirt in front of him. That would not be very best-friend like. That was firmly crossing the territory into something else. Something that felt real.

And I couldn't go there.

Not with him.

"AUDREY!" a voice shouted behind me, and when I turned, there was my friend Sutton. I hadn't seen her too much this semester —probably because of our wildly different majors and the fact that I'd been spending most of my time with Parker.

She was a culinary student, and every single thing I'd ever sampled of hers had been *amazing*. One day, I wanted to be the first customer in the door when she opened a bakery—wherever it was. Her boyfriend, Forest, was on the baseball team, talking about entering the MLB draft upon graduation.

No matter what else happened, I knew they were going to make it. Because he looked at her like she was his very reason for breathing, and there was nothing in this world that would keep him apart from her.

"Hey, Sutton." I was quickly pulled into a hug by my friend.

Sutton White was wearing a pair of ripped jeans, an oversized red flannel, and a pair of Doc Marten boots, with her black shoulder length hair curled in loose waves. And while I spent most days doing a full face of makeup, Sutton always looked effortlessly beautiful with eyeliner, just a swipe of mascara and a bold red lip. I was jealous.

Today, I'd worn one of my favorite pink tank-top dresses, with a white turtleneck covered in little tiny roses layered underneath. It was cute and casual, and I'd left my hair down, just curling the ends before doing my normal makeup routine. "How have you been?"

"Good. What about you? Heard you've been spending a lot of time with a certain lacrosse player."

"Not you, too," I groaned. It had been a couple of days since our date, and it felt like everyone was abuzz with the news of our relationship.

She shrugged. "Athletes talk. Even more than sorority girls do." Sutton cracked a grin. I tried not to dwell on her words. Of course, the boys did. In fact, it wouldn't surprise me if her boyfriend and mine—fake, but whatever—had been in the gym at the same time. Especially since the baseball team and the lacrosse team both had spring seasons.

What I wouldn't give to be a fly on the wall in that locker room... I shook my head to get rid of the thought. There was no part of me that should picture them shirtless and sweaty as they did reps. Even though I wasn't really picturing *them*. There was only one guy who I wanted to see like that.

And I couldn't have him like that.

"Where are you headed next?" I asked her, wanting to change the subject.

Sutton flicked her dark hair back. "I have a pastry class in Carthay Hall." She pointed at the culinary building. "What about you?"

"Rehearsals," I said, looking towards Grimm Center, the home of our theater department. My classes were over for the day, and I'd grabbed a quick bite to eat before heading to the four-hour practice.

In the past, I'd often forgotten to eat on long days like this, being so busy flitting from one thing to the next, but there was something about Parker's presence that made it easier. Maybe it was the way he was always checking in on me. Bringing me food, snacks I'd loved back when we were kids, or going to dinner with me.

It was a small gesture, but it meant so much to me.

"Oooh. I heard the other lead in the musical is your new boyfriend."

"Yeah." I blushed.

She turned to me, raising one dark eyebrow. "You met on Halloween, right?"

"Oh. No. We actually met when we were small. Parker and I grew up on the same street until he moved away. We lost contact for a few years, but he was my best friend when we were younger. We ran into each other again at Halloween and, well..."

"That's adorable, Audrey," Sutton said, squeezing my shoulder.

"No more adorable than you meeting Forest on your first day of college orientation," I mumbled.

They had the perfect fairytale beginning, and I was envious of how easy their relationship was. It was obvious spending any time with them how much they loved each other.

Sutton smiled. "Yeah, I'm pretty lucky." The path forked to where we each needed to go, and I pulled my friend into a hug before we said our goodbyes.

Her words stayed with me as I headed into the rehearsal room.

I wanted that for myself. To love, and to be loved in return.

Maybe one day, I'd find it.

CHAPTER 16

Parker

Audrey nudged me as we stood off to the side, watching the ensemble rehearse on the stage. "How are you holding up?" The three seniors she was friends with— Laura, Mari, and Florence— were all on stage right now, and we watched them dance.

I ran my fingers through my hair. It wasn't easy trying to balance practice and rehearsals, but I thought I was doing a decent job. "Okay, I guess. Coach is still pissed at me. I'm surprised he didn't bench me after finding out."

She frowned. "But you're good. Like, *really* good."

Letting out a laugh, I shook my head. "I'm alright. I mean, for a midfielder, I'm not bad. But Coach and I have an understanding. Part of the agreement on letting me join the team when I transferred here at the beginning of the year."

Audrey furrowed her brows. "And that's... part of why you transferred here? For the team?"

My throat was tight. I hadn't explained it before, because I didn't want to admit it. It made me feel like a terrible teammate who had called it quits. The way she looked at me right now was like I could do no wrong in her eyes. I didn't want that to change. "Later," I murmured, not sure if I was asking her or telling her.

Mary flitted backstage and found the two of us. "You're both on!"

"Oh, sorry." I held out my hand for Audrey. "Shall we?"

We were practicing one of the ending scenes of the musical—the romantic dance after the two main characters were reunited, where they confessed their love for each other. She had on her heels, and I'd quickly found out that rehearsing in sneakers wasn't the ideal footwear, so I'd gone and gotten dance shoes—though I'd found out they actually called them character shoes. They looked almost like dress shoes, though they were more flexible and a hell of a lot more comfortable.

Pretty soon, we'd be rehearsing in full costume. Each time we went through a scene, we'd added more elements. Props, sets, and backgrounds. Lighting. It was a well-oiled machine.

In a lot of ways, the theater department reminded me of my lacrosse team. Every single person was important. We needed everyone for the show to run or to play the game. No single person was more important than the other. Even Audrey, the lead role, couldn't do this without the lighting crew or the person running the sound system.

Just like we needed every member of our team to make plays and passes.

I was grateful for my ability to memorize things quickly. It had come in handy with lacrosse plays, and it was here, too. Both with the script and the songs.

There was also something extremely... freeing about it. Because, for once, I didn't have to worry about anything else. Like I could shut out the outside world and fully immerse myself in this one.

The one where I was the prince who got the girl.

Audrey slipped her arm through mine, her other hand holding her skirt—just like she would once she wore her actual costume. "Let's go, my Prince."

God, and wasn't I just such a sucker that my heart sped up at those words?

Here, with her at my side, it was like I could pretend nothing else was wrong.

"Alright."

"Don't step on my foot this time," Audrey winked.

"One time," I muttered. "I accidentally stepped on your foot *one* time."

Her laugh filled the entire space, lighting me up from the inside out. Then we stepped out onto the stage, gliding effortlessly into our first steps.

At first, I'd struggled to stay on rhythm. Learning the choreography for the entire musical had been a lot, especially when it was all new to me. But practicing had helped, and I was grateful that the weight room for student athletes was empty late at night since had ample open space for me to practice alone.

If anyone ever caught me, I'd deny it, but it was making me better. I felt more confident in my plays during lacrosse practices, too. Maybe because dancing was improving my balance, making me more surefooted.

Whatever the reason, I was having fun.

I spun Audrey, my eyes not leaving her form as she twirled in a perfect circle with her hand in mine before I brought her back into my arms and dipped her.

And then we'd seal it all with a kiss.

True love's kiss, granting the leads their *happily ever after.* That was what this musical was all about. The happy ending between the long-lost Princess and the Prince who risked everything to save her and bring her home. They'd met again by chance, but despite all the obstacles, every threat to them being together, they persevered.

I got a sudden flashback to when we were younger, Audrey sitting on the couch next to me in my childhood home. We'd just finished eating quesadillas and watching *A Pup Named Scooby Doo,* and my mom had asked if we wanted to watch something else before we headed outside to play. Audrey had requested a princess movie.

"But we always watch those girly movies," I'd groaned. *"I want to watch something else."*

"This one has a dragon, Buddy," my mom said, pointing to the cover. *"The prince even has a sword. What do you think about that?"*

Scrunching up my nose, I'd finally agreed. *"Okay... But only because he has a sword."*

Even back then, I'd loved dragons, elves, and warriors. Princes, too, some of the time. At least the cool ones who would do anything to save the day. Jumping through fire, fighting off the evil villains, and at the end of the story, they'd always save the princess.

I wanted to be like that, too. To always save the princess from harm.

When I looked at Audrey, she was beaming. She was wearing a little pink romper with ruffles. Though it had strawberry stains from an earlier snack, she didn't seem to care. *"Yay!"*

And even though I'd been young, I'd known that I'd agree to whatever dumb princess movie she wanted me to watch because it made her happy.

I ignored all the ways this musical seemed to mirror our own story because no matter what was going on between us, it was fake.

Thankfully, no one around us knew that. So I kissed her like I would if I were her boyfriend. If I was the prince who'd just saved her from an evil dragon.

It was a kiss I was all too happy to take, keeping her lips against mine, coaxing her mouth open with slow, lazy kisses, though all I wanted to do was deepen it for real.

Everyone else reset, except all I could focus on was the violet-eyed beauty in front of me. "Audrey—" I murmured, still holding her close, even when we broke apart. Her lips were pink, shiny, and I wanted to touch them. To run my thumb over her bottom lip.

She giggled. "Parker, you can let go of me now," she whispered. "We're all done. No need to keep acting."

"Who said I was acting?" I said in a low voice against her ear, glad no one was around us for the moment.

Audrey blushed, and I chuckled. "Come on, let's head out. I gotta get some food before practice."

"Okay," she murmured, letting me hold her hand as we headed to the student union to grab a bite to eat. Luckily, neither of us had to change—besides our shoes—so it was easy to put our street shoes on and then grab our bags.

"What were you thinking about earlier?" Audrey nudged me as we walked.

"You remember when we were… oh gosh, what was it, five and six? Maybe six and seven? You used to come over to my house after school was out and we'd watch movies."

She tilted her head to the side. "Vaguely."

I laughed. "Do you remember what your favorite one was?"

"The one where the handsome prince saved the day?"

That could have explained a thousand movies, but somehow, I knew we were thinking of the same movie.

"Yeah, Rosie Girl." I slung an arm around her shoulder, tugging her tight to me. Pressing a kiss to her forehead, I just smiled. "That's the one."

She hummed. "I hadn't thought about that in a long time. It's funny that we ended up doing a musical of it, huh? That we're starring in it together?"

Funny? It felt a bit like fate. Like we were destined to end up here together, back in the same place.

"At least I don't have to fight an actual dragon," I said with a laugh as I wrapped my hands around her waist, pulling her in close to me and resting my forehead against hers.

Audrey bit her lip. "Yeah, that might have been a little harder." I could hear her breathing change like she was affected by this. By me. "Parker," she breathed out, standing up on her tiptoes, bringing her lips closer to mine. Like she wanted me to kiss her.

I dropped my head, about to press my lips against hers when —"Audrey!" A voice shouted, coming up behind us on the sidewalk.

My girl groaned, dropping back onto her feet as I let her go. She spun, coming face to face with two girls who I was pretty sure I recognized from her sorority house.

"Hey, guys." She smiled at them. "What's up?"

"Peggy and I were just heading to grab something to eat." The girls barely even paid attention to me, all of their energy focused on their sorority sister. They're both wearing their letters, Pi Rho Sigma embroidered onto a sweatshirt in flowers, and I curl a hand around her hip.

Peggy nods. "Are you hanging out at the house tonight? I think we're having a movie night. Suzie and I were just discussing snack options."

Audrey turns to look at me. "Oh. I don't know. Parker and I were…"

"It's okay, sunshine," I offer. "You can go hang out with the girls. I don't mind." I press my face into her hair, inhaling her sweet strawberry scent. "Besides, I have practice later."

"Alright. But we need food first." She intertwines her fingers through mine. "See you later."

I smiled when we resumed our walk, and she poked at my face. "What's got you smiling like that?"

Her. Because she'd chosen me, and there was no denying the warmth in my chest that I felt from that.

"No reason," I murmured. But I didn't let her go. I just kept her next to me, enjoying the idea that, fake or not, she would choose me.

"You're just full of secrets, aren't you, Parker Maxwell."

"Nah, Audrey Rose. I'm an open book, but only for you." I winked at her, sliding my hand into her back pocket as we kept walking.

She laughed, pinching my side. "We're not acting anymore, so you don't need to be so sweet."

I placed my lips against her ear. "But we're always acting, aren't we, sunshine?"

Or maybe it was the opposite. Maybe it was that we were never acting. Fake or not, musical or not, I just wanted to be by her side. To run my fingers through her beautiful, golden locks. To have those pretty eyes on me. To feel her dainty hand in mine, her fingers interwoven with mine. For her scent to surround me daily.

But I had to stop imagining it.

"Right," Audrey said, giving me a tight smile.

It was a reminder that to her, none of this was real. I needed to remember that.

She took a deep breath. All I could think about was how, before we were interrupted, her lips were almost on mine. How she'd initiated it. Audrey had *wanted* to kiss me.

That was a good sign. Right? It had to be. If she wanted to kiss me, then maybe she wanted more.

God, I was a fucking idiot. Because I was dreaming about my best friend, my fake relationship, turning into something real.

Even though I knew it would never happen.

I kept dreaming anyway.

CHAPTER 17

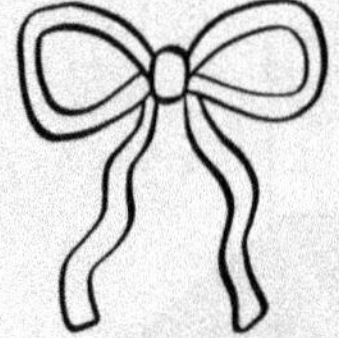

MARCH

The days had flown by, and it felt like spring had finally arrived on campus. The cold winter air that had been lingering for weeks was finally gone, and I could finally almost not wear a coat outside. *Almost.*

Though that hadn't stopped me from pulling out my skirt collection. The tights would keep me warm in the mornings until the chill in the air dissipated.

Spring break had come and gone, and the last week had been surprisingly good. Duke hadn't bothered me, though I still noticed him staring daggers at me during rehearsals, I was always with Parker before and afterward, so he hadn't been able to corner me again.

And if Parker was a little extra on the PDA whenever my ex was around, I wasn't complaining. Turns out I really liked kissing my best friend. It didn't mean anything, of course. Parker always reminded me that we were just acting.

Damn, he was good at it.

The man in question nudged me at my side. "Whatcha thinking about?" He was wearing his favorite red hoodie, one I'd seen him wear countless times this year, and a pair of athletic shorts like he'd just come from the gym.

"Nothing." I blushed. There was no way I was admitting to Parker that I liked it when he kissed me. *Nope.*

"Come on." He gave me a brilliant, blinding smile, flashing his perfect teeth. Like he was the perfect male specimen, his body perfectly sculpted and honed for *perfection.* Sure, I hadn't seen him without his shirt on, but I could guess. I'd seen the way he was on the lacrosse field. "I wanna know what you were thinking about, Audrey. Tell your boyfriend." He slung his arm around me, tugging me tight to his chest.

"Parker," I groaned, hiding my face behind my hands. "You. I was thinking about *you.* There. Are you happy?"

His chest puffed up. "Am I happy that my girlfriend was thinking about me? Of course I am, sunshine."

"*Fake* girlfriend," I muttered, low enough that no one could hear me. Not that anyone was around us, anyway. It was a quiet afternoon on campus. Most people were still inside for class.

He pressed his lips to my forehead. An action that was feeling more affectionate the more he did it. And I didn't want him to stop because secretly… I loved it.

"Parker?"

"Hmm?" He looked over at me, eyebrow raised in question.

"So…" I bit my lip. "I've been meaning to ask you about spring formal." I started, knowing full well the event was coming up later this month. It was one event I helped plan in my position with the sorority.

He raised an eyebrow. "What about it?"

"Well, since everyone thinks we're dating, you should come with me." I turned my body fully to look at him. "You know. As my date."

"Okay."

"Okay?"

"Yeah." He shrugged. "I'd love to come as your date, Rosie."

For some reason, I had a feeling he didn't mean it in a fake way. A shudder ran down my spine. "Cool."

Parker smiled. "You know, I have games the next few weekends."

I fumbled with my fingers, trying to find something to do other than look at him. "Yeah," I responded, hoping my voice didn't betray the emotion I was feeling.

It was funny that he acted like I hadn't written his entire game schedule down in my planner before the semester had even started. Once he'd sent it to me, I'd made sure I knew when they all were. This weekend, he had an away game.

Now that everyone thought we were dating, I tried not to miss any of the home games. Just to keep up appearances, of course. Not for any other reason.

"Are you going to miss me, Rosie Girl?"

I didn't think I needed to answer that. But the worst part was that, of *course,* I would. I'd miss him way too much. But I needed some distance. Needed to remind myself that this wasn't real.

So I didn't answer. Because I didn't trust myself to tell him the truth.

ELLA WAS CROUCHED UNDERNEATH ME, making a few more alterations to my final act costume as I stared in the mirror. She'd been involved with this project from the beginning, down to designing all of the costumes for the musical, and then the costume design majors had all been working on them.

"This is amazing, Ells." Of course, it fit me like a glove, but I'd just been lucky enough that the seamstress and I had identical body measurements.

She waved a hand at me. "Don't move, or I'll accidentally stick you with a pin." My twin had decided after getting the dress on me that it needed more detailing.

"Sorry." I ran my hands over the pink flowers and rhinestones on the bodice, which also flowed down into the poofy skirt. "It's just so pretty."

It was my first time seeing this one since it was finished.

"You ready for dress rehearsals to start?"

"More excuses to wear this pretty thing?" I said, doing a little twirl. "Duh."

My twin smiled. I'd long since given up any hope of her being on stage with me. When we were younger, we'd done community theater together, but Ella had quickly realized she preferred being behind the scenes than in the spotlight.

"Alright, take it off now. I'll finish the last details and get it all ready to go." She undid the back so I could

I gave her a fake pout. "You mean I can't wear it for the rest of the day?"

"Off." My twin poked me in the arm. "Don't forget I know where you sleep."

"Used to be right next to me," I muttered under my breath as I slipped the dress off over my head.

Ella winced. "I'm sorry. You know I didn't want to move but —" My sister looked so guilty. Like it was her fault she'd ended up as the sorority president mid-way through last semester after our last one had dropped out of school. Ilene had recommended she move into the empty suite upstairs, and there had been no way I was letting her turn that down just to share a room with me.

A laugh burst out of me. "I don't blame you, Ella. Are you kidding? The president's suite is awesome. I just get lonely sometimes." Or I did. Before Parker. Now, though, it didn't feel like I even had time to be lonely. Turns out a fake boyfriend was very helpful in that regard.

Pulling my dress on over my head, I opened my arms, and Ella stepped in. We wrapped each other up in a hug that felt like home. There was something about spending time with my twin that always made the world right itself again. Like any problem we faced was going to be alright if we were together.

Maybe it was some super crazy twin sense, but when we pulled apart, she was studying me intensely before she said, "So, how's everything going with Parker? You two seem very cozy." Ella's smirk practically filled her face.

"I—" Was it hot in here, or was it just me? "It's good. I think."

"You think?" She raised an eyebrow. "You don't know?"

"Like you knew with Cam?"

Ella scoffed. "That was different, and you know it."

"Oh, I do, do I?"

"Mhm." She sat at the table, hand sewing a few sequins on a different garment instead of looking at me. "We had a one night stand and I thought he was just some playboy fraternity guy. I had reasons to be hesitant, Ro."

"Or maybe you're just excellent at running away, Ells. And look at you now. You two are like five minutes away from running off and eloping, I swear."

She rolled her eyes. "Slow your roll there, babe. I'm perfectly happy with where we are right now."

I hummed in response. "Sure, sure."

"You and Parker though… it feels a lot like you were meant to be. Why else would the universe have dropped him back into your life?"

My heart sank. Because she didn't know the truth. That none of this was real. "I thought I was the hopeless romantic?" I asked, raising an eyebrow.

She shrugged, tugging her needle through and tying the thread in a knot. "Guess Cam's changed me." A contented sigh slipped from her lips. "I just want you to be happy. After everything last year with Duke, you deserve that."

"I am happy." Mostly.

Ella hummed in response, clearing up her workspace. "I'm all done for the day. You ready to head out?"

"Yeah." I grabbed my bag off the ground. "Should probably go get some work done. I have a paper and presentation next week."

"Are you going to come to the Delta Sig party tomorrow?"

I shrugged. "Probably. I don't have anything else going on." Also known as, I didn't have a good excuse. Parker had an away game this weekend. *Are you going to miss me, Rosie Girl?* I'd changed the subject instead of answering, even though I should have said yes.

Of course I was.

"You should really bring your boy to one of them. I'm sure Cam would enjoy getting to know him."

"He's not—" *mine.* Not really. I bit my lip. I couldn't say that. "He's pretty shy," I said instead. That was true. I'd seen him around other people. He was quiet and reserved most of the time. Until he was with me, and then he seemed to come out of his shell.

Was it just because he was comfortable with me? Sure, we'd grown up together, but there was more to it than that.

"Still." Ella smiled. "Bring him sometime. It'd be fun."

"Yeah," I agreed. "I will."

Because even if it was fake, I wanted him to be by my side —always.

IT WAS ALMOST strange to be in the fraternity house now after going to multiple parties at Parker's house. But my twin sister was here, and so was most of my sorority.

Still, I felt Parker's absence, and I couldn't even explain how strange it was to be without him now. I'd gone from not seeing him for nine years to rekindling our friendship to being attached with him at the freaking hip, and I missed his presence. We'd been texting ever since he got on the bus, heading to New York for their away game. I'd tried to keep up with it today as best as I could, but it was harder not being able to watch the game.

I still had no idea what was going on in the games, but it was cute how he kept trying to teach me. Still, I followed along better than I had before, and at least I knew when to cheer for my guy.

Right now, all I wanted was to go slip Parker's jersey on, bury my nose into it, and pretend like it still smelled like him. It didn't—of course—and I resisted asking him if he'd wear it again just to pick up his woodsy, spicy scent. There was something majorly wrong with me. I was blaming my hormones. Otherwise, being this needy for my fake boyfriend slash best friend would have been certifiably insane.

Sutton came back from the kitchen, handing me a fresh drink. "Thank you," I murmured, taking a sip.

It wasn't a strawberry lemonade—not like the ones I suspected Parker kept stocked in his fridge just for me—but it wasn't beer, either, so I couldn't complain. It might have made me a basic girl, but I'd much rather have a sweet white wine than beer. I scrunched up my nose just at the thought.

"You're welcome," Sutton said, giving me a soft smile with her glossy red lips.

"Where's your boy?" I asked, surprised they weren't glued together.

She looked over to the other side of the room. Cam and Ella had just come downstairs, and her hair looked a little rumpled. I definitely didn't want to know what they'd been up to in his room.

Forest was with James in the corner. They were both the athletes in their friend group. The baseball season had just started, while the football team was done for the year. They'd been on fire this season, making it to the playoffs, though they hadn't won the championship.

We chatted for a while about how our semesters had been going when a noise interrupted us.

Everyone was staring across the room as a brunette with a now soaked white shirt and a red face got into Adam's face. She looked familiar, though I wasn't friends with her, I was pretty friendly with most people I met across campus. "You..." She scowled. Adam's empty beer cup was still in his hand, and he looked a little sheepish. "You asshole!" The words could be heard above everything else, and I winced.

"Sorry, beautiful." Adam clearly chose the wrong thing to say, his playful smirk making her even angrier. "Can I help you clean up?"

Her face just got redder. Like she was imagining what exactly those words could mean. It wasn't a secret that Adam was a bit of a player on campus, ever the flirt.

"No!" The brunette threw her hands up in the air like she couldn't believe what she was hearing, turning and storming out the front door. I was in her path, so I heard a muttered, "Prince, huh? More like a *Beast*," under her breath.

I did my best not to giggle.

Cam went over to Adam, who did his best to look remorseful. "It was an accident."

"Was it?"

"What, you don't believe me either?"

My sister's boyfriend just shook his head. "Just take the L, dude. That girl probably hates you now."

A sigh escaped Adam's lips as he looked toward the door—where she had escaped. "Yeah. Probably." He looked disappointed, and I couldn't help but notice a lingering attraction there. But maybe I was just reading too deeply into it. It was the hopeless romantic in me, after all.

"Come on, big guy," Cam said, looping an arm around Adam's neck. "Let's go get you some water."

"I'm not even drunk," his friend muttered under his breath, but I also noticed he didn't put up a fight with Cam either.

Sutton wandered over to my twin, the two of them chatting, as I pulled out my phone, looking over my text thread with Parker.

PARKER

Miss me yet?

AUDREY

Ha. You wish.

Yeah, Rosie Girl. I do.

You all ready for the game?

Yeah. They're a good team, but hopefully our offense can beat their defense.

I'm sure you'll be great. Good luck tonight.

Even if I'm not on the sidelines, I'm cheering for you.

Thanks, sunshine.

What are best friends for?

I stashed my phone away. He'd never responded to my last message, so I figured he'd been busy getting ready for the game. Hopefully I'd hear from him later tonight once they were back at the hotel.

Finding Ella, I went to stand next to her as Cam walked away, leaving her with blushed cheeks. Cam went to find Forest, leaving the three of us alone.

Her eyes never left her boyfriend, even as he laughed, talking to Forest in the next room.

"You love him," I observed. Honestly, it was obvious to anyone who watched how they interacted. I'd watched her grow closer and closer to him all year. Even if she thought they were hiding it, there was no denying the hearts in her eyes.

She startled. "What?" Ella froze, the drink Cam had made her cupped in her hand.

"He's in love with you too, you know," Sutton added nonchalantly.

As if that wasn't the understatement of the century. It had been obvious for awhile that Cameron loved my sister. We'd all just been waiting for her to realize it. It was in every action—the way he took care of her, supported her, and encouraged her dreams.

"I don't—" My twin shook her head, trying to deny it.

"Ella." I sighed. "I see the way he looks at you." I gave her a look, like, *I know you.* Because I did. I knew the way her brain worked just as well as I knew mine. Sometimes it felt like we knew what the other was thinking. We didn't finish each other's sentences, but I liked to think we could. And I always knew how she was feeling.

"And how does he look at me?" Her voice was quiet, but filled with… hope? Wonder?

The way I wanted someone to look at me. Like I was the most important person in their life. Like they couldn't imagine going a day without being next to me. "Like you're the moon and he's been gazing at a starless sky his whole life. Like he needs your air so he can breathe. So…"

"Audrey." Ella was blushing. "I get it. You don't have to be such a hopeless romantic."

I'd always been one. And I knew that would never change. "Is that so bad?"

"No." Her voice was quiet as her blue eyes met mine. "No, it's not."

I dipped my head, reaching out a hand to squeeze hers.

No, it wasn't. It was never bad to believe in love. It was the one thing that could conquer all. I wasn't naive enough to believe that Parker would ever love me like that. We'd promised each other at the beginning that we wouldn't fall in love with each other, after all.

But one day… I shut my eyes, letting out a deep breath. One day, I hoped my dreams would come true.

That one day, I'd find a love like that for myself.

CHAPTER 18
Parker

PARKER

Hey.

AUDREY

Hi.

Just got to the hotel.

I collapsed onto my bed. I was sharing a room with Samuel tonight, but he'd already stepped out of the room to call his girlfriend, leaving me with my thoughts. Replaying the game in my mind, I tried to go over what went wrong. How I could improve for next time.

The truth was, I'd just been distracted.

We'd been sloppy in this game, almost losing it, but we'd recovered. The final score was 14-12, another Castleton Chipmunks win, with less than a minute left on the clock. We'd fought hard all four periods, thankfully coming out on top.

I stared at the photo of Audrey that I'd set as my lock screen. Her hair was half-up in a ponytail, wearing her favorite pink sweatshirt with a pink ribbon tied around her hair, and she looked so perfect. She was the most beautiful girl I'd ever seen, but it was more than that. It was everything about who she was. How she was so outgoing, so sweet and caring with all of her friends. She was pure sunshine, inside and out. The nickname was fitting in so many ways.

A thought occurred to me briefly: if I called, would Audrey pick up?

Were we there yet?

Maybe. But I couldn't stop thinking about her last text earlier. *What are best friends for?* And damn, I knew that was all she saw us as—despite her lovely blush a few days ago when she'd admitted she'd been thinking about me—but it still hurt knowing she only saw me as a friend.

Groaning, I rolled over, stuffing a pillow between my arms as I watched the dots appear on the screen.

AUDREY

How was the game? I tried to check on the score, but couldn't figure out where to watch it.

PARKER

It was okay. We won, but lost the lead a few times. Definitely not where I would have liked to be.

Oh.

What about you? How was your night?

Good. At a frat party with Ella and some of the girls. Wish you were here.

So you *do* miss me.

Shut up.

Make me, sunshine.

I was smiling at my phone as I laid on my hotel room bed. It was ridiculous how much I enjoyed talking to her when, with everyone else, I'd rather just hole up in my room and read a book or play a video game. I had a new fantasy novel on my bedside table—one I hadn't even touched on this road trip, because I'd been too busy texting my girl.

PARKER

Call me when you're back from the party. I want to hear your voice.

AUDREY

Don't you need to get some sleep? I thought you had an early bus ride home.

Doesn't matter. Call me anyway.

A few minutes later, my phone rang, and I barely even let it ring once before I'd picked up.

"Hey."

"Hi." Audrey sounded breathless. "I'm just leaving now."

Rolling over to lay on my back, I stared up at the ceiling. "You didn't have to leave just to talk to me."

"Eh. I was ready to leave, anyway. Besides, it was winding down."

"Gotcha. Anything fun happen?"

"Not really. Cam's friend Adam bumped into a girl and accidentally spilled his entire cup of beer on her, and now I'm pretty sure she hates him."

"The one that was on the ski trip with you?"

"Yeah," she responded. "He's the ginger haired one. Anyway, I definitely didn't miss the heat between them. Or the way Adam's gaze lingered on her as she stormed out. They would be the perfect enemies to lovers story if you ask me."

I burst out laughing. "What?"

"You know? It's a super common trope, especially in romance novels. It's even better in fantasy when they're actual enemies. The line between love and hate isn't far apart." Audrey let out a dreamy sigh.

"And you want something like that?" I asked, hating myself just for saying it. But damn if I didn't want to know her every fantasy. Her dream guy.

There was a pause on the other end of the phone, and then Audrey said, her voice a little rough. "No, I don't think so. I'm not sure I could do the enemies part." Her voice grew quiet. "I get my feelings hurt too easily."

"Rosie…" I murmured, wishing I was there next to her.

"Besides, I think after Duke, I need to be friends with someone first. Otherwise, I don't know if I'd trust them not to hurt me."

"But you trust me, right?" I held my breath.

Her response was instant. "Of course, Parker. I'd trust you with anything. You're my best friend."

"Okay. Good." I should have felt relieved, but I rubbed at my chest. At the ache there. "Listen, Audrey, I should probably try to get some sleep." We'd head back to Castleton on the bus tomorrow, and then we'd do it all again on Wednesday, but at least it was a home game.

It was almost midnight, and we'd been on the phone for a while.

"Right." Audrey yawned. "Me too. I'll see you when you get back? Dinner?"

"Yeah," I responded, knowing I'd never turn her down. "Of course. I'll text you."

"Night, Parker," she said, her voice soft. "Sweet dreams."

"You too, sunshine."

Little did she know my dreams that night would be filled with her.

"You're late," Audrey said, looking down at the lock screen of her phone. I puffed up my chest at the photo on it of me. It had been over a month since we'd started fake dating, and I liked that she'd kept it. It was a photo of us from my first game of the season, Audrey in her Castleton sweatshirt and me in my jersey after the game. I hadn't even noticed anyone taking it, but damn, I loved it.

"Sorry," I mutter, drawing my hand over my face. "Practice ran long, and coach made us run a few extra drills."

"It's okay. You're lucky this is the last practice before dress rehearsals start."

"Right. Shit." After this, I'd also have to change before we started.

Audrey patted my shoulder, and I pulled her close, dropping a kiss to her lips. Just in case anyone was watching.

"What was that for?" Audrey whispered.

"Can't be too careful," I said with a wink, before heading over to where I was supposed to wait for my cue when the scene began.

Rehearsal went by fast, and by the time we were done, I was completely exhausted, especially when combined with lacrosse practice, and I desperately needed another shower.

But Audrey gave me that face, and I knew I wasn't going back to the house straight away. Not that I'd complain about spending more time with her.

We walked to the commons, and I reached out, interlacing our fingers together. I'd never held hands with another woman before Audrey. Not even Millie, my ex. But with her, it felt right.

It felt like this was where I was supposed to be.

I picked our adjoined hands up, kissing the top of hers. "You know, we missed our one-month anniversary?"

"Parker." Audrey rolled her eyes. She looked around, dropping her voice to a quiet whisper. "We can't celebrate an anniversary. We're not actually dating."

"So? Who's stopping us? The fake date police?"

That made her laugh. "You're ridiculous."

"For you," I agreed.

Audrey's cheeks turned that adorable shade of pink. "Are you... are you flirting with me?"

"Yeah. Took you long enough to notice, Rosie Girl." I squeezed her hand.

She was quiet, and I kept her hand in mine as we entered the cafeteria, not letting her go for even a moment.

GOOAAAAAL! My fists pumped into the air as the ball I threw made it into the net. *The Castleton Chipmunks have scored the winning goal!*

"Fuck yeah!" Sam screamed in my ear. "Good goal, man."

I was suddenly enveloped in a team hug, all of us on the field packed together in one giant huddle. "We did it!" Taylor shouted, all of us in a cluster of celebrating on the field. "Another win!"

I looked over to the stands, trying to find the golden-haired girl who was wearing my jersey. Throughout the game, whenever I'd looked up, I'd found Audrey's eyes intent on mine. Like she was watching *me*.

Over the last month since our first game of the season, I'd been trying to teach her more about how lacrosse worked. Obviously, she still didn't understand everything, but I did my best.

We only had a little over a dozen games total during the season before the playoffs, and each one would impact if we'd make it or not. So far, we'd only lost one, and I hoped we could keep it that way.

The last week had been grueling. Rehearsals were intense, and so were practices, which meant I'd been staying up late to study and get all of my classwork done, barely falling asleep before I had to get up and do it all over again.

But I knew I wouldn't trade any of it to see my girl as happy as she was running down to the field, her blonde hair flying in the wind as she rushed down to the edge of the field. I opened my arms, and she practically threw herself in them, letting me pick her up and twirl her around.

"You won!!" Audrey screamed, her hands intertwining around my neck. "I'm so proud of you."

"Damn right, baby," I said, tightening my grip around her waist. "All of those goals were for you."

"Parker…" my girl murmured, her eyes darting down to my lips a few times. Like she wanted me to kiss her.

It was fake, but in this moment, it didn't feel like it. Audrey in my jersey was a sight I'd never be able to get out of my mind. Because it was too fucking *right*, seeing my name written out across her back.

Letting her body rest against mine, I brought her down to her feet. The toes of her cute pink sneakers sunk into the grass as I cupped her chin, bringing our lips together.

She responded eagerly, molding her body to mine as she kissed me back with as much passion and fervor than I could have ever imagined.

Her tongue dipped into my mouth, and I groaned at the taste. Cotton candy and strawberry soda—always so sweet.

"Audrey," I groaned, hating that I had to stop this. Thank fuck for the athletic cup I wore, otherwise everyone on the field could see how much she was affecting me. And as much as I wanted it to continue, I didn't think coach would be too pleased to see me making out with my girlfriend on the field. "We should, um, stop."

She nipped at my lip as we pulled apart, giving me a tiny nod as she slid down to her feet. It was a reminder of how much smaller she was than me, how I towered over her. "You're right," she murmured, though her voice was breathier than it had been before.

"You're coming to the party tonight, right?" I asked, tugging on the bottom of my jersey down from where it had ridden up on her frame.

"Yeah." She nodded. "Of course. I wouldn't miss it."

"Good." I grinned. "I'll see you there, then."

"I should get going," Audrey said, turning to look at the field.

I caught an eye of my number on her back, and I was practically salivating. "Mmm." I bit my lip. "Turn around. Let me see my name on your back, Rosie Girl. Show me whose girl you are."

I'd never been this possessive over a girl before, but something about her in my jersey really did it for me. I needed to think about something else, so I didn't have to take a cold shower.

She blushed, but did as I asked. I swept her blonde curls over her shoulder and placed a kiss on the crook of her neck. "I'm yours, Parker," she whispered.

"Mine," I agreed.

Because make no mistake… She *was* mine, and I was going to prove that to her.

CHAPTER 19

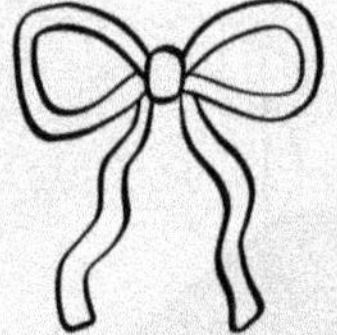

M y cheeks were still warm after earlier, but despite that, I hadn't taken his jersey off. I was wearing white jeans and my favorite casual tennis shoes, my hair pulled half up with a pink ribbon.

Butterflies fluttered in my stomach, and I knew it wasn't nerves. No, it was because something about tonight had felt so *real*. The way his face had lit up when he'd seen me running towards him, picking me up and spinning me around in his arms before kissing me…

And oh, that *kiss*.

I barely had my hand ready to knock on the door when it was pulled open to Parker standing there, leaning on the doorframe. "Hey." He leaned in, kissing my cheek.

"H-hi," I said, feeling suddenly shy. Which wasn't me. I wasn't the one who was quiet or shy. Except that suddenly, the way he was looking at me had me feeling like maybe earlier hadn't been a fluke.

The last few weeks, we'd barely even seen each other between sorority events, classes, and the musical. It felt like the only time we did was in the theater building or at dinner. His practices would often run long, and that didn't even take into account his away games.

"I've missed you," I admitted, wrapping my arms around his waist as we walked inside.

"She finally admits it," Parker said with a grin, pulling me in tight and pressing his lips against the crown of my head. I liked how we fit together like that—how if he stood behind me, he could wrap me up and tuck me under his chin completely. "You saw me earlier, though."

I hummed in response, enjoying his body heat.

"Let's go." Instead of heading into the kitchen like I expected, he headed for the stairs, tugging me up behind him.

"Oh," I squealed.

"What?" Parker looked back at me.

"Nothing, I just…" Somehow, going into his room with just the two of us now felt incredibly *real*. Before, this was fake. Now… I wondered if maybe we were going to pick up where we left off earlier on the lacrosse field.

He interlaced our fingers and marched me up to his bedroom, and I decided I liked this Parker. A little bossy, but still undeniably sweet. And I really wanted more of the dominant Parker. Because I trusted him wholly, implicitly. I knew he wouldn't hurt me. That he cared about *me*. When he bossed me around, all it did was make heat pool in my stomach.

Thoughts I should *not* be having right now. Even if the way he'd kissed me earlier set every nerve in my body on fire. When he brushed his hand against mine, it felt like fireworks exploded on my skin.

His bedroom door closed behind us, and I looked around, anywhere but at him. I'd been in his bedroom dozens of times before, but it had never felt like this—like the energy in the room was *charged*. Like if I looked at him, at his lips, I was going to do something I would regret.

"So…" I started, trailing off when Parker walked to his desk, holding up a bag of food.

His cheeks were warm. "I wasn't sure if you had eaten dinner, so I ordered Chinese. Hopefully that's okay?"

Okay? That was more than okay. I blinked rapidly, trying to get rid of the moisture pooling in my eyes, as if anything could stop them now.

"Fuck." He stepped closer, cupping my cheek. "Are you okay? Rosie Girl, I didn't…"

I shook my head. "No, it's not that. It's great, actually. I—I've never had anyone take care of me. Not like this. I just…"

Parker wiped under my eyes with his thumbs. "I've got you, baby."

I was starting to realize that. It was the little things with him—I didn't have to ask him for help, because he was there before I even could. He knew how I liked my sandwiches, how I took my coffee. Somehow, he anticipated my thoughts and needs before I did. And he always put my needs before his own.

No one had ever treated me like this. Like I was something special.

And he was just my *fake* boyfriend.

My chest was warm, those butterflies at full force as I pressed my cheek against his chest. "Thank you," I mumbled. "You're too good to me." I couldn't address the elephant in the room. That this felt a lot like we were actually dating. Because I was worried if I did, it would break the spell. And I wanted to be here—in his arms, in his room, wearing his shirt. I wanted to be the girl on the sidelines with fifty-nine painted on my cheek, screaming for the first boy who'd ever had my heart.

"You deserve nothing less than everything, Audrey."

I looked down at my feet, trying to hide my blush.

"Let's eat," Parker said, guiding me onto his bed.

I ran my hands over his comforter, the soft gray fabric comforting against my skin. In all the time we'd spent together, I'd never thought about it before. How comfortable I was in his room, laid out across his bed like I belonged there. Heat flared in between my thighs as I thought about him joining me. How it would feel if we'd continued that kiss from earlier, with him between my thighs and—

Parker made a sound in the back of his throat.

"Don't look at me like that, Rosie," he murmured, his voice low. A shiver ran through me. Fuck, did that turn me on? *Yes.* I was surrounded by his scent—his comforting, soothing scent, and I wanted to get lost in it. In *him.*

I just stared at him as he opened up a box of sweet and sour pork and shoveled some onto a plate, adding white rice and noodles before handing it to me. "Here." His eyes were filled with heat as I took the plate from him. "Eat," he murmured. "Then we can go downstairs and hang out with everyone else."

But what if I didn't want to go back downstairs?

What if I asked him to kiss me again? To really kiss me. Not as something fake—but as something real?

Shoveling in a bite of food to stop myself from asking the stupid questions, I couldn't hold back my moan at the tangy and delicious flavor as it exploded in my mouth. The chicken was perfect: tender, soft and juicy, and I closed my eyes, savoring it.

Parker's cheeks were tinged with the slightest shade of pink when I reopened them to take another bite, finishing the entire plate in no time.

Huh. I guess I had been starving. I hadn't eaten at the game, too excited to leave my seat during the short intermission, and I'd only grabbed a granola bar at lunch today.

"Sorry," I whispered, embarrassed at my display.

He crossed his leg over his knee, shaking his head as he took another bite of his dish. I assumed it was probably teriyaki chicken, because that was his favorite. "You don't have to apologize to me." His bore into mine and I swallowed, my mouth suddenly feeling dry.

I'd never felt like this before in all the time we'd spent alone, but I couldn't help but notice how attractive he was tonight. The way his hair looked like he'd run his hands through it a few hundreds of times, his tight t-shirt that clung to all of those well-honed lacrosse muscles. His thighs, stretched and visible to me from the spot where I perched on his bed.

"I'm gonna… I'll be right back," I murmured, sliding off his bed, needing a moment to myself.

"What do you need?" Parker stood up, setting his plate aside. "I can go get you something."

Shaking my head, I waved him back down. "It's fine. I'm just gonna run to the bathroom and grab some water."

And maybe some fresh air, too, because the heat I was feeling right now was unreal. Maybe if I cooled down, I wouldn't feel like I wanted to straddle his lap and ride him until I came.

Fuck, it had been so long since I'd had a good, non-battery operated orgasm. My vibrator did the trick, but it didn't compare to the real thing. Only my last boyfriend had been selfish and never cared about getting me off first, so I'd been taking care of myself longer than I could even recall.

"Okay." He curled his finger around a strand of my hair before tugging on it slightly. "We should go rejoin the party, anyway."

Now that he fed me, it made sense that he'd want to go join his friends. Even if I could have stayed up here alone with him all night. Listening to him talk about whatever book he was currently reading or the video game he'd been playing was infinitely more exciting to me than listening to his teammates, but I couldn't exactly say that to him. He'd probably think it was weird.

Secretly, I liked that he loved swords and dragons, and always played the hero in any story. It shouldn't have been sexy, but his secret nerdy side was absolutely attractive to me.

"Yeah." My voice was breathy, and I hoped he didn't notice. "Probably. Otherwise, your teammates are probably going to think we're getting up to something in here."

He raised an eyebrow. "And would that be so bad, Audrey?"

I didn't know how to answer that. Would it be so bad if people thought that? Or would it be so bad if we did *get up to something*?

But I couldn't clarify.

"See you down there," I murmured instead, pushing his door open and leaving him inside his room.

THE SPRING AIR and the bottle of water I'd snagged from the fridge instantly made me feel better, and I sat on the steps of the porch, enjoying the calm that was outside.

Inside, it was chaotic—lacrosse players everywhere, as well as god knew who else from campus. For a Wednesday night, there were a lot of students here.

All I wanted to do was disappear back into Parker's room, but how could I after I'd practically run out of there like a scared kitten?

"This isn't you, Audrey," I scolded myself. Maybe someone would think it was weird if they walked by and saw me talking to myself, but for once, I didn't really care what anyone else thought of me.

The only person whose opinion I cared about was Parker, and he'd made it clear time and time again that he liked me just the way I was.

"So, why are you being a coward?" I whispered to the night.

Because I was. I was too scared to admit what I was feeling was real, so I was hiding from the man who knew me best.

I sighed, staring up at the stars. Wishing I could ask them for help. Maybe tomorrow I'd call my mom. She always gave the best advice. Right now, I could use it.

My thoughts were so jumbled up, and I was so lost in them, that I didn't hear the pair of footprints walking up the sidewalk until there was a pair of legs standing right in front of me.

"I'm sorry," I squeaked. "I'll move so you can get—"

"No need." The voice instantly sent my hackles rising, and I looked up to find the one person whose face I didn't want to see tonight standing in front of me.

Duke.

My voice was tight. "What are you doing here?"

"Friends on the team invited me."

I paled. "What?" Of course, he had friends on the lacrosse team. I should have known that, but it wasn't like he introduced me to his friends. He'd kept me isolated, emotionally dependent on him. I hadn't seen how emotionally abusive he was until it was too late.

Standing up, I went to go into the house. "Sorry, my boyfriend is waiting for me—"

"Your boyfriend?" He grabbed my wrist, pulling me back *hard*, so I stumbled down the steps and into him.

"Ow!" I cried, wincing as my ankle rolled underneath me.

He didn't even seem to notice that I was in pain, or how my eyes filled with water as he tightened his hold on my wrist. "*I'm* your boyfriend, Audrey."

Suddenly, I was pinned against the siding of the house, a position that felt all too familiar with earlier this semester.

"Are you delusional?" I yelled. "How can you not get it through your head that I. Broke. Up. With. You?"

God, why was there no one around right now? Maybe if I screamed loud enough, someone would come from inside and then there would be proof. "I'll scream," I said, deadpanning. "And I'll tell everyone on campus what you did. How you cheated on me. No one will even want to come near you after that."

I opened my mouth, only to have him cover it with his hand. My eyes widened.

"You're not going to do that." He narrowed his eyes. "You see, Aud. Girls don't break up with me." A slimy grin spread over his face. "I don't care if you say you're with that lacrosse player now." He eyed my jersey with distaste. "You'll come running back to me before long."

I whimpered a little, unable to move as he held me tight against his body. His body spray was potent, and the smell was enough to make me gag. Ugh, how much had he even put on? It was nothing like the way Parker smelled—woodsy and masculine all at once. No, this was all wrong.

There was no way I'd be going back to this possessive, controlling, manipulating jerk.

His hand was still covering my mouth, and I bit down, not hard enough to break the skin but enough to startle him, so he let go of me. "The fuck!?"

He reached out, the palm of his hand making contact with my cheek, and I flinched. No matter what had happened before, he'd never hit me. Not like this.

Tears rolled down my eyes, and I stepped backwards, wrapping my arms around myself. "Leave me *alone*, Duke."

Clarity filled his eyes, and he was suddenly crowding in front of me, his hands gently. "I'm sorry, baby girl. I didn't mean to hurt you. I just—I miss you. Please. Forgive me. Come back to me."

"No." The word was barely more than a whisper. "Just—just go."

And for once, he finally did what I asked, and I turned to go inside.

To look for my safe space—the only place I wanted to be right now.

Parker's arms.

CHAPTER 20

Parker

Has anyone seen Audrey?" I asked the living room full of my teammates. We'd won the game and that meant the guys wanted to celebrate, the party now in full swing. But there were way more people here than we'd discussed, and I was concerned that it was getting out of hand for a weeknight.

"Parker!" Samuel slurred. "About time you showed up, man. We can't celebrate the winning goal scorer without him actually present!"

"Dude," I dropped my voice low. "Are you drunk right now? Coach is going to kill us if we show up with hangovers tomorrow at practice."

I was one-hundred-percent sober. Hadn't had a drop to drink all night. How could I, with Audrey in my room, looking like temptation incarnate?

I'd been hard as a rock all fucking night, especially with Audrey sprawled out over my bed, wearing my jersey, looking like an angel with her golden hair spread out around her. All I wanted was to touch her. To pull her into my arms and kiss her again. After our kiss earlier, I was pretty sure she felt the sparks between us, but my lack of experience made me feel at a loss for words. What was I supposed to do?

"I'll be fine." Sam's voice brought me back into the present. The living room, with my team. Right. I blinked at him. "Just need to sleep it off and I'll be right as rain tomorrow." He slung an arm around my shoulder. "Anyway—"

"Have you seen Audrey?" I repeated, feeling a bit more frantic. It had been what felt like twenty minutes since I'd seen her last, when she'd slipped out of my room saying she needed water and the bathroom. I knew there was no way she would have taken this long. Plus, I'd looked for her all over, and I hadn't seen her in the house anywhere.

"I think I saw her go out front maybe ten, fifteen minutes ago?" Taylor piped up. "She had a bottle of water and her cheeks were flushed."

"Why didn't you say that earlier?" I rolled my eyes, turning to go towards the front door. But when I got to the entryway, there was Audrey. Shaking, with her back pressed to the door.

I narrowed my eyes, coming to stand in front of my girl. She was wearing my jersey, her gorgeous golden locks gathered into a high ponytail with that sparkly pink scrunch she always had on, and even if it was fake, I couldn't help my instinct to protect her. Not when her eyes were watering and there was a red mark on her cheek.

"Who did this to you?" I gritted out, unable to keep the violence out of my voice.

And I *knew*. I knew without asking. Because it was obvious from the way she was trembling.

"Parker—" she whimpered, reaching her hand out to grab mine as if that would help calm me down. But, fuck, I could still see the marks on her wrists from where he'd grabbed her. I saw red.

"It was fucking Duke, wasn't it? He put his hands on you?"

Audrey nodded, tears spilling from her eyes.

"Fuck, baby," I said, opening my arms. "Come here."

She did, collapsing into my hold as I wrapped my arms around her, rubbing soothing circles down her back. "It's okay. It's going to be okay."

"He's never—" she hiccuped. "He's never done that before. He'd never hurt me."

"Where did he go?" My words were sharp. *Lethal.* I flung open the door, intending on getting payback for her.

Coach was going to fucking kill me if I started a fight, but I didn't care. Not when this asshole was trying to hurt my girl. Not when it was my job to keep her safe.

My girl. Mine.

"Parker." Her small hand grabbed mine, interlacing our fingers. "Please," she whispered. "Don't go after him."

I rubbed my thumb over the back of her hand. "He can't keep doing this to you, Audrey. I just—"

The steps on the porch creaked, and there was her ex. Pushing her behind me, I tried not to notice the way she was still cupping her cheek. *He'd hit her.* He hit her, and now he needed to pay.

"Aud, I just wanted to—" Duke started.

I shook my head. "No."

"No?" He raised an eyebrow, like he was questioning my command.

"*No.* Don't talk to her, don't look at her, don't even fucking *think* about her. You hurt her. But here's the thing, Duke. She's not yours. She's *mine*. And I don't intend to let her go. Not ever. So if you ever so much as lay a finger on her again, I'm coming for you. And you won't like it if I do. No matter how much money your daddy has, I can assure you, mine has more. I'm not afraid to fight you." I'd done my fair share of research into Duke Prescott, who was only one minor infraction from being expelled from CU. This wasn't the first time he'd harassed a girl, but I would make sure it was his last.

He scoffed. "Like you can touch me."

"Try me." I crossed my arms over my chest.

He lunged, but I had the upper hand. Predominantly, because I was sober, and I was sure he'd been out drinking. There was no way he wasn't on something.

My fist met his jaw, and he went down, collapsing backward into the door frame.

"Parker!" Audrey gasped.

For me. Not for her shitty-ass ex. I didn't even make sure he landed okay, just closed the door. He was someone else's problem. Not mine. Right now, my priority was the girl in front of me who was shaking like a leaf.

"Are you okay?" Audrey asked, and I pulled her into my arms.

"Me?" I laughed, smoothing down her hair. "Are you okay?"

She melted against me. "I will be now."

Damn right she would.

I scooped her up into my arms, happy when she didn't protest at me carrying her as I moved into the kitchen to grab an ice pack and a treat I'd gotten Audrey earlier. Luckily, since we were college athletes prone to pulling joints and muscles, we had plenty. Snatching one up, I carried her through the crowded living room and towards the back of the house.

"My room or the back room?" I asked her, keeping my voice low. Soothing.

"Your room." She snuggled her face into my neck, and damn, I was content to keep her right here for the rest of all time.

Her eyes fluttered shut as I headed back up the stairs to my room.

"This is nice," she murmured. "Why don't we do this more often?"

"Me punching your ex?" I asked, earning me a laugh from the girl in my arms. "I can do that any time you want, baby."

"You know what I mean."

I was pretty sure if I could see her cheeks, they'd be pink, but she kept her face buried against me.

Kicking open my door, I shut it behind us, walking over to

my bed and setting her down on the edge. Handing her the ice pack I'd kept tucked under my arm, I watched as she guided it up to her cheek.

I ran my hands through my hair, begging for some self control, before taking a seat beside her. "You okay?"

"Yeah. It doesn't really hurt anymore. Just stings a little." Audrey bit her lip before climbing onto my lap, wrapping her arms around my neck. "I can't believe you did that." The ice pack was discarded at her side.

"Of course I did," I said, curling my hand around her hip and holding her protectively. "I'm never going to let anything happen to you, Rosie Girl. I promise." That she'd gotten hurt tonight at all—and on my turf, at my party—was enough to tear me up inside.

"I know." Her smile was sweet. Soft. "I've always known that, Parker. You're my best friend."

Your best friend shouldn't be thinking about how much he wants to kiss you right now, I thought to myself. "Of course I am. World's best fake boyfriend, right?"

She hummed in response, and I didn't care if no one was around. If no one was watching us. If none of this felt fake. "Any girl would be lucky to have you."

The idea of any other girl touching me, of having anyone else with me like this, felt wrong. It was my Rosie I wanted, not anyone else.

I dragged my thumb across her lower lip. "But they don't."

"Hmm?" Her eyes were lidded.

"Have me," I murmured. "They don't have me. You do."

She nodded.

"Because you're mine," I said, marveling at how soft she was. All those curves, her beautiful golden hair, her pretty pink lips— all of it was soft. I wondered if she was soft all over. God, I wanted to touch her. To worship her body.

"Parker," Audrey whimpered.

"What do you want, baby?" I asked, running my finger over her cheek. Wishing I could take her pain away.

"Kiss me."

Like there was any world that I'd tell her no.

I pulled her in closer to me, bringing the hand not holding her hip to her neck, guiding her mouth to mine. After tonight, I needed it. I craved her like I'd never craved anyone else. Like I couldn't get enough. I wasn't sure I ever would.

The sweet treat I'd bought for her fell out of my pocket, tumbling onto the bed beside us, but I didn't even care when the kiss deepened, and Audrey moaned into my mouth as our tongues met. She nipped on my bottom lip, and I sucked on her tongue. Neither one of us seemed to want to be the first one to break the kiss.

I was too aware of the way she was straddling my lap, her heat pressed against my aching cock. The only thing separating us was our jeans and underwear. Damn, I wouldn't be able to last with her on top of me.

How could I? Not when it felt so good to taste her, to hold her like this. Her fingers ran through my hair, raking her fingernails against my scalp in the most delicious way.

She writhed on top of me, like she was desperately seeking friction as I devoured her mouth. Each movement made me harder until I was practically weeping in my pants.

When we pulled apart, her lips were swollen, both of our breaths coming out in little pants.

Audrey sucked in a breath as her hips involuntarily rocked against mine, her eyes widening as she felt my erection pressing against her. "Oh."

I groaned as she experimentally rocked against me again. "Rosie Girl, I'm not going to be able to hold back if you do that."

She fluttered her eyelashes. "Then don't."

"What are you saying?" I whispered, aware of every line we were crossing. Best friends. Fake relationship. And yet none of it mattered as she ground down against my cock.

All I could think about was how good this felt, and how I wanted more. Her hands wrapped around me. My tongue running over every inch of her body. To lose myself in her. I already knew no one else would ever compare to her.

"Make me forget about him," Audrey said, her words so soft I wouldn't have been able to hear them if I weren't directly underneath her. "I don't want to think about him. Just us. Just you."

"You and me," I agreed, pressing a kiss to her neck to keep the other words in. *Because I'm yours.*

She tugged my t-shirt out of my jeans, smoothing her palms up my abs. Her eyes lit up as she traced each ridge with her fingertips. "I feel safe with you. Comfortable. Like we could do anything—try anything, and I know I'd be okay."

Yeah, she would. Because I'd put her first. I might not have much experience with this, but I knew enough. And God, I'd do anything she asked.

I whipped my shirt off, throwing it to the floor so she could continue her perusal with her hands. "You can. Anything you want, Audrey."

"Anything?" Her voice was breathier this time.

"Yeah. Tell me what you need."

She bit down on her lower lip, those teeth peeking out in such an adorable way. "I need…" Audrey blinked up at me, her eyes unfocused with lust. With *need*. "To come."

"Use me," I offered.

"What?" Audrey's voice comes out all breathy. I watch her swallow, then look back at me. Her eyes are wide, intensely focused on me.

"Use me, Audrey. Take what you need."

I rubbed my erection against her, a little moan slipping from her lips.

"It doesn't have to mean anything," I said, digging my fingers into her thighs. "Just let me take care of you."

"It doesn't mean anything," she agreed. "And it doesn't change anything."

And yet, somehow, I knew it would change everything.

Adjusting our positions, I rested my back against the headboard, dragging her along to keep her with me. Audrey's hands came to my shoulders, and with my hands on her hips, we started working in tandem. She rolled her hips against me, and I thrust up against her, painfully hard. My dick was all too eager to be inside of her, but that wasn't happening tonight. He needed to not get his hopes up.

"Touch me," she whispered, grabbing my hands and guiding them up her stomach, over the soft skin, to the bottom of her lacy bra. "Please."

I nodded, my thumbs brushing over her hardened nipples before I cupped each of her breasts in my hand, squeezing softly —tentatively. Even though I wanted to rip her shirt off, to bare her to me and see those perfect tits with nothing concealing them, we weren't there yet.

She was making the sweetest noises as she rubbed herself against me, and somehow dry-humping in my bedroom had topped the charts for the single best sexual experience of my life. Not that I had a lot to measure it against.

"Fuck," I groaned. "Audrey—" I shut my eyes, trying to think of un-sexy things. Things that weren't my girl in my jersey or the breathy sounds she made every time my hips met hers.

She whimpered, still moving back and forth, her hips working in overtime as she chased her orgasm. "I'm so close."

I took her lips with mine, not caring about anything else as we ground against each other. Fuck, it felt incredible. Losing myself in the kiss, I let passion take over, working us higher and higher. My hips thrust up, and she met me stroke for stroke as I coaxed her mouth with my tongue in tandem.

Audrey's head fell back, and she let out a low moan as she came. I wasn't far behind, unable to hold back as I felt the telltale signs of my own orgasm ripping through me.

"Fuck," I muttered, looking down at my lap.

"Did you just—" Audrey giggled.

"Dammit, Rosie," I groaned.

Yeah, I'd just come in my jeans like a teenager who'd never touched a girl before. In some ways, I was. My cheeks felt warm, embarrassment dotting them. I wasn't ashamed of what we'd done, but all of this was new to me.

Audrey nuzzled her face against the crook of my neck, one of her hands resting over my heart, my chest still bare. "That was… amazing. That's never happened to me before."

I blinked. "Really?"

"Mhm. Orgasming just from rubbing against each other is basically unheard of in my world. Normally I had to, um…" Audrey blushed, her cheeks growing pinker by the moment. Like she'd only just realized what we were talking about. "I had to get myself off," she whispered, not meeting my eyes.

"For the record, that's never happened to me before either," I joked, needing to see her smile again. "I don't normally make it a habit of coming in my pants."

She giggled, and I grinned at her, feeling relieved. This hadn't changed everything between us. We were still *us*. Best friends who could laugh about the absurdity of the situation.

And that was good. Better than I could have asked for, really.

Because it meant I still had a chance. I hadn't fucked this up completely.

CHAPTER 21

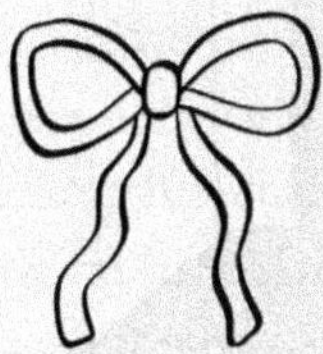

Audrey

Parker went and cleaned himself up, changing into a pair of pajama bottoms. I stayed perched on his bed, my body practically floating on air after that orgasm. Dry humping each other felt more incredible than I could have ever imagined, and after feeling his impressive erection through his pants, I was sure sex with him would be even better. Incredible.

God, I shouldn't be thinking like this.

But it was mutual—and we'd agreed it didn't mean anything. That it didn't change our agreement.

We were still fake dating, best friends who also now helped get each other off. That was fine, right?

I bit my lip as he settled back onto the bed, sitting next to me and bumping my hip.

"I should go," I whispered, feeling suddenly self conscious.

He reached out and grabbed my hand, interlacing our fingers together. "Stay." His eyes were pleading. "Please?"

"Okay," I agreed, letting my head rest on his shoulder.

He said nothing, and we just relaxed in the silence, Parker wrapping an arm around me and playing with my hair as I leaned on him.

I needed this. Needed *him* right now. "He's not going to stop, is he?" I finally whispered, speaking the words I hadn't dared utter ever since we started this.

Parker let out a sigh, leaning his head against mine. "I don't think so, sunshine."

My eyes filled with tears. "It's not fair, Parker. All I want is to live my life. But he's everywhere." A sob escaped from me, and I hated it. Hated being this vulnerable and *exposed*, like my entire heart was out for the world to see.

Except, it wasn't. It was just Parker. Parker, who was rubbing soothing circles on my back. Parker, who knew the exact words to say, whispering in my ear that it was okay. That he was by my side. That I didn't do anything to cause this.

I ran my fingers over my cheek. "I still can't believe that he hit me." The words were a whispered admission. Some part of me, however small—the part that stayed with him for so long— never expected him to lay a hand on me. "I mean, I know I bit him first, but still."

Parker burst out laughing. "You did *what?*"

"He had his hand over my mouth and wouldn't let me go. I would have screamed, but—"

"What the hell is wrong with him?"

I bit my lip. "Maybe he just needs help. Are you sure he'll be okay? He went down pretty hard."

"Is it bad if I say I don't care?"

I laughed. "Honestly, no. But what about *you*, Parker?"

He sighed, like he knew exactly where I was going with that. "Coach won't be happy with me. But I knew that risk when I did it. Especially since all of my teammates were here. It would be better coming from me."

"But..." I frowned. "Will you get in trouble?"

"Don't worry about me, sunshine. It was worth it. But... will you please talk to someone about this?" He asked, those amber eyes looking at me with so much *care* that my chest heaved. "I can't stand knowing he *hurt* you." His voice cracked.

I nodded. "Yeah. I'll talk to Professor Woods." I'd kept her in the loop since the beginning of the semester—minus the whole fake dating arrangement with Parker. But she knew he wouldn't let me be. I'd done my best not to be alone with him, but even that wasn't enough if he was going to corner me like this.

"Good. I'll go with you to talk to campus safety, too, if you want me to."

"Please," I whispered. Something that told me that doing it with him, having the courage to talk about what happened with Parker by my side, holding my hand, would be significantly better than trying to do it alone.

"Okay." He wiped his thumb over my tender cheekbone. "I'm with you, Audrey. I'm always going to be by your side."

I believed him. "What did I do to deserve you?" My eyes filled with tears once again, but this time it was happy ones.

"Do you remember when we first met?"

"No."

He hummed. "I do."

"You do?" I blinked. My family had moved into that house when Ella and I were still small, but I remembered little past that. Only that in all of my memories of the neighborhood, he was there.

"Yeah." Parker grinned. "There were a lot of other kids around, but none close to my age. I was too young for the big kids and too big to hang out with the babies." He scoffed. "Then my mom told me there were two twins moving in next door to me, and they were only a year younger. I was so excited. And then I found out you were girls." He scratched the back of head. "I just wanted someone to play with, you know? Someone who would ride around on bikes with me. Who would play with action figures and nerf guns and swords. And then you moved in."

"And?"

"And there you were, dressed in a little pink overall set. Your hair was in pigtails, and then you *smiled*. And I knew."

I was pretty sure I wasn't breathing. "You knew you wanted to be my friend when I smiled?" Turning my head to the side so I could look up at him, I raised an eyebrow.

He shook his head, wrinkling up his nose. "No. I knew that none of that mattered, because my life was going to be changed forever."

"Ella was there too, you know." She'd always been around when we were younger.

He hummed in response. "But she wasn't the one who rode her pink bike to the park with me every day after school. She wasn't the one who came over to my house and watched cartoons and movies. You two couldn't be more different if you tried. And even if you wore the same outfit, I'd always know it was you. So yeah, Rosie Girl, you do deserve me. Because you're the first friend I ever had. And the only one I've ever wanted to keep."

He pressed his lips to my forehead.

"You were my first friend too, you know. Besides my sister. And the first that really felt like *mine*. Because I didn't have to share you."

Parker winked. "Never will, Rosie Girl."

I hummed in response.

Finally, he said, "So he... never got you off? Never made it good for you?" His eyes looked murderous, and I knew he hadn't forgotten what I'd said before.

I shook my head. "It's never been easy for me... with someone else."

He laughed. "Audrey. No way. You're telling me that after you came just from grinding against my lap?"

Blushing, I dipped my head. Normally, I was too in my head. And maybe the partners I'd been with just hadn't put in that effort to get me off, either. But with Parker, it had been different. Like we'd been working towards a mutual goal. *Together.*

Maybe it was because that was how we'd always done

things. Ever since we were little, we'd worked together—building forts, assembling his legos, even scratching our names into the gigantic tree behind his house.

But no one else understood me like he did.

"Maybe I'm just too much," I murmured.

He worked his jaw, eyes narrowing. "*What?*"

"I'm too much. That's what Duke told me. That all the pink and the glitter and… everything about me." My eyes stung, and I tried to shake the tears away before they could fall. God, I was a mess tonight.

"Fuck, Rosie." He shook his head. "You believed him?"

Did I? Not really. I hadn't changed who I was. But the words had stuck with me. "Maybe he's right. Maybe I am." I shrugged.

"Fuck that." Blinking, I looked at him. Parker looked furious. For me.

He was pissed *for me.* Not at me. Because that was the kind of guy Parker was. I knew he'd defend me no matter what, but this was different.

"You're not too much, Audrey. You're fucking perfect." I was speechless. *Fucking perfect.* No one had ever said that to me before. Parker grabbed my hand, pulling me into his arms.

"I—" I shook my head. "I'm not perfect, Parker."

"Yes, you are." He nipped at my bottom lip. "Those noises you made, the way you came undone for me. You're so responsive, baby. It makes me want…" He shut his eyes, groaning.

"What?" I whispered, running my hands up his abdomen. "What do you want?"

"Fuck," Parker groaned. "Rosie—" He squeezed his eyes shut, his hands stilling mine. "We should stop."

I blinked, lowering my top back down. "What?"

"It's been a long night. And I don't want us to make a decision we'll regret."

He didn't want this?

After earlier, I was practically ready to throw myself at him.

God, I was an idiot. Just because I was feeling it didn't mean he was.

"Right. Um. I'm gonna go," I whispered, feeling mortified. Standing up from the bed, I collected my things,

"Audrey—"

I couldn't do this right now. "Good night, Parker. See you at rehearsals."

"He *what*?" I was sitting on the couch of Laura, Meri and Florence's apartment, stuffing my face with a slice of funfetti cake. Laura's face was red as I told them all what had happened with Duke the night before. "God, that asshole. I can't believe he came to the lacrosse house even knowing you're with Parker." She was knitting a green scarf without even looking at the stitches, which was almost mesmerizing to me.

These three girls had been like older sisters and mentors to me since I started in the theater department, always offering me advice or a hug when I needed it. They lived right off campus, and it had been easy to crash their evening study session.

Maybe I just didn't want to face Parker after how he'd turned me down after what felt like the best orgasm of my life. I wanted more, but obviously, he didn't.

"I've heard he's been getting in with the wrong crowd this year. Drugs, partying all the time..." Meri refilled her glass of wine.

I frowned, looking down at my socks. They had little pink kittens on them, wearing bows. "He was never like that before. I mean, he drank, but it wasn't like this..."

"Have you talked to anyone?" Florence asked from the kitchen where she was popping in a tray of cookies. She was always baking something when I was over here.

"Yeah. I went to campus safety today and told them what

happened. And I have a meeting with the dean of the fine arts department and Professor Woods tomorrow."

"Wow. Do you think they'll suspend him?"

Meri scowled. "They should. If not, I'll give him a piece of my mind."

Part of me wanted that. Part of me was also scared that he would retaliate against me for speaking out. I'd told Professor Woods that earlier, after class. Luckily, Duke hadn't shown up for rehearsals tonight—maybe because he was sporting a black eye.

"*He's going to be mad,*" I whispered. "*What if he—*"

"*Why don't you let me take care of him, Audrey? He's not here for the right reasons, and we both know it.*" He'd only tried out for the musical because he knew it was my dream. Because he wanted to stalk and haunt me even here, in my safe space. Theater—the drama department—wasn't his thing.

"*Still, I just...*" I thought about how he'd been the last few times I'd seen him. I shut my eyes, wishing I was stronger. A single tear dropped from my eye, and I cursed softly. I hated crying in front of people. I definitely didn't want to cry in front of my professor.

She rubbed my shoulder, looking at my wrist. "*He scared you, honey. Put his hands on you.*"

I nodded, wincing. "*Yeah. He did.*"

"*Let me take care of it. I know this has been an ongoing issue, and I think it's something that needs to be addressed now.*"

Professor Woods had given me a hug before I left, reassuring me that everything would be okay. Even though nothing felt okay.

"Maybe. I think so." I hugged my knees to my chest.

"And Parker?" Florence asked.

I raised my head up. "What about him?"

"How's he been taking all of this?" She raised an eyebrow. "His girlfriend got hurt, after all."

"Oh." Right. That was what she meant. "He was the perfect gentleman. Carrying me up to his room, giving me an ice pack, taking care of me..." My cheeks were warm.

Kissing me, letting me rub against him until I fell apart in his arms... *Super casual things that friends do, you know.* Except I couldn't say those things, because they thought our relationship was real.

And it felt a lot less like *just friendship* anymore.

PARKER HAD his hands shoved in his pockets when he came towards the bench I was sitting on outside of the athletic center. It had been two days since the party, and the lacrosse team had another game tomorrow. The bruise on my wrist from how he'd grabbed me had mostly faded, and luckily, the slap against my cheek hadn't left a mark. Still, I felt raw. Exposed.

He let out a sigh, plopping down next to me, running his fingers through his damp hair.

"I got benched."

"I'm so sorry, Parker."

"No, it was worth it." His gaze was set on mine. "What happened today?"

"They've scheduled a hearing with the disciplinary committee, but he's on a one week suspension from all campus activities. Apparently, the only thing he's allowed to do is go to class."

"And the musical?"

A sigh of relief slipped through my lips. "Since he's not enrolled in the theater program, he's been removed from the cast and banned from the theater building."

My fake boyfriend—because I needed the reminder—wrapped an arm around me, tugging me tight against his chest. "Thank fuck."

Neither one of us mentioned the fact that if he got permanently kicked out of CU, we wouldn't need to do this anymore. Pretend to be a couple.

Because I didn't want to stop.

I didn't want to go back to before.

Before I knew what it was like to be in Parker's arms. What it was like to kiss him—really kiss him.

I didn't want this to end.

CHAPTER 22

Parker

axwell. Late again." He looked up at me from his watch as I jogged onto the field, in full practice gear. Shit. "Sorry, coach. Rehearsals ran long."

I'd already been benched once—having to sit out the entire last game—and I felt like shit for letting my team down. But I knew coach's zero-tolerance policy on violence, and yet it was hard to regret it after what he'd done to Audrey.

It was worth missing a game, though, considering he was now facing suspension and had been removed from the musical cast completely. The school had also received information about some of the other girls he'd been harassing, a packet of information that had been slipped anonymously under the door of the disciplinary department's door.

"If you can't keep up with the team, Parker, you'll lose your scholarship. Want you at the top of your game for the away game next week."

I gritted my teeth, holding back the words I wanted to say. Because it hadn't been affecting my game. We'd still been winning. "I know, coach. I'll be better."

He slapped my shoulder, and I jogged on the field, joining

my team for warm-ups before taking my place in mid-field for scrimmages.

Stephens gave me a nod, and I felt myself relax. Maybe it was because I'd been spending more time with the team, but I had grown closer to the guys over the last few months. Now, instead of strangers, they felt like friends.

It was a good feeling.

Now, I just needed to make it through the performance weekend, and then all of this would be over. We had less than a month until then, and that also meant Audrey and I's fake dating deadline was rapidly approaching.

But I couldn't lose her. After the other night, I knew our attraction was mutual. The way she'd come apart in my arms, how she'd been comfortable enough with me to let go. How she could be herself with me.

I wanted everything with her. Wanted this to be real. But I couldn't fuck this up. Not with the musical, and not when I could lose her. I was completely in over my head, and yet not one piece of me regretted this.

GOD, I was fucking exhausted. We'd played hard and won our game tonight, but it had been a close call there. I wasn't playing at the top of my game, and I knew it. My mind was a jumble of thoughts. Everything felt so insurmountable. My feelings for Audrey, and whatever was going on between us, were more important to me than lacrosse. Thankfully, my grades weren't slipping, and I'd stayed on top of my studies.

The real problem was how I was going to juggle games and dress rehearsals as we got closer to the musical. It was getting more demanding, even if I had the entire script memorized practically forwards and backwards.

Sighing, I plopped my earbuds in, putting on the playlist

Audrey had made on my phone as the bus drove back to Castleton's campus.

Back to my girl. I hadn't told her we weren't spending the night tonight, because I was hoping to surprise her with dinner.

I'd put a stop to going any further the other night, and I owed her an explanation for that. She deserved to know *why*. Not that I didn't want to—I *did*, more than ever, but I had no experience. Besides kissing, I'd never gone farther than second base. Audrey and I dry humping till we came the other night was the most erotic experience of my life.

And we hadn't even taken our clothes off.

But I wanted her to know what it meant to me before she did. Because if she gave me that—letting me worship her body —I wanted it to mean something to her. It meant everything to me.

Trying not to think about those perfect tits underneath my jersey, I distracted myself by going through our plays tonight in my mind, thinking about what I could have done better, so I'd be more prepared for the next game. Anything was better than being hard on a bus full of my teammates.

Our bus was just pulling back onto campus when my phone buzzed.

AUDREY

Hey, Dream Boy.

PARKER

Dream Boy?

Mhmmmm. You have a silly nickname for me, so that's my silly nickname for you.

Audrey.

Are you drunk?

A liiiiittle bit.

Where are you at?

Whyyyy? Is my fake boyfriend going to come
swoop in and save me?

Rosie.

Youdon'thaftacome.

Pl;sea

You're scaring me, baby. Where are you?

???

Audrey. Answer your damn phone.

Fuck. She wasn't responding to me. Why hadn't we shared locations with each other yet? That was something I was fixing as soon as I found her tonight. That way, I'd always be able to find her if she needed me.

Dialing a number I had never needed to use, I let out a sigh of relief when she answered almost immediately. "Hello?"

"Ella?" I asked, my knee bouncing in worry.

"Yes? Sorry, who is this?" I heard girls laughing in the background.

"It's Parker."

"Oh! Sorry, Parker. What's up?"

"Are you with Audrey? She was texting me, but she stopped responding."

"No..." I could almost hear her frown. "I'm out with Cam. I know some of the girls were talking about going out tonight to the bar, but Ro hadn't mentioned anything to me. Hold on, lemme check her location." I could tell she'd pulled the phone away, and then she came back. "Looks like she's out at the Red Rose bar. Need me to send you the address?"

"Nah." I shook my head, even though she couldn't see me. "I know it. Thanks, Ella."

"Of course, Parker. I'm glad you're with my sister. You seem to make her really happy."

I cleared my throat. "Thanks. I'm trying."

It was all I wanted, and yet I constantly felt like I was fucking it up.

"Listen, I gotta go. We're pulling back into campus."

"Bye, Parker. Say hi to Audrey for me."

Saying goodbye, I shoved my phone into my pocket as we hung up, not even blinking at Ella's assumption that I was going to go after my girl. Of course I was.

I didn't like the idea that she was drunk and alone. Not after what had happened with Duke. She needed someone to watch her back as she let loose. That someone was me.

Hurrying off the bus without saying anything to my teammates, I grabbed my duffel as soon as I could, hurrying to head out to my car.

"You heading to see your girl?" Samuel asked, knocking his shoulder into mine.

I dipped my head.

He nodded. "I know Coach has been giving you a hard time, but I gotta say, it's been good to see you like this."

"Huh?" I blinked.

Sam followed me out to the parking lot. "Last semester, you were quiet. But after Halloween, after you found your girl, you've been different. I know you're juggling a lot, but you've been playing good, Maxwell. I'm impressed."

"Thanks. I—" I ran a hand through my hair. "It was hard for me after last year. Things with my last team didn't end great. I guess I just forgot what it was like to rely on other people."

He nodded. "We're here for you, man. And if you want to talk about it…" He patted me on the back. "I'm here."

"Thanks, Sam. You're a good guy."

My teammate tilted the brim of his baseball cap. "See you at home."

"Yeah." I smiled. Because it really felt like home. "See you later."

It was time to go find my girl.

STEPPING INTO THE BAR, my eyes immediately narrowed onto my blond-haired beauty giggling around a table, surrounded by a few other girls I recognized from her sorority. They had a round of shot glasses in front of them, all blushed cheeks and shouted whispers.

I headed over to her, her eyes lighting up as she caught sight of me.

"Hey!" she shouted. "It's my boyfriend. Look, everyone! My boyfriend is here."

God, she was beautiful. She'd pinned back some of the front pieces of her hair, and she was wearing a tight fitting pink tank dress and a pair of heels that made her legs look a million miles long. There weren't enough words to describe how gorgeous she was—tonight and every night. Even in leggings and no makeup, I thought she was the most stunning woman in any room.

"Hi, baby." I leaned in, kissing her cheek.

"Why are you here?" Audrey tilted her head. "I thought you wouldn't be back until tomorrow?"

"Change of plans. The bus came back tonight. I wanted to surprise you."

"Oh."

"And then my *girlfriend* was drunk texting me, so…"

"Oops?" She gave me a guilty smile. "Sooorryy."

I bent down, pressing a soft kiss to her lips.

She hummed. "Mmm. Hi."

Laughing, I brushed her hair back behind her ear. "You said that already."

"Oh." She giggled again. "Maybe I had a little too much to drink."

"Come on, Rosie Girl. Let's go home."

She leaned against my shoulder, her eyes drooping sleepily. "Home?"

I kissed her forehead. "Yeah."

"Okay." She turned to her friends. "Parker's taking me home. Night."

"Night, Audrey." Suzie waved at us, Peggy leaning against her side. I didn't know the other two girls, but I tipped my head at all of them before wrapping an arm around Audrey's waist, heading outside of the bar.

She yawned as she got into my car, letting me buckle her seatbelt. I rounded to the other side, the two of us driving in a comfortable silence towards the lacrosse house.

By the time I had pulled in and put the car in park, Audrey had fallen asleep. A smile curled over my face as I took in her sleeping form, curled up in my car. I closed my door quietly, rounding the car to open hers. Unbuckling her, I picked her up in my arms, closing the door behind me and locking my car before heading into the house.

Some guys were still downstairs, but I didn't pay them any mind. No, my only thoughts were on the sleeping beauty curled up against me, her face nuzzled against my chest. God, she was beautiful. So perfect and right and *mine*.

She stirred as I opened the door to my room, closing it behind us. Her violet eyes blinked open, staring up at me. Audrey's hand reached up, brushing against my jaw.

"Look at you. My knight in shining armor coming to save the day," she mumbled.

"I'll always save you, sunshine."

Setting her on the edge of my bed, I bent down to take her shoes off, letting them fall to the floor.

She smiled. "If I'm dreaming, I don't want to wake up."

I chuckled. "Not a dream, baby." Her eyelashes fluttered as I pulled her into my arms. "Come on, we gotta get this dress off of you so we can go to bed."

There was no way I was leaving her alone tonight. Especially not when she was all alone in the sorority house.

"Arms up," I said, not wanting to yank the dress off and hurt her.

Audrey lifted her arms, and I tugged the tight dress off her body, doing my best not to look at her bare skin, knowing the only thing she had on was her bra and underwear.

"Turn around, sunshine," I murmured against her ear. She complied, and I toyed with the strap of her bra. "On or off?"

"Off," she murmured, covering her breasts as I flicked open the clasps, letting the straps fall down her arms.

I grabbed my red hoodie, pulling it over her arms and loving the way it fell down to mid-thigh, practically dwarfing her frame.

Audrey turned around and stepped closer to me, her fingers fumbling over the button on my jeans.

"Rosie." I put my hand over hers, stilling the motion. "We're not going to do anything tonight."

She pouted. "Why not? Do you not want me?"

Dammit. "You're drunk." And there was no way I would take advantage of a drunk girl. And I respected her too much to let her do something she'd regret later.

Her teeth came out, digging into her lower lip. "The other night..." Her voice was all breath. "Did you not... like it?"

Fuck. Fuck that she even thought that. "It's not that."

Audrey frowned. "Then what is it?"

I sighed, bopping her on the nose. "Tonight, we're going to sleep. Tomorrow, when you're feeling better, we'll talk, okay?"

She nodded, yawning again as I pulled the comforter back on my bed, extra thankful in this moment that I didn't have a twin sized bed. "Parker?" Audrey whispered as she climbed into my bed, her hair spread out across my pillows.

"Yeah, sunshine?"

"You'll be here when I wake up, right?"

"Of course I will." I frowned. "Why wouldn't I be?"

Her eyes shut as she snuggled into the pillow. "In my

dreams, you're always gone when I wake up."

I ran my hand over her hair. "Good night, sleeping beauty." I pressed my lips to her forehead, unable to stop touching her. "I promise I'll be here when you wake up."

"Okay," she murmured, curling up and quickly falling asleep.

I watched her for a few moments, satisfaction flowing through me at the sight of her in my bed. There wasn't a single other person I could imagine here. It was like she was meant to be here.

Like all along, without knowing it, I'd been waiting for her.

CHAPTER 23

Audrey

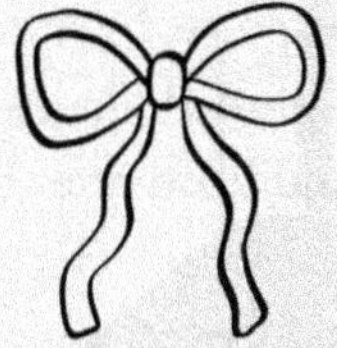

For the first time all semester, I felt like I was sleeping on a cloud. The bed was cozy and warm, and I hugged my pillow even tighter.

Except. Wait. I opened my eyes, holding my breath like that could postpone the inevitable realization. My pillow didn't normally wear a t-shirt. And it definitely didn't have those muscles.

How did I get here?

The last thing I remembered was the bar I'd gone to with my sisters. Where I'd—shit. I'd been doing shots all night, and at some point, I'd pulled out my phone, texting Parker.

It was all coming back to me now. How he'd shown up, sweeping me off my feet and bringing me back to his room. The way he'd carried me into his room, before he undressed me so carefully, averting his eyes as I slipped off my bra and he dropped his sweatshirt over my head.

The sweatshirt I was still wearing, even though it had ridden up my thighs, leaving my panties exposed.

It was red, like his favorite color growing up. I wanted to steal it out of his closet next time he was gone for an away game, to remember this moment. How close I felt to him in it. Parker was curled around me, holding me tight against his body as he slept.

I took in the sight of him, letting my eyes linger on his face. God, he was handsome. I wanted to reach out and trace the sharp lines of his jawbone, brush my fingers over those soft lips.

It had been stupid to go out drinking last night, but after the week I'd had, all I'd wanted to do was forget. Forget about Duke and how he'd ruined the perfect time we were having. Forget about how scared I'd felt, pinned against the house.

Forget about Parker, and how, after basically offering him my body, he'd rejected me.

But last night… he'd said we'd talk, didn't he? I wasn't sure I was ready to hear his explanation.

"Audrey Rose," he murmured as I continued to stare at him. His eyes were still shut, like he was still asleep, but he tightened his hold around my back, bringing me in closer to him.

And pressing his generous morning wood against my stomach. *Oh,* boy.

"Hm?"

"I can practically feel you staring at me even with my eyes shut," he said, little more than a mumble. "Go back to sleep."

It was still dark outside, so all I could do was comply. Besides, he was so warm that my eyes were already drifting shut again, sleep taking me quickly.

All I could think as I fell asleep in his arms, is that *this wasn't a dream.*

"Hey, sleeping beauty," a deep voice whispered against my ear. "I'm going to run and grab breakfast."

"Mmm?" I blinked open my eyes, finding him standing over me, wearing a Castleton University crewneck and a pair of sweatpants.

Damn. He looked good in those.

He pressed his lips to my forehead, and I practically melted into the pillow.

"Want me to come with you?" I mumbled, not actually wanting to get out of his bed. Because it was too warm. Too comfortable. And here, I didn't have to think about the mortification of last night.

He chuckled. "No. I just didn't want you to wake up alone."

"Oh." I smiled, yawning and stretching my arms out. "Get me something?"

"Of course." Parker brushed a piece of hair behind my ear.

Curling my arms around his pillow, I buried my nose in it, inhaling his scent. God, this was absolutely surreal. I was in his bed, and we'd been cuddled up all night. Parker had held me in his arms as we slept.

Nothing had happened, and he'd been the perfect gentleman last night. He could have just taken me back to the sorority house, but he'd brought me back here.

What did it mean? My head swirled with possibilities. The other night, he'd stopped us before anything could happen, despite the ache between my thighs and how I had so desperately wanted to straddle him once again.

But he was right. We shouldn't complicate this with sex. *Right*? Or maybe...

Twenty minutes later, I hadn't gotten back to sleep. In fact, I was wide awake when Parker came back in the door, carrying a bag that smelled suspiciously like cinnamon rolls and two coffees in a coffee carrier.

Sitting up, I let the sheets fall to my waist.

"Mmm," I practically moaned at the scent in the air. "Gimme." Reaching out my hands—like I was a toddler, instead of a twenty-one-year-old college student who much definitely had a better vocabulary than that—I practically sighed in relief as he put the cup in my hand. "You're my hero." I sipped the cup, the sweetness of the white chocolate mocha hitting my tastebuds.

He chuckled. "Anything for you."

I gave him a soft smile, drinking my coffee before digging into the cinnamon roll, the sweet treat practically melting in my mouth.

He watched me with rapt attention, a look of satisfaction on his face even as he drank his own coffee and ate the breakfast he'd picked up for himself.

When we'd both finished, he blew out a breath. "About last night..." Parker said, sitting down next to me, running his hands through his hair. I knew by now that he did that when he was nervous, and it was so adorable.

"It's my fault," I offered. My voice was low. Resigned. "I know you're just my fake boyfriend, and I basically forced myself on you—"

"Fuck. Audrey. *No.*" He shook his head. "It's not like that."

"Okay." I bit my lip. "Then why?"

His head dropped, like he couldn't make eye contact with me. "I'm not—" He blushed. And *oh my god*, Parker was blushing. "I'm not exactly experienced. With girls."

"But..." I cocked my head. "I thought... You *have* had a girlfriend, right?"

I hated thinking about him having been with someone else. That someone else had gotten to see him like this. Hold his hand. *Kiss him.* The flash of jealousy that surged through me was new.

I'd never considered myself a possessive person—not until now. Not until Parker.

"Yeah, but we didn't... Go all the way." He cleared his throat. "I didn't stop us because I don't want you, Audrey. I just didn't want to disappoint you."

He hadn't...? With anyone?

"I'm a virgin, Audrey."

I blinked. "Oh."

He ran his fingers through his hair, blowing out a deep breath. "Yeah."

"I didn't know."

"How could you?" He cupped my cheek. "I didn't tell you. Maybe I just didn't want to make it some big thing. It's not like I'm waiting for marriage or anything. It just didn't feel right before, with anyone else. And I've always been so busy, with sports and everything." The corner of Parker's lips tilted up in a hesitant smile. "But maybe, all along, I was just waiting for you."

"Parker." I shut my eyes, nuzzling my face into his hand. "I don't even know what to say." God, the sincerity in his tone was making me *melt*.

I was waiting for you. Words I'd never known how much I wanted to hear. But suddenly, they changed everything.

"Does it bother you that I'm not?" I whispered, my eyes fluttering open. "That I've been with other people?"

He flinched. "No. Of course not, Audrey."

When I'd first started college, I'd hooked up with a few people before quickly realizing it wasn't for me. I got attached too easily, imagining my entire life with someone after the first date. After that, I'd only slept with people I'd been in committed relationships with. And after Duke, well... There hadn't been anyone.

"We can take it slow," I offered. "If you want to." His jaw clenched. "Or... maybe we should just focus on the musical right now."

That was the right thing to say, but when I looked at Parker, his eyes were dark. "I do want to," he said. "I just don't know how to do this. And I don't want to fuck it up, Rosie."

"You won't," I promised. Because I wasn't sure it was possible for Parker not to excel in every single thing he did.

He rubbed his hands over his sweats. "How do you know?"

This time, it was me who cupped his cheeks. "Because it's *you*, Parker. And I know you." His cheeks were dotted with the faintest of pink, and it was endearing.

"Guess you do, huh? You probably know me better than anyone."

"Yeah." I liked that. I practically preened at the words. *Better than anyone.* I liked him better than anyone, too. "You know, formal's next weekend."

He nodded. "Yeah." Parker tapped on his forehead with his finger. "Got it all up here."

I laughed, throwing a pillow at him. "Okay, dork."

"Hey, my good memory comes in handy. I'm a quick learner." He smirked. "*Really* quick."

My cheeks heated at the insinuation. How quickly he'd gone from quiet and shy to flirty.

That was when I remembered that the only thing I was wearing was my underwear and his sweatshirt, his sheets, and as much as I wanted to go further, now wasn't the time. Not after last night.

"Well, this was fun." I got up, pulling his sweatshirt down to mid-thigh, covering everything. Scrambling off his bed, I pressed a kiss to his cheek. "Thanks for breakfast."

"Okay?" He raised an eyebrow. "That's it?"

"Uh-huh. We're taking things slow, remember?" I quirked an eyebrow. "So I'm going to go home and get ready for this week, and then I'll see you later." Nodding my head a few times, I took in Parker's face. He looked shocked.

"So, are we just going to pretend like this never happened?" He rasped, moving to stand in front of me. His frame towered over mine, his brown hair falling onto his forehead as his eyes captured mine, demanding attention.

"No," I murmured.

Standing up on my tiptoes, I kissed him softly, pulling away to look at his eyes. Did he know how I felt? How desperately I wanted him? How I was trying to be patient because I wanted this to mean something to him like it did for me?

Neither one of us said a word. But his amber eyes bore into mine, and for a second, I thought he was going to pull away. Like we'd just leave it there.

But Parker wrapped his hand around my neck, and then he pulled me back into him, his lips descending on mine. It wasn't like my soft, uncertain kiss. No. He devoured me with his mouth, passionately kissing me like he couldn't bear not to.

Like he wouldn't let me go.

His tongue slipped inside, and heat pooled between my legs.

When we pulled apart, his lips brushed down my neck, and I tilted my head back, letting out a small moan.

"We can still do other things," he said against my skin.

I nodded. *Yes,* was right on the tip of my tongue, but I couldn't seem to get the word out.

"Tell me what to do," Parker said, his lips caressing my neck in open-mouthed kisses. "Tell me how you like it. I want it to be good for you."

"It will be," I reassured him, cupping his jaw. *Because it's you.*

"Rosie," Parker groaned, sliding his hand up my thigh underneath his sweatshirt.

I widened my legs for him, an open invitation for him to touch me. His fingers were hesitant, exploratory, as he dragged them up my inner thigh and over the thin fabric of my panties. I whimpered as he ghosted over my clit, not giving me what I needed.

He hooked his fingers in the waistband before dragging my panties down my hips and kneeling in front of me. Spreading me wide, he kneeled in front of me, pushing the sweatshirt up to my waist and just staring at my bare pussy, perfectly on display for him.

"God," he murmured, his rapt attention focused on my slit. "You're so beautiful. So pink."

I blushed. "Parker..."

"Tell me what you like," Parker repeated, looking up at me from between my thighs. His soft, brown hair was right there, and it was all I could do to bury my fingers into it. He pressed his lips against the soft, sensitive skin of my inner thigh, eyes still locked on mine. "Want to be your good boy."

A groan slipped from my lips. "You can—you can use your

mouth," I panted, already so turned on. Needing this. "Taste me."

"Fuck, yes," he groaned, leaning in and licking a line up my entrance, like a hesitant first taste. "I've wanted to do this for so long," he muttered against my cunt. I was dripping wet for him, more turned on than I'd ever been in my life, and he hadn't actually done anything yet.

But then he spread me apart with his fingers, lapping at me with his tongue like he was dying of thirst.

"So wet." He swirled his tongue inside, and I wasn't sure I believed him when he said he'd never done this before. "Is all of this for me, baby?"

I nodded. Being surrounded by his scent, tucked into his bed and wearing only his sweatshirt, had made me incredibly horny.

Parker pulled back, looking up at me. "What else?" His eyes were dark, pupils blown with desire.

"Your fingers," I moaned. "I need—" Biting my lip, I held back from practically begging him for more.

He slid a finger inside of me, groaning as I clenched around him. He pumped it a few times, his eyes studying my face like he was trying to gauge my reaction, before adding another finger. "Good?" He asked as he crooked his fingers.

I gasped at the sensation. "Yes. And then my clit—" I let go of his hair so I could bring my finger to that bundle of nerves—showing him what I liked.

Parker hummed, pulling his fingers out of me and spreading my wetness around, circling my clit with his fingers.

"I think I've got this now," he mused as I let my head fall back when he thrust both fingers back inside of me at the exact moment his lips closed over my clit, licking and sucking it. Each flick of his tongue against me and pump of his fingers was bringing me higher and higher.

My knees were shaking, and he picked up each of my legs, dropping them on his shoulders before pushing us back against the wall, moving those fingers inside of me in a steady rhythm.

"Don't stop," I cried. "I'm so close." I buried my nails into his shoulders, letting every sensation run through me as he took me for a ride.

He ate me out like a fucking champ, letting out groans all while fucking me with his fingers. *So good.* It had been so long since anyone had touched me like this, and my body was absolutely wound tight. Ready to explode.

"Come for me, baby," he murmured, the vibration against my clit too much.

I cried out, unable to hold myself back as I let go, my orgasm bursting through me like the sun rising into the sky, and I let myself ride in the moments of bliss as he continued working his fingers inside of me.

When I opened my eyes, he withdrew his hand, planting my feet back onto the floor before standing up. My juices coated his fingers, and he hummed, slipping them inside his mouth as he sucked them clean.

"So sweet. You taste like the sweetest thing I've ever had. Delicious."

Holy shit. My cheeks were warm, but I couldn't look away. Hot. He was so damn hot.

"How?" I asked, not even formulating words. Because that was *incredible.*

"Said I was a virgin, sunshine, not that I was a prude." He winked.

I let out a giggle. Then my eyes drifted down, seeing the massive tent in his sweatpants. I reached out, brushing a finger over his impressive erection. There was a part of me that was ready to drop to my knees right here. I wanted to see it, to return the favor—to taste him like he had tasted me, but he put his hand over mine as I cupped him through the material.

Frowning, I looked up at him.

Parker gave me the tiniest shake of his head. "That was just for you." He pressed his lips against mine, kissing me roughly, letting me taste myself on his tongue. "I'll take care of myself later." He brushed a piece of hair back behind my ear. "Feeling better?"

I nodded, wrapping my arms around myself. "I should probably get back to the sorority house. I have a meeting later today." I hated to leave after that, but I also needed time to process what had just happened. What we'd just done.

How it felt like we'd changed something between us forever.

But I like this new version of us.

He looked down at my frame. "You look good in my sweatshirt."

"Maybe I should keep it, just like your jersey." I buried my nose in the neck, inhaling deeply. I never wanted to wash it.

He kissed me again. "Maybe you should." Parker's eyes drifted down my bare legs. "Do you want a ride back?"

I nodded, then something occurred to me. "Can I also borrow some, uh… pants?"

The idea of doing the walk of shame in my dress and heels from last night was mortifying, but would anyone think twice about me wearing my boyfriend's clothes? *No.*

He chuckled. "Sure. Hold on."

A while later, after rolling a pair of his sweats so they wouldn't fall off my hips and a steamy make-out session in his car, I couldn't keep the smile off my face as I walked back to the sorority house.

"See you later, Rosie Girl," Parker said, as I closed the door. "And I can't wait to be your date next weekend."

CHAPTER 24

Parker

I f I had died and gone to heaven, this would have been one hell of a way to go. Singing a duet, a love song, with the girl I wanted the most. The girl I always thought I couldn't have. Because she was my best friend.

Except there was nothing in the world that compared to the other night when I'd had my mouth on her, tasting her sweet pussy, hearing her moan as I brought her pleasure. *Me.* No porn could ever compare to the sight of my Rosie, flushed from the orgasm I'd given her.

If I wasn't careful, I was going to get addicted to it.

Thoughts I definitely should not be having at a dress rehearsal because this costume was *not* meant to hide an erection. The pants were black, practically molded to my thighs, and I wore a brocade vest over a black tunic. Every bit the Prince I was playing.

Except my thoughts were not as chivalrous as my character, who was supposed to be serenading the girl whose heart he was trying to win.

"Parker," Audrey whispered as I swept her up into my arms, practicing the dip. "You okay? You look like you're in pain."

"Oh." I grimaced. "Yeah, I'm fine. Just thinking about…"

Fuck, what could I say that wasn't *her?* There were too many people around us on stage to admit I'd been thinking about carrying her out of there like a caveman and burying my tongue in her backstage or in the dressing room. "Lacrosse," I finished lamely. It wasn't a complete lie. I had a game at the end of the week, after all.

She gave me a little eye-roll as we went through the next steps of the choreography, breaking apart before coming back together again as I twirled her into my arms.

The music ended and the two of us held our poses—my hands on her hips and hers holding the lapels of my vest.

"Good!" Mary said, watching us from the audience. "Parker, make sure you look at her lovingly. You love her, but she doesn't know that yet."

I did.

I did love her.

Not that there was a chance in hell I was going to risk messing this up by telling her. Because Rosie, my Rosie Girl, she meant too much to me.

"Right." I nodded, looking down at Audrey. Her violet eyes were focused on mine, and I reached out to brush a small piece of bang out of her eyes.

"Yes! Just like that."

How did I explain to her I wasn't even acting? That I was just looking at my girl the way I'd always wanted to?

"Let's take that number one more time from the top! And then we'll be done for the day."

"Parker…" Audrey whispered, her fingers sliding down my torso before we pulled apart.

"Hmm?"

She bit her lip. "Never mind. Let's do this."

I dipped my head low against her ear. "Did I tell you how beautiful you look in your costume yet, sunshine?"

Her cheeks went pink as she looked down at the pink glittery fabric. "No."

I winked at her before heading back to wait for the music to reset. "Always are."

LATER THAT WEEK, the stadium was full of screaming sports fans, but there was only one I cared about. The same one who I'd spent the last week with dancing around on stage.

"Parker!" There was Audrey, standing at the edge of the field, wearing my jersey and a short skirt. I jogged over to her, pulling her into my arms and kissing her deeply.

We were having the best damn season of my career, and I was pretty sure I owed that all to Audrey. My girl in the stands, cheering me on, was the best motivation I'd ever had. I wished my parents were here, too, but at least I had her.

The worst part about away games was knowing she wasn't watching. We had a fairly evenly balanced schedule of home versus away games, and I was thankful this wasn't pro sports where we had to be on the road for days at a time.

Her eyes fluttered dreamily when we pulled apart, her fingers clutching my jersey over my chest pads. "That was some kiss."

"Gotta remind all of them whose you are." *Mine.*

Audrey's smile was bright. Dazzling.

"Come home with me," I whispered against her lips.

"Hmm… Is there a party tonight?"

I shook my head. She tilted her head, her eyes widening with realization. And then—*heat.* Desire. I knew I wasn't mistaking that in her gaze.

"Okay," she mumbled, nodding her head. "I will."

"Wait for me," I said, kissing her again. "I just have to change out of this."

I was about to get my uniform off faster than I ever had in my entire life. I needed a shower, but maybe I could convince her to take one with me. Later.

Audrey just nodded.

Hurrying to the locker room, all I could think about was my girl. Even as coach talked to the team, nothing could bring me down from my bubble.

I'D DRIVEN home from the field in record time. Audrey had been waiting for me, just like I'd asked. Something settled in my chest, seeing her waiting for me. *Contentment.* I'd never had a relationship like this before, where it was so fulfilling and also so easy being together.

Opening her car door, I held out a hand for her as she stepped up on the curb. She blushed, interlacing our fingers, and I tugged her in behind me into the house.

Once I got to the stairs, it only took a second before I had her over my shoulder, my hand on her ass to keep her skirt from flying up.

"Parker," Audrey giggled. "Put me down. What will your teammates think?"

Like I fucking cared.

Once I got into my room, thankful for the hundredth time this year for the private suite, I slid her down my front till she was back on her feet before pressing her against the door.

She was gorgeous, with her pink lipstick and flushed cheeks, those blonde curls pulled up into a high ponytail with her favorite pink scrunchie. Gorgeous and mine.

Fisting *my* jersey in my hands on either side of her, I just stared at Audrey. "You don't know how much seeing you in my jersey affects me, baby."

She blushed. "You like it that much?"

"Of course I do. It's hot as fuck." I ran my lips across her exposed collarbone. "My name on your back, like you're all mine."

"I am," she murmured. "I am yours."

I groaned. "Fuck, I like hearing that."

There was no one else for me. No one but this sweet, sunshine girl with her blonde hair like golden rays and her deep violet eyes who wore my clothes like they were always meant to be hers. I wanted to toss her over my shoulder like a caveman, to keep her where no one else would steal her away from me.

She gasped as I pressed my cock into her, already half-hard. "Look at what you do to me, Rosie. How can you ever doubt how much I wanted you?" Just one look at her, and I was like this. These days, it didn't take much. The smell of her strawberry shampoo, the sweetness that always followed her. It was everything. Every damn thing about her. Even her smile.

Audrey shook her head, her eyes falling shut as she let out a low moan. "I—I didn't know. I thought all of it was fake."

"Does this feel fake to you, Rosie?" I asked, pulling her panties aside and pushing two fingers into her without preamble. "My fingers inside of you as you wear my number?"

"No," she cried, clenching my fingers as I plunged them in and out of her needy cunt.

She was my obsession, but it was more than that. She was my damn salvation. She was everything I wanted and everything I couldn't have. Every dream made real.

"Fuck, you're so responsive." Keeping her pressed against the door, I worked my fingers inside of her, a series of breathy moans slipping from her lips as I brought her higher and higher. "So wet for me. Such a good girl."

She tightened around me, and I knew she was close. But I wanted her to come on my tongue this time. I pulled my fingers out, drawing a whimper out of her.

"I want to taste you again," I murmured, inching her backwards onto my bed until she had to bend her knees and sit on the edge. "Want to bury my tongue in your pretty pink pussy. Wanna feel you clenching around my tongue."

"Parker," she gasped as I ran my nose over her panties.

"Can I?" I looked back up at her. "Can I go down on you again?"

"Like you need to ask."

I flashed my teeth, grabbing her knees and pulling them apart, humming with satisfaction as I saw the color of her underwear. Pink cotton greeted me with a little lace waistband, and I nipped at the inside of her thighs with my teeth before looking up at her. "Can I take these off?"

"Yes." She dropped her head back. "Please."

Dragging them off slowly, Audrey squirmed underneath me as I took my sweet time with her panties. I dropped them to the floor before kneeling in front of her, taking my time to explore her fully. Last time, I'd been rushed. This time, I wanted to take my time with her. To learn exactly what brought her pleasure. To bring her to the edge, over and over again, until she was screaming my name.

"You're so fucking beautiful, Audrey. Look at you." I parted her folds, unable to tear my eyes away. She was beautiful. She'd propped herself up with her elbows, wearing only my jersey, and fuck if that wasn't a turn-on. I reached down, squeezing my cock in my pants, trying to ease the ache.

No matter how much I wanted it, I wasn't going to be inside of her. I'd take care of myself later—in the shower—just like I'd done the last time I'd had my mouth on her.

We were going slow, like she'd said. And because I didn't want her to think she was some quick fuck to me. Not when she was everything.

"Touch me," she begged, writhing with need.

Who was I to say no to that?

I swiped a line up her entrance, circling her clit a few times before replacing my tongue with my thumb. Applying pressure as I rubbed it just like she'd shown me, I thrust my tongue inside her cunt, lapping up all of her arousal. Her back arched as she let out a cry.

Whatever assholes she'd been with before hadn't taken the

time to make sure she was getting off, and I fucking hated that. When she told me she had a hard time orgasming with anyone else, I couldn't believe it. Because she was so responsive to my touch.

She was always so wet and eager, squirming against my face as I tasted her thoroughly.

Audrey's thighs tightened around my head, and I groaned. "That's it, baby." Her hips rocked into me, each movement pushing me into her mouth. "Want you to come on my tongue. Soak my face."

She did just that as I pressed down harder on her clit, giving her what she needed as I thrust into her with my tongue, dragging it through her wet cunt over and over, teasing her insides as her pussy pulsed around me.

I groaned as my mouth flooded with her come, drinking every last drop.

"Fuck," she moaned, collapsing onto my mattress as I pulled away. "You're so fucking good at that."

I grinned against her, pressing kisses to her inner thighs. "Told you I was a quick learner."

CHAPTER 25

Audrey

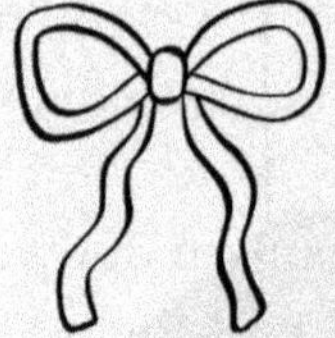

*I*t's *always the quiet ones.* That's what everyone always said. But I didn't expect him to talk so *dirty.* I was pretty sure I could come from that alone. How was he so good at this? He was a quiet, shy nerd, and yet he played with my body with such precision. The first time, he'd asked me to tell him what I liked. Tonight, he'd taken charge, and I liked giving him control over my body.

I liked when he praised me, too. Or called me *his.*

Like I really was his girlfriend.

I didn't really know what we were doing, but I couldn't find it in me to care. Not when it felt this good, when I was panting after crying out his name loud enough that his entire house probably had heard me.

He ran his hands through his hair as he stood up, looking at me.

My eyes narrowed on the bulge in his pants.

Parker was hard. For *me.* From going down on me. And I *really* wanted to return the favor this time. Wanted to touch him. Taste him. To make him come the way he had for me.

Sliding off the bed, I kneeled in front of him.

"Audrey," Parker groaned. "You don't have to—"

"I know," I murmured, unzipping his pants. "I want to."

I'd never particularly *enjoyed* giving blowjobs before. Maybe because with Duke, it felt more transactional. Honestly, sex with him was never great. Looking back, I questioned why I even stayed with him for so long. Why I let him make me feel so small.

Parker didn't do that, though. He made me feel like I was cherished. Valued. Appreciated. *Loved.*

Outside of this room, our relationship was all fake. I knew it was. And yet, I couldn't help but wish for more. That he'd love me. That this was real.

That at the end of the day, he'd pull me into his arms and we'd dance in the cotton candy clouds until the end credits rolled. But this isn't a fairytale.

Still, I wanted him to know how special he was. Wanted him to be cared for.

Pushing his pants and boxers down his hips in one movement, I freed his length fully. God, he was big. And the tip was glistening, a drop of pre-cum oozing out. I traced a pink nail over his cock, and Parker shivered from the motion.

"Fuck, Rosie," he groaned. "What are you doing to me?"

Darting out my tongue, I swiped it over the head before moving my attention down the length, coating him in my saliva. I looked up at him through my eyelashes, blinking as I took the head into my mouth, running my tongue around the rim.

Wrapping my hand around his shaft, I slowly pumped him as I sucked lightly, my cheeks hollowing out.

"Harder," he gritted out like he was trying to hold himself back.

His hand wrapped around mine as he squeezed tighter, both of us working him in tandem.

With my free hand, I ran my fingers through my folds, gathering up the wetness and rubbing it over my clit, moaning as I took him in deeper.

"Audrey." He cursed. "Fuck." Parker's free hand wrapped

around my ponytail, tugging it back, forcing my eyes to meet his. "That feels so good. There's no way I'm going to last."

I pulled off of him. "It's okay," I said, my voice hardly more than a rasp. "I want to make you feel good. You can come if you want." I fluttered my eyelashes. "Let me taste you, too."

He groaned as I sealed my mouth over him once again, flattening my tongue and breathing through my nose as I took inch after inch of his thick, hard cock.

"You're fucking incredible," Parker encouraged as I gagged a little, unable to take him too much deeper. Still, he took over, wrapping my ponytail around his hand as his hips started to thrust.

And I let him. Because fuck, being on my knees in front of him, watching him throw his head back in pleasure as he used my throat… I'd never felt more sexy. More desired.

Like he was losing his mind with need as much as I was.

But he was also careful not to go too deep, like he knew there was only so much I could take. Because as much as I wanted to deep throat him, there was no way I could. But Parker didn't seem to mind.

"I'm gonna come," he grunted, his cock swelling in my mouth. He pulled out to the tip, but I kept my lips closed around him as he spilled in my mouth, rope after rope of his cum settling onto my tongue. And the face he made as he lost it, his eyes closed in pleasure… a shiver ran down my spine.

I ran my tongue over my lip as I swallowed, making sure I got every drop.

And then Parker pulled me to my feet before kissing me, not caring that he'd just come in my mouth. That I tasted like him.

"That was—wow." He laughed. "You okay?" He wiped his thumb under my eyes, gathering up the moisture I hadn't even realized was pooled there.

"More than okay," I nodded, smiling at him. "That was fun."

He chuckled, pressing a kiss to my forehead. "Want to stay tonight? We don't have to do anything else, but—"

Parker didn't even need to finish the thought before I answered, "Yeah."

Because I liked sleeping in his arms.

And because I wanted to soak up these moments for as long as I had them.

Laying across Parker's bed days later, I twirled a strand of hair around my finger as I looked up from the notes I was studying for one of my upper division theater classes. They were written in my favorite pink sparkly pen, and I traced a manicured nail over the paper.

Parker was quiet and withdrawn tonight, and I didn't know why. But I wanted to make it better. Wanted him to talk to me, so I could understand what was going on inside his head.

We didn't keep secrets from each other. Not as best friends.

And not as whatever we were *now*, either. We still hadn't had sex, but that hadn't stopped us from doing other things. Including kissing a lot.

"Parker."

"Yeah?" He looked up from his architectural textbook. We were both studying on his bed, both unable to go even five minutes without touching the other. He'd play with my hair, or I'd rest my feet in his lap.

"What's wrong?" I poked at his arm. "And don't tell me nothing because I know you. Something's on your mind."

Parker sighed. "My old team is playing us in two weeks."

"Oh?" I frowned, sitting up against his pillows. "Shouldn't you be excited to see your old friends? You were with those guys for three years, after all."

"Yeah." Parker shut his eyes, dropping his head to my lap. "I was. But…"

Running my fingers through Parker's hair, I massaged his

scalp. He hummed, his eyes closed like he was enjoying my hands on him.

"Parker," I murmured, keeping my voice low, like I was trying not to spook a horse. "What happened?" I'd suspected there was something, but he'd never told me. Even when I'd asked about his reason for transferring, he'd avoided the subject.

Was he… embarrassed? Because he didn't need to be. I knew that whatever the situation was, he hadn't told me for a reason.

He took a deep breath, his amber eyes blinking open to look into mine. "My ex-girlfriend cheated on me."

"The fuck? She cheated on *you?*" God, that fucking sucked. I'd been there, and it was the worst feeling in the world. But also on *him*? He was the biggest cinnamon roll boyfriend on the planet. I couldn't imagine why anyone could have him and look elsewhere for more.

He chuckled. "Yeah. But that wasn't even the worst part. It was *who* she cheated on me with." His eyes were glued to the ceiling instead of on me.

"Who?" I hated to ask, having a bad feeling I knew exactly what he was going to say, but I wanted to keep him talking, so I just kept running my hands through his silky soft light brown strands.

"My teammate. We were close. Like brothers. And, fuck, I wasn't even upset that she cheated." He pinched the bridge of his nose. "How fucked up is that? I was—still am, actually— upset that he'd broken my trust. We got into a fight on the field. Lost the game because of it. I cost our team the championship, Audrey." He was choked up. "Because she wasn't getting enough attention from me, so she turned to him, and I—"

"Hey," I reassured him. "It's okay."

Parker frowned up at me. "It's not. I never should have let that happen. I should have—"

I stopped petting his hair. "Parker, have you talked to anyone about this?"

His cheeks were dotted with pink. "I'm talking to you, aren't I?"

"I mean like… a therapist, babe. Someone who can help you work through all your feelings." I gave him a sad smile.

He shook his head. "No." Parker sighed. "I know I should. I just…"

"I know." Slinging an arm around his shoulder, I leaned my head against his. "But I'm here whenever you want to talk."

"Thank you, Audrey," he said, closing his eyes. "You have no idea how much I appreciate that you're in my life."

"Always," I responded, meaning it. "No matter what happens, I'll always be here for you, Parker."

We sat in silence for a while after that, just holding each other on his bed. Words weren't needed, not when we had each other.

Running my fingers through my curls, I separated out the ringlets, making them look like pretty waves. I'd finished Ella's hair and makeup already, sending her back to the event—though I suspected she'd end up making a pit stop at Cam's first, with the amount of texts they'd been sending back and forth.

It was officially the date of the spring formal, and with the way everything had been developing between Parker and me over the last week, it felt so much more real.

Like this really *was* a date.

We were still pretending to be in a relationship, and yet it was so much *more*.

Parker was picking me up at the sorority house, and then we were driving over together.

A lot of the girls had already left the house, leaving it much quieter than it had been an hour ago. I slipped my heels on, looking at my outfit in the mirror.

My floor-length gown was a dusty rose color, adorned with sparkles, and the neckline of the dress had roses that went all the way around. I'd fallen in love with it when I saw it, and it had been an obvious choice.

I got little butterflies as Parker's text came in, letting me know he had arrived.

Heading downstairs, I opened the front door, seeing him standing on the stoop in a suit and tie. Damn, he looked *good*.

And his tie... It was the color of my dress. He had matched *me*.

"Hi." He stepped in, pressing a soft kiss against my cheek.

I tucked a strand of hair behind my ear. "Hey."

"Wow." Parker's jaw dropped open. "You look..."

"Good, right?" I did a little spin for him, loving the way my pink formal dress rippled around me. "Does it get the fake boyfriend stamp of approval?"

He made a show of looking me up and down, and then nodded. "It's beautiful, Rosie."

My cheeks warmed. I like that he called me that. Not Aud. I always hated when people shortened Audrey. Ella called me Ro, short for my middle name, Rose. And Parker... Parker had always called me Rosie. His childhood nickname for me somehow held more meaning now.

"Thank you. You look very handsome yourself."

He adjusted his lapel. "Have to look good as your boyfriend, don't I?"

I giggled as he held out a hand, placing mine in his. Parker kissed the top of my hand. "Shall we?"

Nodding, he interlaced our fingers together, the two of us walking hand in hand to his car.

There was a giddy excitement I felt holding his hand like this, one that I tried to ignore before. But I couldn't ignore how much I liked it when he called himself my boyfriend, how much I liked him being the one by my side in everything I did.

Instead of Parker moving to open the car door for me, the way he always did, we stood facing each other, his eyes sweeping over my face like he was taking all of me in.

I couldn't help but do the same, studying his face. Those beautiful amber eyes, the streaks of gold in them even more apparent this close up. His long eyelashes, those cheekbones that anyone would be jealous of. His strong jaw. Those soft, kissable lips.

He was gorgeous.

And he was mine. My best friend. My everything.

"Audrey."

"Hmm?" I tried to ignore the butterflies as he tucked a strand of hair behind my ear.

He smiled. "I'm going to kiss you now."

"O-okay," I whispered, tilting up my face as he cupped my cheeks, bringing his down to meet me.

We'd kissed so many times, and yet, losing myself in this one was easy. Because it felt different.

There was a gravity here that I'd never felt before. Like maybe all this time, we'd just been circling around this. As if whatever trajectory we'd been on had been leading us here.

And I never wanted it to end.

CHAPTER 26
Parker

The venue for the sorority's spring formal was decked out in decorations to match the Moonlight Masquerade theme they'd picked. Everything was midnight blue and silver, and everyone was grinding and dancing in the middle of the room, under a ceiling of twinkle lights that almost looked like stars.

There were sorority girls and their dates everywhere, most in long, floor-length dresses and carrying masks, but in all honesty, I barely noticed them.

I only had eyes for one girl.

The one on my arm, whose eyes were wide as she took in the decor. The one who looked like a fairy princess tonight in her pink dress that sparkled with each step.

Audrey's sister was somewhere in the room—along with Cam, Ella's boyfriend, whom I still hadn't met—but I was content to just stay in our little bubble.

Because when it was just us, it was real. When other people were around, it was all an act. That felt backward, but it was true.

Some of her sorority sisters waved over at her, shouting her name. I recognized two of them as Suzie and Peggy, who I'd seen often over the last few months.

She gave me a tight smile. "I'm gonna go say hi."

Audrey was one of the most outgoing, extroverted people I knew, but I also knew how draining it could be for her. How she felt like she had to be happy all the time. That her role was to be the peppy, cheerful one.

There was a reason I liked my space. That I took longer to make friends, to warm up with people. I was perfectly happy staying behind and reading a book instead of going out to clubs or parties. But for her, I'd gladly put on a suit and tie.

I pressed a kiss to her cheek. "I'll go grab us something to drink, and then if you need me to rescue you, just give me the signal."

Audrey raised her eyebrows. "What's the signal?"

Chuckling, I leaned over, dropping my lips against her ear. "You'll know, *baby*."

Her cheeks turned the sweetest shade of pink as I walked away, heading to the refreshment table. I noticed she watched me go, her eyes glued to my ass.

I was definitely teasing her about that later.

"Having fun?" Ella asked me, coming to stand next to me.

"Depends on your definition of fun," I laughed, watching Audrey talk in an animated fashion, her face practically glowing with happiness. "But yeah. I am."

She gave me a small smile. "You're good for her."

"I hope so." Filling a glass with punch, I took a sip. The likelihood that someone had spiked it, considering all the fraternity guys here, was high, so it was worth a taste test first.

My girl's twin nudged my side. "No, you are. Audrey's always smiling, but for a while there, I could see how sad she was behind it. And then you came back into her life, and she started laughing again. You mean a lot to her, Parker. You always have."

"Thanks, Ella. She's lucky to have you as a sister."

Ella shook her head. "I'm the lucky one. She's always been the one that dragged me along to everything. Even joining the sorority was Audrey's idea. But I'm grateful because it led me here. If I hadn't been president, who knows if Cam and I would have met or ended up together? And Cam... he's it for me. I know he is." She bit her lip. "Audrey's got a big heart, but she's also a hopeless romantic. She dreams big. Just... don't break her heart, okay? I don't know if she can pick up the pieces a second time."

Don't break her heart? "That's the last thing I want," I reassured her.

Not that Ella had any idea what we were really doing. How we'd promised each other that we wouldn't fall in love with each other. That none of this was real. *For her.*

It was fake for her. Even if it wasn't fake for me. Not anymore. It hadn't been in a long time. Maybe not ever.

Because I'd wanted Audrey Rose ever since she walked back in my life.

"I care about her," I told Ella. "I always have."

When had I started loving her? I didn't even know. All I knew was I'd felt this way for a long time. I'd loved her growing up, but it was different now. I was *in* love with her.

"I know." She squeezed my shoulder, looking around the room. "I gotta get back to Cam, but have a good night. Take care of her."

"Always," I promised.

"Night, Parker." Ella waved to me as I wandered back over to my girl.

I found her surrounded by even more girls than before, everyone laughing and smiling. I looped an arm around her waist, pulling her against me. "Having fun?" I whispered in her ear, holding out the drink I'd brought for her.

"Hi, *baby*," Audrey said, taking the glass from me and sipping at the punch. The girls all giggled at our open display.

Pressing a kiss to her neck, I let her finish the drink before taking the empty glass and setting it on a nearby table.

"Want to dance?" I asked Audrey, holding out my hand to her.

"Yes," she replied.

"Sorry, ladies." I flashed them a perfect grin. "I'm going to steal away my girl now."

"Have fun!" Suzie shouted after us.

"But not too much fun!" Peggy added on.

Audrey wrapped an arm around my waist, practically collapsing into a fit of giggles as we headed to the dance floor.

Once her hand was in mine, my other resting on her waist as she leaned against my shoulder, I took in her expression. Eyes bright, a sparkle in them as she stared up at me.

"You good, Audrey?"

She nodded. "Even better now. But thank you for saving me from the interrogation."

"Of course." I chuckled.

"They were asking me about *you*, you know."

"Oh?" Smirking, I pulled her in tighter against me. "What about, sunshine?"

She ran her tongue over her bottom lip. "I'm not sure you want to know, Dream Boy." Her voice was breathy, and damn, I liked it when she called me that.

"Oh, now I *definitely* need to know, Rosie Girl."

She fiddled with my suit jacket as she hummed against me, both of us swaying in time with the music. "If you really must know, they brought up the night you stormed into the bar and carried me out of there. Pretty sure they were just jealous." Audrey patted my chest like she was feeling me up. "I mean, have you seen yourself?" She whistled. "Whatever girl you end up with is going to be really lucky, Parker."

"Right." My face fell. Because the girl I wanted to be with was standing right in front of me. Fuck. How could she not know that I wanted her? That she was the only person I saw when I imagined my future?

Because you haven't told her, my brain reminded me. *Because you're scared of losing her.*

Both of those things were true.

We kept dancing, moving in a slow circle

"Anyway, I didn't tell them about anything else between us." Her cheeks were pink. Fuck me, why did I have to find it so damn adorable? "I didn't want anyone to get the wrong idea, you know."

"And what is the wrong idea, Audrey?" I brushed my nose against hers. "Just so I know. So we're on the same page."

She bit her lip but said nothing, her violet eyes holding mine.

I dipped my head, lowering my words to barely more than a whisper. "You didn't want your friends to know I know what you look like when you come, hm? How you're such a good girl for me, fucking my fingers and imagining I'm filling you up? That all I can think about is the fact that I've tasted you—twice—but I still haven't seen you naked? Or is that not something your boyfriend would think about?"

Audrey's breath stuttered when she responded, "I thought we were taking things slow."

"We were." I pushed my stiff cock, already aching in my dress pants, against her. "But maybe I don't want to do that anymore, Audrey." Because I already knew I wanted her. That I wanted this. I wanted her to want that, too.

"I thought we were pretending," she said with a gasp. "That this was f-fake."

"Does this feel fake to you?" I groaned against her mouth. "I'm so tired of that word, Audrey. I think we should retire it from our vocabularies."

"You're my best friend," she insisted. "I can't lose you."

"Audrey." I squeezed her hand, looking around the two of us, and then pulled her off to the side. "You'll never lose me. Okay?"

"Okay." She nodded.

I wanted to tell her more. About how I felt about her. That this wasn't fake for me. That I loved her. But it was too soon, wasn't it?

Ella told me not to break her heart.

So instead, I just kept her in my arms, letting the music say the words I couldn't.

Hoping like hell that she'd choose to stay with me once all of this was over.

That I was enough for her.

Because she was the only one for me. And she always had been.

APRIL

"Can you try the lift one more time?" Mary asked, biting the end of a pen as she watched Audrey and I. We'd been practicing this piece of choreography for months, and today, we just weren't nailing it. Maybe something was off.

Maybe it was just the aftermath of this weekend that had us off-balance.

We were deep into technical rehearsals, and I couldn't believe how close we were getting to the actual musical performance.

It was insane to think that pretty soon, performance week would be here. Honestly, part of me couldn't wait for it to be over so I could breathe again. The last few weeks, I'd had three or four hours of lacrosse a day, plus four hours of musical rehearsals.

I'd barely had time to spend with Audrey. Normally, we had dinner together, though sometimes that was just spent in silence, shoveling food in before we headed to the theater building.

And what would happen when this was all over? Would she still want to do this?

I nodded, and Audrey looked at me, frowning. "Can we have a moment first?"

Our student director nodded. "Sure. Let's take a water break."

My girl grabbed my wrist, pulling me offstage and into the wings.

"Are you okay?"

"I—" I thought about the unanswered text on my phone. *I'll be there for the game next weekend. Can we get together and talk?* Did I want to see her? To talk about what had gone wrong in our relationship? No.

I just wanted to move on. Castleton had been my fresh start, and I was happier now. It wasn't just Audrey, though feeling like I had finally found my person certainly helped. The guys back at my old school had been like my brothers, and when that trust had broken, when they'd taken Raf's side over mine, it had hurt.

"Honestly, no." I scratched the back of my head. "I've just got a lot on my mind. It's messing with me."

She wrapped her arms around me, unprompted. "I'm here for you, you know. Whatever you need."

I kissed the top of my forehead. "Thank you. Best girlfriend I could have asked for."

Her eyes glittered with emotion. Maybe she noticed I didn't say *fake.*

Tilting her chin up, I stared into those violet irises for a beat before pressing a soft kiss against her lips. "It's my ex."

"Your ex?" Audrey repeated.

"Yeah. She texted me. Apparently, she's coming to the game this weekend."

"What?" Her eyes widened, and she furrowed her brows. "But... why?"

I sighed. "That's the question of the hour, really. I guess she wants to talk."

"Do you think she's trying to get you back?" Audrey wrapped her arms around herself. She was wearing a pretty pink wrap sweater over her dress today, all of her hair piled on top of her head in a tight bun except for her bangs and a few strands in the front.

God, she was beautiful.

A snort slipped from me before I could stop it. "She'd be stupid to try. I don't want to be with her."

Audrey fidgeted with her sleeve. "You don't?"

"No." I curled one of her loose strands of hair around my finger. "I don't."

I didn't want my ex—I wanted her. I hoped she knew that.

She let out a breath. "Okay. Should we go try that lift again?"

Kissing her again, a little deeper this time, I intertwined our fingers. "Yeah. Let's go, sunshine."

Her smile was enough to brighten my entire day, all thoughts of my ex and my former teammates coming here forgotten for now.

My heart was racing as I stood in midfield, waiting for play to resume. It was the third period of the game, and we were up by two, but it wasn't a big enough lead for me to feel comfortable. We'd won the last face-off, but lost the ball, and the opposing team had gotten the last goal.

We both had our best face-off players out there—Taylor for CU, while Dallas, one of my old buddies, was on the opposing side. The two met in the middle, leaning down toward the ball as the ref made the call, holding position until the whistle blew. Finally, we were back in play, both battling for the ball. Taylor pulled it away, sending it towards me, and I was immediately in motion.

Scooping up the ball, I rocked it back and forth with the head, keeping it in place as I raced to the net. The shot clock was ticking, telling me I had less than sixty seconds left to attempt a shot on goal.

I could see Samuel out of the corner of my eye, ready to take the pass as the other team's players caught up with me. Lining myself up to send the ball to him, Raf came out of nowhere, swinging his stick forcefully at me, taking the wind out of me.

The ball fell to the ground, and I winced, thankful for all the protective gear on my head and chest. Though I was sure at the angle he'd gotten me, I'd have a nasty bruise on my arm later.

A whistle blew, thank fuck.

"Rhode Island number thirty-three, two-minute penalty for slashing!" The ref made the hand signal, and Rafael glared at me as he headed to the penalty box.

Samuel came up to me, patting me on the back. "What the fuck was that for? That felt personal."

I took a long pull from my water bottle as I sat on the bench. "It was." How could I explain my girlfriend had cheated on me with him? I didn't know why he was trying to get revenge on me, though. It should have been the other way around.

Except, I didn't care. Maybe I should, but I didn't.

He raised an eyebrow as Derek came over, standing in front of us. "You good, Maxwell?"

I nodded. "Will be, after we kick their asses."

"That's my boy." He pumped his fist in the air. "Let's get 'em."

CHAPTER 27

Audrey

O h god," I gasped. "Do you think he's okay?"

Parker had taken a hard hit from one of the other players. I was sure it wasn't easy to face your old team. That they were still in the same conference was crazy enough. Let alone everything that had happened with his ex-girlfriend and old teammates.

"That looked like it was on purpose," Ella observed. My twin sister was with me in the stands, a fact that made me happier than I could express. She was wearing a pale blue Castleton Chipmunks t-shirt and jeans, while I was wearing Parker's jersey and my favorite white swishy skirt. It was a beautiful day —the sun was high in the sky, and everything felt *right*.

Rehearsals this week had been amazing. Especially when we'd hidden away and kissed behind the curtains, and I felt like a giggling high schooler sneaking around with her first boyfriend. I hadn't even been this smitten with the actual first guy I'd dated, which is how I knew everything with Parker was different.

And I was happy. So happy.

But also, a little worried about my man.

The player who hit him was sent to the penalty box, and I bit my lip, watching Parker head back to the bench. Normally, he played a longer shift before heading back, but I was sure they were just making sure he was okay.

"It gets a little rough sometimes," I admitted to my sister. "Sticks and all of that. But that's why they have helmets and all that padding." Still, at least the helmet protected his face. I would hate for anything to happen to his smile. God knows the hockey players lost enough teeth for the rest of the student athletes.

Ella nudged me. "So, how's everything been going between you two? You know we haven't really talked about it."

"Like you and Cam, huh?" The semester had been so busy, it felt like we had barely seen each other lately. Still, she was my twin sister, and we'd always been so close.

She blushed. "He told me he loved me."

"And?" I bumped my shoulder into hers in return.

"And I said I loved him too." Her blue eyes were bright, Ella's face glowing with happiness.

"When did this happen?"

My twin looked at the ground, ignoring my eyes. "Before formal. When his dad was in town."

"I can't believe you didn't tell me sooner!"

She rested her hand over her heart. "I still can't believe it's real, honestly. But everything's been amazing. And we're looking at places to move into next semester."

"Wow." My eyes widened. "That's big."

She nodded. "Yeah, but I'm ready for it. It's been a busy year, being the president, and I think it'll be nice to spend our senior year living in one place. Plus, then I don't have to keep sneaking in and out of the fraternity house to spend the night with Cam." Her cheeks were even redder this time. "What about you?"

"Well, it's..." I worried my lower lip into my mouth. "It's great. But we haven't, ah..." I blushed.

"What?" She frowned.

"We haven't had sex yet," I whispered.

"Why not?"

"I don't know… I want it to be special for us." For him, since it was his first time. I didn't want it to be some rushed or hurried encounter because my first time definitely hadn't been sunshine and roses.

Ella nodded. "It will be, though. I mean, just look at him. Plus, the way he looks at you? Wow."

God, he was glorious. He'd taken his helmet off, running his fingers through the light brown strands, squirting water from his water bottle on his face.

I fanned myself. "Yeah. He's…" I practically moaned, just thinking about how good it felt when he went down on me. It felt like we hadn't had a spare moment together lately—not since the formal—but god, I was wet just thinking about it. "I never could have expected him."

"That's how I feel about Cam. That's how I know you two are going to make it." She rested her head on my shoulder. "I'm really glad you've found your person, Audrey."

I had, hadn't I? He was everything to me. My best friend, my boyfriend. And it felt fast, but I knew that what I felt for him was different than it had ever been before. Because I'd never felt this overwhelming affection and warmth in my chest just from *looking* at someone before.

Maybe she was right.

I smiled. "Thanks, Ells. I think I needed to hear that."

"Anytime, Ro."

Her childhood nickname for me made the warmth in my chest expand even more, and we settled back in, watching the game and cheering when our team blocked a shot on goal by the opposing team.

Finally, the third period came to an end—luckily, we were still up by two, since neither team had gotten another goal in the last few minutes as we'd been talking.

Unfortunately, there was only a two-minute break before the next period started, so I couldn't head down to check on Parker.

THEY WON, luckily without too much incident. There was a point that I thought Parker and the same guy who had gotten the penalty before were going to get into a fight, but it was clear that he was holding himself back. I didn't understand why they'd go after him. Parker was the one who got cheated on. He was the one that should be upset.

But maybe they were pissed that he'd left the team?

I picked at my nail beds as I headed down towards the field. Ella had given me a long hug before she left, promising to talk soon, and I'd needed that. Needed this moment with my twin.

It was strange to think that at some point, we'd part ways. We weren't sharing a room anymore, but we still lived in the same house. Next semester, we wouldn't even have that. She'd be living with Cam, and I'd… what? Still be living in the sorority house?

We didn't have to live there, especially as seniors, but we could. Except, I liked the idea of having my own space. Liked the idea of Parker and I being able to spend time with each other *alone*, without worrying about anyone hearing us. Without having to leave the door open or stay in common areas.

I hadn't even thought about where I'd live next semester until Ella had brought it up, but suddenly, I was eager to make plans. Parker and I, though… it was too soon, wasn't it? We hadn't even talked about what we were. What this was.

Even if it wasn't fake anymore.

I stood on the edge of the field, smiling as Parker ran over to me like always, dropping his helmet on the ground before picking me up in his arms and spinning me around. It was practically our tradition now, and I giggled, a giant smile filling my face.

"That's my Rosie Girl," he said, his gaze holding mine. "Thanks for coming."

"Of course. You couldn't drag me away. Especially since you

taught me about the crease, and I understand what's going on now." I cupped his cheeks, looking at him in concern as I scanned him for injuries. "Are you okay? You got hit pretty hard."

"I'll be fine, sunshine," Parker reassured me, setting me back on the ground but keeping his arms wrapped around me. "Nothing I haven't dealt with before."

Still, watching him get hurt wasn't fun. Standing on tiptoes, I leaned in close to his ear. "I'll make it all better later," I murmured, pressing my lips against his neck.

He dropped another kiss to my lips. "Looking forward to it."

Someone cleared their throat, and we pulled apart a few inches to see who it was.

A girl approached us, but it wasn't anyone I recognized. She must have come from the other team because she was wearing their school's colors. "Hey, Parker."

From the way he stiffened, I had a pretty good idea of who he was. Parker's ex.

"Millie." He just dipped his head.

She was absolutely gorgeous, with dark hair that she had twisted back away from her face, wearing a black and purple jersey that I assumed belonged to her current boyfriend.

"Hi." I stuck out my hand towards the girl. "I'm Audrey. Parker's *girlfriend*."

"Oh." She looked between the two of us for a moment. Like my hand on his chest and his wrapped around my waist didn't spell out enough. "I see. I'd come over to ask if you'd gotten my text, but…"

A text? I looked at Parker, hoping the look of confusion didn't show on my face.

"I did. But I don't need to talk, Millie." He looked at me. "I've moved on. I'm happy now."

She sighed. "Look, you don't have to forgive me. I know what I did was crappy."

I scoffed. That was an understatement. "You think?"

Millie glared at me, her eyes screaming, *did I ask you?* "Still, you left the team. Raf was your best friend."

"Was he? Because in my world, a best friend wouldn't fuck your girlfriend." Parker's tone was like a sword slicing through thorns. Lethal. With no room for argument.

She blanched and then shrugged. "It's not like you would, either."

My jaw dropped. How *dare* she? I stepped forward, ready to fight her myself, when Parker placed a hand on my back. I looked up at him, and he just nodded. Like he had this.

"I told you I wanted to take things slow. You were the one who asked me out. I'm sorry that I couldn't give you what you wanted, but that was your choice."

"Because I *liked* you!" His ex shouted. "God, is it so bad to want your boyfriend to pay attention to you? Raf does. He spoils me with presents and dotes on me. That was all I wanted. Someone to care about me. But you never did."

"I'm sorry," Parker said, shaking his head. "It was never you, Millie. It was always me."

I couldn't imagine Parker not doing those things because he'd always done them for me. But maybe there was a deeper reason. Something I hadn't even let myself consider yet.

Millie turned her attention to me. "It's because of *you*," she said in a whisper. "I recognize you. From the photo."

"Mills—" Parker cut her off, a slight shake of his head.

My eyes widened. "Photo?"

The guy who'd hit Parker during the game came around, slinging a shoulder around Millie and interrupting us. "Everything good here, babe?" He kissed her cheek.

"McKennon," Parker said, his voice like ice. "What's your fucking problem?" He tightened his grip around me. "Did you seriously think trying to antagonize me was a good idea?"

"Well, it's not like you would talk to me. Either of us. I know Millie texted you." He shrugged. "You ran away from the team, from our friendship, without even talking to me. I just wanted…"

"Raf…" Millie said, patting his stomach. "It doesn't matter. Not anymore." There was resignation in her voice, and I wondered how hard that must be. To accept that your boyfriend never really gave you the time of day. She'd fucked him over, but maybe it hadn't been fair to her either. She wasn't the villain—it was just a bad situation.

Even if my insides burned with jealousy, thinking about the two of them together. Even if I wanted to gouge her eyes out just for looking at *my* man.

"We were brothers," Raf said. "I thought you'd be the one standing next to me at my wedding one day."

Parker looked across the field, towards his team. Samuel was with his girlfriend, the two of them laughing, and some of the other guys I knew were also crowded around, celebrating. "I've learned a lot about friends this year, Rafael. And the thing is, I would never hurt a friend the way you betrayed me. I don't regret transferring. Above all, because I found Audrey, and there's nothing I wouldn't do for her."

I blushed, feeling the sincerity in his words.

"I'm sorry," he offered again. "But I don't think we can be friends."

Raf nodded, not saying another word.

"Bye, Millie." Parker nodded at her. "I hope you have a good life."

"You too, Parker." She looked at the two of us, still standing so close together. "I hope you got everything you wanted."

"I did."

My insides were warm. Gooey. I definitely wanted to show him my appreciation now.

Sliding my left hand into his, I squeezed tightly as they walked away. "Are you okay? After all of… that?" I gestured in front of us.

"God, you're fucking incredible, do you know that?" he

rasped against my ear. "Don't know what I did to get such an amazing girlfriend."

I hadn't even done anything but been there for him, but I suspected that was all he needed. Someone to stand by his side.

Running a hand up his jaw, I pushed my fingers through his hair. "The better question, *baby,* is what didn't you do?"

He nuzzled his face into the crook of my neck. "Want to go home?"

I nodded, poking at his chest, still covered in his pads and equipment. "But go change first. You're all sweaty."

Sweaty, and yet… delicious. He was so hot like this, and I was practically salivating at even the faintest of touches.

He smirked, nipping at my lips. "Okay, baby. Meet you at the car." Parker handed me his keys.

I grinned, already looking forward to showing him just how much he meant to me when I got my mouth on him. As much as I was dying to have sex with him, I couldn't deny that the foreplay had been better than anything I'd ever experienced before, and I was content with that.

For now.

THIS WAS IT. Our final full dress rehearsal. The musical was next week.

And Parker was… not here. He was late. I was already dressed in my costume for act one, the brown fabric of my skirt billowing around me as I stood at the door, biting my lip.

I knew he'd been stressed with lacrosse, and his coach wasn't going easy on him, but we'd made it work. He'd been here all semester. Except for now, with so little time left.

"Where is he?" Professor Woods said with a frown, looking down at her watch.

"He said he had practice but that he'd be here," I said, shaking my head.

She squeezed my arm. "It's not the end of the world. We can send in the understudy to run lines with you."

I nodded. "Yeah. That makes sense."

The understudies for both our roles would still perform the musical during one of the other shows, but if Parker wasn't here for any reason, then I'd play opposite him instead. Luckily, it wasn't Duke.

That was my saving grace. He'd been kicked out of CU for the semester and told not to come within one hundred feet of me or he'd be charged with stalking. Ever since all of that had ended, I'd felt more comfortable around campus.

Still, I didn't want to perform with anyone else. I had in rehearsals—we both had—but it wasn't the same chemistry I felt when we performed together.

Parker might have been an athlete, but he was mesmerizing on stage. The grace and poise he brought to the table—plus his singing voice? It was enough to have me dropping my panties and begging him to eat me out.

Something he'd done last Saturday after his lacrosse game, making me come twice before he'd let me touch him. Even if we still hadn't had sex, or even taken our clothes off, things between us were so hot and heavy that I knew it was only a matter of time before we did.

CHAPTER 28

Parker

I'm so sorry I'm late. Fuck." I grimaced, coming to a stop outside of the dressing room.

Mary, the student director, just shook her head at me, a clipboard in her hand. "Hurry and get changed! We had to prep the understudy. They're about to go on stage."

I shoved my backpack in a locker, already stripping out of my athletic shorts and sweatshirt to pull on my costume. Ella had fitted me in it, making alterations, and even though I felt a little ridiculous in the get-up, I had to admit I looked every bit the part.

Final rehearsal? We had this.

I caught Audrey's eye as I stood in the wings off stage left. She was on the opposite side, her entrance coming from the right. While I wasn't in the first scene, she had her reveal after the beginning where they explained the Princess's birth and origins, about how she was hidden away to protect her.

Her theater friends were on stage, the three seniors who doted after her like big sisters. At one point, they'd cornered me, telling me they'd kick me in the balls if I hurt their precious little rose. I was slightly terrified of them, so I'd agreed, even if I didn't plan on hurting her. Never.

Ella was in the back, flitting around and checking everyone's costumes to make sure they were all perfect. From what I understood, she'd designed all of them, though she hadn't had the role to make every single costume of the show—that would be too much work for any one person. Before I'd volunteered to do this, I'd known very little about musical theater. Now, I felt like I had a much better idea of what was going on.

She gave me a thumbs up, and I smiled. I was glad Audrey's twin seemed to approve of us. Especially since they'd always been close, and that meant we would always be in each other's lives.

If I had anything to do with it, we would.

I'd been trying to plan something special for Audrey after the performance weekend was over. Unfortunately, lacrosse was getting in the way. I already couldn't wait for the season to be over, but once it was, it also meant the semester would be too. Which meant less time together, not more.

There had to be a better solution to that problem, but I wouldn't go there now. Not when we still had so much to figure out between us.

Audrey's eyes met mine, and her face lit up. *That's my girl.*

I grinned, waving at her, and she almost missed her cue to go on stage because she was so busy staring at me.

Ella chuckled next to me.

"What?" I asked, watching her sew a few extra stitches into one of the ensemble's bodices.

"She doesn't even see it," my girl's twin murmured. "But damn, I've never seen her like this. So smitten. You two are so cute, it almost makes me sick."

"Thanks. I think?"

She patted my shoulder. "Go get her. Be her knight in shining armor."

I wasn't sure if she was talking about the musical—or about real life.

Audrey flopped down onto my bed, wearing one of my lacrosse t-shirts.

"How are you feeling?" I asked her, pressing a kiss to Audrey's forehead before going over to switch off the overhead light. "With opening day being tomorrow and all."

I could count the nights on one hand that she'd spent in her own bed over the last week. Maybe it was just because we were trying to spend time together, even as the semester ramped up and we got busier and busier. Neither one of us wanted to be apart.

Still, we fell asleep as soon as our heads hit the pillow.

"Good, I think. It's still a little surreal, you know? But I'm excited. And it sounds like they almost sold out the theater, which is always good."

I hummed. "Of course they'll be there for you, sunshine." Because her people showed up for her.

Slipping under the sheets, I drew her close to me, burying my nose in her hair so I could inhale her sweet scent. There was probably something wrong with me that I got hard just from sniffing my girlfriend's hair, but damn, I wanted her.

It was like an unspoken vow between us. We hadn't talked about it. To be fair, there wasn't time for anything else, considering how late rehearsals finished each night and I had to get up early every morning for practice. I was barely fitting in my gym session every day, let alone studying for my architecture degree.

Not for the first time, I questioned why I was getting such a difficult degree, but I loved what I was learning. I always thought it was fascinating, planning and designing buildings. One day, I'd get to oversee the construction of something I'd built, and that thought excited me more than I could properly describe.

It would be worth it, in the end. Plus, I liked the idea that I could work almost anywhere with my degree. It meant that if

Audrey wanted me to follow her to New York as she chased her dreams of being on Broadway, I could. I'd already started researching firms in New York City, finding internships I could apply to, and starting the processes. After all, in just over a year, I'd have my degree and my certification.

And though I might have had family connections, since my dad knew people in just about every field thanks to his job in finance, I wanted to do it myself.

Audrey let out a little yawn. "Do you think your teammates are going to come watch you?"

"Probably." They'd teased me a little about it at the beginning of the semester, but now, I think they thought it was cool. Plus, the single ones had realized how many girls there were in the theater department and had sniffed around. "They haven't told me when, though."

She cuddled up against my chest. "You know, you make a fantastic pillow."

"Happy to be of service, baby." I played with her hair, enjoying the act of just holding her. Fuck, I loved her. So damn much. It was practically bursting out of me, wanting to tell her.

Not yet. The musical was almost here, and I'd tell her after that.

"You know, I just remembered something," Audrey whispered. "Millie said something about a photo of me?"

"Oh. Right." I switched back on the light, untangling us so I could get out of bed. I hated leaving her arms, but I knew this was important.

Grabbing my wallet, I pulled out a piece of paper I'd kept in there for years.

I held it out for her, watching as she unfolded the photo that I looked at often in the years we were apart.

"This is—" She looked up at me, eyes wide with surprise.

"Us," I answered. We were eleven and twelve in the photo, our final summer together before I moved away. She had pigtails and a cute pink gingham dress on, beaming at the camera next to me.

Audrey shook her head. "What does this mean?"

"I didn't realize Millie had seen me looking at it. I found it when I went home for break freshman year of college in some old stuff. And I don't know… I just kept it with me after that. Kept *you* with me all this time, even when we didn't talk." I shrugged.

"Parker." Her eyes were filled with tears. "This is so sweet. Damn you."

I rubbed my thumb under her eyes. "I know now why there wasn't anyone else, Audrey Rose. Why I never wanted to be with anyone else. Because all my life, it's always been you. I was always waiting for you." Tipping her chin up, I brought our lips together, repeatedly, until she opened for me, letting me slip my tongue inside. It was unhurried, like both of us knew we had all the time in the world to get lost in each other.

Even though it felt like our time was running out.

She hummed, her eyes already getting droopy once again. I knew she was exhausted, and we both needed our rest.

Resting my chin on her head, I tucked her into my body, the two of us falling asleep just like that. Like we were always meant to be right here, together.

OPENING NIGHT.

What a *rush*. It was strange to think that we were here.

I hadn't seen Audrey in the last few hours, but I knew she'd been here early to help with hair and makeup. That was the thing about my girl—even after she did her own, she always helped the others who needed it, and every transformation was stunning. It somehow enhanced each person's individual beauty instead of distracting from it or covering it up. Like she was a makeup fairy, flitting around and dusting her magic all over them.

The thought made me smile because that was just who she was. She didn't even think about whether she should help others. She just did.

She was a star in every way, shape, and form. The brightest damn star in the sky. That was why she was my sunshine.

"Five minutes!" One of the tech crew called out.

"Be right there," I responded, running my fingers through my hair one last time.

And then I grabbed my surprise, heading next door to set it up for later. Knocking on the door, I poked my head in to make sure everyone else had exited before sneaking into the women's dressing room.

I found Audrey's makeup kit and stuff in front of one of the mirrors, pulling a vase of pink roses out from behind my back and leaving them on the counter in front of the bright lights. Fluffing the flowers, I made sure to position it so the note with her name was in the front. Hopefully, no one else would mistake them as theirs.

Hurrying out and back to the theater, I found Audrey peeking out of the closed curtains.

"Do you see anyone?" I whispered.

She jumped back. "Oh. Parker." A pretty pink blush formed on her cheeks. "Hi."

"Hi." I tucked a strand of hair back behind her ear. Her act one costume was more woodland princess compared to her act two dress, but she looked stunning in both of them.

I resisted kissing her, though, because I didn't want to mess up her stage makeup.

"You look beautiful."

"Thank you. You look very handsome yourself. My dashing prince."

"Don't forget your knight in shining armor," I joked.

"Ah, yes. But you haven't slayed the dragon yet, remember?"

I nodded at the curtain. "So, anyone we know?"

Audrey bit her lip. "I saw my parents. A ton of my sorority sisters. And…"

I raised an eyebrow. "And?"

"Maybe you should look yourself."

I laughed. "Alright."

Taking her position and parting the curtains just barely—enough to get a small peek—I saw what felt like an entire row of my teammates.

Here for opening night.

"Well, fuck." I rubbed at my chest. "I didn't expect that."

She giggled, the sound melodic, drifting through the air.

"Positions, everyone!" Mary said, walking through and doing her last-minute checks. But I knew everyone was in place. She ran this place like a tight ship. The orchestra, the lighting team, the sound team—everyone was a finely tuned piece of the puzzle. And they were all necessary for tonight to go off without a hitch. Without every single one of them, there was no way for the performers on stage to shine or for my girl to absolutely dazzle the crowd.

"Happy opening day, Rosie Girl."

"Happy opening day, Parker. Break a leg." She winked.

And then we headed separate ways, the introduction music playing as the show was announced and the curtain opened.

I watched the opening number from the wings, unable to keep my eyes off of Audrey the entire time she sang.

My star, my everything.

CHAPTER 29

Audrey

atching from the side stage as my friends—my theater family, really—performed was nothing short of magical. There were very few scenes in the show where I wasn't on stage, so each moment of break I had involved some sort of costume change, modification, or switching out of props. We'd rehearsed each piece so much, from staging to running through it, that it was practically second nature now.

I couldn't imagine doing anything but this with my life.

Maybe one day, after I was ready to settle down with someone, that might change, but I loved musical theater. My parents hadn't quite understood at first. I knew Ella was in the same boat with her career. It wouldn't be easy, but it was so fulfilling. Seeing the audience's faces light up, the way the crowd reacted to each shift in music, all of it was exhilarating.

But the pride in my parents' eyes as they watched me dance and sing meant more to me than anyone else's. This wasn't my first role, but it was my first leading one, and I was so touched to see them there. Cam was sitting beside our parents, looking surprisingly calm even though I knew my dad could be a little overbearing. Ella was in the back, helping with changes for the ensemble that had multiple roles.

Most people had no idea how much truly went into a production like this, even for college.

And Parker.

God, he was incredible.

I loved him more than I could even describe. Maybe he felt it, too. I hoped he did.

Technically, this was it. Our deadline. Because originally, we'd only agreed to fake date until the end of the musical. Even though we'd only been fake dating to get Duke to leave me alone. Not that it had worked until he'd been suspended. And yet, we kept up the ruse.

Except it felt like everything had changed.

What was happening between us? We hadn't talked about it. Except for the last week, I'd slept in his arms every night. He'd confessed to me he'd been waiting for me, even when he didn't know it.

I mean, *swoon*. How could that not make your heart melt?

All I wanted was to pin him down and have my way with him, but I knew the real reason we hadn't gone further yet. There was something unspoken between us. Like we both wanted it to mean something.

Would he end it now that the musical was over? We didn't need to fake date anymore. If I confessed how I was really feeling, would everything be different? I didn't want anything to change.

Because I loved the way we were.

During intermission, my sister found me in the dressing room, wrapping her arms around me. I'd already started redoing my hair, fixing it for my second act dress.

"You're so amazing up there, Ro. I'm so damn proud of you."

"Thank you." My eyes filled with tears. "But look around us, Ells. This couldn't have happened without you."

She gave me a huge smile as we pulled apart. "I know most

people can't imagine doing college with their siblings, but I'm so glad I have you. That we've gotten to take classes together and experience everything at CU together."

I shoved her arm. "Don't get all sappy with me now. You can't make me cry before I have to go back on."

She let out a little giggle. "Did you see Cam is out there with our parents? He insisted on coming even though I'm not actually *in* the musical."

"Yeah." I re-pinned a few of my curls. "Of course he is. You could walk him like a dog, babe."

My twin chuckled, and I bit my lip, looking at her through the lit up mirror.

"Ella…" I dropped my head onto her shoulder, letting out a deep sigh. "How did you know?"

"Know what?"

"That Cam was the one." Biting my lip, I looked up at her. "That you loved him."

"For a while, I didn't. But it was in every action of his. The way he took care of me. The way he was so patient with me, loving me while he waited for me to catch up. I pushed him away because I was scared, but when I stepped back, I realized that he'd been there for me all along. He understands me in a way I'm not even sure I understand myself. And he loves me even with all of my flaws. Maybe even more so because of them. So I guess I just… knew." She cocked her head. "Is this about Parker?"

"How'd you guess?" I said, a watery laugh coming from me. But I wasn't going to cry. *I wasn't.* "But we're not like you and Cam. Parker and I are best friends. And…" I lowered my voice. "It was all fake."

"Was it?" My twin asked, raising an eyebrow.

I ran my hands over my bare arms, hugging myself. "Yeah. At least… I thought it was. And then it stopped feeling fake, and it felt so… *real.*"

"And what do you want now?" Ella asked. "Because if you want him, if you love him, you need to tell him, Audrey."

I nodded. "I—"

"Hey, Audrey," a girl in the ensemble came over, holding a vase with pink roses in them. "I think someone left these for you. They were on your station with all of your makeup, but I know you haven't gotten over there yet."

I'd been so busy talking to Ella that I hadn't even noticed.

"Oh." I ran my fingers over the flowers. "They're beautiful."

My sister squeezed my shoulder. "Tell him," she insisted.

"I will," I promised. After the show.

When we were alone—that was when I'd tell him how I felt. That I wanted more. That I wanted everything.

Including him.

THE LIFT WAS FLAWLESS. And the kiss? Perfect.

The curtain closed after we took our final bows, the entire crowd—a completely packed theater—cheering for us.

Opening night was done.

"We did it!" someone cried, and everyone cheered. Hugs and laughter filled the stage before everyone headed back to the dressing rooms to get out of their costumes, hanging them up so they'd be ready for the next performance.

And there he was. Parker. My boyfriend. The fact that it was supposed to be fake was something I was trying really hard to remind myself of.

He opened his arms like he knew exactly where I wanted to be.

Running, I threw myself into them. He caught me, spinning me around as I looped my arms around his neck.

"You were amazing, baby."

I blushed. "Thank you. Not so bad yourself, Parker Phillip."

"Audrey Rose, I believe we survived the first night."

"Now we just have to do it like four more times," I joked.

Parker chuckled. "With you, that'll be easy." He rubbed his nose against mine. "Best partner I could have asked for."

"How'd you get so good at this?" I asked, raising an eyebrow.

He smirked, curling his hands around my waist and pulling me closer. "I stopped acting."

"What?" I gaped. "That doesn't make any sense. You're *supposed* to be acting."

Parker shrugged. "Don't need to. Turns out I'm pretty good at this boyfriend thing without even trying."

I took a step back, fisting my hands in my dress. "But I'm… I'm just your fake girlfriend, right?"

"Rosie." His voice was tight.

I shook my head, looking at the floor. "It's my fault. I knew what this was going into it, and I shouldn't have gotten my—"

He kissed me to shut me up, and my eyes widened.

"Rosie Girl." Parker's fingers brushed my chin, forcing me to look up into his. "Will you stop freaking out and listen to me?"

Worrying my bottom lip into my mouth, I nodded.

There was no one else around, and Parker kept his hold of my chin, those gold-flecked eyes staring into mine.

"When we agreed to do this, to fake date, we set a deadline. Yeah? That we'd do it until the end of the musical so Duke would leave you alone." I nodded, still not saying anything, because my heart was in my throat. "But he hasn't been here in over a month, baby, and here we are. Still dating."

"Yeah." I bit my lip. "But—"

"Audrey." Parker silenced me with the *tsk* of his tongue. "We're together." He dropped his head, burying his nose in my hair and inhaling. Just like he did every night when we shared his bed. "I hate being apart from you, and we've spent almost every single night together lately, and I—" His words were a balm to my anxious heart. I'd needed to hear them, and now that I had, well…

"Parker," I responded. "Shut up and kiss me."

He scooped me up into his arms, complying with my request. His hands dug into my hips, and I curled mine over his shoulders, standing on my tiptoes despite my heels that added a good two or three inches, and I moaned as his mouth covered mine hungrily, his tongue tracing my lips, sending shivers of desire racing through me.

I let out a small moan as he crushed me against him, and then—

Someone turned the lights out.

A giggle burst free from me. "We should probably go."

"Yeah," he rasped. "Let's get out of here."

THANKFULLY, the dressing room was empty when we got back to it, and Parker carried us both inside, flipping the lock behind us before his mouth slammed back onto mine.

He pressed me up against the door, his lips delving to find mine, kissing me thoroughly. Passionately. *Hard.* It was a claiming kiss. The straps of my dress fell off my shoulders, and Parker's knee was between mine.

"Parker," I moaned against his mouth, rocking against his leg to get some sort of relief.

When he pulled away, I nibbled on his lower lip.

"Fuck," he groaned, pulling my lips back to his and brushing his tongue over mine, again and again, until I was a panting, writhing mess. "I just can't hold myself back with you."

I ran my lips down his neck. "So don't. You don't have to hold yourself back. You can have me."

Parker's eyes were dark with need, and I wanted him to lose control. To take what he wanted—because what I wanted was *him.*

Cupping his erection, I practically drank in his sharp exhale of breath. "I want you," I murmured, stroking him over his pants.

I needed these damn costumes off *now*.

He groaned. "You have no idea how badly I want you. But I don't have anything on me. And I definitely don't want to fuck you for the first time in a dressing room."

Letting out a whimper, I nodded. He was right, and I knew it. I wanted our first time to be special, after all. But I also wanted to show him how much this meant to me. That he'd done all of this for *me*.

Toying with the straps of my dress, I let them fall down my shoulders, leaving them bare for him.

"You're the most beautiful thing I've ever seen," Parker said, coming to stand in front of me and pressing his lips against my skin.

Turning around, I swept my hair over one shoulder, exposing my back to him. "Will you… unzip me?"

I could hear him swallow roughly, and then his fingers brushed over my spine, finding the hook and eye and undoing it before dragging the zipper slowly down my skin. It was torture in the best way, igniting all of my senses.

My dress fell from my hips, leaving me in just my nude leotard that I wore underneath my costume. I shimmed the rest of it off, picking it up and draping it over the chair next to me.

"My parents are probably wondering where we are," I whispered, catching Parker's eyes as he undid his brocade vest, sliding it off, and then undoing the black jacket he wore underneath.

He groaned as he took in my body. "Fuck. I know." His hands came up, cupping my breasts through the leo. "But all I want right now is to taste you."

My eyes fluttered shut as he pushed the fabric down, exposing the cups of my bra, and then he pushed that off too, freeing my tits to the air. With the first swipe of his tongue over my nipples, they were hard, and I let out a small moan.

"We need to change," I said, hardly more than a whimper as he sucked one of the hardened peaks into his mouth. "Parker— oh my *God*."

"It's a crime that I haven't gotten my mouth on these before." With his free hand, he flicked my other nipple with his thumb before pinching and pulling at it in the most delicious way.

"I know." I shut my eyes, enjoying the feeling of his tongue and teeth as he nipped, sucked, and soothed my breasts.

Why had we never done this before? It was like there had been some invisible line we hadn't crossed. If we weren't naked with each other, the orgasms hadn't meant anything. But now, this meant so much more.

"Just let me make you come, and then we can go see your parents," he begged.

How could I say no to that when I was already soaked? Nodding, Parker picked me up in his arms, carrying me over to the little couch in the middle of the dressing room that I'd never been more grateful for.

He kneeled in front of me, unstrapping my heels and sliding my feet out of them before dropping them to the floor—each hitting the ground in a thunk—before he stood back up, his eyes tracing every inch of my body as he peeled the leotard off the rest of the way, not even letting me help him pull it down my thighs.

"I need you," I begged, unhooking my bra from behind and letting it join my base layer on the floor. "Please."

Pushing me down to a seated position, he pulled my legs apart, not even bothering to take off my tights. No, instead, he ripped the fabric over my crotch, pushing my panties aside so he could plunge two fingers inside of me.

"*Yes*," I cried out.

"Fuck," he panted against my lips. "You're so wet. You needed this, huh, baby? Need your boyfriend to fuck you with his fingers?"

Whimpering, I nodded, letting the sensations take over as he put his mouth back on my tit, sucking and lavishing them with attention as he worked his fingers inside of me. Each stroke brought me higher and higher, and I was so close to coming apart in his arms.

"Good girl," he praised. "Taking my fingers so well. But you need more, don't you? Don't worry, I won't make you beg for it." He added a third finger, and I was so blissfully full.

Parker rubbed his thumb over my clit, bringing his mouth up to mine as I screamed his name. Like he knew I wouldn't be able to hold back.

I was languid in his arms, practically floating on air after that orgasm, and then he dropped fully to his knees, burying his head between my legs as he drank up my release, licking me clean. And fuck, I was already so close to another orgasm. If he kept this up, it wouldn't take much more.

"Can you come for me again?" He rasped, pulling away from me for a moment so I could see my wetness shining from his lips. "I've been such a good boy, haven't I, Rosie Girl?" He dragged his tongue over my entrance, flattening it against my clit before swirling it in a circle. "I want you to soak my face."

And then he delved back inside me, using his tongue and mouth to bring me back to the edge, palming his cock through his costume pants. I was sure he was painfully hard, but I already knew from experience that he prioritized my orgasm over his own, like it gave him pleasure to see me satisfied. And fuck, if that wasn't the hottest thing of all.

I was limp, boneless, and well sated when he finally pulled away, giving me one last lick before readjusting my panties over me. My tights had a giant hole in the crotch now, but at least no one would notice that during dinner.

Still, my cheeks were pink as we re-dressed, pulling our street clothes on.

Parker licked his lips. "So sweet." He caught my eye and

winked. "Don't worry, baby. There's more where that came from later."

I couldn't *wait*.

CHAPTER 30

Parker

I love the flowers, by the way," Audrey murmured after we cleaned ourselves up. She'd pulled on a casual, flowy pink dress while I'd put on a pair of jeans, wishing I'd brought something nicer for dinner. "Thank you. You didn't have to do that."

"Of course I did." Dipping my mouth down to hers, I kissed her, letting her taste herself on my mouth. Fuck, having Audrey's sweet essence in my mouth as we went to dinner with her family was probably the worst idea I'd had. It was going to be the only thing I'd think about all night. My cock was aching, straining against my pants, but I didn't let myself come. Because I hadn't earned it yet. So, I'd be good tonight.

Because she deserved more.

I knew she wanted our first time to be special, and I did too. I wanted it to mean something for both of us.

Threading our fingers together, we both headed back out to the main lobby area, finding Audrey's parents and Ella waiting for us.

"Is Cam coming to dinner?" Audrey asked her twin.

She shook her head. "He has a giant test he had to study for, so he had to run."

"Oh, that's too bad," I said, meaning it. I was a little bummed that I still hadn't officially met Ella's boyfriend, though I was sure it would happen soon enough.

"It's good to see you again, Parker," Audrey's mom said, her eyes a little glassy. "You're all grown up and so tall now."

I cleared my throat. Leah and Stephen Ashford had been like a second set of parents to me growing up. Maybe one day, they'd be my in-laws. I hadn't imagined seeing them again tonight, but I was glad they were here. "It's good to see you too, Mrs. Ashford."

"Please." She smiled. "You can just call me Leah."

Audrey's dad stuck out a hand for me to shake. "Heard you've been taking good care of my daughter."

"Yes, sir." I shook his hand, his firm grip not deterring me in the slightest. He was tall and well-built, but I was taller. Plus, I was used to egos from being an athlete. I looked him in the eye, not cowering.

Stephen Ashford finally nodded. "Good, good. Well, shall we eat? Leah made us a reservation at a little Italian place down the road. We wanted to celebrate both of our girl's special day."

Ella blushed. "It's really Audrey's, not mine, Dad. I wasn't even in the show."

"Nonsense," her mom said. "You designed all the costumes, and Audrey was the lead. Those are both a big deal."

Audrey reached out, squeezing her twin's hand, before coming and slipping an arm around my waist. "Are you okay with this?" She murmured.

I knew if I said no, that she would understand. That she wouldn't push. But I was. I was ready for this. Everything that came with being in a relationship with her. If I could make it work while faking it, I knew nothing would stop me when it came to the real thing.

"Of course," I said back, squeezing her hip. "Anywhere you are, that's where I'll be."

Her responding smile was how I knew this was all worth it.

ON SUNDAY, after the last performance of the musical, all the cast gathered for a party at one of the seniors' houses. I was surprised anyone had any energy left, but drinks were flowing and the music was playing loud enough that individual conversations couldn't be heard.

Audrey was leaning against me on the couch, her head resting on my shoulder. I hadn't even had to coax her into sitting on my lap this time—she came here of her own free will. And there were plenty of free spaces to sit.

We couldn't stop touching each other. But we hadn't gone all the way yet, either. The musical was exhausting, and after we'd gotten back from dinner with her parents the first night, Audrey had passed out before she'd even changed into her pajamas. Also known as my shirt because she hardly wore anything else. And every night since it had been more of the same.

Call me crazy, but I just wanted some alone time with my girlfriend. The party was fun, and everyone was having a good time, but I was ready to go.

"Having fun?" I murmured in her ear as she took a sip of the strawberry lemonade cocktail I'd gotten her. Unlike the frat parties or lacrosse parties, there were a ton more fruity options here, which was good for my girl. I hadn't had anything to drink tonight, even though we'd walked here and didn't need to drive home.

"Yeah." She hummed.

I brushed a strand of her blonde hair over her ear. "You can go hang out with your friends, you know. I'm okay here." When had we become that couple who was too busy canoodling in the corner to talk to anyone else?

Audrey sighed, resting her forehead against my chest. "It's okay. I see them plenty in class, anyway. I hate that you have an away game next weekend. I wanted to spend some time with just the two of us." She bit her lip. "You know…"

"I know." I smoothed my hand over her hair. "But I won't be gone that long. And the season is almost over, which means everything is going to calm down soon." Though we were in the runnings for the playoffs, and if we won, we'd be going to the championship, and that would mean a lot more games left to play. For the team, I wanted to win, but selfishly, I wanted to have more time to just relax with her.

She sighed. "The semester's almost over, though. And then…"

"Then what?" I finished her thought.

Audrey nodded. "Exactly."

"I wanted to do something special next weekend," I admitted. "Take you out to dinner. A *real* date. The whole nine yards."

"You've already done that for me, Parker," she whispered against my lips.

But it was different. Because before, this hadn't been real. I ran my hands up her thighs. "Still. Wanted to make sure we did it all right."

She giggled. "You're just a big softie, Parker Phillip."

"Mmm." I brushed my lips over hers.

"Get a room, you two," Ella remarked, walking by and smirking at us.

Audrey stuck her tongue out at her big sister.

"We could, you know," I rasped against her ear.

"What?" She blinked.

I swallowed roughly. "Get a room." Sure, my bed was comfortable, but I wasn't sure I wanted to know that my teammates were on the other side of the wall the first time we had sex.

Not to mention, I just knew I wouldn't last long once I got inside of her. These days, it felt like all it took was bringing up the image of her naked, those pretty pink nipples hard and wet from my mouth, and I was coming two pumps later in the shower.

There was no way I wanted to embarrass myself like that.

"If you want..."

Audrey cupped both of my cheeks. "Parker..." Her voice was soft as she kissed each of my cheeks before dropping one against my lips. "I hope you know I don't need anything special or fancy. I just want you, okay?"

I nodded. "Next weekend?" I squeezed her thigh.

She bit her lip, a little moan slipping free. "*Yes.*"

A FEW DAYS LATER, my duffel bag stowed under the bus and backpack in hand, I loaded the bus for one of our last away games of the academic year. The playoffs didn't start until mid-May, so we'd be focusing on finals along with the last few games we had for the rest of the semester.

Grabbing my earphones, I got ready to stick them in so I could listen to my new fantasy audiobook as soon as we got going.

Samuel stuck out his hand for a fist bump. "How are you feeling, Maxwell?"

I bumped him back with my fist. "Good. A lot less stressful since the musical is over."

"That's right! Damn dude, that was amazing. You were really great up there. Didn't know you could sing so well." He slid into the row across from me, and I knew I wouldn't get any relaxing done on this road trip. Damn. It was better when I'd been running late from rehearsals all the time.

Taylor popped up from the row in front of me. "You could seriously make a career out of it."

Chuckling, I shook my head. "That was a one time thing. Just for Audrey."

"Well, it was worth it if you got the girl out of it, wasn't it?" Samuel asked.

"Yeah." I grinned. "It was."

"We should go on a double date sometime. I think Dani would love that."

"Sure. But maybe like… next semester?"

He laughed. "Fair enough."

"I can't believe this season is almost over as it is. The exhaustion has basically seeped into my bones at this point," I said.

A nap would be great. In fact, if I could sleep until finals week, that would be even better.

The other guys laughed. Derek, our team captain, got on the bus and sat in the row behind Samuel.

I nodded at him. "How's it going, man?" I'd thanked them all for coming after the opening night of the musical. Part of me still couldn't believe the way they'd shown up for me. Even if it had taken some of my attention off the team, they'd supported me. That meant more to me than I could properly express.

All this time, I'd thought of my last team like brothers until everything had gone down with Raf and Millie, but looking back, they were never as close as this team was. They wouldn't have dropped everything to watch me sing and dance in a theater performance.

Transferring here had been the right call all along. I was glad to be a part of this team. Though some of them would graduate next month, I had one more year, and I wanted to make it count.

"You know, the usual. How do you think Coach is going to be tonight?"

We'd been on a winning streak, so the extra practices and drills he'd been having us run felt excessive. Though even I had to admit they were successful as long as we kept winning. So I shrugged.

"I've heard he's having problems with his wife. Maybe that's why he's been so hard on you, Maxwell," Taylor offered.

"Fuck if I know," I muttered.

"I don't think that's why," Derek offered. "I think he's been watching you, Parker. You're a skilled player. Especially after you bonded with the team. You're good at reading passes and creating opportunities to score. I'm pretty sure he's had his eye on you for captain next year."

"Captain?" I repeated, my eyes practically bugging out of my head.

"Yup. But don't tell him I told you that." He grinned. "I'd be happy to leave this team in your hands, Maxwell."

"Thanks, Stephens." I looked around at all of them, even the teammates I wasn't as close with as these three. "I'm really grateful I ended up at Castleton and met all of you. This has been a great season." I meant it. Even without Audrey's presence in my life, I'd had a fantastic time playing lacrosse with all of them.

And I was going to take these last few games to soak it all up and savor each moment.

THE NEXT DAY, we played hard. All of us knew what was at stake —the playoffs. A potential championship. None of us wanted to lose that. So we'd given them as few opportunities to score as possible, stealing the ball whenever we could and trying to make as many shots on goal as we could. We were on fire.

It wasn't surprising, considering how harmoniously we all worked together. Offense and Defense were at the top of their game.

"That was fucking amazing," Samuel said, slinging his arms over Derek and I. "We're going all the way to the top, baby!" He shouted the last words from the top of his lungs in the parking lot as we returned to the hotel.

"Yeah, yeah," I laughed. "Don't go jinxing us."

He rolled his eyes. "Not possible. We're too good."

"Too cocky," Derek said.

Samuel grinned. "My girlfriend's not complaining."

"Ew." I pushed him off of me, still laughing even as I feigned disgust. "Don't need to know about your sex life, Samuel."

"What about yours?" He smirked at me. "Isn't that your girl?"

"What?" My head whipped up to where he was pointing.

Sure enough—there she was. A Castleton University hoodie on, a pair of jeans, and her white leather sneakers. Her cheeks were pink and her smile bright as our eyes caught. And fuck, how could I stay away?

"See you later," I said, already jogging over to my girl.

My arms were already open when she met me in the middle, and I wrapped her up in a hug.

"What are you doing here?" I asked, unable to hide the surprise from my voice.

Her voice was all breathy. "I missed you."

I chuckled. "I missed you too, baby, but I'd have been back tomorrow."

She hummed. "Maybe I just couldn't wait anymore." Her eyes were full of heat as she took in my appearance, her gaze lingering over one specific part of my body. While Coach insisted we show up to games looking nice and in suits, more often than not, we left wearing sweats after we showered.

I knew how much she loved these gray sweatpants.

"Mmm." I pressed my nose into her hair. "But I'm sharing a room, sunshine."

"I'm not." Audrey slipped a room key into my hand. "Later," she murmured into my ear. "Come up to room 259."

I swallowed roughly.

"I'll be waiting." She pressed a kiss to my cheek and then disappeared into the elevator—to her room upstairs, where she'd be waiting for me.

Holy fuck.

I pressed my hand over my heart. *Tonight.* This was happening tonight.

CHAPTER 31

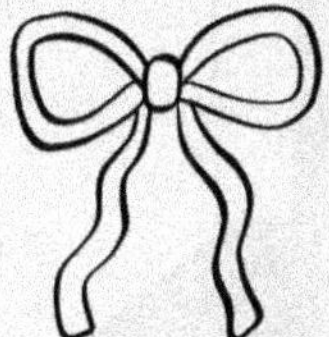

Audrey

Was this plan insane? Certifiably. And yet, there was no denying that I was tired of waiting for this. For him. What were we waiting for? Something special? It would be special because it was us.

Because of all the feelings overflowing in my chest.

Love. I loved him. Capital L, no mistaking it.

There was no way to deny that, not anymore.

So I'd driven up here to see him and booked a hotel room.

I'd gone and watched his game, sitting in the visiting students' section and watching his team absolutely destroy the home team. No one had warned me how hot and bothered I'd get by watching my boyfriend play his sport. Because the lethal focus and the determination on his face as he ran towards the goal before throwing it into the net?

God, I was a mess.

I'll be waiting.

Parker's face when he walked into the hotel and saw me had been worth every part of this plan. Every dollar I'd spent on the hotel room where I now sprawled out over the king bed, presenting myself like a meal for him to feast on.

There was a box of condoms on the nightstand, as well as a bottle of wine and a bowl of strawberries. A girl couldn't be too prepared, right?

My clit was aching, begging for my touch, clenching in anticipation for the main event. Finally, *finally*. We both wanted this so badly. And that we'd waited this long was a testament to how much we cared about each other. Loved each other, even though we hadn't said the words.

And as much as I wanted him to know, I wanted tonight to be special first.

I heard the mechanical lock on the door as the key was used, and my heart fluttered. *Parker.*

"Hi." I played with the ends of my hair, left down in loose waves.

"Audrey." His eyes traced over every inch of my body. "Fuck. You look so good in my jersey."

The only thing I was wearing was his jersey, which had his last name on my back and his number on my body—because I was his.

"Hi, Dream Boy." I ran my tongue over my lips.

"Rosie Girl," he groaned. "You're the dream."

I fluttered my eyelashes. "Come here."

Parker reached down, pulling off his sweatshirt and giving me the briefest hint of his muscled abs.

Biting my lip, I held back a groan at the sight. Fuck, he was hot. Tall and fit and every girl's wet dream. But he was mine. All mine.

"That's my girl," he rasped, as if mirroring my thoughts. "My Rosie. You're so perfect."

Trailing my fingers up my thighs, I shook my head. "That's you."

Parker climbed onto the bed, still wearing his sweats and a tight white t-shirt that clung to his body. Those damn gray sweats that did nothing to hide his erection. Every time he'd worn them, I'd practically dropped to my knees in front of him, begging for his cock. No regrets. I knew what I wanted, and what I wanted was him.

Tonight, though, I didn't want him in my mouth. I wanted him inside of me.

He kissed me—tenderly at first, like a casual exploration of my mouth—before it turned deeper. *Hungrier*. Like he wanted to devour me whole.

His hands pried my thighs apart, skimming over my bare skin at my entrance. "Shit. You're not wearing any panties?"

I shook my head.

He ran his fingers through my slit, gathering up the wetness. "You're fucking soaked."

"Parker," I moaned as he brought the same finger up to his mouth. It was *erotic*.

The fabric of his jersey rubbed against my nipples, and I watched him lick my juices off of his skin.

He pressed his erection against my core, still covered by fabric. I needed more. Needed his clothes off.

"What does my girl want?" He asked against my skin, teeth skimming over my earlobe.

"You," I gasped out as he rocked against me again. "*Everything*. I want everything, Parker."

He groaned as I slipped my hands under his shirt, tugging it up his stomach. He helped me by crossing his arms and pulling it off over his head, a move that had no business being that hot. It was magic; I swear. At the very least, I was entranced by his bare skin.

"These too," I responded, sitting up to push at the waistband of his sweats. Parker helped me tug them down, leaving him in just his boxer briefs. "Need them off."

My breath caught in my throat as he ran his fingers through his light brown strands, pushing them back off his forehead. His hair was still a little damp from his shower, his amber eyes bright as he took me in.

He swallowed roughly, his tone turning serious. "I... I want to make you feel good. But I'm nervous that I'm going to do something wrong, or that I won't be very good, and—"

"I know." I cupped his cheeks. "But I trust you. I want you."

A groan. "Fuck, baby. You're too good to me." He pushed his jersey up over my hips, bearing my lower half to him. "I'm probably not going to last very long the first time. But I want it to be good for you."

"It will be. Everything you do to me feels good, Parker." He had no idea. I'd never been with someone who *gave* as much as he did. Like my pleasure was his sole focus.

He laid down on the bed, dragging me so I straddled his stomach. I was hyper-aware of how wet I was as I planted my hands on his pecs.

"Come sit on my face, Rosie," Parker urged me, gripping my hips. "I need to make you come first."

"Oh." I squeaked as he lifted me up, settling me on top of his mouth. Planting my knees on either side of his head, I hovered above him.

"*Sit*," he commanded, grasping my hips and pulling me down until his tongue breached my entrance, running up my slit.

I let out a little gasp as his lips closed over my clit, sucking and applying the most delicious amount of pressure as his grip on me kept me pinned down against his body.

It didn't take much till I was crying out, rocking my hips in time with the movements of his mouth as he alternated between thrusting his tongue, brushing his teeth over my clit, and sucking it into his mouth.

It was too much. It wasn't enough.

"Parker," I cried out as the orgasm burst through me. He licked me through it, lapping up my release, and when I came back to my senses, he pulled me back down against his chest.

He tucked my hair behind my ear. "Fuck, I'll never get tired of that."

"Me too," I hummed, shimmying backward until his cock

pressed against my ass, already hard. Bending down, I pressed my lips against his, tasting myself on his tongue. "I want you," I begged. "I want to feel you."

He nodded, and I climbed off of him to grab a condom from the box as he tugged his boxers off, finally freeing his length.

It was the first time I'd ever seen him completely naked, and it was glorious. All those muscles, his body toned from lacrosse and all the time he spent in the gym.

"Here," I murmured, handing him the foil packet, finally drawing my eyes away from his body and up to his face.

Parker smirked, taking it from me and setting it on the bed between us. "Like what you see, sunshine?"

I blushed. "I—"

He laughed, and it instantly made me feel better. It was a reminder that the man I was sharing this moment with was my best friend. My boyfriend now, but that solid foundation of friendship was the reason I was so comfortable around him.

"Come here, baby," he said, patting the spot on the bed next to him as he sat up. I climbed over to him, sitting on my knees.

"Hi," I whispered, my eyes focused on his cock. God, it was big, pre-cum already dripping from the head. I'd never really thought of one as beautiful before, but his was. I'd had him in my mouth before—multiple times—but something about this moment felt so different.

"Hi." Parker reached out, tracing the details of my face before running his finger over my collarbone. "Put it on me?" He murmured, looking at the condom between us.

I nodded. The intimacy in this moment was enough to set my body on fire.

Reaching down, I wrapped my hand around his length, pumping it a few times before I bent down, running my tongue over the tip, lapping up the liquid there. He let out a guttural groan, and it was only then that I finally ripped open the packet, rolling it down his length.

I'd always used condoms with previous partners, even

though I was on birth control, but I already wanted to know what it would feel like to have him bare inside of me.

I groaned as I climbed onto his lap, pressing a kiss to his lips before positioning his tip at my entrance. I sank down a few inches. It was an adjustment to take him in since he was so much bigger than me, but I already felt so full, even with barely more than the tip inside me.

Parker brushed his thumbs over my nipples, the fabric rough against my bare skin as he cupped me over his jersey. "You're so fucking perfect."

Rocking my hips against him again, I took him a little deeper, letting out a moan. "You're so big." I shut my eyes, trying to work him into my body.

"But look how well you're taking me. And you're going to take every inch, aren't you, baby?"

I whimpered as I wiggled down another few inches. Parker's eyes were focused on where I was taking him into my body, but he hadn't moved yet. I suspected he was holding himself still, knowing that when he moved, it would be over.

But I was perfectly comfortable taking the lead.

"Audrey," he groaned, resting his forehead against my shoulder. "You feel so good."

His hips thrust up, an involuntary movement, and I gasped as he settled inside me, burying himself to the hilt. Fuck, I was so full. I'd never been with anyone this big before, and he felt incredible. Like I'd been made just for him.

The perfect fit.

Parker wrapped his arms around my back, holding me tight against his body, keeping his cock buried deep inside me.

"Fuck. Fuck, fuck, fuck." He chanted, tangling his fingers in the jersey's hem. "Give me a minute. I just need this to last."

I chuckled, nodding as I ran my fingers through his hair, soothing him. "It's okay even if you don't."

Wiggling my hips, Parker let out a grunt. "Audrey. *Fuck.* That's just mean."

He grabbed the hem of his jersey, guiding it up and off my head, practically tearing it off my body. "I love fucking you in my jersey, but I want to see all of you."

Nodding, I eagerly agreed with the sentiment.

His eyes were focused on my tits as he reached out, cupping each one as he tenderly rubbed each one with his thumb before pressing his lips to the swells of each breast.

"Perfect," Parker murmured.

And then, without warning, he flipped us, positioning me against the pillows as he pulled out, leaving just the tip inside, before thrusting back in.

"*Oh,*" I cried out. "Yes."

Parker was clenching his teeth, and I could tell how desperately he was trying to hold himself back. But he didn't need to.

I reached out, guiding his fingers to my clit, the two of us beginning to work it in tandem even as he continued rocking his hips, driving me higher and higher. The room was filled with the sound of us, skin smacking against skin, as we made love for the first time.

"Don't stop," I panted. "I'm going to come."

"Thank fuck," he groaned, still rubbing circles against my clit, giving me the delicious pressure I needed. "I'm not going to last much longer."

He leaned down, giving me his lips, and white burst across my eyelids, bright and *dazzling* as I came. I could feel my pussy clenching around him, and more curses fell from his lips as he followed right behind me, my orgasm triggering his own. I could feel him swelling, growing harder before he came, losing himself in my body.

Parker collapsed onto me, his weight like a warm blanket, and I wrapped my body around his.

"How was that?" I whispered in his ear.

"Mmm." He responded. "Ask me again in twenty minutes. I think you've killed me. I think I just died, and I'm in heaven now."

I giggled, wiggling my hips as I felt him soften inside of me. We'd need to clean up, but for now I was content to stay just like this, safe and warm in his arms.

The only place I wanted to be.

CHAPTER 32

Parker

All of my senses filled with her. Audrey Rose. My Rosie. She tasted like strawberries and sugar and smelled like roses, and I was inexplicably lost in her.

She was mine. My girl. The only one I'd ever wanted, and I'd given her every part of me.

Fuck, but it had been incredible. I'd barely been able to keep from coming as she wiggled her sweet body onto my dick, watching her cunt stretch around me even as my jersey stayed on her body.

I wanted to do that again. And again, and again, and again.

"Audrey." I nuzzled my face into her neck. "Why haven't we been doing that from the beginning?"

She laughed. "I don't know. Feels a little silly now, doesn't it?"

Pulling out, I went to the bathroom to get rid of the condom and clean up. Audrey slipped in behind me, pressing her naked body against mine as I stared in the mirror, resting my palms against the cool countertops.

"I watched your game, you know," Audrey whispered. "I was there."

I frowned, looking back at her. "I didn't see you."

She gave me a little mischievous grin. "I know. I didn't want you to."

"Mean."

Audrey ran her fingers up my abs, her nipples pressed against my back as she kissed my shoulder. "I wanted to surprise you. If you knew I was at the game, it wouldn't have been a surprise."

I hummed, enjoying the attention she was giving my body. So was my dick, already half hard and standing at attention. One time was *definitely* not enough.

"Still, I like seeing you there. In my jersey," I said, letting out a groan as she wrapped a hand around my shaft. "But this was—fuck—definitely a good surprise."

"I can wear it again while you fuck me if you want," she said, wiggling her eyebrows as I watched her through the mirror, her hand moving up and down as she pumped me slowly.

Damn, I loved that idea. And I definitely wanted her on top of me next time. My eyes darted to the large tile shower behind us, and I turned, scooping her up in my arms. "I have a better idea," I said, reaching in and turning the hot water on.

"The shower?" She asked, raising an eyebrow.

I laughed. "I've always wanted to shower with you, Rosie." Pressing a kiss to her nose, I let her slide down my body until her toes hit the floor. My cock pressed against her soft stomach. She was all curves and smooth skin, a sharp contrast to my lean and muscular body. I was fucking obsessed with her.

Running my hands up her sides to relish in the feel of her skin, I moved us underneath the warm water, letting the spray run over our bodies.

It was heavenly, especially as I picked up Audrey's shampoo off the ledge, the strawberry scent filling the air as I squeezed out a drop onto my palms before massaging it into her hair.

She closed her eyes, letting out a soft moan as I raked my fingers over her scalp. "That feels so good," she murmured.

"I want to take care of you," I said, tilting her chin back to wash the shampoo out of her hair. "I always want to take care of you. Even though I know you don't need it because you're incredible and independent."

"Maybe I like it when you take care of me," she said, opening her eyes after I'd finished rinsing. "You're the only person who I've ever been with who makes me feel like I'm not a burden, but a—"

"You're not," I interrupted her, cupping her chin. "It's a *privilege* to take care of you." I pressed my nose against hers.

She gave a contented sigh as I spun her around, using her conditioner and smoothing it over the ends of her long, blonde hair.

After it was also rinsed out, I picked up her body wash, filling my palms with an ample amount before rubbing them together.

Audrey held eye contact with me as I ran my hands over her body, washing her thoroughly, dragging my thumbs over her nipples and then down, down, rubbing over her thighs and entrance.

My cock was aching, painfully hard from exploring her body with my hands.

"Parker," she whimpered as I rubbed my finger back and forth over her clit. "That's so—" Her head fell back as I dipped it inside, giving her just up to my knuckle. "More," she begged. "I need more."

"Do you need me to fill you up, baby?" I rasped against her ear. "Make you a sopping mess as I take you here in the shower?"

"Yes," she cried, her pussy gripping me like she was trying to suck me in deeper.

My cock was fully on board with this plan, and I pressed her against the shower wall, burying my face in her neck and sucking on her skin as I positioned myself at her entrance. Except—

"Shit," I groaned. "We don't have any condoms in here."

Audrey gave me a hesitant smile. "If you want, I, um… I'm on birth control. And I got a test after, well… you know. I'm okay with it if you are."

"Fuck, baby. Are you saying I can slide into you bare?"

She nodded, nibbling at her lower lip. "I want to feel you." Audrey wrapped her arms around me, sliding her hands down my back, letting them rest against my ass as she squeezed. "Please. I've never…" Her eyes fluttered. "I want to give you a first. Like you've given me yours." Standing on her tiptoes, she pressed a kiss to the side of my mouth.

I spun her around, pressing her against the shower wall. "Hands up, baby." This position gave me the perfect view of her cute little ass, something I hadn't taken enough time to appreciate in the past. I squeezed her cheeks lightly, running my knuckle down her slit before taking my length back in hand.

"Oh." My girl gasped as I pressed the head against her entrance. She was still wet from earlier—sinking my finger inside of her had confirmed that.

"Fuck," I groaned as her wet heat enveloped my cock. God, this was nothing like before. Sinking inside of her bare felt incredible. Like I could feel the way she was wrapped around me as I fed her inch by inch of my hardened cock.

She was going to ruin me. No—she already had. I'd been ruined for anyone else long before I'd ever sank inside of her. Maybe the first time we'd kissed under pretenses of practice. I'd do it all a thousand times over if it brought us to right here, right now.

"You don't have to go slow," she panted, looking at me over her shoulder. "Fuck me hard. Please," she begged. Audrey wiggled her hips, trying to force me deeper inside, and I responded by slamming into her, feeding her my entire cock in one hard thrust.

"Is this what you wanted?" I asked, pressing against her wet body as she let out a moan.

She arched her back as I pounded into her deeper, thrusting over and over again as I experimentally swiveled my hips, testing her reaction. I might have been a virgin up until the last hour, but I was finding that learning Audrey's body—the spots that made her cry out and how to make her feel good—was better than anything else I could have imagined.

Her cunt spasmed around me, gripping me tighter, and oh, fuck, it felt good. If I hadn't already come once tonight, I would have lost it right then and there. Clenching my teeth, I focused on making her come again before I did. Reaching around us, I rubbed my thumb against her clit.

"Come for me, sunshine," I rasped against her ear, feeling her shiver in response.

She let go, her pussy giving me a vice grip, milking me for my own release as her folds pulsed around me. *So good.* I groaned, feeling the telltale signs of my release coming on from the base of my cock, my balls tightening with need.

Pulling out, I let out a deep grunt as I spilled my cum over her back and the supple swell of her ass, painting her with my seed.

"Damn." I swiped a finger through it, running my fingers through it to spell out my name before pulling her into my arms so I could wash it off of her. As much as I wanted to be a caveman and let her sleep with my scent all over her body, I also wanted her to be comfortable.

Audrey collapsed against me, letting out a little yawn.

I chuckled, picking her up as soon as we were both clean and setting her down on the bathmat so I could towel her dry before carrying her back to the bed.

Neither one of us bothered putting our clothes back on. I just slid in beside her, enjoying the feeling of her warm, naked body next to mine.

And we both promptly fell asleep in each other's arms.

A few hours later, I had to sneak back into the room I was sharing before curfew checks. Coach might have cut me slack for starring in the musical and dating Audrey—both of which had been major distractions from his point of view—but I knew his policies when traveling with the team. Staying in my girlfriend's room wouldn't have gone over well. Besides, I'd need to get on the bus with everyone in the morning.

We all arrived together and left together, no exceptions.

So as much as I wanted to stay in Audrey's arms, I'd left her a note on top of my red sweatshirt that she'd had stashed in her bag, pressed a kiss to her forehead, and headed up to the third floor.

My Rosie Girl,

I'll see you back on campus. Last night was incredible, and I'm not sure I'll ever forget it. Maybe you don't realize how crazy I am about you, but it's true. It was never fake to me. All this time, I was just waiting for you.

Drive safe. I have your location now, so I'll track you in case anything happens. Still, call me when you're back. Miss you already.

Your Dream Boy

The last few weeks of the semester were always crazy, but this year, a certain amount of calm had descended over me. Like nothing could pop the bubble I was in with Audrey. She was my girl, and the sex was incredible. Though she hadn't spent every night in my bed, I liked that this was real.

She was it for me. I was in this for the long haul. Even if that meant exposing the deepest truths of my heart to her.

We hadn't said I love you yet, but I could feel it in every action. Every time we came together, making love in the quiet of my room. It was all around us, and yet... why were we holding back?

Practice was over for the day, and I'd already finished classes and hit the weight room, which meant I was free for the evening. Sure, I still had to study for finals that started in just a few days, but at least I had some free time.

I headed towards where my girl had told me she'd be, walking faster than normal because I missed her. God, I was a sap, missing her after only a few hours apart, but I couldn't help it.

Entering the coffee shop, I saw her blonde hair and the cheery pink outfit she was wearing today. Audrey's love for pink never failed to make my chest warm.

My face lit up as I headed towards her. She couldn't see me from this angle, but as I approached, I saw she was sitting with Ella. I frowned as I realized I could hear their conversation.

"So, what's going on between you?"

"I don't know, Ells," she sighed.

"But you said it was all fake, right?"

"It *was*," she murmured, taking a sip of her iced coffee. "But I don't know."

I froze. She didn't know what? How I felt about her?

Fuck. I needed to fix that.

Audrey's twin rubbed her back. "I told you everything would work out."

Instead of saying hi, I headed back to the lacrosse house, knowing I needed to show her exactly what she meant to me. How much I wanted this—for the long haul.

Fuck this. If Audrey didn't think I was serious about her, didn't see that I was in this, that was my fault. And I had to show her she was wrong. We were good together. There was no one else I wanted by my side. In my bed.

In my heart.

Because I loved her. Loved her more than I'd ever loved anyone. Before Audrey, I hadn't really understood what it meant, but I did now.

Love was too small of a word for what she meant to me.

CHAPTER 33

Audrey

Twisting a strand of hair around my finger, I watched students hustling by on the sidewalk outside. It was the end of dead week, so even though we had classes, I'd already turned in or finished all of my projects and papers for this semester. Finals started on Monday, and I couldn't *wait* for summer.

Except for the small, somewhat pesky problem that I had no idea what I was *doing* for the summer. And to make things worse, Parker and I had been dancing around the subject. I was dying to know what he wanted to do, but for some reason, I couldn't come right out and ask.

We were together, spending as much time with each other as we could, but was he ready for more? I knew I was.

"So, what's going on between you?" My twin asked, popping a piece of blue raspberry candy in her mouth. It was her guilty pleasure, even if it turned her tongue blue.

"I don't know, Ells," I sighed, running my finger over the rim of my cup.

"But you said it was all fake, right?" My sister furrowed her brow.

"It *was*," I murmured, taking a sip of my iced coffee. "But I don't know…" It wasn't anymore. And if the note he'd left me was any indication, it had never been fake to begin with.

My eyes connected with hers, and she gave me a look of understanding.

Ella rubbed her back. "I told you everything would work out."

"I love him," I said, biting my lip. "I probably have for a long time. And even though I'm pretty sure he feels the same way, neither one of us has said anything. And we—" I blushed.

She gave me a devious smile. "Had sex?"

I nodded. "And it's *so* good. Like, mind-blowing orgasms *good*."

"So, what's the problem?" She always knew me so well.

I frowned. What *was* the problem? A laugh burst out of me. The problem was I was over-thinking this. I was thinking like the Audrey I'd been months ago, before Parker had come back into my life. Before he'd shown me how good it could be together.

Maybe you don't realize how crazy I am about you, but it's true. It was never fake to me. All this time, I was just waiting for you.

"Oh, god. I'm being that insecure girl, aren't I?"

"Tell him," she insisted. It wasn't the first time she'd said that, and I knew she was right. "I'd suggest sooner rather than later, but that doesn't seem to be your style, does it?"

Rolling my eyes, I looked down at my cup again. "What would you think if I didn't spend summer at home this year?"

When I met her blue eyes, they were understanding. Sure, we were identical twins, and we did everything together, but this was different. "Cam and I have already talked about what our summers will look like. I have my internship and so does he. But we're going to make it work, doing long distance till we can move in with each other next semester. So if you want to spend it here or with him, I wouldn't blame you, Ro."

I wrapped my arms around her. "I love you. You're the best twin ever, you know that?"

She chuckled, returning the hug. "I love you too."

"I gotta go." I winked at her, grabbing my bag and heaving it over my shoulder. "Talk to you soon!"

"Tell him how you feel!" Ella shouted after me.

I waved my hand at her, already planning the perfect way to tell the man I loved how much he meant to me.

"WE DID IT!" I cheered, throwing my arms up as we all piled out of our final for our musical theater class.

"Another year down," Mary said, pumping her fist up in the air.

Everyone laughed, and a bittersweet feeling settled in my bones. My finals were done, which meant the semester was officially over. I couldn't believe that I only had one year left at Castleton. After that, we'd be out in the real world. Getting jobs. Even if that meant waitressing or working some other small job until I could land a role on Broadway.

This year had been good to me. So good.

Tonight, I was heading to a party with Ella, Sutton, and a bunch of our other friends to celebrate the end of the semester.

Parker wasn't sure if he'd make it on account of a lacrosse meeting. I didn't really understand why they needed to have one today, but he'd just kissed my forehead this morning at breakfast, reassuring me that everything was going to be great.

He'd finished his last final yesterday, and I was jealous. Of course, I had a class that had the last possible final exam time slot. Luckily, part of finals in musical theater class were awards, and it had mostly felt like one giant party.

Heading outside, I stared at the academic quad. April was almost over, and it was warm enough outside that I was comfortable enough in just a dress and flats. My favorite attire. I could layer like no one's business—I had to if I wanted to wear dresses year round—but I loved the simplicity of late spring and summer even more.

Tilting my head up to the sky, I soaked in the sun's rays.

I had an appointment later today to get the keys to my very first apartment.

Hopefully, *our* first apartment. It was probably crazy to do this as a surprise—one that also required me being extra *sleuthy* to get Parker's information and the paperwork necessary—but I wanted to show him I was all in.

This was probably the wrong order, but when had we done anything right? Our relationship had started out fake, anyway.

This proved it was *real*. That we weren't just a temporary fling. He was good to me—so good to me, taking care of me like it was his job—and it was my turn to take care of him.

The lease started immediately, and that it had even been available was kismet. Sure, it was only a one-bedroom apartment, but there was enough room for both of us. We'd have a kitchen, a washer and dryer, and, most importantly, no sorority sisters or lacrosse teammates on either side of the wall.

And the shower was *beautiful*.

I'd leaped at the chance to sign the lease when I'd found out the price—within my budget, considering it was less than living in the sorority house—and saw the unit in person the other day.

So who was I to say no?

I was taking the future into my own hands.

Now all I had to do was ask my best friend, my boyfriend—the love of my life—to move in with me.

CHAPTER 34
Parker

Audrey was at a party with Ella and Cam's friends, but I couldn't wait. Not when I knew exactly what she needed to hear. Plus, I'd just found out that we had officially made the playoffs. We made the fucking *playoffs!* My fist pumped into the air, but the person I wanted to share this with the most wasn't here.

My fingers fidgeted with the small jewelry box in my pocket. I'd bought her this before the musical, but I hadn't found the right time to give it to her yet. It wasn't much—one day, I'd buy her an engagement ring and ask her to be mine, the way I'd wanted since I was little—but it represented *her*.

Hopping in my car, I drove to the house, ignoring how fast my heart was beating in my chest.

I didn't even bother to knock. Opening the door to the house, I scanned the living room. The guys were all there—but no Audrey. Hearing a laugh coming from the kitchen—her laugh—I nodded to them before heading that way.

Like she was the sun, and I needed to orbit around her, drawn to her very presence.

"Parker?" Audrey blinked. "What are you doing here?"

But instead of answering, I pulled her into my arms.

And with my hands wrapped around her hips, keeping her body plastered to mine, I dipped my head down, taking her lips with mine. Kissing her with everything I had. I poured all of my love into that kiss, hard and unrelenting. I kissed her like she was the air, and I'd been suffocating.

Like it was the last damn kiss of my life.

But this wasn't the end. Not of us. Not for us. No, this was just our beginning.

I swept my tongue over her lips, and Audrey opened, letting me inside, before her arms wound around my neck, fingers digging into my hair as she tugged me in tighter.

The world narrowed down, and it was just Audrey and I. I didn't even care that all of her friends were watching us make out, that they'd seen me maul her like a bear. Because fuck, I needed her.

Lifting her into my arms so I could kiss her deeper, I wrapped my hands under her ass, not breaking our connection for one single moment.

Someone cleared their throat, and Audrey pulled away, her cheeks pink. The color of her wardrobe. My favorite fucking color on the planet.

She'd asked me once what my favorite color was. I'd answered red because it was a pleasant color and a decent answer. But really, it was the color of her cheeks when she blushed. The color she wore every single day, like an addict. The color of her bedsheets. Her pretty pink lips when I'd just kissed them.

"Fuck, Dream Boy," Audrey whispered. "That was some kiss." God, every time she said that, all I wanted to do was kiss her again and *again*.

I leaned my forehead against hers for a breath. "What do you say we get out of here?"

She nodded. "I think that's a good idea." She rubbed herself over my erection, and I groaned.

Yup. That was a great idea. I didn't need any of them to see how hard making out with her had gotten me.

Addressing the room, I finally said, "Um, hi." I was sure a blush covered my own cheekbones as I set Audrey back down on her feet. "I'm just gonna, uh, borrow my girlfriend now, if you all don't mind."

After adjusting myself—discreetly—I slipped my hand into hers, guiding her out the door I'd just come in.

I didn't even pay attention to their reactions. No doubt, it was a surprise. None of them really knew what had been going on between us.

Fake, until it suddenly wasn't.

It was real. So fucking real. Hadn't I proved that over the last few weeks?

"Parker," Audrey finally said, tugging at my hand as I reached my car. "What was that?"

I turned to look at her, taking in her appearance. Swollen lips, her dress slightly askew on her frame from the way I'd had her in my arms. Beautiful.

Mine. So perfectly mine.

"That was me coming to see my *girlfriend,*" I repeated it. Like maybe that would help her get it through her head.

She blinked. "What—"

"I love you." The words were out there before I could think better of it. "And I couldn't have you go on for one more second, thinking I didn't. I told you, this was never fake for me. To me, it's always been real." Audrey's eyes were locked on mine, the pretty violet irises swirling with unshed emotion. "It's *always* been you, Rosie. In every dream, every vision, you were the one I wanted by my side."

"Parker..." She bit her lip, holding back a laugh.

I frowned. "What?"

"I'm just trying to figure out why you felt the need to barge in there, sweep me off my feet, and give me a grand declaration of love. Not that I don't appreciate it, because I do, but—"

"I heard you," I admitted. "Talking with Ella."

She furrowed her brow. "You did?"

"Yeah. That you weren't sure how I felt." I scratched the back of my head.

"Oh. Parker." She giggled. "That's not what I was saying."

I frowned. "You weren't?"

"No." She beamed. "I was saying I love you, and I think I have for a long time."

"You do?"

"Of course I do."

I wrapped my arms around her, pulling her against me. "Thank fuck."

She responded by wrapping hers around my neck. "You're so ridiculous."

"I'm new to all of this," I responded. "Remember? You've gotta cut me some slack. I've never told a girl I loved them before."

The smile she gave me was enough to make my heart stop beating in my chest.

"I think after Millie, I was hesitant to open up to people. To my teammates and the idea of love. Because that betrayal runs deep. But you've been so patient with me. And yet, you have my entire heart in your hands, Rosie Girl. You've had it for a long time."

"Me too," she said, her voice breathless. "I was so scared of getting my heart broken again that for the longest time, I didn't see what was right in front of me. Or maybe it was that I didn't let myself see it. But you've always been the one for me, Parker Phillip Maxwell. I've known it since I was eight years old, and damn if I was going to go one more minute without telling you how much I love you. I'm *in* love with you."

I was floored. Because damn, if we hadn't been on the same wavelength. "I think we both need to get better at expressing our feelings earlier," I said, chuckling.

"Probably," she murmured, pressing her palm against my cheek.

I brushed a strand of hair behind her ear. "Now, I have everything I could have ever asked for. I'm in love with my best friend, and she loves me back. My teammates are my friends, and they have my back." I pressed my nose against hers. "Plus, I'm going to be the Captain of the lacrosse team next year."

"What?" Audrey shrieked, jumping up and down. "You should have led with that! That's amazing! Congratulations, baby."

Smirking, I leaned down, kissing her softly. "You were more important. The most important thing in my life."

She hummed, kissing me back.

"Now, do you want to go back inside and celebrate with my friends, or do you want to go back to your place and we can do some celebrating of our own?" Audrey raised her eyebrows suggestively.

"Back to my place," I agreed. *Definitely.*

WE'D BARELY BEEN BACK in my room before I was slamming the door shut, tugging her dress off over her shoulders. My shirt followed, and then my jeans as Audrey unhooked her bra and shimmied out of her underwear—shedding our clothes and all our barriers. This was real, raw. And it felt so special to be with her like this.

"Parker," Audrey moaned as I pressed kisses down her neck, over her collarbone, before kissing her shoulder and sucking the skin into my mouth. I liked the idea of marking her so that everyone knew she was mine.

I wanted to memorize her body with my tongue, to trace her curves, every inch of her I hadn't before. She stood in front of me, completely naked, and I just stepped back to take her in.

Her tits, the perfect handful to fit in mine. Her hips, soft with those little dips, just begging to be gripped. All of her was perfect. Those pretty pink lips. Her cute little butt. That silky blond hair that she loved to wear down, blonde curls tumbling over her bare skin.

"You're so beautiful," I murmured, unable to look away.

Audrey's cheeks deepened in response, taking a step forward to reach out her hands towards me. I let her explore the way I just had. Taking all of me in. Her small, soft hands wrapped around me, sliding down, her eyes glued to the tip of my shaft.

"How is it that no matter how many times I have you, I still want more?" She whispered, wiping her thumb over the bead of pre-cum that oozed out.

"You're asking *me*?" I chuckled, dragging a finger between her legs. "I'm insatiable for you, baby. I'd have you for breakfast, lunch and dinner if you let me. Spend all day buried between these thighs."

I dipped my finger into her slit, finding her wet and ready. "You're already ready for me, aren't you, my Rosie Girl?"

She whimpered as I pushed two fingers into her at once, scissoring them between her folds. It wouldn't take much to have her falling apart beneath me. We were both too worked up. Maybe there was something about saying those three little words to each other that made everything feel heightened.

We'd been experimenting, trying different positions to see what felt best, but there was still one I wanted to try.

"This time, I want you on top," I said, cupping her breasts with my hands as I flicked my thumbs over her nipples. "I wanna watch these pretty tits bounce in my face as I fuck you."

She nodded, eagerly agreeing and I tugged her over to the bed, laying down and patting my chest.

"Ride me, baby."

This time, I knew would be hard and fast. We were both wound too tightly for anything else. But later, I'd take her slow and tender to show her just how much I loved her.

Audrey climbed on top of me, positioning my cock at her entrance, sinking down on me. Every time, I couldn't believe how fucking good it felt inside of her. Would it always just keep getting better?

I gripped her hips as she took me to the base, sheathing me fully inside of her. Her knees were positioned on either side of me, giving her the perfect leverage to work me back and forth, in and out.

"Look at you," I cooed. "Look how well you take me."

From this position, I could see her stretched around me, watching as she rocked back and forth, her hips moving as she sought more friction.

Her eyes closed, hands planting on my chest as she let out a few short pants. "I'm so *full*."

I chuckled, and she started rocking her hips back and forth, grinding her clit against me, letting out a cry every time she hit the base. Watching her chase her own orgasm was hot.

So was the way her tits jiggled every time she bounced on my cock, moving up and down. Grabbing her hips, I helped guide her motions, rolling them over and over as I thrust up inside of her, knowing I wouldn't last too much longer.

Sitting up, I kept one hand on her hip as I cupped her breast with the other one, sucking a nipple into my mouth, lavishing it with attention.

"It's too much," she groaned. "I need—"

"I know what you need, baby." I switched to her other nipple, unable to stop my hips from keeping that steady rhythm, fucking into her. "Touch your clit. Make yourself come."

She nodded, bringing her hand down between us. The tips of her fingers ran over my cock, wet from her ministrations, before she felt the place where her body took me in.

I let out a groan as she pressed her fingers apart, rocking her palm against her clit. "S' good," she slurred. "How does it keep getting better?"

She took the words right out of my mouth.

I gritted my teeth. "I'm gonna come, baby. I can't hang on much longer. I just need—"

Audrey came before I could finish that thought, crying out my name, her back arching and pushing out her tits as she let go. She contracted around me, still rocking her hips as wave after wave of her orgasm ripped through her body. Damn, if that wasn't satisfying.

Following close behind her, I held her tight to me as I roared my release, pouring inside of her. I felt like a caveman every time I did it, unable to hold myself back as I filled her with my cum. After I softened, I pulled out, watching our combined releases drip out of Audrey's pussy. Scooping it up, I pushed it back inside of her. Nothing would come of it, not now—but it was still hot as hell.

"Round two?" Audrey asked, her fingers dancing over my bare chest as she snuggled her body against me.

"Later," I promised, laughing as I brought her mouth to mine, letting my mouth express just how happy I was that she was mine.

"You know, we haven't talked about what happens now that the semester is over," Audrey said, her fingers curling with mine as we lay naked in my bed, face to face. I thought I liked this part the best—the intimacy of *after*, when we were cleaned up and cuddling. When she let me hold her and we just talked about anything and everything.

"We'll figure it out," I promised her as I played with her hair. "It's not like I can't drive up to you this summer."

"That's true. Or…" She hesitated.

"Or?" I asked, tilting her chin up with my finger, her eyes capturing mine. Holding my interest. She looked shy and reluctant—and I knew she was neither of those things.

If anything, I was the shy one, content to be quiet and reserved. Before her, I was completely comfortable sitting back and watching. Now, well… everything felt different.

"Well, Ella's got an internship this summer with the costume design department at the theater company back home. And I don't know your plans, but…"

"I did an internship last summer with an architecture firm, so now it's just a matter of applying for something after graduation."

"And where, exactly, are you hoping to end up?" Audrey fiddled with her hands in her lap. Her voice was filled with cautious optimism, and I held in a chuckle.

I rubbed up her hip, settling protectively on the inside of her thigh. "Why, sunshine?"

"Maybe it's too early to hope we'll be in the same city, but…" Those purple eyes locked on mine. "A girl can dream, right?"

"New York City." I smirked. "Every firm I applied for is in New York."

"But…" Her eyes scanned over my face as she processed what I said. "You couldn't have known we'd end up together?"

"Maybe not. But I hoped. You were always my dream, Rosie Girl. Why do you think I held onto your picture all of those years?"

Her cheeks were pink, a sight that made me grin extra wide.

Reaching over to my nightstand, I slid it open, grabbing the surprise I had for her. Kissing her flushed cheek, I placed the small box in her hand.

"Parker." She gasped. "What's this?"

I shrugged. "Open it."

It was a gold star pendant on a dainty chain—something I'd seen and had instantly thought of my girl. In the middle was a small diamond, and it sparkled when it caught the light.

"A star?" She blinked. "I don't—"

"It's you," I explained. "I'm sure one day you'll have your own star, but for now, you're mine. And that's how I think of you. My sunshine. My star."

"I have something for you, too," she admitted, her eyes

watery. "It might be crazy. And it's definitely big." Audrey bit her lip. "You can say no. If you don't want to, I just—"

"Audrey." I pressed my lips to hers to get her to calm down. "What is it?"

She pressed a key into my palm.

I blinked. "Huh?"

"Will you move in with me?" She sat up on her knees, perched in front of me. "I signed the lease already, and it's ours." Her throat moved as she swallowed, and I could tell she was nervous. "If you want to."

"And we'll share a room?" I asked.

"Uh-huh."

"And a bed?" I raised my eyebrows suggestively.

"Yes."

"And we can be as loud as we want?"

That one made her laugh. "I mean, the neighbors might not appreciate that, but…"

"Yes, Rosie. There's nothing I like more than the idea of waking up next to you every day. Every night you spent apart from me was miserable, anyway." I kissed her, softly at first, before giving her my tongue. "Yes, I'll move in with you."

And just like that, we were moving in together.

CHAPTER 35

Audrey

Everything was moving fast, but it felt like we were exactly where we were supposed to be. My heart was full, the random butterflies still bursting through me at moments just like this one.

Because there was Parker, standing outside on the sidewalk, holding a bouquet of pink roses with that smile that he only wore for me.

Meeting him halfway, I came to a stop in front of him, wearing a pair of denim shorts and a cute pink polka dot top tied in a knot at my waist. It showed the slightest sliver of midriff, but it was a warm day for May, so I was perfectly comfortable. I'd been unpacking the last of the boxes from my room at the sorority house, working up a sweat.

My boyfriend handed me the flowers, and I took them automatically, staring down at the beautiful roses.

"What are these for?" I asked, burying my nose in them.

"Can't a guy buy his girlfriend flowers without needing a reason?" Parker looped his arm around my shoulders as he walked me back inside. "Especially when they just moved into their first apartment together?"

I shrugged, hiding my smile as I held the flowers tighter to my chest. "I suppose."

"That's my girl," he said, nuzzling his nose against mine.

Fake girlfriend or not, I'd *always* been his girl, hadn't I?

As of today, it was officially summer. My bedroom in the sorority house was now empty. Parker had moved out of the lacrosse house, too, and since neither one of us had *actual* furniture, we'd bought ourselves a bed. The rest of the furniture in the apartment was thankfully supplied by both of our families, who were very eager to pawn things off onto us.

Our apartment was basically fully furnished, though, so I couldn't complain. My childhood desk sat next to Parker's. The spot where I'd written our names in a heart with a Sharpie underneath my desk was still there, feeling like a wonderful twist of fate. We'd lost each other for so many years, but then we'd found each other again. Maybe the universe had known what it was doing when it gave me Parker as a child. Like it knew one day, he'd be my everything.

"I love you," I murmured against his ear as we walked into our apartment together.

Parker's face lit up like it always did when I told him how I felt. "I love you too."

I leaned against him, feeling grateful beyond words.

He wasn't completely off the hook from lacrosse yet since they had the playoffs starting next week. Luckily, I'd be able to catch every game—well, as long as they kept winning—and I was so excited to scream for my man. His parents were going to come down too, and even though it had been a long time, I already couldn't wait to see Mrs. Maxwell. She'd been so good to me when we were younger, and Parker had assured me she was ecstatic that we were together.

It was going to be the best summer ever, and it was all because of the man by my side.

"What are you thinking about?" Parker asked as I sighed happily, resting my head on his shoulder.

"How lucky I am."

Ella and I had talked every night since she'd left for the summer, and we really talked. She told me about Cam, about how they'd been talking about the future, and I shared about everything that had happened over the semester with Parker and I. Well, almost everything. Some moments were too special to share.

Still, I was *deliriously* happy. It should have been illegal to smile this much.

"Me too." He scooped me up into his arms, carrying me the rest of the way into our apartment.

"Put me down," I giggled.

He flashed his pearly white teeth at me. "Nah. Think I'm going to carry you around everywhere from now on, Rosie Girl." Parker winked.

I rolled my eyes, loving the attention. The way he doted on me was sweet. I didn't have to second guess his feelings for me, because he showed me every day how much he loved me through his actions and his words.

"You know…" I murmured, cupping his cheeks. "We haven't christened our new bedroom yet." I wiggled my eyebrows.

"And here I planned to feed you," Parker said, making a *tsking* sound with his tongue as he dropped me on my feet.

I hummed for a moment as if thinking it over. "Bed first," I responded. "Food later."

He laughed, and damn if it wasn't my favorite sound in the entire world.

What I'd learned in the last week was that Parker's teammates really *loved* to tease him about us. He'd invited a few of the guys over to our place after practice this week. They were all spending a lot of time each day on the field and in the gym, so I knew how important it was for them to have some time to relax and unwind, too.

Samuel was quickly becoming one of my favorites, mostly because he and Parker were the closest and I liked how wholesome their friendship was.

"He tried to deny how into you he was from the beginning," Samuel said with a laugh. "But it was so obvious from the moment he saw you at the Halloween party that you two were going to end up together."

I looked over at Parker, who was sipping a Gatorade at the kitchen counter. He had the faintest of blush on his cheekbones, and I winked at him. All the guys had come here after practice, so they were all in athletic shorts and t-shirts, given the temperature outside.

"Honestly, I'm surprised it took you two as long as it did to start dating. We all had bets on when it would happen," Derek chimed in.

"Oh? You took bets?"

"Yeah. I think I had one month." Derek chuckled.

Taylor shrugged. "I had two weeks."

Samuel sighed. "Who knew it would take over three?"

"She was my best friend, you guys," Parker said, rolling his eyes and walking over to us. "I had to approach with caution. Like a lion pouncing on his prey."

I giggled when he jumped on me, wrapping his arms around my stomach and pulling me down onto his lap. "But it was all worth it in the end, huh?" I asked, cupping his cheek.

"Yeah." He pressed a kiss to my cheek. "Definitely."

"Ugh, gross," Taylor said, covering his eyes. "You two are disgusting. I'm way too single for this."

Derek laughed, smacking the back of his head. "No one said you had to come over, man."

He crosses his arms over his chest. "I didn't want to get left out."

Samuel looked at me, shrugging. "At least you didn't have to share a wall with this one." He hooked a thumb towards Parker. "It wasn't exactly quiet."

It was my turn for my cheeks to turn pink. God, I did *not* want to think about him hearing us have sex.

Parker's hand tightened over my thigh. "You say that like you're not just as loud with Danielle."

"Oh, shit," Taylor snickered. "Get him."

I wiggled on Parker's lap, trying to get comfortable.

"Audrey." His words were rough against my ear. "Unless you want to make this worse, don't do that."

Why—*oh*. I giggled. He was hard. *"Sorrryyy,"* I turned just slightly, batting my eyelashes at him.

He banded his arm around my waist, keeping me tight against him, and we stayed like that as the guys chatted. Warm and secure in his arms, I grew drowsy, finally drifting off.

I woke up when Parker shifted me in his arms later, saying goodbye to his friends. It had grown dark, the sun already setting in the sky. Considering it had been early evening when they'd come over, I had been out for a good amount of time.

"Sorry." I yawned. "I guess I'm still tired after the events of last week."

"You're fine." He chuckled. "I had fun today. Thanks for agreeing to have the guys over."

"Of course. It's your place too." I tilted my head, looking at him funny. "And they're your friends. Besides, I like them. They might enjoy teasing you, but they're good guys."

Parker nodded. "I know. Part of me has always known it, I think."

He shifted me so I'd be straddling his lap, each leg on either side of him.

"So, you really liked me, hm, Parker?" I wound my arms around his neck, loving teasing him myself. "Embarrassing."

Red spread up his neck and ears. "Rosie..." His voice was deep. "We're dating."

"Still." I leaned in to kiss the tip of his nose. Running my fingers up through his hair, I gently scratched my nails over his scalp. He closed his eyes like he was luxuriating in the sensation.

"Imagine my surprise," I whispered. "When I saw the hottest guy at that party and he turned out to be the kid I used to play in the mud with. The one who watched *A Pup Named Scooby Doo* with me after pre-school and cried when I wanted to watch Christmas movies. The one whose name I doodled on my sketchbook next to mine with a heart around it. And you were still you, but also… This." I dragged my nails up his abdomen. "A gorgeous, handsome man, but still my best friend."

His deep laugh settled in my lower region, my body already sparking to life with desire. "God, trying to just be friends with you was the hardest thing I've ever done. I wanted to kiss you from that very first moment." He pushed my t-shirt off my shoulder to kiss my bare skin. "You've always been the most beautiful woman in every room you're in."

I batted my eyelashes. "We really were so oblivious, weren't we?"

Parker cupped the back of my neck, pressing a soft kiss to my lips. "I love you, Audrey Rose. So fucking much. Like my heart might actually burst inside."

"I love you, Parker Phillip."

Our soft and gentle kissing quickly turned into more. Rocking my hips against him, I was overly aware of his hardening erection underneath me. How the only thing that separated us was my thin panties beneath my skirt and his workout shorts.

"I want you," I murmured, staring into his beautiful golden flecked brown eyes. That wonderful shade of amber that felt like my entire world.

"Bed?" He asked, shifting his hands to grip my hips.

I shook my head, pulling the t-shirt off over my head. "Don't want to wait. Just want you inside me."

Parker groaned as I slipped my hands inside of his shorts, his cock popping out. God, he was gorgeous. Long and thick, but somehow the perfect size. I ran my thumb down his length before circling the crown.

When I looked up at him, his eyes were dark.

"Put me inside of you," he ordered. I liked it when he was all bossy and dominant. It was so far from what I expected when he'd confessed that he'd never had sex before, but I liked the growly in charge Parker as much as I loved the sweet, shy one.

Pushing my lace panties to the side, I lifted my hips, guiding him into me. We both let out a moan as I sank down onto his length, and it was glorious. I loved feeling this full.

Dropping my head back, I slowly rolled my hips against him as Parker sucked my nipple into his mouth through the lacy pink bra I was wearing. It was a matching set, and I swear every time he saw my panties were pink, there was a spark in his eyes.

He reached around my back, flicking the clasp even as he kept his mouth on me. The straps slipped down my arms, and then I shimmied it off, dropping it behind me. I loved the way his eyes roved my body, taking in my pink nipples that were hard from his ministrations.

Like I was sexy. Beautiful. *His*.

Sometimes I felt ridiculous, all of my pink and sparkles, but then I remembered how much Parker loved it when I was truly myself, and I realized I didn't care what other people thought. I dressed the way I wanted because it made *me* happy.

And it didn't hurt when Parker looked at me with desire in his eyes, either.

I rocked against him, each movement slow and sensuous, as he thrust his hips up to meet me, and it didn't take long at all before we were coming together, our bodies wrapped around each other on the couch, like nothing in the world at all could tear us apart.

Looking into his eyes and kissing him tenderly even as he remained inside of me, I knew nothing ever would.

CHAPTER 36

Parker

Here we were. The Castleton Chipmunks lacrosse team had made it through all the rounds of the playoffs, and we'd made it to the championship game.

After everything I'd been through this last year, I couldn't believe I was here. Maybe I was lucky because all of it—everything I'd gone through—had brought me here. To Audrey Rose. To the love of my life.

She always had been. And I knew deep in my bones that I'd been waiting for her. That it wouldn't have been like this with anyone else.

Because the girl in the second row, screaming for me, wearing my jersey with my number painted on her cheek—she was the best thing that had ever happened to me.

She was the reason I was going to be captain of the team next year. Because somewhere along the way—while pretending to be her boyfriend and acting in a starring lead in a musical, for fuck's sake—I gained the confidence I needed all along. And I forgave myself for everything with Millie.

Without Audrey, I never would have realized just how dull my life had been before. I hadn't truly been living or enjoying the world around me. I'd just been going through the motions:

class, practice, the gym. It had been a life, but not one that brought me joy.

My ex and I had never been right for each other, and I hated it took her cheating on me for me to see that. But she wasn't a bad person. I might not have wanted to be friends with her again, but I could see how she must have been hurting. Our relationship had made sense—we had a class together, and she liked me. I liked her well enough, so when she'd asked me out, I'd agreed. But I'd never given her the attention that she deserved. Because the *passion* wasn't there.

Not like it was with Audrey.

But it was more than that with her, too. Audrey and I had this deep foundation we'd built together of trust and respect. We didn't keep things from each other—not the important things. How easy would it have been for her to never tell me about Duke? But we had.

"Let's do this!" Derek shouted. "Castleton Chipmunks on three!"

Laughing, I threw my hand in, and we all screamed for our team.

It was the most intense sixty minutes of game play of my life, even as I played in five-or-so minute shifts. On the field, I had to adopt that lethal calm, blocking everything out. On the bench, my heart was in my throat as I watched my teammates pass the balls or try to block the opposing team's play.

And down to the final minute of the game, when Taylor passed me the ball and I ran with it towards the net, launching it with nothing to lose—I knew this season would be one I'd never forget.

My girl was waiting by the side of the field, like always, beaming in my jersey.

"You won." Audrey's face was beaming as she stood next to my parents—and hers.

"Hi, baby," I said, dropping my gloves and helmet onto the ground so I could pick her up and twirl her around. Audrey's laugh lit me up inside, and I set her back on her feet. I wanted to kiss her, but with both of our families here, I'd wait until we were alone.

"We're so proud of you, Parker," my mom said, wrapping her arms around me in a hug.

"Good job, son." My dad patted me on the shoulder, the pride on his face practically radiated through.

"Thank you guys so much for coming," I said, feeling a little choked up. "It means so much to me."

Even Ella and Cam were here, coming down for the weekend to help support me. I was touched. Cam and I had finally met the day after the big party—we'd all gone out for brunch—and we'd instantly started talking about sci-fi and fantasy series we liked.

In short, everything was great. Better than great, even.

I pushed my fingers through my hair—damp, since I'd been sweaty after running around on the field for four periods—and looked at my family. My blood, and the one I'd made. It felt right that we were all here.

"So we thought we'd all go out to dinner and celebrate. What do you think?" Dad tugged my mom into his side, wrapping an arm around her shoulder and tugging her to him.

I nodded. "Sounds great, Dad."

Audrey slid her hand into mine and wrapped her other arm around mine.

"The team is getting together later tonight for one last hurrah before everyone goes home for the summer." I looked down at her. "Do you want to go?" Audrey gave me a little pout, and I dropped my lips to her ear. "Don't worry, we'll have some alone time later."

Her lips tilted up in a coy expression. "Alright." She stepped up on her tiptoes. "But only if you promise to make it up to me."

"Leave the jersey on," I murmured into her ear. "I want to see you in it as I—"

Audrey wrapped her hand over my mouth to keep me from talking, scolding me with her eyes.

Chuckling, I kissed her palm. "Later," I promised.

DINNER HAD LASTED FOREVER, and I'd barely made it two drinks at the party with the guys before I was dragging Audrey out of there, desperate to be alone with her.

If I'd have had my way, I would have been inside of her as soon as I stepped off the field, but our families were important, and I hadn't gotten to spend much time with my parents all year.

Audrey was in my arms, her lips on mine, as soon as the door shut behind us.

God, she looked so pretty tonight. There was a pink shimmer over her eyelids, and she'd pulled her hair up with a cute pink ribbon.

"I need you," I panted, pressing open-mouthed kisses to her neck before sucking on the skin there.

"Then have me," she said with a gasp as I pushed her panties aside, roughly plunging two fingers inside of her. Thank fuck, she was wearing a skirt. I loved the easy access, especially compared to the pants she'd worn in the winter.

Plus, I loved watching it swish as I walked behind her, admiring her cute little ass.

Audrey let out a whimper as I pushed her up against the door, her head falling back. "Parker," she cried. "I need—"

"I know what you need," I mused, pulling my fingers out and lifting her into my arms so I could carry her into our bedroom.

Dropping her on the bed, I didn't waste a single second, stripping my clothes off before tugging her skirt and pretty pink undies down and pushing my jersey up past her hips. I groaned at the sight of her spread out for me.

Just like our first time.

"Fuck," I groaned, using my fingers to spread her open. "Look at you. So wet and perfect for me. Your pussy is the prettiest shade of pink, Audrey." Dipping down, I brought our lips back together, kissing her roughly as I pushed my fingers back inside of her, making sure she was ready for my cock.

The little breathy noises she was making were going straight to my cock, standing at attention and begging to be inside of her as I continued to fuck her with my fingers.

When I could feel her getting close, I pulled them out. She let out a little whimper as I sucked them clean, keeping my eyes locked on hers.

"How do you want me?" Audrey fluttered her eyelashes, running her fingers down her body before bunching the jersey up at her waist.

"On your knees," I ordered. "Let me see my name on your back as I fuck you. Jersey stays *on*."

She scrambled up on her hands and knees, raising her ass into the air and giving me the perfect few of my last name across her back.

One day, it would be hers, too. It was crazy to already be thinking about marrying her one day, but I couldn't help it.

There was no one else I could see in my future. Not when we fit just right together. She made me a better person in every possible way, and I wanted to give her everything.

Kneeling behind her on the bed, I spread her cheeks wide, massaging her cute little ass with my hands.

"Parker," Audrey moaned as I continued to lavish attention everywhere but where I knew she needed it. "Get inside of me."

Knowing neither one of us could wait much longer, I positioned myself at her entrance, driving deep inside of her with one shallow thrust.

"Did you need my cock, baby?" I asked, holding her hips, keeping my pelvis pressed against her backside.

She hummed in response, tightening her pussy around me, and I groaned. "Fuck. Feels so good."

I gave her a light smack against the ass, and Audrey let out a small moan, so I did it again. Not quite enough to cause pain, but enough that I could tell it brought her pleasure.

"More," she begged.

"So beautiful," I rasped, gathering up her long blond streaks in my fists and tugging them as I snapped my hips into hers, over and over again, fucking her hard, just like she wanted.

I'm panting, trying to hold myself back, trying to think about anything except for how good it felt like this, how tight and wet she was as I buried myself inside of her.

And all the while, as I pumped inside of her, my eyes were glued to my jersey. The thing that proved she was *mine*. She had been from the very first moment she'd put it on.

It was that thought that I kept in my mind as I brought her to a climax and as I followed behind. That she was mine.

I was hers, and she was mine, and no championship in the world was as good of a prize as the blonde in my arms screaming my name as both of us descended into utter bliss.

It was the weekend, and for once, we didn't have anywhere to be. It had been a little over two weeks since my team had won the championship game, and I was practically floating on air. Everything was different.

Because I had the girl.

She was mine. My Rosie Girl.

My sleeping beauty, who had fallen asleep in our bed. The one we shared. In our apartment. Living together still felt surreal. I'd loved having her in my room whenever she stayed over this semester, but this was different. No sneaking out. No worrying about getting caught.

Our clothes hung together in the closet, and it felt domestic as fuck to make breakfast for her every morning and dinner together every night.

If there was one thing about my girl, it was that she was *not* a morning person. Since the season was over, I went for a run every morning to stay in shape, but I let my girl sleep.

I couldn't imagine life any differently. Twenty-two, and I could see my future clearly. Audrey and I were already living together, and after we graduated next year, we would do life together. I'd started talking with firms in New York City, and hopefully, one of them would give me a job offer. She was already looking for casting notices and trying to find an agent who would help her get cast in a role on Broadway. And while my girl knew it might not be easy, it was what was in her heart.

And I never wanted her to do anything other than follow her passion, to reach for the stars. Because she was a star, so brilliant and bright, and I wanted to help hold her up.

A small smile curled on my lips as I watched her, not wanting to disturb her as the movie played. Her blonde hair was sprawled out over our bed, and I couldn't help but play with it, running my fingers through the soft strands.

"Mmm," Audrey moaned, nuzzling against me further in sleep. "Parker…"

I ran my thumb over her cheekbones, tracing each inch of her face like I could memorize it from touch alone.

Finally, her eyes fluttered open.

"Hey." I shifted my position, sitting up against the pillow so I could watch her fully.

"Sorry I fell asleep," she whispered.

"It's fine, sunshine," I said, kissing her forehead. "I like watching you sleep."

She blushed. "Stop saying things like that."

"Like what?" I asked, knowing I was playing coy and trying to hide my smile.

She playfully smacked my arm. "You know what I mean. Don't pull an Edward Cullen. And I don't need true love's kiss to wake me up."

"No, but does it hurt to try?" I grinned. That was always her favorite fairytale growing up. After the prince had slain the dragon, he found his princess, his true love, and woke her up with a kiss. A smirk covered my lips. "The dragon was slayed, after all. And you love me. So I guess what they say is true. And they all lived happily ever after."

Audrey smiled. "I think I can live with that."

So could I.

Pulling her into my arms, I nuzzled my face against her neck, letting her sweet strawberry scent wash over me. Letting the knowledge that she was my happy ending—that despite everything, we were here together—rush over me, filling me with warmth and love beyond comparison.

Her eyes drifted closed again as she fell asleep in my arms.

"I love you," I murmured against her ear. The words could never express the enormity of what I truly felt, but they were a start.

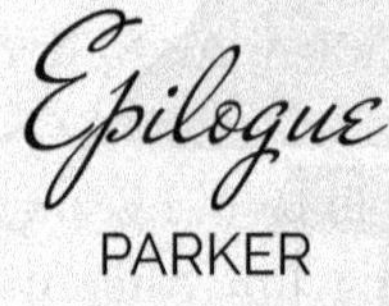

Epilogue

PARKER

ONE YEAR LATER...

Stepping off the stage with my diploma in hand, I took a deep breath. *I did it.* As of today, I was officially a graduate of Castleton University with my Bachelors of Architecture. Five years went by in the blink of an eye. These last two, all I wanted was to slow time down. To be able to cherish the memories we were making. The time I got to spend with her.

But that wasn't how life worked. It came at you, a hundred miles per hour, whether you were ready or not. Just like a ball goes into the net. Sometimes, you missed. Sometimes, you got the goal.

Or, in my case, the girl. The perfect girl who I didn't deserve, but was sure as fuck glad I had.

Heading back to my seat, I looked around the room. Somewhere in the crowd were my parents, sitting next to Audrey's. It felt right that they were sitting together. Like we were back where we started. Except this time, we weren't just neighbors or best friends. We were together. Calling Audrey my girlfriend—my *real* girlfriend—for this last year had been the biggest joy of my life.

Especially living in our apartment together off-campus. After living with other people for multiple years, there was nothing better than coming home to her every single day.

Something I couldn't wait to do for the rest of our lives.

The ceremony ended, and we all shuffled out of the arena to greet our family and friends.

Audrey's blonde hair shone in the sun, illuminating her like a golden halo surrounding her. She'd unzipped her gown, showing off the pink dress she wore underneath, along with the star pendant I'd given her. Her cap was decorated in pink roses, glitter, and butterflies, and it was so *her*. God, I loved her.

I loved every single bit of her.

How could anyone ever think she was too much? She was everything.

"Parker!" my girl exclaimed, catching sight of me.

I gave her a dopey smile. "Hey, Rosie Girl." I opened my arms, and she flung herself into them.

Just like she'd done after every home game this year. Just like she had after the school musical last year, when things had gone from fake to real. Though they'd always been real to me.

I'd loved her since I was just a kid, and that would never change. She was my sunshine, a golden glow that brightened every day. She was every star in the sky.

Wrapping her up, I buried my nose in her hair, inhaling her sweet strawberry scent. God, she always smelled so good. She made everything better.

When we pulled apart, her eyes shining with unshed tears as she looked up at me, I kissed the tip of her nose.

"Don't cry, baby." I wiped away the tears with my thumb, cupping her cheeks with my hands. Holding my entire world between them. "We made it."

She laughed. "I'm just so happy. I can't help it."

"I love you, Rosie Girl," I said, pressing a soft kiss to her lips.

Leaning down, I rested my forehead against hers.

Audrey smiled. "I love you too, Dream Boy."

Every time she called me that, I couldn't help but chuckle. That we'd both liked each other all along, that neither one of us had wanted to make a move because we didn't want to ruin the friendship, was just so *us*. But we'd found our way together.

She was my first, and if I had my way, my last.

Ella and her boyfriend, Cam, were standing off to the side, the latter holding a gigantic bouquet of white flowers in his arms.

I had flowers for Audrey too, though I'd left them for later, wanting to have our own special moment. I wasn't asking her to marry me—not yet. We were still young, and we had plenty of time. But I wanted to celebrate graduating, being together, and the future we would share just the two of us.

I saw Audrey eyeing her twin, and I knew what she wanted.

"Go see your sister, baby," I whispered in her ear. "I'm not going anywhere."

She hummed in response, pressing a kiss to my cheek. "I know. You're stuck with me, Parker Phillip Maxwell."

"Like there's anything in the world I'd rather be, Audrey Rose Ashford."

She pressed another soft kiss to my lips before running towards her sister, shouting, "Ella!"

"Ro!" Ella grinned, moving her flowers out of the way so my girl didn't crush them as they hugged tightly. Even though they'd been sitting together at graduation, walking one after the other, I wanted them to have this moment.

I stood back, letting them hug it out.

"Congrats, man," Cam said, coming to stand behind me as the two shared their own conversation. Like they were in their own world.

"You too," I nodded. "Ready for the real world?"

His eyes didn't leave Ella's as he said, "Yeah. I can't wait."

"New York's going to be great," I answered, meaning every word. I'd never imagined myself living in the city, but I'd landed an incredible opportunity working with one of the architecture firms there, and Audrey was going to pursue her own dream: Broadway.

The two of them were moving to the city as well. Ella had gotten an internship working with a costume designer, while Cam was working for a prestigious law firm in the city.

For the twins, I knew this was like a dream come true. They were close—even closer now, after this last year.

Maybe it was the fact that they were both in a serious relationship, and neither one of them had to hide their feelings anymore. We'd gone on more double dates than I could count, and now I considered Cam to be one of my best friends, too. Audrey would always be number one, however.

"Hi, Audrey," Cam said, sticking out his hand toward my girlfriend.

She just rolled her eyes, pulling him into a hug instead. "We're practically family now, Cameron. And in our family, we hug."

He laughed, and after they pulled apart, the Ashford parents came over, taking photos of the two girls in their pink and blue dresses, their caps decorated with flowers, sequins, and glitter. Ella's featured a silver sparkly high heel, which was fitting with what I knew of how she and Cam met.

"Let's get one with your boyfriends," Audrey's mom shouted. My parents were standing side by side with Audrey's, their phones also out to snap pictures.

I pulled Audrey into my side, wrapping an arm around her hip, as Cam did the same for Ella. We took pictures of the four of us, and both couples individually.

My girl beamed, turning her head up to look at me. "Thank you."

"For what?" I tilted my head.

"For finding me." She closed her eyes, sighing happily. "For making all my dreams come true."

I pressed a kiss to her forehead. "You were always my dream, Audrey Rose."

We took our photos, and the rest of Cam's friends joined us with their girlfriends. James and Adam's girls weren't graduating this year, but we piled in for a photo of the ten of us all the same.

It was crazy to think that two years ago, when I'd stepped foot onto this campus, I hadn't had a single friend. And then I'd run into Audrey at that Halloween party, and everything had changed. Now, I had friends on the lacrosse team who were more like brothers. Ones I was sad to say goodbye to. They'd been loyal, steadfast guys—ones you could trust out on the field.

And Cam's friends had become mine, too, thanks to Audrey pulling me into their group. The last year, we'd hung out more than I could count at one of our apartments, laughing long into the night. It filled a part of me that had been broken. The guy who left Rhode Island, coming to Castleton for a new start, was gone. In his place was a better Parker. One who knew what it was like to love. To be loved, truly, for who you were. To have friends you could count on.

After another thirty minutes of chatting, I was growing impatient for my surprise.

"What do you say we get out of here, sunshine?" I asked, leaning down to whisper the words in Audrey's ear.

She was breathless as she answered, "Yes, please."

I grinned. "Good. Because I want to get my girl alone so I can show her how proud I am of her."

Audrey blushed. "Parker—"

"You know you love it." I winked, placing my hand on her lower back.

Quickly saying goodbye to her family and mine, I guided her to the parking lot, not taking my hand off her. Part of me just wanted that connection—to have her warmth—because it grounded me, steadied me and reminded me that this was real and not just a dream.

Because for so long, I'd dreamed of this. Having Audrey as mine. And I wasn't going to fumble this opportunity. Not now—

not ever. I opened my passenger side door for her, helping her in before shutting it.

"Where are we going?" Audrey asked as I settled into the car. Reaching over, I grabbed her seatbelt and buckled her in. Just like I had from our very first *fake* date. Now it was just tradition. She still blushed, her cheeks going that adorable shade of pink I loved so much.

"It's a surprise," I answered, not wanting her to know what I had up my sleeve yet.

"You know I don't need any surprises," Audrey answered, looking over at me and studying my face.

I still hadn't turned the ignition on, so I turned to face her. "I know. But I want to, Rosie Girl. Okay?"

She leaned over and pressed a kiss to my cheek. "Okay."

I slid my hand onto her thigh, squeezing it lightly.

As we drove, Audrey stared out the window. "It's surreal, right? That it's all over. I can't believe we're moving in two weeks," she said with a sigh. "Where did the time go?"

"It's bittersweet," I agreed. "I'll miss this place. But mostly sweet—because I still get you."

"You're ridiculous." She blushed. "Are we still going to the party later?"

I nodded. Cam's friends had planned a graduation party—one last hurrah. "Yeah. I just wanted some time alone with you first." Picking up her hand, I kissed her knuckles.

"Mmm. I can't complain about that."

Between her parents and mine being in town the last few days, we hadn't had much time to ourselves. We were all going out to brunch tomorrow to celebrate, so I didn't feel too bad about ditching them today.

"Didn't think so."

She laughed as I pulled into the parking lot in front of the apartment building where we'd lived for the last year. It was a quick drive to campus, which had been convenient for getting to class.

Pulling a silk blindfold out from my door, I turned to Audrey. "No peeking."

"Okay, what are you up to?" She asked, but let me tie the soft fabric over her eyes, blocking out her sight.

"Told you," I said against her ear. "It's a surprise." With one hand on her back, I guided her to our apartment door, quickly unlocking it and stepping inside. "Wait here," I said, leaving her right inside the front door to finish the last few details, turning on the lights and grabbing the things I'd stashed out of the fridge.

"Okay," I announced a few moments later, coming around to take the blindfold off. I'd left my cap and gown on the counter, ditching my suit coat but staying in my dress pants, button-up shirt, and tie.

It was pink. Because I had to match my girl. I grinned as she looked around.

"What's this?" Audrey asked, her eyes growing wide as I took her cap and gown from her as well, handing her a bouquet of pink roses.

Just like I'd given her on our first date.

"Parker..." She let out a small gasp.

I'd strung fairy lights from the ceiling this morning after Audrey had left our apartment and scattered pink rose petals in a path toward the pink blanket set up in the middle of the living room. There was an ice bucket with a bottle of champagne in it, a plate of strawberries, and those little cotton candy bombs that made your drink sparkly and sweet.

Something I knew Audrey would love.

"It's our last night here," I said, wrapping my arms around her waist and resting my chin on the top of her head. "I wanted it to be special. One last memory."

She hummed into my hold, letting me sway her in my arms. "This is too much." She buried her nose into the roses, inhaling deeply. "Thank you."

"You're welcome, Rosie." I kissed the top of her head. "Now

come on." I tugged her towards the blanket, sitting down and pulling her between my legs. Grabbing the bottle of champagne, I quickly popped the cork and then filled two glasses before grabbing the cotton candy bombs.

She laughed as I dropped them in, and the champagne swirled with pink glitter. They were also strawberry-flavored.

"Okay, I'm obsessed. Where did you even get the idea to do this?" Audrey asked, staring into the glass.

I smirked. "I know you, Audrey. You're my best friend, but more importantly, you're the love of my life. How could I do anything other than show you just how much I love you?"

She laughed, and the sound was music to my ears. "Parker…"

"Alright, I admit. I overheard some girls talking about it while I was waiting for you to get out of class the other day," I sheepishly said. "I thought you'd like it."

She swirled the liquid in the glass, watching it move. "I do."

"To us," I said, holding up my glass. "To our future."

"To us," Audrey agreed, clinking it together.

Humming, I took a sip of the concoction. It tasted the way Audrey always smelled, so fucking sweet and so damn perfect. And mine. All mine.

I was filled with such a sense of rightness. Like of all the places in the world, this, right here, was where we were supposed to be.

Together.

We both finished our drinks, and my girl snuggled up against my chest, taking a sip and running her tongue over her lips. "How could I have ever doubted that we could be more than friends?"

"I don't know. I guess it was a good thing I was an idiot and asked you to fake date me, huh?"

"Imagine, one day, when we tell our kids this story."

"Our kids, huh?"

Audrey blushed. "Yeah. Eventually." We hadn't talked about our future

Leaning down, I rasped against her ear, "I like the sound of that."

"I told you, you're stuck with me, Parker Maxwell."

"Maybe you're the one stuck with *me*, Audrey Rose."

One day, I'd ask her to be mine. To marry me. But not yet. That wasn't what tonight was about. Tonight was about us. Taking another step towards our future together.

She hummed, taking a long drink of her sparkling pink drink. "Once Upon a Time, there was a boy and a girl. And they were very best friends."

"Once Upon a Fake Date," I corrected. "And the boy loved the girl very much, but he was afraid to tell her. He didn't want to ruin their friendship because he liked having her sunshine in his life. Liked all of her pink and the glitter she left behind."

Audrey giggled. "Well, the girl loved the boy, too. She'd been doodling his name in her notebook since she was little. Hoping to marry him one day. But then he moved away. And she didn't see him for nine years."

I didn't need a summary of the rest. I remembered every vivid detail since running into her at that Halloween party I'd been dragged to. Her pink witch costume. The song she'd been humming when I found her outside. How everything had fallen back into place like we'd never spent any time apart.

"I like the beginning of our story, Rosie Girl. But I think the rest is going to be my favorite part." I leaned down, kissing her softly, tasting the strawberry champagne on her lips. The cotton candy was sweet, sugar particles clinging to her lips. Pulling away, I ran my tongue over her bottom lip. "Mmm. Delicious."

She blinked up at me, lust clear in her eyes. Pressing a kiss to her neck, I slipped the strap of her pink dress off her shoulder.

"Yes?" I asked her, waiting until she nodded before slipping off the other strap and kissing her bare skin. "God, I fucking love you. So sweet. So perfect for me."

We were cheesy and ridiculous, but I wouldn't have it any other way.

But this wasn't happily ever after—not yet. We were just getting started.

For the rest of our lives, this was exactly where I wanted to be. Right next to her.

Right next to the love of my life.

Extended Epilogue

AUDREY

SEVERAL YEARS LATER...

A bouquet of pink roses sat on my dressing table, a note attached to the top.

Rosie. My heart fluttered. Picking up the note, I slid the card out of the envelope, tracing my fingers over Parker's careful penmanship.

> *Come out to the stage, baby. I have a surprise for*
> *you. There's a dress and shoes waiting for you in the*
> *closet. Put it on and come find me. I'll be waiting. -P*

I rested my hand over my heart. What was he up to? The man never failed to find ways to surprise me. In the little ways—bringing me flowers home, surprising me with my favorite food—and the big. Like this. I loved him so much. A smile curled over my face.

When I opened the door, I found a beautiful pink dress, covered in pink flowers and sparkly material, that reminded me of the one I'd worn in the school musical all those years ago. A note, this one in my twin sister's handwriting, was attached to the hanger.

> *Ro,*
>
> *When you first told me about you and Parker, I knew you'd met your one. The man you were going to have your happily ever after with. You deserve this so much, Audrey. I love you, and I'm so happy to be your twin sister. When Parker reached out to me and asked me to make this dress for you, there was no way I could say no. Because I'd do anything for you.*
>
> *I don't have to say I hope you love it because I already know you will. Because I know you as well as I know myself.*
>
> *Thank you for doing life with me. I'm so grateful every day that you're my sister and that we're here together.*
>
> *Ella*
>
> *PS: Don't forget the shoes.*

I looked down at the bottom of the closet, finding a pair of sparkly gold heels. They reminded me of Ella's favorite silver pair, and I couldn't help my squeal. This morning, Ella and I had gone to the spa, where we'd been pampered all day, had our nails done, and then she'd taken me to get my hair and makeup done. Suddenly, I had a feeling I knew what all of this was about.

My stomach was full of butterflies in the best way, and I got changed in a hurry, thankful for the zipper so I could get the dress on myself before buckling the straps of the gold heels.

It was perfect. Combined with the makeup and hair, I looked like some sort of woodland princess. Maybe that was the idea. But it was so *me*, and I felt so loved by the two most important people in my life. Of course, my boyfriend would get my sister in on this.

When I stepped out onto the stage, I expected to find Parker waiting for me, but it was empty. I frowned, looking around. This place had become my home over the last year, even though I still had my sights set on a bigger stage—one with my name on the marquee.

A few of the set pieces had been pulled down, but the only thing in the middle of the stage was a piece of paper on the floor.

I bent down to pick it up, looking over the words.

Once Upon A Fake Date
By Parker Maxwell
[AUDREY stands alone on stage while PARKER enters from stage left.]

What was he up to?

As if on queue, there he was.

Dressed in a suit with that damn light pink tie that I knew for a fact he only wore to match me. He had other ones—maroon, red, dark gray, but whenever we were going somewhere together, he insisted we match. He was so handsome. My Parker. The man of my dreams. I'd loved him before I even knew what love was, and now, here we were. Living in New York City together. I was working as an actress in off-broadway performances while he'd landed a great job as an architect at a prestigious firm in the city. He got to design some amazing high-rise buildings, and I knew his favorite part was showing them to me in all stages of the build, especially when they were done.

"Hey, Dream Boy," I whispered, still holding the script in my hand. "What's going on?"

He grinned. "Follow the script, and you'll see."

I cleared my throat, turning the page and starting to read from the top.

PARKER: There she is. The girl of my dreams.

There was no paper in my boyfriend's hands. Clearly, he didn't need one as he repeated the words from the page.

"There she is." His eyes lit up, the gold inside practically sparkling with mirth. "The girl of my dreams."

"Have we met before?" I read off the paper.

"Maybe we have," Parker responded, holding out a hand for me.

I slid my hand into his, ignoring the weight of the moment. The words were reminiscent of us. Things we'd shared with each other before. There was meaning all around us. In every single thing he ever did.

"There's something familiar about you."

He hummed, guiding his hand over my head and giving me a small twirl. "You've known me all your life, Rosie Girl."

I smiled. "So I have."

It was cheesy—but in the best way—a way that felt so true to who we were.

"They say if you dream a thing more than once, it's sure to come true."

I didn't say anything. I just nodded.

"Well, all my life, I dreamed about you."

My eyes filled with tears as I read the next line.

[PARKER gets down on one knee.]

"Parker..." I whispered, looking down at him, the script now completely forgotten. I didn't need to be told what to say. Not when he was down on one knee in front of me, about to say words I could have only dreamed about.

"Audrey Rose Ashford," he started, squeezing my hand, still

clasped in his. "There hasn't been one single moment of my life that I didn't love you. These last few years with you have been the best of my entire life. You fill my life with so much sunshine. With all of your sparkles and your pink, and I wouldn't ask for it any other way. There's no one else I would get on stage and sing with. No one else I would make a total fool out of myself and write a script for, either. When I say I would literally slay a dragon for you, I think you know I mean it." He winked. "Once upon a time, I asked you to be my girlfriend."

"*Fake* girlfriend," I clarified, trying to blink away the wetness in my eyes even as I made the joke.

He snorted. "It worked, didn't it?" Shaking his head, he pressed a kiss to my knuckles. "Now, I'm asking you to be my wife."

All the oxygen had escaped my lungs. I definitely wasn't breathing. Not as Parker pulled a little pink box out of his suit jacket, popping it open to reveal a beautiful diamond ring. Nope. Definitely not breathing.

Parker gave me his signature grin, looking up at me with love shining in his eyes. "Will you marry me, Rosie Girl? Will you make me the luckiest man alive and live happily ever after with me?"

"*Yes*," I nodded, tears falling rapidly. "Yes, yes, yes!"

He scooped me up in his arms, twirling me around before setting me on my tiptoes and kissing me passionately. His lips coaxed mine apart, and everything in the world faded away. It was just him and I—this man that I loved so much. The man who would be my husband.

When we broke apart, Parker rested his forehead against mine, grinning. "What do you think? *Audrey Rose Maxwell* has a nice ring to it, doesn't it?"

It sounded better than nice. It sounded like all of my dreams had come true.

"I can't wait to marry you," I said against his chest, staring down to look at my new ring. The rose gold band looked like vines, with little diamonds embedded in the leaves, and a large princess-cut diamond sat in the center of the band, with a pink diamond set on each side. It was gorgeous, and I couldn't look away. "I've wanted to marry you since I was twelve years old, Parker."

He laughed. "I have you beat. I think I told my mom I was going to marry you when I was nine. Mom thought I was crazy, but look at us now. I was right."

My fiancé kissed me again, softer this time.

"You did all of this for me?" I asked, looking around the stage.

Parker nodded, running his hands through his light brown strands of hair. "Yeah. I had some help, obviously." He cleared his throat. "The script was all me."

"Thank you," I murmured, placing my hand over his heart. "I loved it."

"Yeah?"

I hummed in response. "Though I think you need to dial it back a bit on those acting lessons, Dream Boy." I winked at him. "Getting a little too sappy."

He smirked. "I told you I'd give you your happily ever after, didn't I? This is just me making good on that promise."

I rested my head against his chest, soaking up all his love. He had promised me that, and I knew he meant it.

It was why I had given him my heart from the very beginning.

PARKER

The cotton-candy skies were brilliant, streaked with the golden glow of the setting sun. I was captivated, unable to look away, sipping at the beer in my hands and marveling at how far we'd come.

I'd promised her a happily ever after, but today truly felt like the start of that.

All our friends were here—gathered in the large tent, string lights woven above the dance floor where I could still hear everyone singing and laughing.

Out here, though, staring out across the grounds, all I felt was the calm peace of knowing I was exactly where I was supposed to be. That my life was perfect in every way imaginable.

"What are you doing over here?" Audrey asked, coming to stand at my side.

She wrapped her arm around my waist, and I couldn't help but smile as I pressed a kiss to her forehead. I was staring off into the sunset, the river in the distance. We were at a castle upstate, which was everything I could have imagined it to be. It was spring—her favorite season—and flowers were in full bloom around us, painting the landscape a beautiful hue of vibrant colors.

Placing my hand on her hip, I tugged her in tighter next to my body. "Just appreciating the view." But now, I wasn't staring out at the gardens.

I was staring at Audrey.

The love of my life.

And, as of a few hours ago... My beautiful *wife*.

Her white lace dress showed just a hint of cleavage at the top, hugging the top half of her body before the fabric spilled down around her waist and hips. When I'd seen her walking down the aisle towards me, I'd lost my train of thought. Everything. She was my everything.

"This place is beautiful," she finally agreed. "I'm glad we picked it."

I looked down at the gold band on my finger, wiggling it. "I'm just glad I finally get to call you my wife."

On her finger was the ring I'd proposed with last year, when I'd almost made a fool of myself begging the director of the Broadway show she was working on to let me propose there, setting up the whole scene and even roping her twin sister in to help.

"I love you," she murmured, leaning her head against my chest.

Ella and Cam had gotten married last summer, and they were now expecting a baby boy. She was six months along, though she still insisted on wearing her favorite pair of heels to serve as Audrey's matron of honor today.

We were some of the last of our friends to tie the knot, though it wasn't for a lack of wanting. We'd both known since graduation that we'd end up here one day but had wanted to be secure in our jobs. After Audrey had landed her first leading role in a musical, I knew it was time.

And here we were. She was doing amazing things, and I was so proud of her.

"Love you too, my Rosie Girl," I said, pressing a kiss to her forehead.

Audrey's cheeks were pink when she looked up at me. "Do you think we should head back up there?"

"Probably." I gave her a little smile, tucking a strand of her blonde hair behind her ear. She'd worn it down, all curled and pretty. "I'm sure they want us to cut the cake."

"Oh, Ella definitely does." She laughed, weaving her fingers through my hand as we started walking. "She's been craving cake since this morning."

I hoped that would be us soon. Though if she wanted to wait while she continued being an absolute star in her show, I didn't mind that either. But I liked the idea of having a little girl who looked just like Audrey. Could already imagine taking her to Central Park Zoo, to the New York City Ballet, and carting her around on my shoulders wherever she wanted to go.

"What are you smiling about?" Audrey whispered. We'd almost gotten back to the tent.

"Our future," I replied.

The way she looked at me made me feel like I had butterflies in *my* chest.

We cut the cake, everyone cheering as Audrey pressed a large forkful to my lips. No smashing it in each other's faces here. The strawberry filling was sweet and perfect, and the cake was that perfect consistency—moist and light, perfectly melting in your mouth.

When it was my turn, I dug the fork into the cake, getting a small bite and bringing it up to Audrey's lips. Her lips closed around it, sliding slowly off the utensil, her tongue darting out to lick the frosting off. But I used my free hand to wrap around her waist, tugging her in closer to me and kissing her deeply, tasting the cake and frosting from her mouth.

God, it was heavenly. The taste of her—of strawberries and champagne—flooded my tongue, and I was content to stay just like this.

"Get a room!" Samuel shouted. He and I were still close now, even after graduating, and I was grateful to have a friend like him.

"That's the plan," Audrey said, winking at me.

I could feel the warmth spread up my neck and over my ears, and I was sure the tops of my cheeks were pink.

She giggled. "Should we dance, husband?"

"I'd like nothing more, wife."

And we danced, the sky a beautiful mix of pink and blue. A crown of gold eclipsed my bride's head as I twirled her around the dance floor, the familiar steps from the musical in my mind.

The Happily Ever After waltz.

It was fitting because it was ours.

Our Happily Ever After was finally here, and it was beautiful.

The End.

Want to read a bonus scene of Audrey and Parker at the Tony's with Ella and Cam? Click here to sign up for my newsletter to download it or follow the link below! https://dl.bookfunnel.com/e7dpjm2x4e

Castleton University will return in 2025 with Izzy & Adam's Story: The Bookworm and the Beast.

Acknowledgments

Thank you to everyone who has read this book and supported me. I truly couldn't do this without all of you and the help of some amazing people.

Mary Ellen, who drew the beautiful color, which is truly the prettiest pink of my DREAMS.

My Alpha Readers, who I asked about 5000 questions to making sure I got everything as accurate as possible: thank you for being some of the best people I know. I love you all so much.

To my bread girlies (you know who you are): thank you for keeping me going and being willing to try out whatever my new hyper fixation craft is with me or willing to help with whatever I need, including being my emotional support person at signings. I love you and our friendship so much.

To Autumn, for all the work you do for me. What would I do without you??

Finally, thank you to my parents, especially my mom (who I will let read this book, despite my constant mortification over her reading any of my spicy scenes): thank you for being the most supportive parents I could have asked for throughout my author journey, including going with me to signings and being willing to travel wherever I need to go just so I don't have to be alone. I know it's been a long road, but I wouldn't be here now without you both.

And to my brother, (who won't ever read this), thank you for letting me ignore you every time I'm on a deadline and can't do anything. Sorry.

Also by Jennifer Chipman

CONTEMPORARY ROMANCE

Best Friends Book Club

Academically Yours - Noelle & Matthew

Disrespectfully Yours - Angelina & Benjamin

Fearlessly Yours - Gabrielle & Hunter

Gracefully Yours - Charlotte & Daniel

Cousins Coffee Club

(Best Friends Book Club Generation 2)

Uniquely in Love - Ellie & Owen (coming spring 2025)

Castleton University

A Not-So Prince Charming - Ella & Cameron

Once Upon A Fake Date - Audrey & Parker

The Bookworm and the Beast - Izzy & Adam (coming summer 2025)

A North Pole Christmas

Elfemies to Lovers - Ivy & Teddy

PARANORMAL ROMANCE

Witches of Pleasant Grove

Spookily Yours - Willow & Damien

Wickedly Yours - Luna & Zain

Bewitchingly Hers - Eryne & Barrett (coming fall 2025)

SCIENCE FICTION ROMANCE

S.S. Paradise

A Love Beyond the Stars - Aurelia & Sylas

A Passion Beyond the Galaxy - Kayle & Leo (coming soon)

About the Author

Originally from the Portland area, Jennifer now lives in Orlando with her dog, Walter and cat, Max. In her free time, you can find her with her nose in a book or going to the Disney Parks. She loves writing romance heroes who fall first and hard for their women. Jennifer writes Contemporary Romance, Paranormal Romance, and Sci-Fi Romance.

Website: www.jennchipman.com

- amazon.com/author/jenniferchipman
- goodreads.com/jennchipman
- instagram.com/jennchipmanauthor
- facebook.com/jennchipmanauthor
- x.com/jennchipman
- tiktok.com/@jennchipman
- pinterest.com/jennchipmanauthor